A FORCE OF TWO . . .
CRACKING DOWN ON CRIME,
SMASHING EVIL AT ITS SOURCE!

For high-stakes action, thrill-a-minute adventure, and pure, nonstop excitement, you've come to the right place! You'll find it all, the total crime-busting package, in . . .

THE HARDY BOYS CASEFILES™
COLLECTOR'S EDITION

Your favorite teenage detectives
in three of your favorite stories.

Don't miss it.

Books in THE HARDY BOYS CASEFILES™ Series

THE HARDY BOYS™ CASEFILES

COLLECTOR'S EDITION

Beyond the Law
Spiked!
Open Season

FRANKLIN W. DIXON

Aladdin Paperbacks
New York London Toronto Sydney

ALADDIN PAPERBACKS
An imprint of Simon & Schuster Children's Publishing Division
1230 Avenue of the Americas, New York, NY 10020
Beyond the Law copyright © 1991 by Simon and Schuster, Inc.
Spiked! copyright © 1991 by Simon and Schuster, Inc.
Open Season copyright © 1992 by Simon and Schuster, Inc.
Produced by Mega-Books, Inc.
All rights reserved, including the right of reproduction in whole or in part in any form.
THE HARDY BOYS and colophon are registered trademarks of Simon & Schuster, Inc.
THE HARDY BOYS CASEFILES and ALADDIN PAPERBACKS
are trademarks of Simon & Schuster, Inc.
Manufactured in the United States of America
First Aladdin Paperbacks edition December 2005
2 4 6 8 10 9 7 5 3 1
ISBN-13: 978-1-4169-1828-8
ISBN-10: 1-4169-1828-0
These titles were previously published individually.

BEYOND THE LAW

Chapter

1

"YOU HAFF ZE DOCUMENTS?" Joe Hardy's blue eyes twinkled as he gave his older brother a lop-sided grin. With an expert twist of the steering wheel, he parked their van in front of Bayport's police headquarters.

"I've got the documents." Frank Hardy held up a thick manila envelope, shaking his head at Joe's hokey accent. "You sound like something out of a bad late-night move." He opened the van door and stepped out into the warm day.

The police headquarters at the top of the stairway before him was a squat, solid-looking building. Its thick, redbrick walls looked as if they'd stood in the middle of Bayport forever. Frank remembered that when he and Joe were kids, they'd joked that headquarters must have been the first thing built in town and that Chief Collig had gotten his start fighting Indians with his boys in blue.

Over the years Frank and Joe had been at headquarters many times, running errands for their father. Fenton Hardy was a private detective, and his investigations often involved his working closely with the police. Frank and Joe tangled with criminals, too, but they usually found themselves competing with the law.

Frank smiled. Chief Collig and the rest of Bayport's Finest found it hard to accept the idea of teenagers solving crimes. But that hadn't stopped him and Joe from putting a lot of crooks behind bars.

"Let's give these papers to the chief," Joe said as they headed up the front steps. "He has to sign off on them before Dad's license can get renewed." Another grin swept his broad, good-humored face. "A simple enough job."

An answering smile appeared on Frank's dark, handsome features. "At least it's dry work. Anything to stay above water." Frank was talking about their last adventure, *Deep Trouble,* in which they'd faced claim jumping and murder while diving for sunken treasure.

Frank pushed the heavy door open and stepped into the cool lobby of the building, grateful to be out of the late summer heat. Frank could hardly believe school would be starting in a little more than a week.

Frank looked around and decided that this place must have been something to see—about fifty years earlier. Now, though, the decoration seemed old-fashioned. The tall inquiries desk just ahead of him looked ready for another fifty years' work, though, even if it was dented and scarred.

Behind the desk and peering down at them was Patrolman Con Riley. A wry smile appeared on his square, ruddy face. "Well, what can we professionals do for Bayport's youngest crime-busters?" he asked. Con was the closest thing to a friend they had on the force, but he was still a cop. Frank couldn't expect a welcome with open arms.

"Can we see Chief Collig, Con?" Frank asked. "Dad sent us with some papers that have to be signed for his P.I. license. So if we can just get them in and out—"

Con shook his head. "I don't think that's a good idea. The chief's in a meeting with the new police commissioner, Mark DeCampo." He frowned. "That guy has really been getting the chief's goat. I guess the chief just hasn't been himself since his wife passed away."

Frank nodded. He and Joe had gone with their parents to the funeral services and been surprised at the turnout. They'd learned that Beatrice Collig had done a lot of good for the community. Although the new wing on the library carried the name of a rich contributor,

3

Bea Collig was the one who'd led the fund-raising drive. She had organized work-study programs to keep kids in school. And thanks to another plan she had championed, many of the younger police officers were taking college courses.

"Mrs. C. was like a mom to all of us on the force," Riley said sadly. "We miss her, but it's hardest on the chief. His temper has been terrible ever since she, uh, went."

"His temper?" Joe said in disbelief. "Don't take this the wrong way, Con, but how could you tell? Chief Collig is always blowing up at something."

Frank nodded. The chief was well-known for his short fuse, and the Hardys had lit it often by interfering in what Collig considered police business.

"Oh, sure, he gets *red* angry a lot," Con agreed. "His face turns red, he yells a bit, then he calms down. That's normal. No, I'm talking about how he gets *white* angry. All the blood leaves his face, his voice gets quiet, and he talks all polite-like. But when he's done, you feel about this tall." Con held up his hand, his thumb and forefinger about an inch apart.

"What's bugging him so much?" Frank wanted to know.

"Oh, it's the new city government. At first I was glad to see honest people in office. I

4

believed in the idea of cleaning things up after that last bunch was kicked out and convicted."

From the look on his face, Con had changed his mind, Frank decided. "But there's a problem with this purer than pure image. All the new bigwigs want to be seen on TV, uncovering corruption. You know how they've reorganized the Sanitation Department and the mess they found in the school lunch program. Now DeCampo wants to find some corruption on the force. So he went and brought in his own—"

All of a sudden Con's face changed, he sat straighter in his chair, and his voice became very crisp. "No, I'm sorry, the chief isn't available right now," he said to the boys. "You'll have to— Oh, hello, Captain Lawrence."

"People to see the chief, Riley?" A man in a carefully tailored police captain's uniform appeared beside the desk, almost soundlessly. Frank stared. The guy looked almost like Hollywood's version of police brass. Under a cap whose visor was covered with gold braid, the man's graying hair had been cut to look professional but stylish. His teeth, gleaming in a quick smile, were so white that Frank suspected they'd been capped. The face above the insignia of rank was a little too thin to be handsome but probably looked great on TV.

"Perhaps I can help," the man offered.

"Uh, I don't think so, Captain Lawrence,"

Con said, his voice tight. "The chief will have to sign off on these papers. They're the local approval for Fenton Hardy's private investigator's license. This is Frank and Joe—"

"Hardy?" Captain Lawrence's face suddenly grew cold. "I'm not fond of private eyes, not even the famous Fenton Hardy. And I've heard about you two—the so-called Hardy boys. Kid vigilantes have no business in modern crime control."

Lawrence stepped abruptly away. "I'll be in my office, studying reports," he told Con over his shoulder.

Riley sat stiffly at attention until the man was gone. Then he leaned over the desk, speaking softly. "That's the clown DeCampo has sicced on us," he said in disgust. "Captain Parker Lawrence. Get a load of him—'crime control.' Whatever happened to enforcing the law? He'd rather give the streets to the creeps while he makes cops miserable with investigations by his Internal Affairs Unit."

"Internal Affairs?" Joe repeated. "Aren't those the guys who go probing for crooked cops?"

"That's right. DeCampo's convinced that if the politicians in town were crooked, then the cops have to be, too. So he imported Captain Lawrence to spy on us. And Lawrence tried to get *me* to work as a snitch for him."

"What did you say?" Frank asked.

"I said no, and then I told the chief. He called DeCampo, and that's why they're in there." Con pointed down the hallway behind him to a pebbled-glass door with the word *Chief* in gold letters.

As they watched, two shadows appeared close to the glass, and voices were raised, so Frank and Joe could hear.

"Yeah, Mr. Commissioner. I suspected it was *your* efforts." Chief Collig's voice was as sharp as a knife.

"I mean the *administration's* efforts to clean up the force," Mark DeCampo quickly amended.

"No, I think you were right the first time," Collig returned angrily. "It's *your* efforts to get on TV, like all the other administration crimebusters. Well, let me tell you one thing, pal. You're trying to uncover something that's not there. And your grandstanding is hindering this police force. How do you expect cops on the beat to do their jobs if they always have to look over their shoulders? And why? Because a bunch of clowns are trying to find corruption that doesn't exist. If people don't trust my officers, they can't do their jobs."

"It's not a question of trust, Collig, but of control."

"Now you're saying I can't control my own people? Or is it that *you* want to control them?"

7

DeCampo's voice turned nasty. "Don't push me, Collig. You're the last major official left from the previous administration, the only one who's not in jail. I could get lots of support to make it a clean sweep," he said threateningly.

"Those crooks didn't appoint me!" Collig's voice was an angry roar.

"Yes, but you worked with them." DeCampo raised his voice to drown out Collig's. "And if you work in the mud, you're bound to get dirty. Hey! What—?"

Frank and Joe stared, amazed, as the two shadows started scuffling.

"I don't believe this," Joe began. His words were cut off as the door to the chief's office suddenly flew open. For a second Mark DeCampo stood facing the hall, framed in the doorway. Frank had seen the police commissioner on TV, but never like this. The man's expensive suit was rumpled, his tie askew, and his handsome face mottled purple with anger. He stumbled a couple of steps down the hall, from the force of being thrown out of the office. "You're finished, Collig," DeCampo choked out, turning back to the office. "You pushed it too hard this time."

Chief Collig gripped the doorframe, breathing hard, his big, stocky frame rigid. Frank noticed that the sleeves on Collig's uniform shirt were rolled up, the muscles on his arms rippling as he tried to calm down.

"Pushed it, DeCampo?" Collig glared at the police commissioner, his face pale. "You're lucky I didn't punch your smug face in for that crack."

Collig raised a clenched fist. "Nobody says that Ezra Collig isn't honest. *Nobody!*"

Chapter

2

FOR A LONG MOMENT the two men stood and glared at each other. Both Joe and Frank leaned against the front desk, trying to appear as inconspicuous as possible. Joe noticed that Con Riley had his head down, too. None of them wanted to be noticed by the two angry men.

Joe didn't even turn as Mark DeCampo stormed down the hall and out the front doors of the building. From the other end of the hall, the door to Chief Collig's office closed with a thunderous slam. The Hardys lifted their heads and raised their eyes toward the closed door. Joe wondered if this was how survivors of heavy shelling felt as they poked their heads up to see where the artillery had been fired from.

Con Riley cleared his throat. "Well, the meeting's over. If you want to go in now, I guess you can.''

"No way, Con." Frank shook his head. "Mount Collig might erupt all over again. Especially if he knew we witnessed his last outburst." He passed the packet of papers to Riley. "Why don't you wait until the chief has calmed down a bit, then give him these to sign. We'll pick them up later—maybe tomorrow."

Con gave them a wicked grin. "Well, if you're sure . . ."

The Hardys hurried out of headquarters like witnesses who didn't want to be tapped for questioning. Joe was sure that when the chief cooled off, he'd be very embarrassed about blowing up. After all, he'd physically thrown Mark DeCampo out of his office. He certainly wouldn't feel better if he discovered he'd had an audience.

When they'd climbed back in the van, Joe finally broke the silence. "Do you believe what happened?" he asked as he started the engine. "That was some show the chief put on. I've seen him mad before, but he never lost it like that."

"Not only that, it's *who* he lost it with," Frank said, frowning. "Strictly speaking, Mark DeCampo is Collig's boss. He could fire the chief for what happened today."

"But he wouldn't," Joe predicted confidently. "He'd have to give a reason, and somehow I

11

don't see him complaining in public that Collig bounced him out of his office." He grinned. "DeCampo may want to get on television, but he doesn't want to look stupid."

"It's not as straightforward as that." Frank shook his head. "DeCampo is a politician. He knows there's more than one way to skin a cat."

Joe glanced over. "What do you mean?"

"I mean DeCampo won't fire Collig right now. But he'll be looking for a reason—any reason— to give the chief his walking papers."

"Fat chance of that," Joe scoffed. "Collig has been running that force for years, and he does a great job. Just a couple of months ago he got that award for being one of the best cops in the country. How can DeCampo touch him?"

"All he needs is one little incident to make Collig look bad," Frank said. "The rest of city hall will line up behind him to get rid of the chief."

Joe was a little shaken. "But that—that sounds crooked. I thought this new bunch was supposed to be honest."

Frank shrugged. "It's still politics. And the new bunch is a lot more honest than the old one. Remember what happened when *they* had a political problem."

Joe remembered only too well. Maybe this city government set up committees and dumped on Collig, but the old guard played rough. They even murdered the city manager when they thought he was about to reveal some of their dirty deals. By sheer bad luck the hired killer bumped into Callie Shaw, Frank's girlfriend, while making his getaway. That had put Callie, Frank, and Joe on the hit list, and they'd come frighteningly close to getting killed.

Of course, they'd finally cracked the *See No Evil* case, and by catching the hired killer, they'd launched the scandal that brought the old city government down. In a way, the Hardys had helped to usher in the new government—including Mark DeCampo.

"It's almost funny," Frank said. "Every time we ran up against Collig in a case, Collig got furious with us. Now he's being accused of that same kind of corruption we uncovered in the government."

"So *you* think," Joe said. "The chief's got nothing to worry about."

"What about those threats DeCampo made?" Frank asked.

"You mean that 'clean sweep' crack? What's he going to do? He has no proof that Collig's corrupt."

"DeCampo just has to make Collig look bad," Frank said. "He just needs to make people doubt Collig."

"Collig's got a great reputation," Joe responded. "Who'd doubt—"

"You did, during the *See No Evil* case. That's

why we didn't bring the cops in until the very end."

"Yeah, but—" Joe decided to shut up. They drove the rest of the way home in silence.

Fenton Hardy was not happy to hear that his papers were still at police headquarters. He was even less happy when he heard why.

"DeCampo told Chief Collig he was finished? He threatened to fire him?" He shook his head in disbelief. "What for?"

The boys explained about the new Internal Affairs Unit and DeCampo's accusations of corruption.

Fenton Hardy surprised his sons by throwing his head back and laughing. "The Bayport force? Corrupt? No way. I was a cop myself in New York. I've known a lot of cops—honest ones and not so honest. Seen all the setups and scams. I've even helped break some up."

His expression grew more serious. "I'd know if anything crooked were going on here. So would Ezra Collig. He's an honest cop if ever I saw one. And I've never seen anyone so down on crooked cops."

"So you think he'll be around tomorrow when we go to pick up your papers?" Joe gave Frank a smug smile as he spoke.

"I certainly hope so," Fenton said. "Of course, with politics and politicians, you can never be sure."

Now it was Frank's turn to act smug as the smile disappeared from Joe's face.

Joe spent the afternoon working on the van. He had a suspicion that the engine's timing was a little off. He usually felt better working with his hands when things were disturbing him.

They couldn't really be thinking of getting rid of Chief Collig. It would be like removing a local landmark.

Joe tried to imagine what the police force would be like without the chief. For all his life— or at least, all the time he'd been investigating crimes—Collig had been there. Usually the chief had acted more like the enemy, an obstacle to solving a mystery. He definitely didn't like competition. He'd get furious when the Hardys contradicted him on a case, and often he'd gnash his teeth when the Hardys turned out to be right.

But the chief also knew good work when he saw it, even when it drove him crazy. For Joe, Collig represented the local law—tough, hardworking, and, Joe was sure, totally honest.

As he bent over the engine with his testing gear, he hesitated for a second. What a shock it would be if the chief lost his job so soon after losing his wife.

Joe set to work, and after a while the questions receded to the back of his mind. There was a job to be done here. Hands and tools moved carefully, tuning the engine.

At last he had the van's engine purring perfectly. "Yeah!" he said, listening to the solid sound. "It runs like a big jungle cat."

"Hey, Joe!" Frank stood in the doorway between the house and the garage. "Come in here. You have to hear this!"

"I've got—" Joe began.

"Forget about the tools! This won't wait!"

Puzzled, Joe followed his brother into the house, wiping his dirty hands on an old rag.

The television was on in the den, the last minutes of an ad for WBPT's "Evening News Hour." The face on the screen was so clean-cut, a choirboy would look sleazy beside it. A deep, serious voice was saying, "Our new newsman, Rod Vernon, brings the hard-hitting style that made him a network news star to Bayport—"

"You can say that again," Frank said grimly.

The pounding newsroom music on the ad faded, only to return again as the show resumed. Joe glanced at his watch. The Bayport "Evening News Hour" had begun.

The camera zoomed in for a tight close-up on Rod Vernon, showing off blue eyes, neatly combed blond hair, and a jaw just rugged enough. His perfect features were set in a very serious expression as he stared out at his audience.

"Tonight's lead story will be a shock to most area residents. We've discovered that a major figure in Bayport's crime-control establishment may be a criminal himself."

Joe stared as Vernon's face was replaced on the screen by a stock-film clip of Chief Collig in his dress uniform. "Information received by us indicates that Chief Ezra Collig of the Bayport police force was fired from his first law-enforcement job."

The picture of Collig's face froze on the screen as Joe stared. "Apparently," Vernon went on, "Collig had been taking bribes from local businesspeople."

Chapter

3

FRANK AND JOE STOOD in stunned silence while they listened to the whole lead story. Only when the anchorman's face appeared on the screen, talking about the latest state budget crisis, did they move.

"This is getting weirder and weirder," Joe said. "What do you think of what that Vernon guy was saying?"

Frank abruptly turned off the TV. "I'm more interested in what he *wasn't* saying," he finally replied.

"What do you mean?"

"All of Vernon's 'story' was a rehash of his intro line," Frank explained. "He had nothing new to add after the second sentence."

Joe frowned. "He gave the name of the town where Collig worked—Millerton."

"And the fact that thirty-five years ago Ezra Collig joined the police force there. Then, six months later, he quit. Fine—that's in the public record. But this stuff about collecting bribes . . . there's no record of that—only Vernon saying it, very seriously. If you ask me, he's slicing the bologna mighty fine. I bet he rushed his big exposé onto the air without checking it out."

"So maybe Vernon's wrong," Joe said, a glint of hope in his blue eyes.

Frank shrugged. "Maybe. We can only wait and see."

By the next morning, though, all of Bayport was buzzing with the story. The Hardys were amazed to discover how many people were willing to believe Rod Vernon's accusations. Even the *Bayport Times* had come out with a special edition about the corruption allegations. The front page showed a photo of an incredibly young-looking Ezra Collig. He stood uncomfortably at attention in an ill-fitting police uniform, his eyes focused to the right.

"Looks like he's staring right at the headline," Joe said, holding up the paper while his brother paid for it. Indeed, Collig seemed to be reading the big black letters beside him: "Holding the Bag?"

The boys were standing at the entrance to the

Bayport Mall. Frank had made plans to have lunch with his girlfriend, Callie Shaw, and then to head over to police headquarters to pick up Fenton Hardy's papers.

Inside, the food court was full of people. Frank had to keep Joe from crashing into people as he read the story. Joe finished and folded the paper. "Nothing new in here. It basically reports that Vernon accused Collig on the air of being a bagman—collecting bribes. All that's new is this picture. The caption says it dates from Collig's days on the Millerton force. Oh, and it tells where Millerton is."

"I looked it up on a map last night," Frank said.

"Well, for people like me, who didn't," Joe said, "they give a little map. Hmm. I'd say he moved about as far from that town as he could and still stay in the same state. Funny."

"Oh, hilarious." Frank glanced at the story. "Did the *Times* try getting in touch with the Millerton police?"

Joe held out the paper. "Yeah. According to their records, Collig worked for about six months, then resigned on very short notice. So Collig wasn't fired, the way Vernon said."

"But he did leave," Frank said, frowning. "Which will start everyone wondering if there's a cover-up. They'll figure Collig left Millerton under a cloud." He sighed. "I just hope that cloud doesn't rain on the chief's parade."

Frank forced his way into the lunchtime crowd filling Mr. Pizza. Callie had managed to grab a table; she waved to the boys, who quickly joined her.

"What's up?" Frank noticed that his girlfriend's pretty face had a little more color than usual.

Callie shook her head, her blond hair flying around her shoulders. "It's the radio. They're playing—well, just listen."

The rock song blaring from the pizza joint's speakers came to an end, and the disk jockey came on. "And now we've got a request from yet another of Police Chief Collig's many admirers. Good choice—it may be where the chief ends up. So let's give it up for the King—"

A moment later Elvis Presley began singing "Jailhouse Rock."

"The station's been doing that ever since I came in," Callie said, "which is a pretty lousy thing to do to the chief, if you ask me."

Frank got up and went to the counter to order a pie and sodas, then called the manager over. "Hey, Tony."

Tony Prito was an old pal of Frank and Joe. He dropped the wad of pizza dough he'd been working on into some flour and came over. "How's it going?"

"Not bad. Think you can get another station on the radio, though? Callie's getting a little annoyed at the Collig trash-a-thon."

"Yeah? Well, *we* like it," one of the kids at the counter said loudly. Pizza grease gleamed on his chin. "This is my favorite station, and Howie Starr is my favorite deejay."

"That's right!" other voices said.

Bolstered by the show of support, the greasy-chinned spokesman faced off against Frank. "Maybe you're not as hot a detective as you think, Hardy. After all, you've been sucking up to the police for years, and you never figured that Collig was a crook."

"Yeah!" more voices called.

Frank managed to hold back his anger and keep his voice even. "From everything I've heard so far, there's no proof the chief is a crook."

"The news guy on TV wouldn't have called him one if it wasn't true!" somebody yelled.

"That shows what you know!" Joe Hardy jumped up from his seat. "I have a buddy over at WBPT, a cameraman we used to work with. He shoots the in-studio stuff for the 'Evening News Hour.' You've seen all those ads about what a hotshot network news reporter Rod Vernon is? Ever wonder why he's doing local news in Bayport? He's a troublemaker and got sent down to the minor leagues. The guy likes to come up with big scandals, but about a third of the time he practically invents them."

Frank was a little surprised at his brother's statement. He'd noticed Joe spending time on

22

the phone that morning but hadn't dreamed that he was checking up on Rod Vernon.

The kid with the greasy chin stood silent for a second. Then his face brightened as he came up with a comeback. "Yeah, well, that means the guy is *right* about two-thirds of the time, and I think he's got the chief pegged."

More voices joined in, egging Greasy-chin on.

"What do you guys know?" Callie shouted angrily. "You've never even met Chief Collig!"

"We saw him at school for anticrime assemblies," one kid said. "I never liked him."

The song on the radio had changed to another "humorous" request—Johnny Cash's "Folsom Prison Blues." Then the hourly news came on.

"Still no comment from Chief Ezra Collig on the bribery accusations made by Bayport newscaster Rod Vernon—"

"See?" The kid at the counter finally wiped his greasy chin. "If he's innocent, why doesn't he come out and say so?"

The voice of the radio announcer continued as Frank and Joe walked back to join Callie. "We've made repeated inquiries at Bayport Police Headquarters, but the only response we've had came from Captain Parker Lawrence of the Internal Affairs Unit."

Joe shot Frank a worried look. Why was Internal Affairs involved?

Then came Lawrence's voice. "Police Commissioner DeCampo has asked for a thorough and fair investigation. I shall be appointing my best people—''

"For a political hatchet job," Frank said in disgust. "DeCampo has his incident to get rid of Collig now, and he can have the guy he hired do the job. All he has to do is drag his feet on this so-called investigation and let the media hang Collig out to dry."

"But we know the chief would never do the things they're saying," Callie objected.

"Just look at them." Frank jerked his head at the hooting crowd in the pizza joint.

"Kind of scary," Joe said quietly. "Like that moron saying, 'I heard it on TV, so it must be right.' "

Frank stared at the newspaper, taking in the picture of the young Ezra Collig. He couldn't have been much older than I am, Frank thought. The face was much thinner, but those were definitely Collig's features.

Frank's eyes narrowed with a sudden thought. "I wonder where the *Bayport Times* got this picture. It sure was convenient."

"Maybe they were working on the story already," Callie suggested.

"Uh-uh," Frank said. "What they've got here in print is only what Vernon said on TV, plus what they could pick up in a quick phone call to the Millerton police."

He turned to Callie. "Do you think your

friend Liz Webling is working at the *Times* today?"

"Why don't we go and find out?" Callie said.

"After we eat," Joe added.

There was almost half a pizza on the table when they did leave. None of them had much of an appetite, after all.

After a quick drive downtown Callie, Frank, and Joe found Liz Webling at the *Times* offices, pounding a typewriter and frowning. She seemed happy to leave her job and talk for a few minutes. "Dad always sticks me with the boring stuff, like typing up the notes from the school board meeting," she complained.

"Want to try something a little hotter?" Callie said. "How about the Collig story?"

Liz's dark eyes sharpened. "What have you got on that?" she asked. "All we have is Rod Vernon's word, plus a call we made to the Millerton police."

"And an old photo of Collig," Frank pointed out. "Was that an old file thing?"

Liz shook her head. "No. We got it last night." She went to a nearby desk and pulled out a file folder. Inside was an old black-and-white photo—the picture of the young Ezra Collig. A box had been drawn on the picture in grease pencil. "That's where we cropped the shot," Liz explained. "We didn't want to use the whole picture."

"Hey, it's only half a picture," Joe said, fin-

25

gering the right-hand side. There was no border—whatever had been there was snipped away clean.

"That's the way we got it," Liz said. "I remember wondering what Collig was looking at."

"What do you mean, you got it last night?" Frank asked.

"A messenger delivered it just a bit after the newscast," Liz replied.

"Something for you to make up a front page around," Frank said suddenly. "Somebody is really pressing all the media buttons around here. We're definitely looking at a setup."

"Setup? Who?" Liz scooped up her notepad. "Are you guys investigating? Do you have any suspects in mind?"

"No comment," Frank said hurriedly.

Liz grimaced in disappointment. "Give me a break here, guys," she said. "Here I am, minding the store while everybody goes to the big press conference at the cop house. And you hand me a story—"

"Press conference? At police headquarters?" Frank broke in.

"Yeah." Liz blinked in confusion as her three visitors whipped around and headed for the door.

"How are we going to get in?" Joe wanted to know.

26

"We play it dumb—we're just three kids coming in to pick up Dad's papers."

As he led the way to police headquarters, Frank found the street in front of the building full of news vans. "Looks like a riot," he whispered to Joe and Callie as they slipped through the entrance. The lobby was jammed. Camera crews elbowed one another, jockeying for position in front of the booking desk. Behind them were the still photographers. A late reporter jostled Frank as he ran past him to join the crowd. The guy acted like the last wolf to get to the deer.

Confronting the whole media mob was a lone police officer—Con Riley. He looked as if he wished he were anywhere else, Frank thought. "Will you folks please stop shoving?" he shouted over the noise. "I've already told you, Chief Collig isn't in."

"Then who's holding the press conference?" Frank recognized Rod Vernon in the middle of the crowd. His blond hair was immaculately moussed and brushed into a shining helmet, and his WBPT news blazer was perfectly cut and unwrinkled, but there was a nasty expression on his choirboy face. "I don't like dealing with underlings—"

Behind Con, down the hall, the door to the chief's office opened and Mark DeCampo stepped out. Frank wondered how anyone could believe the smile on the man's tanned face. Marching

27

behind DeCampo was Parker Lawrence, the life-size toy soldier.

"I'd like to thank our friends in the media for taking the time to attend this briefing," DeCampo said. His "media friends" were all busily aiming minicams, cameras, microphones, and cassette recorders at him.

"I'll keep my comments brief," DeCampo said. "In response to the questions being raised about Ezra Collig, I have suspended him from the office of chief of police, pending a full investigation."

Frank did a slow burn, watching DeCampo turn to his Internal Affairs stooge. "In the meantime, Captain Parker Lawrence will run the investigation—as well as the Bayport police force."

Chapter

4

FRANK WAS TOO STUNNED to move, but the media hounds around him sprang into action. Hands shot up, and questions were shouted. "Mr. Commissioner!" they chorused. "Does this mean you believe the charges of bribery?"

Mark DeCampo was too polished a politician to fall for that. He ignored the questions, instead turning the conference over to Captain Parker Lawrence. Frank had to admit that Lawrence was quite a performer. For the next forty-five minutes he showed himself to be honest, true, forthright—all the best Boy Scout virtues. At the same time, however, Lawrence did his best to stick a knife in Chief Collig's back.

Inwardly Frank seethed, but he knew that all

he could do for now was listen to Lawrence's rhetoric.

Lawrence never mentioned Collig's guilt or innocence. He just made nice noises about bringing the investigation to a speedy conclusion.

When the newspeople began asking how long the investigation would take, however, Lawrence gave them a lot of double-talk. And he asked to be addressed as Acting Chief Lawrence.

When the reporters realized they weren't going to get anything more, they disappeared with surprising speed. So did Lawrence, once no more cameras were around.

The Hardys and Callie found themselves alone in the big, old-fashioned lobby, except for Con Riley behind the booking desk.

"So what did you think?" Con asked quietly. He threw a glance over his shoulder toward the chief's office. "I think this guy is gonna slaughter the chief, then hang the pieces out to dry." He wrinkled his nose as if he'd just detected an extremely bad smell. "Acting Chief, my foot. He's the boss now, and he intends to stay in that office. With him running the investigation— and that rat DeCampo taking care of the political side—they'll do it."

"Con, we hate to bother you now, but what about—"

"Your dad's papers!" Con smacked himself in the forehead. "I got them in to the chief yesterday, but I don't think he signed them." He frowned. "And I don't know if it's a good idea for me to check right now."

"Don't worry about it, Con," Frank said. "We'll ask Dad what he wants to do."

"You might have to get them signed by the Acting Chief." Con gave a grim laugh. "Do you think that would make him an acting P.I.?"

Con became deadly serious and almost pleaded. "You guys have to stick your noses into this one. You *have* to!"

Frank opened his mouth, but no words came out. "We'll do what we can," he finally said. Callie and Joe silently followed him out of headquarters. They walked to the van, and Frank drove Callie to her house. Then the Hardys headed home to report the latest to their father.

"I can't get over Con asking us for help," Joe said from the passenger seat.

Frank nodded. "It's almost scary to think Collig might need it." He paused for a second. "But I think he does. There are too many people after his hide—Vernon, Lawrence, DeCampo. Take your pick of whoever started this mess."

"You left out 'all of the above,' " Joe told him as they reached their street. He shook his head. "I think we've got to do something, Frank. I mean, Chief Collig can be a pain in the neck. He drives me crazy half the time, but—"

"Hey, the other half you drive him crazy," Frank cut in.

"But he's not a man who'd take bribes. I can't

believe he's guilty." Joe glanced at his brother, but Frank said nothing.

"Well, do you?" Joe asked.

"I wonder how this story got started," Frank finally said. "And why the chief isn't saying anything in his own defense." He sat a little straighter in the driver's seat. "But I think we definitely should look into this whole mess. Until then, well, let's say I'm keeping an open mind."

"I always thought you had a hole in your head." Joe grinned as they pulled into the driveway.

They found their father in his office, hanging up the phone.

"There's still a holdup over your papers," Frank reported. "Looks like Chief Collig didn't sign them yesterday. And today—well, he wasn't in his office."

"Not surprising, after the witch-hunt that's being stirred up." Fenton Hardy scowled. "As a matter of fact, I was just trying to reach Collig at his home. He has to make some sort of statement."

"Dad, what's he going to do?" Joe asked.

"Make it clear that he's innocent," Fenton said. "Collig is no crook. I'd stake my reputation on that. But I think he's going to need help proving it."

The boys' father gestured toward the phone. "But Collig's phone has been busy for the last hour. He probably just left the receiver off the hook.''

"So what do we do now?" Joe said.

"We'll pay him a visit." Fenton gave them a ghost of a smile. "Besides, maybe we'll be lucky and discover he brought my papers home with him."

He got up from his desk chair. "No time like the present. We'll take my car."

Chief Collig lived at the edge of town. Frank stared out the car window at the stone and plaster houses in the quiet neighborhood. But as they rounded a curve in the road, the peace and quiet abruptly disappeared in a welter of parked cars and a milling crowd.

"Now we know where all those media people went after the press conference," Frank said, recognizing two of the TV vans that had blocked the street in front of headquarters.

Now they were blocking the road in front of Collig's house. Camera crews, photographers, and reporters crowded onto the chief's lawn.

Frank realized there wasn't enough room on the road for Fenton to get through. They came to an abrupt stop and climbed out, leaving the car to block the road even more. Frank found himself staring down dozens of camera lenses.

Rod Vernon was in the lead, his video operator at his side. "Outside the home of embattled Bayport police chief Ezra Collig, we find famous private detective Fenton Hardy."

Why do these news types always have to hang idiotic tags on people? Frank wondered. It's not enough to call Collig the police chief. He's got to be "embattled." Just as Dad has to be a "famous private detective."

Vernon gave them a friendly grin as he shoved a mike into Fenton's face. "Can it be that the police chief feels so desperate that he's turned to outside help?"

Fenton didn't reply.

"So you aren't coming to see Chief Collig?" Vernon pressed.

Frank stared at the guy's face. Those choirboy features were still set in a smile, but the eyes were like those of an animal—an animal that had smelled blood.

"No comment," Fenton Hardy said. "Now, would you please move your van so we can get by?"

"Yeah," Joe added. "Tell your guy to stop wasting film and our time."

As soon as he told the video operator to cut, Vernon stopped wasting his smile on them, too. He didn't bother to hide his annoyance as he sent his sound man to move the WBPT van.

With the road cleared, Fenton and the boys slid back in and drove on.

"How are we going to get in the house with that mob in front of the place?" Joe asked.

"Not through the front door, that's for sure." Frank glanced from the crowd of media people

34

to the road ahead. "The road curves a bit more, winding up into the hills. We could probably park out of sight up there, then cut across on foot to Collig's backyard." He looked over toward his father. "Feel up to a little cross-country trek, Dad?"

Fenton Hardy smiled. "Let's head for the hills."

They drove on, following the road up a hillside. Fenton pulled the car over in front of a small yellow bungalow. Below them they could see a thin row of trees, separating the yard behind the yellow house from the Collig backyard.

"No fence—that's a piece of luck," Joe said.

"And there don't seem to be any newspeople hanging around the back," Frank added.

His father stared at the grassy slope. "They haven't mowed this part of the lawn recently, but it looks fairly straightforward. Let's hope the folks who live here don't think we're burglars."

They left the car, moving silently past the yellow house. Frank held his breath as they passed dark windows. Then he had to concentrate on keeping his footing. The slope was steeper than it seemed, and he found himself skidding on the long grass until they reached the cover of the scrubby set of trees.

Peering around the bushes and thin tree trunks, they checked out the open space of Chief Collig's backyard.

"Nothing to hide behind at all," Fenton Hardy said. "Let's hope Vernon and his merry crew are all hypnotized by the front door. I don't want them asking us more stupid questions."

Frank took a deep breath, then dashed across the carefully tended back lawn to the rear door of the house.

"I sure hope the chief is home," Joe muttered as they ran. "We'll look real stupid banging on the door of an empty house."

Ten feet from the door, they discovered the house was occupied, all right. The back door flew open.

There stood Chief Collig, a wild look in his eye—and a .38 caliber police revolver in his hand.

Chapter

5

THE HARDYS MOMENTARILY FROZE under Ezra Collig's gun. As recognition came into the chief's eyes, the weapon went down, and a shaky hand came up to rub his forehead.

"I was in the kitchen, keeping away from that pack of vultures parked on my porch," Collig said. "When I saw people in the yard, I decided to come out and . . ." He suddenly became aware of the gun in his hand and stopped speaking. "Uh, I was going to warn them off."

Fenton was serious as he and the boys entered the house. "You should be glad we *weren't* newspeople," Fenton told the chief. "A picture of you waving a gun at them would have been front-page material."

Collig shuddered and put the gun in a drawer.

"I can imagine the headline—'Is Chief Losing His Mind?' " He dropped into a chair and stared out through the mesh curtains on the room's big picture window. The kitchen must have been a more recent addition to the old house. Frank saw an ultramodern range and all sorts of appliances for processing and preparing food.

"You don't know what it's like," Collig said, still staring out through the curtain. "I haven't had a moment's peace since that creep Vernon went on TV last night. First came the call from DeCampo, asking me not to come in today. Then the phone didn't stop ringing. I finally took it off the hook." Frank saw the receiver from the kitchen wall phone stuck in a drawer.

"I couldn't get out of the house, not with that crowd outside." Collig's face was bitter. "And it just kept getting larger."

"It will keep growing until you go out and say something. You're the only one who hasn't been heard from in this story." Fenton gazed at Collig with concern. "You realize, of course, that they're going to keep hounding you."

"Hounding me?" Collig repeated. "You make it sound like they've got a right to treat me like a criminal."

"Look, I don't think there's anything to this story. Neither do the boys or a lot of people in Bayport. That's why we're here, to offer our—"

"Help?" Collig cut him off with one angry word. "I've been living in and working in this town for most of my life. Keeping the streets safe, keeping the people safe. If they can't trust me after all that—well, maybe they deserve a tin soldier like Parker Lawrence.

"You never know which are the best years of your life—until they're over," Collig continued. "Those weren't easy years. People don't realize what police work was like, back when I started out. Hardy, you were a cop—what? Twenty years ago?"

Fenton Hardy nodded. "Just about."

"So you know how things have changed. Me, I was an old-timer twenty years ago, with almost fifteen years on the job. It was like another world. Some of the stuff that was a regular part of the job then would be considered criminal today."

Frank almost said that bribery had always been a crime, even back then, but he forced the words back.

Collig's face was grim. "I put in thirty-five years of honest service. Then someone digs up this piece of ancient history to smear me." His hands clenched. "I'm going to find the guy who's pulling this"—he glanced at Fenton Hardy—"myself. And when I track him down, he'll wish he'd never been born."

There was a long, uncomfortable silence after that speech. Obviously, Frank thought, being held a virtual prisoner in his own house hadn't helped the chief's temper.

Fenton Hardy must have thought so, too. "Well, first you'll have to get out of here—and you can't do that until you talk to the people outside."

Collig led the way to the living room. Heading to the window, he twitched back the drape to peek out. The movement must have caught the attention of the newspeople outside. Through the tiny chink in the curtain, Frank saw Rod Vernon's video operator charge forward. He crashed into a blooming rosebush, trying to peer inside.

Hands clenched, Ezra Collig yanked the drapes shut. "My wife planted that bush and tended it for twenty years." His words were quiet, but they simmered with barely contained fury. "And that blasted snoop tramples it down."

Frank was glad that Collig had put his gun away, especially when the man stormed the door.

The Hardys stepped back, out of the line of sight, as Collig opened the door and stepped onto the porch. "I expect you have all been waiting for me to make a statement," the chief began. "Well, here it is. I have no comment on the whispering campaign that is being directed against me."

"How can you really consider it a whispering campaign when all the major news media in the area are carrying the story?" Rod Vernon was in the first rank of reporters, his microphone thrust in Collig's face.

"No comment."

"It would seem that Commissioner DeCampo is taking the allegations very seriously," Vernon pressed. "Are you aware that you've been suspended?"

Collig gave him a look of pure murder. "No comment."

"Could you explain why you left your first police job?" Vernon tried to step around Collig to get into the house. Suddenly he found himself bouncing back from Collig's outflung arm.

"I came out here to make a statement, not invite you into my house to badger me." Collig's voice was ice-cold. "You guys are always ready to yell 'privacy' when cops try to get background on a guy. And your notes are confidential when we want to look at them. But when you want a story, it's fine to come poking and prying into someone's private life, destroying things." He glanced at the trampled rosebush, and his lips became a tight line. "So let me clue you in on something. This is private property, and I want all of you off it—now!"

"Or what?" Rod Vernon asked nastily. "You'll call the cops?"

For a second Frank wondered if Collig was going to burst into a rage. Even Vernon stepped back. But all Collig said was "No comment!"

41

He slipped back in through the door and slammed it in Vernon's face.

It may not have been a successful press conference, but it served its purpose. Most of the media people began packing up and heading off. "I expect a few diehards will stay out there," Collig said, still grim. "At least that so-called human being, Vernon, has left."

He glanced at Fenton and the boys. "I suppose you'll want to be going, too. Front door or back?"

"Back," Fenton Hardy promptly responded. "We had a run-in with Vernon and his friends, too."

Collig led them to the kitchen door and opened it. Fenton Hardy hesitated for a moment before stepping out. "Good luck, Ezra," he said. "And if you need—"

"Hardy, I know you mean well." Collig raised his hand, cutting Fenton off. "But thanks, anyway." He nodded to Frank and Joe.

The Hardys climbed the hill to their car and took off for home. Each was wrapped in thoughtful silence. At last Frank said, "So what do you think, Dad?"

Fenton Hardy shook his head. "I still believe he's an honest man—but an honest man with something to hide."

"What?" Joe wondered.

"Who knows? But something about this affair has Collig bothered and running a bit scared."

They arrived home to find the answering machine on Fenton's office phone blinking. While their father dealt with the message, the boys talked in the kitchen.

"Come on, Frank. The chief is a good guy. Whatever he's worried about—well, it may be nothing. Just an old embarrassment."

"Sure. Whenever I feel embarrassed, I grab a gun and threaten to take potshots at anybody in my backyard." Frank frowned as he poured himself a glass of milk. "Whatever it is, it's really got the chief off balance."

Fenton Hardy joined them. "The Pittman case is heating up," he announced. "That means I have to get on a plane to Florida right away. While I'm gone"—he sighed—"I suppose there's nothing I can say to keep you off the Collig case. I do have a job for you, though. Track down my papers and get them signed, will you? The licensing authority will start to get impatient."

Frank and Joe spent the evening relaxing as their mother, Laura, helped their father get ready for at least a week-long stay. The boys' aunt Gertrude was out of town, so Frank and Joe watched the evening news alone. Rod Vernon had edited his "interview" with Collig into a real hatchet job.

"Even without the gun Vernon managed to

make Collig look like a real looney-tune." Joe's forehead was creased with worry.

"Yeah, but he's still not presenting anything to back up what he said yesterday," Frank pointed out. "Let's pay a visit to headquarters tomorrow to see if the cops have found out anything solid."

The next morning Frank and Joe climbed the steps of police headquarters. Con Riley sat behind the booking desk. Apparently, he'd recovered from the media onrush.

"Well, gentlemen," he said when he saw the Hardys. "What can we do for you today?"

"Any news on our dad's papers?" Frank asked as he walked up to the desk.

"I've got good news and bad news about that," Con replied. "The papers have been found, but they're in the clutches of our acting chief."

Frank lowered his voice, glancing around. "And how is the acting chief doing on his investigation of the real chief?" he asked.

Even though no one was around, Riley lowered his voice, too. "It's supposed to be top-secret," he said. "But Lawrence and his troops decided to start off by questioning old members of the Bayport force." He grinned without humor. "And old cops love to gossip."

Riley shook his head. "But that's all Lawrence has—rumor and gossip. The old-timers say Collig was a real straight-arrow. He wouldn't go for any scams that were considered okay back then. As he rose in rank, he cracked down on those, too."

"I guess Lawrence is disappointed at what he found—or *didn't* find out," Frank commented.

"The best Lawrence has been able to come up with is a gap in the records. There are a couple of months between the time Collig left his job in Millerton and joined the force here in Bayport."

Con pitched his voice so it sounded like that of an announcer doing a commercial for a soap opera. "What was Collig up to? What was he living on? His ill-gotten gains? What terrible secrets will be discovered? Tune in tomorrow—"

"Riley!"

Con jumped. He and the boys turned to look down the hall at the chief's office. There stood a scowling Parker Lawrence. "If you're finished entertaining your young visitors, Patrolman, perhaps you can send them back here." He turned and stepped back into his office.

Poor Con Riley looked like a balloon with all the air let out. "I, uh, think the acting chief wants a word with you," he said.

The chief's office was pretty much the same: big wooden desk, old-fashioned desk lamp, but already a couple of new items had appeared. A computer sat on a table behind the desk, and a TV and VCR faced Parker Lawrence as he sat in the office chair.

45

Great, Frank thought. Now he can tape all his adventures.

Another thing struck Frank as being just the same. The acting chief gave them the same unfriendly stare that Ezra Collig had often aimed at them across this desk.

"I caught the tail end of that—performance—outside," Lawrence said. "You're trying to dig up information about my investigation. I want you to know that I know you and your father were at Collig's house yesterday."

He slammed a palm down on the desk—a fine dramatic gesture. Frank wondered if Lawrence had been practicing at home. "Obviously, you're planning to interfere in this case—but I won't have it!"

Joe saw red. "What are you going to do? Throw us in jail?"

Lawrence shook his head. "No, I'm just expressing my concern," he said in a silky voice. "I wouldn't want you to distract me from my job, because if I get too busy, I won't be able to sign these." He held up the manila envelope full of Fenton's papers.

"It would be a shame if your father lost his license because you wouldn't listen to reason."

"The nerve of that guy!" Joe slapped the passenger-side panel of the van. Lawrence is blackmailing us!"

Frank nodded from behind the driver's wheel.

"But we learned something. Two somethings, in fact. There's an information pipeline between Lawrence and Vernon. We weren't on TV last night. So how did he know we'd passed Collig's house?"

"Do you think maybe Lawrence is the one behind smearing Collig?" Joe suggested.

"Uh-uh," Frank said. "Lawrence may be exploiting and using it, but he's not the brains behind it."

"How do you figure that?" Joe frowned.

"He's a glory hound. Why do you think he has a VCR in his office? So he can see himself on TV. The only thing he cares about is his image. He's not the kind of guy to dig out a story or evidence—he's just a user. If he had solid evidence to get rid of Collig, he'd have it out by now."

"Right," Joe said. "Then who can have started the smear campaign? Who's the brains behind this? Who else do we have? Vernon? DeCampo? Mr. X from planet Y?"

"Judging from yesterday's newscast, Vernon hasn't got any real evidence against Collig, but he's obviously the media connection. Whoever's behind this fed him the initial rumors and stuff."

"So maybe we should keep an eye on Rod Vernon," Joe said, "because he might lead us to a suspect."

A quick call to their contact at the TV station told them where Rod Vernon's WBPT van was.

They arrived at the scene of a fire just in time to see the van pull away. Frank followed cautiously, right back to the television station.

"Great," Joe said as they pulled up across from the station's parking lot. "Now we're stuck on a stakeout."

After the TV van was parked, Rod Vernon didn't head into the building. He cut across the lot to a bright red Porsche Carrera and jumped into the driver's seat. With a throaty rumble the engine started and Vernon headed out.

"At least it's an easy car to spot," Frank said.

They followed the red car through downtown Bayport to the outskirts of town. Just across the bridge over the Willow River, a figure in a trench coat stepped out from behind a tree and waved. Vernon pulled off the road, and the figure slipped into his car.

"The elusive Mr. X," Joe said. "What now? We can't stop on the bridge to check them out."

"We'll pull past, find a place to hide the van, and make our way back." Frank sped up a little, passing Vernon's car. They couldn't get a good look at anyone in the low-slung sports model.

"Over there," Joe said, pointing. "We can park between those bushes."

Frank pulled the van neatly off the road. Then they got out, and closed the doors silently. "Stick to the brush at the side of the road," Frank said. "Don't let them spot us."

He pushed aside some prickly branches. In a

moment he'd have a clear view of who Vernon was conspiring with.

But he didn't get a chance to see. Instead, Frank heard only the roar of a car engine. A black car was streaking across the bridge, heading straight for Vernon's Porsche.

Vernon gunned his engine, slamming the car into gear, and the red sports car roared away.

Both cars screamed down the road in a high-speed chase!

Chapter

6

"CAUGHT FLATFOOTED," Joe said in disgust as the two cars roared past them.

"Well, come on!" Frank shouted, taking off for the van. Joe beat his brother to the door, flung himself in behind the steering wheel, and flipped the key in the ignition. Frank managed to close his door as the van tore out of the bushes.

"Can we catch them?" Frank asked as Joe goosed the gas pedal.

"The dark car, for sure. That's just a regular sedan." Joe was quietly confident of their van. "As for Vernon's Porsche, well, I guess we'll have to be lucky."

They headed down River Road, moving farther away from town.

"There they are!" Frank said as they rounded a curve.

The two cars raced along, far ahead of them. As they whipped along the curves in the country road, the black car stayed right on the tail of the red one.

"Hmm," Joe said. "That sedan has to be a special model, with a muscle engine."

"What we need is a little more muscle in *this* engine," Frank complained. They'd reached a long straightaway, but despite Joe's best efforts, they were hundreds of yards behind the other two cars.

"Hey, I built this van to move fast, but not to challenge every road rocket that comes along." Joe sounded a little embarrassed. "You can't win them all."

As it turned out, they did win one. They were still well behind when a police cruiser came tearing out of the brush ahead of them, siren wailing.

Joe slowed down. No way was he going to pass a cop car while moving well over the speed limit. As they followed, hanging back well behind the action, they saw the police car had the same problem they had had. Not enough speed.

"Looks like a tough chase for the cops," Joe said.

Finally the flashy sports car increased its lead over its black pursuer. The sedan pulled off to the side, and the police pounced, cutting it off.

Moments later the Hardys passed, going at a very slow speed. A red-faced police officer was writing a ticket for a red-faced driver. Joe and Frank both had plenty of time to recognize the man in the black car.

It was Chief Collig.

Later that day the boys learned that Rod Vernon had recognized his pursuer, too. The highlight of the "Evening News Hour" was a report from police headquarters about Collig's speeding ticket.

Joe shook his head and turned off the television. "The chief really blew it this time."

"He blew it for us, too." Frank flopped back on the couch. "If he'd held off for two seconds more, we'd have seen who was in the car with Vernon."

"Cut him some slack, Frank. How could he know we were there?" Joe protested. "Besides, he came up with the same idea you did—tailing Vernon. With a little luck he might have caught the guy in the car. He just has to get used to working the street again. He's a little rusty from running the police force, instead of being out on the streets, investigating."

For two days the Hardys kept an eye on Rod Vernon. They also grew steadily more worried as they realized just how rusty Ezra Collig's surveillance methods were. They could spot the chief a mile off, and so, unfortunately, could Vernon.

Three times during the first day they saw Collig's black sedan roar into humiliating camera ambushes. At one point Vernon's red sports car had stopped to pick up someone from a bus shelter. Collig continued to pursue aggressively. Suddenly the WBPT van screeched out of a side street, door open with a video operator hanging out. Vernon hopped from his car, a mike in his hand, and began asking Collig why he was harassing them.

That was the piece that appeared on the "Evening News Hour" that night.

The next day Collig became more cautious. He borrowed someone else's car to tail Vernon.

He was still spotted, though. Late in the day Vernon led him on a wild-goose chase, then parked in the lot at the Bayport Mall. Pursuing Vernon on foot, Collig ran into the Food Hall—and found another camera crew lying in wait.

"Why are you following me, Mr. Collig?" Vernon asked tauntingly in front of a large audience. "Why can't you let me do my job in peace? Or are you afraid of what I'll find?"

Teeth clenched, Collig wheeled around and walked away, pursued by the camera crew.

"Acting Chief Parker Lawrence has promised me police protection if you continue to harass me." Vernon's smug smile made Joe's stomach churn.

He and Frank were at the edge of a crowd of gawkers who had gathered. The boys made sure they were out of camera range. They didn't want their father to lose his license just because they turned up on Parker Lawrence's VCR.

Joe heard an odd conversation as the camera crew was packing up.

"You know," a young woman with a baby said to another shopper, "that's not fair. Why is this Vernon guy allowed to take Chief Collig apart, but the chief can't even try to find out what Vernon is up to?"

The friend nodded. "I thought maybe there was a case against Collig when they first announced this bribery thing. But we haven't seen any evidence about it on TV—just this Vernon showing poor Chief Collig up."

Frank had obviously been listening in, too. "Let's stop off at Mr. Pizza," he said suddenly.

"What about Vernon?"

"He'll be back at the studio, editing his latest little video footage. I want to catch some more public opinion."

They stopped at the entrance to the pizza shop. Inside, the kid with the greasy chin was chewing on yet another slice. "That was really some show out there. Vernon made Old Man Collig look like a jerk." The kid gave a loud horselaugh.

But instead of joining in, most of the kids in the shop were quiet.

54

"It was a pretty lousy trick, setting him up like that," one girl said.

"Come on! He caught Collig in the act!"

"In the act of what?" Callie Shaw whipped around from the counter, where she'd been getting a soda. "Following someone is no crime."

"It's harassment." The loudmouth tried to drum up support.

"What's calling a guy a crook without any proof?" one of his friends suddenly asked.

"The cops are checking into it," the loudmouth said sullenly.

"They haven't found anything, though. Neither have the TV reporters or the newspapers." The Hardys' friend Chet Morton put his slice of pizza down. "It's beginning to seem as if Rod Vernon shot his mouth off without any facts. I think they call that libel."

The kid chewed on that for a second, then said, "Well, Collig is a public figure. Doesn't that make it all right?"

"And what's Vernon—an unknown? Why can't Collig follow him? He isn't trying to shoot him or anything. He just wants to know what Vernon's doing. Why is Vernon getting so bent out of shape?"

"Unless," Callie said, "he hasn't got anything to back up his bluff."

"Hey, Charlie," Tony Prito said to the kid who'd been sounding off. "You finished with

55

that slice? Maybe you'd like to take a walk in the mall.''

Joe and Frank exchanged smiles as they ambled in for their dinner.

After that evening's telecast of the "Evening News Hour," Joe felt that a lot more folks would be on Collig's side. Instead of destroying Collig, Vernon was making people sympathetic to the police chief.

The next morning's *Bayport Times* editorial asked some very pointed questions.

Why was Rod Vernon making accusations he couldn't support? If he'd been told that Collig had collected bribes, why didn't he furnish specific proof? And why didn't the anonymous accuser step forward?

Frank folded the newspaper after they finished reading. "This time around we'll really have to keep an eye on Vernon," he said. "I'm betting that whoever is behind this will have to meet with him now. The smear campaign is losing momentum. They'll have to try something new."

Joe called his camera operator friend at WBPT, Johnny Berridge.

"Vernon is really catching some heat for this Collig thing," Berridge told him. "I think he's getting rattled. I overheard his assistant calling a local rental agency to get a car. Something tells me he may ditch his sharp wheels for something a little less noticeable."

"Like what?" Joe wanted to know.

Berridge's voice dropped low. "Like a brown sedan, license plate ZWD-one-nine-zero."

"That's a rental plate, all right," Joe said.

"It's parked across the street from the station, not in the lot," his contact went on. "Look, I've got to go. Hope this helps."

All day Vernon drove around in his flashy sports car or rode around in the WBPT van. Frank spotted Chief Collig, back in his black sedan. Vernon must have recognized the car, too, but he didn't try any camera attacks. The two of them, with Frank and Joe bringing up the rear, just drove around all day, an auto version of follow the leader.

At last Vernon arrived back at the station in time for the "Evening News Hour" telecast. Collig pulled into the parking lot, and Frank directed Joe to a spot on the street to continue their surveillance.

"I want to keep an eye on the lot and on that rental car on the street," he said.

They spent a boring hour and a half on the stakeout. Then, Joe exclaimed, "Pay dirt!" Rod Vernon dashed from the front door of the studio and hopped into the rental car.

As the Hardys pulled out to follow, Joe shot a quick glance back into the WBPT parking lot. "Should we just leave the chief sitting there?" he asked.

"He fouled up our chance of seeing who Vernon was meeting the last time," Frank said. "Not again."

This time Vernon headed for Bayport's downtown area.

"He's running out of streets," Joe said. "That's the bay up there."

Following him, they drove through a dingy neighborhood. Frank saw stained brick warehouses with sagging doors, and an occasional cheap restaurant, all closed now.

Joe hit the brakes suddenly. "He's driving out onto that dock."

"A good place to meet. They can guarantee nobody else will come too close."

Joe turned off his headlights and coasted to a stop about a block from the dock. "The corner up there has a broken streetlight," he said, jumping out of the van. "Maybe we can use the shadows to move in closer."

He led the way, half-crouching through the darkness. The street was covered with litter, and it was hard to move without making any noise. He and Frank reached a half-rotted shed at the foot of the dock when they heard somebody behind them kick over an empty soda can.

The Hardys froze as a man walked out from a shadowy side street into the wan glow of a streetlamp. Mark DeCampo!

"So *he's* the one behind all this," Joe whispered.

Vernon got out of his rental car and walked

back to meet the police commissioner. "This isn't too cool," Frank whispered. "If DeCampo is caught setting up a media hatchet job . . ."

The two men met on the dock and started talking. Joe and Frank were too far away to hear any words, but they could see the angry gestures. Vernon glanced at his watch. DeCampo peered into the darkness at the edge of the dock—uncomfortably close to the Hardys.

"Looks like they're waiting for somebody else, who hasn't shown yet," Frank said. "Maybe there *is* a Mr. X behind all this."

Shrugging, Rod Vernon headed back to his car. DeCampo followed, still gesturing.

"They've been stood up," Joe said. "Maybe we should step right up and ask who they're waiting for."

He put one foot on the dock, but that was as far as he got.

The brown rental car burst into flames with a roar, a tongue of fire licking up from the trunk. Joe and Frank staggered back.

The two men on the dock, much closer to the blast, were flung headlong, trapped beside the blaze!

Chapter

7

FRANK AND JOE BOTH LEAPT into action, running full-tilt onto the dock. Vernon and DeCampo both lay unmoving. The rental car was burning uncontrollably, and parts of the wooden dock had caught fire, too.

"We've got to get them away from there!" Frank yelled.

Joe looked doubtfully at DeCampo's dead-white face. "What if he's bleeding internally? We could hurt him."

"If we leave him there and the gas tank goes up, it'll kill him for sure," Frank snapped.

Together, they struggled to drag the two men to safety. Once the injured men were out of direct danger, Joe ran for the van and its mobile phone.

"There's been an explosion on the docks," he reported to the emergency operator. "Two men have been injured—*seriously*."

He joined Frank in giving mouth-to-mouth resuscitation to the two men until an ambulance arrived. The shriek of its siren was a welcome sound, until the Hardys realized it was accompanied by a police car.

When the patrol officers recognized the two casualties, they were on the radio immediately. "You two just stand here," one officer said to the Hardys as her partner called headquarters. Joe noticed her hand hovering by the gun butt at her hip. This is going to be just great, he told himself.

A flood of police reinforcements arrived, red and blue lights flashing in the darkness and sirens screaming. The lead car's door flew open, and out stepped Parker Lawrence. "Just like in the TV cop shows," Joe muttered.

The acting chief marched up to Frank and Joe. "Want to explain what you're doing here?" he asked curtly.

Frank shrugged. "We were following Rod Vernon—as it turns out, to a secret meeting with Commissioner DeCampo."

"Ah—um-hm." Lawrence went from angry to poker-faced as this sank in.

"And then Vernon's car exploded." Frank was on safer ground here. "Obviously, someone planted a bomb to get Rod Vernon—" He paused for a second. "Maybe it was aimed at the commissioner, too."

Lawrence headed for his car. "Equally obviously, we have a strong suspect, someone who considered both men to be his enemies—Ezra Collig."

"Chief Collig?" Joe said in disbelief. "But he's not even here. Vernon arranged to switch cars, and Collig didn't know. He's probably still sitting in the parking lot at the TV station."

"That's a poor attempt to create an alibi— with friendly witnesses." Lawrence glared at them stonily. "You apparently found out about the switch. So could Collig. And I'm sure you know that there are lots of ways to set up a long-range explosion: timers, radio controls—"

He picked up the microphone from his car radio and called headquarters. "Dispatch a car to the WBPT station parking lot. Officers will take in custody a male in a black sedan—Ezra Collig. He's wanted for questioning in connection with the bomb attack on Rod Vernon and Commissioner DeCampo at the docks."

Lawrence hesitated. "Make sure the personnel are I.A. unit members."

Internal Affairs, Joe realized. He wants his own flunkies to arrest the chief.

"As for you," Lawrence went on, "you're coming to headquarters. I want statements from both of you, and then I'll decide whether to hold you as material witnesses."

The Hardys rode in the acting chief's police car—in the backseat, where usually only prisoners rode. At least, Joe thought, we aren't handcuffed.

They had almost reached headquarters when an urgent call came in on the car radio. "The chief—I mean, Ezra Collig wasn't in the parking lot."

Giving their statements to two detectives inside took only a few minutes, but Joe and Frank wasted a couple of hours in Bayport's police headquarters while Parker Lawrence decided what to do with them. Actually, he didn't spend much time thinking. He was too busy directing an intensive manhunt all over town.

As word of the bombing—and the search for Collig—spread, headquarters filled with media people.

When Joe and Frank were finally sent to Lawrence's office, they found him sweating. Joe noticed that the man's usually immaculate uniform was rumpled. This was his first test as acting chief. So far it appeared that Lawrence was fumbling the ball.

He took it out on the boys. "You two are finished on this case," he growled as they stood in front of his desk. "I don't want you getting in my way again."

"I don't see how keeping an eye on Vernon got in your way," Frank said.

"Some good your eye did him," Lawrence sneered. "Or the commissioner."

"If we hadn't been around, they'd probably have burned to death on that dock," Joe burst out. "You should have taken better care of Vernon if he was snitching for you."

"Just out of curiosity," Frank asked, "was DeCampo the one who came up with the idea of smearing Chief Collig? Or was it someone else?"

Lawrence stared stonily at him. Frank continued impatiently, "We know there was no love lost between Collig and DeCampo. We heard DeCampo threaten to fire him. What doesn't fit is that DeCampo and Vernon were obviously waiting for someone on the dock—someone who didn't show."

"I don't have time to listen to this!" Lawrence shouted. "We know who set the bomb—Collig! He proved it by running. He must know by now that we want to question him, and he hasn't surrendered himself."

He cut himself off and glared at the Hardys. When he spoke again, his voice was tighter and higher. "Maybe I should remind you that your father's license is hanging by a thread. If you want him to work again, butt out."

"Sure, we get it, your mind is made up, so you don't want anyone confusing you with facts," Joe said.

"Out!" was Lawrence's only reply.

* * *

It was early morning when Frank and Joe returned home. Their mother was up, on the phone with their father. "Looks like we won't have to call a lawyer to get the boys away from the police," Laura Hardy said. "They're walking in the door now."

"But we've got a real problem, Mom," Frank said. "You and Dad should know about it."

Picking up the phone, he gave a rundown of what had happened in the last couple of days, including Parker Lawrence's threats about Fenton's license. The room was silent when he finished.

Then Fenton said, "Put me on the speaker phone."

"I said I'd stake my reputation on Collig's being innocent," the boys' father said. "Now I'll have to risk my business. Frank, are you sure those two were waiting for someone?"

"That's the way it looked," Frank said.

"DeCampo was definitely looking for someone," Joe added.

"And if we don't do something, Collig is going to be railroaded into jail." Fenton Hardy paused for a moment. "I say go for it, guys." He laughed. "Not that I expect Lawrence to keep my license from me. I've got enough police friends in other towns—or states, for that matter. What do you think, Laura?"

She smiled. "I think you boys had better crack this case. I'd hate to move."

"Thanks, Mom—Dad." Joe was grateful for the vote of confidence, until he realized the size of the job facing him and Frank. How were they supposed to clear Ezra Collig?

After a few more moments of discussing strategy with their father, they hung up.

"I'm bushed," Joe said, yawning. "It's bed for—"

His words were cut off by the ringing of the phone.

"Now, who'd be calling us at this hour?" Laura Hardy said.

Frank picked up the phone to hear Chet Morton on the other end. "Hey, Frank," his old friend said. "I sure hope I didn't wake you, but there's something weird going on out here. Mom and Dad are away, so I'm holding down the fort alone. A little while ago I started hearing noises. I thought of calling the cops, but I'd hate to have it turn out to be a raccoon. Um—but I'd also hate to go out alone and have it turn out *not* to be a raccoon." Chet was trying to sound cool about the situation, but Frank could tell he was nervous.

"We'll come out and help you check around," Frank promised. "We're leaving now."

He turned to Joe. "No time for sleep. Something's gone bump in the night out at the Mortons'."

Joe used the high beams as they drove to the Morton farm. Chet and his family lived out where the real country began. There were no streetlights, but he easily spotted Chet's house. Every window was lit up.

"Glad you guys are here," Chet said, greeting the Hardys at the door.

"What kind of noises are you hearing?" Joe wanted to know.

"Shh! Listen!" Chet peered nervously into the darkness. Then they heard it, too.

Out of the inky night came a fuzzy crackling sound, followed by a sharp click.

"I've heard that before," Frank said. "Recently. But where?"

"Let's get some flashlights and check it out," Joe suggested. Armed with the lights and Chet's baseball bat, they set off across the barnyard. The sounds grew louder as they approached a small patch of forest not far from the road.

"Voices!" Chet burst out.

Frank sped up. "I think I know what this is!" He plunged into the woods, followed by the others. Cutting across the road, he found what he expected.

It was a black sedan, canted at a crazy angle. One wheel was up on a tree root, and the driver's door was open, as if the car had been abandoned quickly. With a blast of crackling static the police-band radio on the front seat came to life: "Headquarters—A-thirteen in position on River Road. No sign of fugitive. Over."

Then came a sharp click as the headquarters' radio operator responded.

"Well, now we know why Lawrence's manhunt was such a bust," Joe said. "Collig was listening in on every one of his orders."

It was only a couple of hours to sunrise when the Hardys found themselves back at police headquarters. Parker Lawrence was not pleased. Besides calling the cops about discovering the car, Joe and Frank had also informed WBPT, the *Bayport Times,* and a couple of radio stations.

Joe grinned at the media people crowding the headquarters lobby. They were having a fine old time with the fact that Collig the fox had so embarrassingly eluded Lawrence's hounds.

The acting chief completely forgot about the media people when he saw the Hardys. "I told you what I'd do if I found you meddling in this case!" he shouted.

"Since when is reporting an abandoned vehicle meddling?" Joe asked. "Especially when it was one you were searching for so hard?"

"Face it, Lawrence," Frank said as cameras and microphones zoomed in on him. "You're after the wrong man. Collig didn't set that bomb. You can't even pin a clear motive on him. We're going to Millerton tomorrow." He glanced at his watch. "I guess I mean today. And we're going to get to the bottom of this bribery story."

In the brief silence that followed, they heard a reporter saying, "This is Bayport Newsradio, live from police headquarters."

When he realized their confrontation was being broadcast live, Lawrence shut up and sent the boys home. They got a few hours' sleep, then, yawning, set off for Millerton.

"I don't get it," Joe complained as they pulled away. "We were pretty groggy by the time we got home. But I'm sure I'd have noticed the gas gauge reading empty."

"We'd better fill up before we get on the interstate," Frank said.

They headed for their usual gas station. Frank paid the cashier while Joe worked the self-service pump.

"That'll do it," Joe said, hanging up the hose. "We were almost bone-dry."

As he started to open the passenger door, a figure suddenly darted out from a patch of bushes nearby. Joe stood frozen as the figure dashed past him, through the open door, and into the van.

It was Chief Collig!

Chapter

8

"WHA-WHAT ARE YOU DOING?" an utterly dumb-founded Joe asked.

"And why are you doing it *here?*" Frank had arrived at the other door. He stared in dismay at their uninvited guest.

"That should be obvious. I'm getting a lift out of this burg." Ezra Collig was calm and confident as he took a seat in the rear of the van. "I caught your little run-in with Parker Lawrence on the radio late last night. I was grabbing a cup of coffee at a greasy spoon outside of town."

He shifted in his seat. "Like you guys, I realized I'd never be able to beat this bombing rap if I stayed in Bayport. Lawrence wants my head on a spike over the door of headquarters. I've got to find someone who can tell my side of the story about what happened in Millerton. That means going there. So, when I heard you two were heading that way, I walked back to town and figured I'd hitch a ride."

"How did you know we were going to be here?" Frank asked.

"Oh, I know where you and your dad stop to get gas," Collig said. "So I just made sure you'd need some. Sorry about that—I owe you for half a tank of super unleaded."

The boys continued to stare in complete disbelief. Why didn't he just get in the van at the house? Joe wondered. Maybe Collig was enjoying playing bad guy a little too much.

Collig gestured for them to get in the van. "Well, come on! If you're going to stand out there and stare with your mouths open, you're going to call attention to us." He glanced at the open doors. "And right now attention is not what I need."

Joe climbed aboard and so, reluctantly, did Frank. "You know, you could land us in trouble—deep trouble," Joe said at last. "I mean, officially you're a fugitive. How many times have you taken a dim view—"

"In other words, how many times have you done this to *me* over the years?" Collig interrupted. "You've just about driven me nuts, helping suspects escape, fouling up my investigations. Well, this time *I'm* the fugitive."

He looked at them pleadingly. "So, why can't

71

you butt in this once, when I really need your interference?''

''The people we've always helped have been innocent.'' The words had burst from Frank's mouth and surprised him almost as much as they did Joe. He glanced from Joe's shocked face to Collig's stony one. He took a deep breath before adding, ''Okay. So I think you're innocent, too. Let's roll.''

They pulled out of the gas station and headed for the interstate.

''A fugitive,'' Ezra Collig mused as they rolled along. ''It's been a long time since I had to pull up stakes and run for it. Sharpens your mind a bit.''

Frank wanted to ask what he meant, but the chief continued, paying no attention. ''Since Bea passed away, I've just been living on the rebound, not really living, just reacting to things. It's funny. Hearing Lawrence order his stooges to pick me up was like a strong slap in the face. Wake up, Collig! You've got a life to take care of!''

Frank took the opportunity to ask some questions. ''Maybe you can tell us some of the stuff that Lawrence hasn't found out yet,'' he said. ''For instance, where did you spend those mystery months between your first job and coming to Bayport?''

Collig looked embarrassed. ''It's no mystery,

really. All Lawrence had to do was check." His ears went red. "I was in high school."

"What?" Joe stared. He *couldn't* have heard that right!

"I was sweeping a store by day and taking night classes to get my high-school diploma." Collig became a little defensive as he explained, "It's not something I wanted spread all over."

"You were a high-school dropout?" Frank asked.

"You make that sound like the title of an old crime movie. You have to remember, things were a lot different when I was a kid." Collig grinned. "No, I'm not going to tell you about wrestling grizzly bears on the way to school. But in those days you could get a decent job even if you didn't finish school. And I don't mean flipping burgers." Collig's lips tightened. "Things were tough at home, and it was time for me to feed myself. I left school in the middle of my senior year. Got a job on a road-building crew."

He smiled at the memory. "It was backbreaking work. Then one day I happened to see an old chain-gang flick. The prisoners in the movie were doing the same work I was." He gave the boys another grin. "So I decided to change careers."

"And you became a cop?" Frank asked.

"The Millerton force didn't have the highest standards," Collig admitted. "If you had two arms, two legs, and enough muscle, you got the job. Being able to write your name was sort of like icing on the cake. It was a different world then, guys, a different world. . . ."

Frank decided to ask about something else that had been puzzling him. "Chief, did you recognize the picture that ran in the *Bayport Times?*"

"Believe it or not, that was me—a lot younger and much skinnier, of course." Collig patted his ample midsection as he spoke.

"I mean, do you remember the picture itself? Where it was taken?"

Collig shook his head, frowning. "There was just a brick wall behind me. Maybe if I saw the whole picture, it would shake a memory loose."

"The picture came to the *Times* by messenger, and it was cut in half," Joe added.

"Cut in half?" Collig sat a little straighter in his seat, a shadow flitting across his face. He shook his head. "Nope. That doesn't ring any bells."

"So how come you went back to school?" Joe asked.

"Ambition," Collig told him. "I wanted a better job as a cop. But I found out the better police forces had stiffer requirements—like a high-school diploma."

He shrugged, probably to chase away the remembrance of those past disappointments. "After getting turned down for the fifth time, I settled in Atlantic Heights, a bit down the coast

74

from here, got a job to keep body and soul together, and enrolled in night school.''

"Why Atlantic Heights?'' Frank asked.

"They have a good police force there, and the desk sergeant was friendly. He said if I got a diploma, he'd see about getting me a job.''

"So you got your diploma,'' Joe said.

Collig nodded. "Believe it or not, I was a straight-A student. Till then I'd never much cared about studying. But now I had a reason to work.''

He smiled at some scene many years distant. "A couple of reasons, actually. I made up my senior year and graduated from Atlantic Heights High. My name's right there in their records, and of course the information is in the records down at headquarters. Lawrence could have found out if he'd just looked.'' Collig frowned. "But he was too busy trying to prove I was doing something crooked.''

"Wait a second,'' Joe said, glancing back at the chief. "You said that after you graduated that sergeant was going to get you a job on the local force. What happened?''

Collig shrugged. "Another sergeant's nephew got the slot instead of me. I don't regret my stay in Atlantic Heights, though. I got my diploma, and there was a cute instructor, right out of teacher's college. Bea Cowan. She made me the happiest man in the world when she agreed to become Bea Collig.''

"You married your teacher?" Joe exclaimed. That's one way to get good grades, he thought to himself.

"Yup," Collig said happily. "I sent out applications to all the nearby towns. The Bayport P.D. asked me to come for an interview and liked what they saw. The rest, as they say, is history."

Frank glanced in the rearview mirror for a look at Collig as they reached the crest of a hill. "Well, that takes care of the time between leaving Millerton and reaching Bayport," he said. "Can you tell us about your first job? Your time in Millerton?"

They went over the top of the hill, and Joe suddenly leaned forward in his seat. "No more time for trips down memory lane," he said suddenly. "We've got major trouble up ahead."

Frank watched the road and became pale. The thin morning traffic was slowing and bunching up as they approached a barricade of police cars.

"A roadblock," he said, his throat dry. "And we've rolled right into it!"

Chapter

9

"IT'S MY OWN STUPID FAULT." Collig's expression was grim as he peered through the windshield. "I was busy yakking instead of thinking."

He growled low in his throat as the van joined the tail end of the line of cars waiting to pass through. "The force has a standard plan for setting up roadblocks. Know who picked this place? Me. I figured right beyond the crest of this hill was perfect—fugitives wouldn't see the roadblock until it was too late."

"Right—just as the cops would see us now if we tried to turn around. It would be like waving a big red flag saying, 'Come and chase us!' " Joe glanced at his brother. "We've got a problem. What do we do?"

"We're in plain view of everyone," Collig

said unhappily. "Even if I bail out, the boys will see me—and they'll know which vehicle I left."

"That's true." In his mind's eye Frank just saw his father's P.I. license fly away.

"I don't suppose we could just ram our way through," Joe suggested.

"Right. No one would notice that." Frank gave his brother an annoyed look.

"I say, just hang tough." Collig left the seat he'd been in, moving to the shadows in the rear of the van.

If the cops open the back door, we've had it, Frank thought, but he didn't have much choice. They'd reached the barricade.

The police officer who approached them had a vaguely familiar face. Frank must have seen him around town. Certainly he recognized Frank. A big grin spread over the patrolman's round face. "Well, well, if it isn't the famous Hardy brothers! Making your trip to Millerton, I presume, as announced on the media."

Frank's insides froze. What if Parker Lawrence had decided to stop them? What if he'd issued orders to have them picked up? The van might well have become Chief Collig's limousine to jail!

Wild thoughts of escape flashed through Frank's mind. Then he realized that the officer was laughing. "You guys did a nice job of making Lawrence look like a twit. It was all over the morning news. Keep up the good work in Millerton. Pass on!"

The officer waved them through. "See you on TV!"

Both Hardys breathed deep sighs of relief. The general dislike for Parker Lawrence in the Bayport force had rescued them! They continued down the interstate.

Behind them they heard dry laughter as Chief Collig returned to his seat. "Well, we lucked out on that," he said.

"Let's hope our luck holds," Frank responded. "I'm too young to die of a heart attack."

"There shouldn't be any more roadblocks. That was the farthest location I ever planned." He paused for a second, then said casually, "You didn't happen to get the badge number of the officer who let you through?"

"Why?" Joe asked. "Do you want to thank him?"

"No," Collig replied. "If *when* I get this mess cleared up, I intend to chew that cop out for letting me escape."

The ride to Millerton took a couple of hours. At first Collig was quiet, having been jolted out of his talkative mood by the near-miss at the roadblock.

Gradually, though, Frank managed to start a conversation again, bringing it around to Collig's days in Millerton. Still, he never worked up the courage to ask Collig outright about the bribery charge. That seemed to be pushing it.

Collig had a huge fund of stories from what he called his rookie days. Some were funny, like when he got fooled into buying ice cream for a supposedly lost little girl. He found out the kid pulled that trick on every new cop who pounded the beat. "She should have weighed a ton from all the ice cream she put away," the chief said.

There were also scary stories such as the first time he'd had to pull his gun. After chasing a burglar for six blocks, the guy turned on him with a knife. "We faced off for a long moment," Collig said. "That stupid switchblade looked like a sword to me. As it turned out, my gun must have looked like a cannon to him because he gave up, and I got my first collar—my first arrest."

Frank felt as if he was getting a peek into another world—one out of the past. "It's all different now," Collig said. "Criminal law and how it's enforced have changed completely. When I started out, there was a lot less hassle about using deadly force. Using a gun in certain situations would have won a promotion and a medal in the old days. Now it would get you thrown off the force. We didn't have to knock and announce ourselves as police when we raided a place. And the idea of reading a card to warn a crook of his rights . . ." He just shook his head.

"Back in those days if you didn't like some

character's looks, you could stop him on the street and toss him. Search his pockets. Today that would be 'unreasonable search and seizure' because I didn't have 'sufficient cause.' When a known thief turned up on your beat, you'd whack the guy in the calf with your nightstick.''

"Just to scare him?" Joe asked.

"No, as crime prevention. If the guy's leg hurt so bad he couldn't run, he couldn't steal." Collig shrugged. "Sooner or later the thief would get the message. He'd grow tired of getting whacked and move along.''

"What did the public think about this?" Frank wondered out loud.

"Most of them thought it was great. Store owners on the beat would give you presents. I knew one officer who brought a little red wagon along on his beat every Christmas. It would be piled high by the end of the day. Restaurants and diners were happy to have cops around for protection. They'd let us in 'on the arm.' We ate for free.''

"Chet Morton would sign up for a chance like that," Joe joked.

"Some guys took advantage, of course. My old partner would take the freshest fruit off stands without paying. He wouldn't even ask." A frown passed over Collig's face as he spoke. For the next few miles he was silent.

"What's the matter, Chief?" Frank finally asked. "Something wrong?"

81

"I was just reminded of something else," Collig said, then added, "the blue wall of silence."

"What was that?" Joe wanted to know.

"If a cop did something wrong, it was settled inside the department, in secrecy. No press releases, no snooping reporters. No one ever wanted the force or any cop to look bad."

Is that what happened to the chief? Frank wondered. Did he do something wrong—something halfway okay in that simpler world but illegal in today's world?

"Sounds as if you had some kind of problem with that wall." Frank hoped he could get Collig to talk about it. Then maybe they wouldn't have anything to investigate in Millerton.

"You could say that," Collig grunted. But that was all he said. He simply sat, tense and silent, for the rest of the ride. Frank knew he still couldn't ask the chief about the bribery charge.

"Just drop me off here," Collig said abruptly as they came to a hill at the edge of town. Frank got his first view of Millerton—a vista of low brick buildings. "I don't believe it," Collig said. "The place has hardly changed."

"Do you want to arrange a place to meet—"

Before Frank could even finish, Collig had jumped out of the van and disappeared into the bushes. He didn't even look back.

Shaking his head, Frank drove into the center of town.

"Why didn't you just ask him about the bribery thing?" Joe wanted to know.

"Why didn't you?" Frank answered.

Joe shrugged, and they both understood it was a question they couldn't ask Collig directly.

"Where to first?" Joe asked.

"Let's try the library. They should have back issues of the local newspapers."

An overworked librarian was not very happy at their request. "I'll have to unlock the Special Document Room for you. The papers from that far back are kept in bound volumes there."

"No microfilm?" Frank said, surprised.

"We keep hoping to get it in the budget, but this is a poor town." A glance around the library confirmed that. Its dingy walls should have been painted years before, there were gaps in the shelves of books, and a lot of the stock seemed to be badly dog-eared paperbacks.

The Special Documents Room turned out to be an airless closet down in the basement. Sighing, Joe took the volume covering the year before Collig's resignation. Frank got down the volume covering the year after.

After a few hours of fruitless searching, Joe closed his book. "There's not a mention, not even a hint, of any police problems. All they were interested in was how the new interstate would revitalize the area's economy."

"I guess they were wrong about that, too." Frank thought of the tired-looking town as he shut his book. "I've covered more than a year after Collig left, and there's no mention of bribery."

"Maybe this was settled behind the blue wall of silence," Joe suggested, "without press releases."

Frank nodded. "Without snooping reporters, either, I bet." He stretched, then returned the volumes to their shelves. "Well, let's try to pierce that blue wall—at police headquarters."

After asking the librarian for directions, the Hardys jumped in their van and drove off.

Millerton Police Headquarters was a smoke-stained brick building, as shabby as the rest of the town. Frank noticed litter tossed around the front steps as they walked in. "We're here to see Detective Preznowski," he told the officer behind the scarred front desk.

A phone call to their father had set the police old-boy system to work. Out came Detective Dwight Preznowski, a short, rotund man. "Come on in here," he said, leading them to an empty squad room. "A pal of mine in Junction City owes your dad, and I owe him. I sat here and waited for you guys, and you made me miss a free lunch—the shoo-flies from Bayport were buying."

"Shoo-flies?" Joe asked.

"That's what we call Internal Affairs people," Preznowski explained. "You know the song— 'Shoo, fly, don't bother me.' "

"So, the Bayport Internal Affairs people are here?" Frank said.

"Yeah, asking questions about Collig and all this ancient history as if it happened two days ago. They're taking us out to lunch to 'ensure our cooperation.' Instead, I'm giving you all that they got." Preznowski walked to a nearby desk, scooped up a thin file folder, and handed it to Frank.

"This is it? His service record?" Frank scanned the two sheets inside. Height, weight— had Ezra Collig ever been that thin? Here was the date Collig had joined the force, his commendations, arrests, and after less than a year, his resignation. The second sheet was a typed resignation letter, painfully citing personal reasons.

"Not very much," Joe said, reading over his brother's shoulder.

Preznowski shrugged. "It's all we've got on paper."

Frank turned back to the first sheet, remembering one of Collig's stories on the ride. "Can you get us the file on"—he checked the record for the name of Collig's partner—"Raymond Bozeman?"

Sighing, Preznowski disappeared into a file room. Soon he was back, with a somewhat thicker file. "Happy?"

"We'll see." Frank ran through the file, scanning dates, commendations, arrests, partners—

85

the last being Ezra Collig. Then he found a resignation letter, dated about a month after Collig's.

"Personal reasons again," Joe said.

"Is there a listing of people who left the force
around this time?" Frank asked.

It took some digging, but in the end the Hardys had a list of seven names, which they
checked against the files.

"One medical discharge, one retirement, and
five resignations, starting with Collig's."

Frank raised his eyebrows at Joe. "All of
them for personal reasons."

Chapter

10

STANDING BY HIS BATTERED DESK in the squad room, Detective Preznowski stared in grudging admiration at the list the Hardys had compiled. "In a couple of hours you two kids have managed to accomplish more than those shoo flies did in the last few days."

He rattled the paper in his hand. "Come on. Let's go talk to the chief." He led Frank and Joe down a corridor to an office marked Chief.

Chief Gilmartin of the Millerton police force was a thin, wiry man with a fringe of white hair over his ears. Frank saw that the man's faded blue eyes stayed sharply on Preznowski as the detective related his story.

"We've had reporters and those Internal Affairs types from Bayport all over here,"

Gilmartin said. "But this is the first solid lead anyone has come up with."

Frank felt a twinge. Was it a solid lead that might lead Collig into more trouble?

"The Bayport I.A. guys are more like accountants than cops," the chief went on. "They have no idea how to dig into a case. Would you believe that they were trying to find records of disciplinary hearings? From *those* days? None of that went down on paper."

Obviously, Frank thought, Chief Gilmartin was a graduate of the blue-wall-of-silence school.

"Were you on the force when Collig was here?" Frank asked.

The chief shook his head. "That was a little before my time. I came on to replace one of the guys on this list." He tapped the paper.

"When I started pounding the beat, a lot of the local shopkeepers were angry at us. They didn't trust the police. And the chief back then, Old Man McClure, set up all new rules. 'No officer shall accept any gratuities,' " he quoted. "I remember, I had to look up what a gratuity was. Why couldn't he have just said, 'no tips'? A lot of guys were nervous. Nobody wanted to talk about why new rules were needed."

He shrugged. "You didn't need to be a great detective to figure some guys must have been shaking down the local merchants. But the stink died down pretty fast. Nobody likes to remember that kind of thing."

"Would it be possible to track down the men who resigned?" Frank asked.

Chief Gilmartin shook his head. "Not from our records. How long were they here? Five, seven—the longest service was ten years. Back then you didn't get a pension till you put in twenty-five years. There was no reason for us to keep track of these guys."

"How about retirees?" Frank suggested desperately. "Maybe some of them would remember exactly what happened."

The chief reached into his desk and came out with a list. "You can make a copy of this. I gave one to the Bayport Internal Affairs guys." Gilmartin didn't look very hopeful. "Some of the men from those days are dead. The rest are all over the Sun Belt. When you're old, winter in Millerton isn't much fun."

Frank scanned the list. He saw addresses in Florida, Arizona, California. "Have the Bayport investigators contacted any of these people?"

"Not on our phones," Gilmartin said firmly. "Money is tight around here. I heard one of them say they could wait till they got back to their office to make the calls."

The Hardys nodded. That fit in with the way Parker Lawrence wanted the case investigated—nice and slow.

"Isn't there anyone in town who might know about that time?" Frank asked.

"Maybe Commissioner Potts," Preznowski

suggested. "The Commish was around in those days."

"The police commissioner?" Joe asked eagerly.

"Ah—no." Chief Gilmartin looked as if his detective had told a joke in very poor taste. "Some of our people call Potts 'Commissioner' as a joking nickname. He's an old, retired officer. A good cop, but I don't think he'd be of much use to you." Gilmartin continued to give Preznowski the evil eye.

"Well, sir, I guess we've taken up enough of your time." Frank was eager to get out of the office before he ran into any of the Bayport investigators. So far they'd been lucky. He also wanted one peek in the records to find out where Potts called home.

A brief search of Millerton's streets led them to the address they'd gotten from the files. Leonard Potts lived in a shabby apartment house on the poor side of a poor town. The Hardys had a shock when the apartment door opened. A raw-boned man with an unshaved chin peered out at them. His body was twisted, one hip leading the other.

"What can I do for you?" he asked.

"I'm Frank Hardy, and this is my brother, Joe. We're looking into something that happened in the police force about thirty-five years ago. Maybe you can help us."

"I was heading out for a little dinner," Potts told them. "You can come along and talk." He

90

set off painfully down the stairs. Frank and Joe followed.

They went to a smoky little restaurant with a long bar down one side. "This place used to be Minty's, a cop hangout," Potts told them. "I still come in for old times' sake." He pointed to the exposed brick wall, where a moth-eaten moose head hung. "We had a regular tradition. All the rookies had their pictures taken with their partner and the moose head. We used to say it looked like Chief McClure." A waitress came, and Potts ordered soup and salad without glancing at the menu. The boys asked for hamburgers. They had missed their lunch.

Potts watched them from his chair. "I guess you notice I go off at an odd angle these days," he said. "I was the longest-service, most-decorated cop on the force. Then one day my partner and I went to check on a stolen car. Punk inside had a nine-millimeter pistol. Killed my partner, put four bullets into me. They did a job on my hip and spine. I came out of the hospital, and they gave me a medal. Told me I could work at headquarters—easy duty.

"Then, one day, I had to go down to the firing range. Somebody shot his gun, and I was under a table, screaming. The force had a big problem—a hero with a medal who couldn't stand guns. They called it a nervous breakdown, gave me a medical discharge. I'm fine—as long as I remember to take my pills."

He took a little box out of his pocket. "Pink, white, blue." Potts washed down each pill with a sip of water. Then he looked at them with red-rimmed eyes.

"So," he said. "What do you want to know about the Millerton police force?"

He started nodding when he heard their story. "Yeah, yeah, I remember those days." He gave them a lopsided grin. "Even if I say so myself, I was a pretty good cop. I had a nose for everything happening on my beat. So I noticed when the shop owners began acting funny—something between hate and fear."

Potts frowned. "I remember getting a meal on the arm, and the diner owner coming out and sounding off about it. 'Isn't it enough that I pay you guys off?' he said. 'Do you have to eat me out of house and home?' " Potts shifted in his seat. "Of course, it turned out to be Bozeman."

"Raymond Bozeman?" Joe asked.

The old man nodded. "He was quite the lad, Ray Bozeman. Everyone expected him to move up when Sergeant Henried retired, because everyone took Bozeman's orders already. But he was too greedy, making money on the side—protection money. Stores began getting windows broken or maybe they'd have a little legal trouble. Bozeman would step in, and then everything was fine."

Potts leaned back, eyes half-closed as he remembered. "Bozeman had a rookie partner.

Every Friday the kid went out, regular as clockwork, to collect the money from the store owners."

The food had arrived, but neither Hardy was hungry now. "Do you remember the rookie's name?" Frank asked. If Potts actually fingered Ezra Collig—

Potts shrugged. "Who can recall after all those years? He was only around a couple of months. Then he left. After that, Bozeman and a bunch of other guys resigned."

Frank and Joe paid the bill, leaving the old man to his soup and salad. "Did I help?" Potts asked.

"You answered a lot of *my* questions," Frank said. But I don't happen to like the answers, he thought.

"I still don't believe it," Joe said as they stepped into the darkening street. "A rookie who was making collections, then was the first to leave the force. We know who it has to be. But why—*how* did he wind up doing that?"

"Boys!" a voice hissed from a nearby alley.

The Hardys turned to see Ezra Collig beckoning them.

"That place you were in—is it still Minty's?" Collig asked when they'd joined him. They shook their heads. "It used to be a cop hangout. I thought some of the old gang might be there."

"Gang?" Frank said a little coldly. "What an interesting word. There was no 'gang' in there,

93

Chief. Just an old man named Potts. He told us about Ray Bozeman and his rookie partner. Oh, yes, and there was also something about extortion and collecting protection money from local merchants.''

Collig focused on the ground. "I know all about that," he said quietly. "I was the bagman.''

Joe and Frank stood silent for a second. They'd been convinced by Potts's story, but actually hearing Chief Collig confess shook them up.

"Wait! You have to hear the whole story!" When Collig raised his eyes, they were wild. "I was just a kid—"

"Oh, no," Joe said, "not the old 'I was just a kid' cop-out.''

Collig glared at him. "I was a raw rookie, just off the farm, and I got chosen as partner by the hottest cop on the force. Ray Bozeman taught me how to be a cop. I thought he was the greatest guy in the world. When he asked me to take over the collections for the Policemen's Fund, of course I did.''

He shook his head at his own stupidity. "I couldn't understand why all the storekeepers seemed so angry at donating to a charity fund. Finally one shopkeeper's daughter exploded at me. 'I thought you were a pretty good guy,' she said. 'Why are you helping to rob my father?' ''

The chief's mouth quirked in a self-mocking

smile. "That's when I learned the Policemen's Fund was mainly a charity for one policeman— Ray Bozeman. He got most of the take and split the rest with his pals.

"I was sick to realize the racket I was involved with. And I was scared, too. How could I go up against Bozeman and his boys? Police work is dangerous enough with a partner to cover your back. When you're fighting crooks in front and can't trust the guys behind—well, it's like being caught in a cross fire. You don't survive."

He sighed. "It was the toughest thing I ever did, but I took my bag of collections straight to Chief McClure. The old man nearly swallowed his dentures, but you have to give him credit. He believed me and promised the situation would be taken care of."

"What happened to you?" Joe asked.

"The chief told me that by turning Bozeman in, I'd turned myself into a target. He's the one who suggested I get out of town. I stayed in touch until I heard that Bozeman and his cronies had left the force. Then I thought the nightmare was over."

"And?"

"And I got on with my life. I tried to get a better job, discovered I needed more education. Then I met Bea. She showed me I could be more than a cop on the beat. I even went to college, got a degree, won promotions. . . ." His voice ran down. "My decision to turn that money in was the turning point that set the whole course of my life. You could say it made me the man I am today."

He looked down at his hands. "Now Bea's dead, and this accusation from my past has surfaced. The mistake I thought I had set right . . . there's no one left who knows the *whole* story. Chief McClure died years ago. He was proud to see where I'd gotten. And Captain Frazee, he knew the score, too, but a heart attack took him a dozen years back."

Frank nodded thoughtfully. "There's no written proof, because they didn't keep records about dirty cops."

"I have no proof of my story at all," Collig said quietly.

"Maybe we could talk with Potts again," Joe began, turning back toward the street.

His words were cut off by three gunshots— and a wild scream.

96

Chapter

11

JOE AND FRANK RAN out of the alley toward the sound of the shots—into the street. They found it empty. Apparently, Joe thought, people in this neighborhood didn't gather to see what was going on when they heard gunfire. No, very sensibly they stayed away.

Wait—the street wasn't completely empty. Joe spotted a huddled figure lying in the gutter. "Frank! Over here!"

Together they raced toward the man in the gutter.

A dark figure leaned out of an alley farther down the block. "Down!" Frank yelled, catching a glint of light on a gun barrel. Four more shots blasted out.

The Hardys hit the ground. Across the street

from them the prone figure let out another wild scream.

"I don't get it," Joe whispered. "Those shots are going way over him. Why—"

Frank had rolled behind a parked car. Rising to a crouch, he dashed from car to car, using every scrap of cover. He peered into the darkness of the alley where the gunman had been.

"You can get up, Joe. The shooter's gone."

An infuriated roar came from the alley they had left. "Are you two out of your minds, running into gunfire like that? You could have been killed!" Collig shouted.

Frank was across the street and kneeling over the crumpled form in the street. "I thought that baggy coat looked familiar," Joe said, joining his brother.

It was Leonard Potts. He lay on his side, all his muscles tensed, his body pulled into a tight ball.

"He doesn't seem to be hit," Frank said, reaching down to touch the man. Potts flinched. The sound that burst from his throat was the whimper of a frightened animal.

"The gunshots!" Joe said in a hushed voice. "They must have set him off again."

Chief Collig joined the boys, staring down. "Len?" he said in shock. "Len Potts?"

For a second the tensed figure on the ground coiled. Potts's lids opened, his eyes not focusing completely as they took in Collig, and he gasped. "Young Collig! Another ghost trying to kill me!"

"Another ghost?" Collig repeated. "What do you mean? What ghost? Who? You've got to tell me, Potts!"

The other man had curled himself into a ball again, a thin whine escaping from his teeth.

Collig turned in desperation to the Hardys. "Did you see the guy who was shooting? What do you think Potts meant?"

"He was just a shadow with a gun," Joe said.

"I have no idea what Potts is trying to say." Frank shook his head, staring at the helpless bundle Potts had become. "I'll tell you one thing, though. The only guy left who knew anything about Bozeman's extortion scheme won't be telling anyone about it soon."

The wail of sirens approached them through the streets.

"Can you tell us anything more about Bozeman?" Frank asked. He turned and found that Collig had disappeared.

Joe followed Frank's surprised gaze. "I guess we shouldn't be surprised," Joe said. "There are lots of alleys around here. And what do you expect a fugitive to do when he hears sirens?"

The Millerton police were the first to arrive. "Hey, it's the Commish!" one of the officers cried. He knelt to check the frail old man's pulse. "It's okay, pal. It's okay."

He turned to the Hardys. "What happened?"

"Somebody fired a gun from that alley over there," Joe said, pointing.

"Someone shot at Commissioner Potts?" the cop said in disbelief.

"We don't know. He was on the ground, but he wasn't hit."

"What kind of sicko would do a thing like that? Everybody around here knows the Commish. Nobody would want to hurt him."

"It looks like somebody was really aiming for his weak point." Joe's face was grim in the revolving red lights of an ambulance that had just arrived. Attendants in white coats were gently shifting Potts onto an ambulance gurney.

Frank turned to the patrolman, who was taking statements on his notepad. "Could you put us in touch with Detective Preznowski?"

Back at headquarters the Hardys stood with Preznowski in a now-crowded squad room. "So you say the Commish actually remembered a little about what happened way back when, huh? What do you know."

"According to Potts, Ray Bozeman was running an extortion racket," Frank said.

"Well, he sure doesn't sound like a model officer," Preznowski said. "So, what do you want?"

"We'd like more information on Bozeman. Maybe you can use your computer to check state records."

"Not now," Preznowski said. "The operator's gone for the day."

Frank lowered his voice. "If you can get me to the computer, *I* can get the information in a couple of minutes."

Preznowski unlocked a tiny room down the hall, where a nearly obsolete computer sat humming. "All I ask is that you don't break the machinery and give a copy of whatever you find to Chief Gilmartin."

Joe watched as Frank took a couple of minutes to get a feel for the machine. "Can you get this to do what we need?"

"Watch." Frank's fingers danced over the keyboard. "Okay. We're into the state data bases." It took a while, but they finally received a fairly complete report on Ray Bozeman's career.

"After he left Millerton, Bozeman got a few more jobs as a cop." Joe scanned through the printout.

"Right," Frank said. "I got that from the state law-enforcement records. I guess lots of small towns would be happy to hire an experienced lawman."

Joe read a little farther down. "Ah. Fired for running various scams. Then he got dirtier and dirtier, until he completely went over to the other side. Convictions for armed robbery—this guy is getting more violent. Then he tried to knock over a bank, got nailed, and caught eight to ten years in the state pen. Where did this stuff come from? The crime and court data banks?"

Frank nodded. "The hot info is at the bottom. I got that from the Corrections Bureau computer. According to them, Bozeman was released a couple of months ago. But when I accessed the parole authority records, guess who hasn't been visiting his parole officer lately? If you came up with the initials R. B., you wouldn't be wrong."

Joe carefully folded up their copy of the printout. "So, we've got the guy who headed that extortion ring all those years ago. Now he's out there somewhere. The question is, where?"

"We've got a whole lot of 'wheres' to wonder about," Frank pointed out. "Where's Collig, for instance?"

Joe gave his brother a troubled glance. "Do you believe his version of the extortion story?"

"I could go either way," Frank admitted. "The facts we know support either case. Nothing's on paper. One thing I'm sure of, though. Collig did *not* try to blow Vernon and DeCampo up."

"Why—" Joe began, then he nodded. "Sure. Maybe it was the same guy we got a glimpse of—the one trying nighttime target practice on Potts."

"Unless, of course, Potts had a deadly enemy who just happened to send a bunch of bullets past him right after he talked with us." Frank shut down the computer. "But I think that's stretching coincidence too far."

They stopped by the squad room to thank Detective Preznowski and to leave a copy of their printout. The detectives in the room were wearing old, cheap, baggy suits. Joe could understand that. His dad used to warn about detecting in good clothes. "Wear a good suit, and you're bound to get mud, crud, or blood on it," he'd say. "Only cops who stay in offices can dress up for the job."

That's why Joe immediately noticed the two men in better-grade suits who came rushing over to snatch up the paper. One, a tall guy wearing a high-fashion suit, looked like an ugly version of Parker Lawrence. The man's hair was cut in the same style as the acting chief's, but he didn't have the same telegenic face. His lantern jaw jutted out as he started reading.

They say imitation is the sincerest form of flattery, Joe thought. This is one ambitious cop.

The other man was short and pudgy, sport jacket open with a sweater stretching over his swelling belly. With his chipmunk cheeks and tiny forehead, he looked like the perfect sidekick, Joe thought.

The guy sounded the part, too. "So who's this Bozeman?" the chubby guy asked, reading the printout.

"He was on the first list these two turned up," Lantern Jaw said impatiently. "Collig's partner, remember? So, he turned out to be a crook. Maybe the boss—"

Sure, Lawrence will find some way to use that to smear Collig some more, Joe thought bitterly.

Preznowski spoke up. "Since you gentlemen already know the Hardys, it's only fair that I introduce you to them. This is Detective Spratt"— he pointed to the tall man—"and Detective Pickerell."

"Keep up the good work, guys." Joe turned to his brother. "Let's blow this joint."

In their van again the boys were silent until they were out of the Millerton city limits.

"Did you get a load of those two clowns?" Joe finally said. "They can't really be detectives. They'd look more at home behind the counter at Mr. Pizza."

"Nope," Frank objected. "Tony would hire brighter help." He steered the car onto the interstate and upped the speed. "I'm not worried about them, but this case is getting to me. Especially since everything we learned in Millerton— except what Collig told us—only makes him look worse."

Behind them a car came roaring up. Frank glanced in the rearview mirror, only to see an old, tan station wagon gaining on them.

"We'll let this guy pass—whoa!"

The passenger-side window of the station wagon was open as it swooped past. A hand appeared, and Frank and Joe both stared to see what it held: a bundle of waxy sticks with a sputtering fuse!

"Holy—" Joe gasped.

The hand let go of the dynamite—tossing it right in the path of the Hardys' van!

Chapter

12

His FACE PALE, eyes glued to the bundle of destruction bouncing on the road, Frank Hardy swerved the van wildly, giving it gas. Whoever threw the dynamite figured nicely, he thought. We're almost on top of it, and the fuse is almost gone. Unless we get around it fast—

The front wheels of the van almost hit the waxy sticks as he steered. He goosed the gas pedal, trying to put as much distance between them and the dynamite as possible.

The road curved, but Frank and Joe still saw the blast behind them. They felt it, too. The force of the explosion hit the van as if a giant hand kicked the rear bumper. The extra speed sent them screaming through the curve, nearly toppling.

Frank fought the wheel as they skidded. He was flung hard enough against his seat belt to bruise his shoulder, but he managed to steer into the skid and, with just inches of roadway to spare, regain control of the van.

Shakily he drove to the shoulder of the road and stopped the vehicle.

"N-nice job," Joe finally managed to say.

"Do we have a small crowbar in the back?" Frank asked. "I think I need help prying my fingers off the wheel."

In moments, however, he was turning the key to start the van up again.

"Hey, you're not going to try to catch the Mad Bomber of Route I-forty-nine, are you?" Joe asked.

"No, but I'd like to put some space between us and that bit of do-it-yourself road work. I hear sirens in the distance. I think Millerton's Finest will be getting tired of finding us at the scene of all the weirdness." They left as fast as the law allowed.

"I don't get it," Joe complained as they drove along the interstate. "We go to Millerton, and first somebody shoots at us, then someone throws a bomb."

"I think that's the same somebody," Frank said. "Either that or the Millerton Tourist Board has a real problem."

"What I mean is, what did we do to deserve

all that attention? We found a list of other cops who quit the force. Then we dug up one of the walking wounded, who told us about the extortion scheme and talked as if Chief Collig were a crook. And we got some info on Ray Bozeman.''

"You could write a great paragraph on 'How We Spent Our Day,' '' Frank told him.

"My point is, that's hardly enough to make someone try to kill us," Joe insisted. "We must have learned something we don't realize."

"Okay, let's go over it again. What places did we visit? The library, police headquarters, Potts's apartment, that restaurant, an alley, headquarters again. Oh!" he suddenly exclaimed, banging his fist against the steering wheel. "We must have been deaf and blind. Collig mentioned the place. Potts actually *told* us. And we didn't catch it."

"What?" Joe asked.

"The restaurant we were in. What did it used to be called?"

"Minty's," Joe remembered. "It used to be a cop hangout."

"Where they had a tradition of taking pictures of new recruits and their partners standing by that moose head. It looked like the old chief, Potts told us, and even pointed to the stuffed head. *Which is hung from a brick wall.* Get it?"

"The picture of Collig that came to the *Bayport Times!*" Joe exclaimed. "It was cut from a larger one." He glanced at his brother. "You think it was a picture of Bozeman?"

"It was something that somebody was afraid would be recognized. And that opens up all sorts of possibilities." Frank frowned over the steering wheel. "For one thing it explains the attacks. What did we learn about on this trip? Bozeman. Suppose Bozeman saw we were getting a little too close to identifying him. We spent a long time at headquarters. Then we went to see Potts. And where did we go next? Minty's! Yeah, I can see Bozeman getting a little nervous. So, he decides to put a scare into Potts to shut him up."

"Maybe he didn't know that Potts has a fear of gunshots," Joe said.

"Or maybe he did." Frank looked grim. "Anyway, we turn up, and he sends a few shots at us, as a warning. But we go back to the police station. So he decides we need to be shut up—permanently."

"Either Bozeman is very shy or he's a nut," Joe said.

"Well, you might be shy, too, if you were the source of those corruption accusations."

Frank glanced over his shoulder. "Let's try this on for size. Ever since we saw Collig and DeCampo fight, we've kind of suspected DeCampo was the one behind the smear campaign. Neither Lawrence nor Vernon seemed to be running things. DeCampo is a born organizer—he ran a great reform campaign. And he had a motive.''

Joe nodded, following Frank's argument.

"Suppose we were wrong. Suppose the smear campaign didn't start with DeCampo. He officially suspended Collig and started Lawrence's investigation the day after the accusations. What if he only jumped on a bandwagon that was already rolling? DeCampo was furious at Collig, and along comes this newsman with a story that might get Collig fired. Vernon would do DeCampo's political dirty work. And DeCampo would even be on TV, fighting corruption.''

"So, you're saying DeCampo didn't start the ball rolling," Joe said. "Vernon did.''

"Actually, Bozeman did," Frank explained. "He probably contacted Vernon with his own version of the bagman story.''

"Nice theory," Joe said. "I can only spot a few dozen holes. How come Bozeman waited all these years?''

"First, he was in jail, and then he probably lost track of Collig. But when the chief got that top cop award a few months ago, he got nationwide publicity." A slow smile spread over Frank's lips. "In fact, most of the stories referred to the fact that he was the only honest man in a corrupt administration. I wouldn't be surprised if that's what gave Bozeman the idea to smear him.''

"The sweetest revenge—I can buy that." Joe

nodded. "But how did Bozeman find us, to cause all this trouble in Millerton?"

Frank shrugged. "He followed us from Bayport. It's no secret we were going to Millerton. Remember how that cop kidded us? Our trip was announced on live radio. All Bozeman had to do was stake out our house until we left."

"But why us?" Joe insisted.

"Because he's scared of us," Frank said. "We turned up on the scene when DeCampo and Vernon were nearly killed. We said the chief was innocent. We were going to Millerton to find out the whole story."

"That bombing is the part that puzzles me," Joe said. "If Bozeman wanted to smear Collig, he needed Vernon and DeCampo. Why blow them up?"

"I think I've got an answer for that, too," Frank replied. "When did the blast happen? After public opinion began swinging over to Collig's side. Editorials were demanding that Vernon reveal his source. If Bozeman came out of the shadows, he wouldn't be a mystery man with dirt on the chief. He'd be identified, and Lawrence—and the media—would check his background. He might even be discredited if it was discovered that he'd led the extortion ring. But if Collig's accusers were murdered, who would be blamed?"

"Collig," Joe said grimly. "It all makes a twisted kind of sense." He glanced at Frank.

"I'll tell you something—if Bozeman has to be this devious, there's still something fishy about his story. I'd say it's a strong bet that Collig told the truth about being an innocent pawn in Bozeman's schemes."

He sighed. "Well, Frank, you've got a real theory. The only problem is, will we be able to get anyone to listen to it?"

They drove on to Bayport and straight to police headquarters. Luck was with them. Acting Chief Lawrence was still in the building when they arrived.

"What do you two want?" he demanded after they knocked on his office door.

"Have your people sent you the new information from Millerton?" Frank asked. "The stuff about the extortion ring?"

Lawrence nodded. "It looks like Collig was involved in dirtier business than we imagined."

"More men than Chief Collig were involved," Frank said. "For instance, there was Ray Bozeman. We have information that says he actually led the ring." He glanced over at Lawrence. "I don't suppose you know who started all the accusations?"

"Rod Vernon," Lawrence said impatiently.

"I mean, who told *him?*"

"I—ah, don't know." Lawrence seemed more than a little uncomfortable.

"Then perhaps you should consider this." Frank began laying out his whole theory of Bozeman as the original—and possibly lying—source of the story.

Lawrence was unconvinced.

"Well? Don't you see?" Joe burst out at the acting chief's doubtful expression. "If Bozeman is so worried about being discovered, it means he has something to hide—something more than the extortion ring. I think this means Chief Collig told us the truth. He was duped into collecting money for Bozeman."

"That's an interesting theory, but the facts still point to Ezra Collig." Lawrence wasn't about to change his mind. "Wait a minute! How could Collig have told you about his connection with Bozeman? You only found out about that in Millerton."

His eyes narrowed into angry slits. "Unless you saw him there—consorting with a fugitive, probably aiding him . . ." He leapt to the doorway, blocking it as he threw the door open. "You!" he shouted to a passing officer. "Take these two into custody. I want them held for questioning."

Chapter

13

THE POLICE OFFICER GAZED at the Hardys a little oddly as he led them away. Frank figured it wasn't every day people were arrested in the chief's office.

Lawrence's voice followed them down the hall. "Get me the Millerton police. . . ." He was already savoring the triumph of siccing the local law on the unsuspecting Chief Collig.

The desk officer was as surprised at this in-house arrest as Frank and Joe's guard. He had to interrupt Lawrence's call to Chief Gilmartin to get a charge.

"They're not being charged with anything," Lawrence said, emerging from his office. "They're just assisting us in investigating the Collig case." He gave the Hardys a sidelong glance.

"Assisting!" Joe burst out. "We tried to assist, by telling you not to go after Collig, but to go after Ray Bozeman. He's the one—" Joe's angry words were cut off as a heavy hand landed on his shoulder.

The man in the suit with the heavy hand was a stranger, but Frank figured out his job from the look on the other cops' faces. Another of Lawrence's Internal Affairs shoo-flies, he realized as the man started leading them away.

"Hold on a second!" Joe resisted the pull on his shoulder. "Don't we get a phone call?"

"There's no need for a phone call." The man's voice was snide. "That's only when people are charged with crimes. You're just answering some questions to aid our investigation."

"You can't keep us here like this! Either charge us or let us go!"

Frank grabbed his brother's arm. "I think Dad would want us to help the police." He stared deep into Joe's eyes. Remember Dad's license, that look said.

Joe shut up. "Okay, let's get the questions over with."

The shoo-fly led them to an interrogation room. He was tall and bland faced, with an expensive haircut and a designer suit. Another would-be smooth character, Frank thought. "I'm Detective Belknap, by the way," the investigator told them with a nasty smile. "Be back in a minute. Don't go away, now."

"All the comforts of home." Frank flopped down on the unyielding seat of a wooden chair and stared around the room. There wasn't much to see: a bare table, walls covered in sound-deadening acoustical tile. One wall was a huge, floor-to-ceiling mirror. "Here's another fine mess your big mouth has gotten us into," Frank added.

Joe felt bad. All too late he realized that Frank had never mentioned seeing Chief Collig. If he hadn't mentioned it, Lawrence wouldn't have had any reason to hold them. "Hey, Frank, I'm sorry—"

His brother raised a hand. "Don't say any more. You know how they set up interrogation rooms." He glanced up at the light fixture, sure there was a bug up there. Then he glanced at the probable two-way mirror, remembering the VCR in the acting chief's office. "Smile. Right now, we're probably on Parkervision."

"If you ask me, the acting chief is more into acting than being chief. He's not investigating the Collig case. He just wants to nail down his new job. And he doesn't want any inconvenient facts getting in his way."

Belknap came in, carrying a notepad. "Okay, let's get down to cases here. What time did you leave for Millerton?"

He continued to ask for every detail of the trip on the interstate. At first Frank thought it was some kind of strategy, a trick to trip them up.

Maybe the acting chief had some suspicions that they'd helped smuggle Collig out of town.

But Belknap didn't pounce on any discrepancies in their stories. He just slowly wrote down every word on his pad. Every time Frank or Joe tried to move ahead, he'd bring them back with some nitpicking detail.

"How many newspaper volumes were in the library?" he asked.

A little farther along, it was, "Was this Preznowski wearing a tie?"

Joe stared. "What difference does that make?" he asked. "If you're that interested, you could ask your own guys who were at his office."

"I want to get the complete story here." Belknap raised his eyes from his pad. "Don't be in such a hurry. We have lots of time."

Frank and Joe understood. This wasn't an interrogation—it was a farce. Lawrence had obviously ordered his flunky to waste as much time as possible. Meanwhile, the acting chief was moving heaven and earth to get Collig captured in Millerton. Maybe Lawrence thought they were in cahoots with Collig. In any case, he was making sure they couldn't get to a phone to warn Collig.

In a weird way, though, the boring questions set off Frank's mind to reexamine the events of their trip. "So this Potts guy looked at Collig and saw what he thought was a ghost?" Belknap said. "What were his exact words?"

" 'Young Collig—another ghost trying to kill me!' " Suddenly Frank sat bolt upright on his uncomfortable chair. "Of course! *Another* ghost!"

Joe and Belknap stared at him. "What are you talking about?" Joe asked.

"Potts looked at Collig—a guy from his past— and saw a ghost. But he'd seen *another* ghost that night—the guy who shot at him. And there's nobody left around here from those old days but—"

"Ray Bozeman!" Joe mouthed so Belknap wouldn't hear him. "We suspected it, but this would be solid evidence! If we can prove that he shot at Potts, then Lawrence will have to take your theory seriously," he finished up in a whisper. He turned, eager to plead their case with Belknap. Then his shoulders fell. "But we can't prove it. Potts is the only one who saw Bozeman shooting at him. And the last time we saw him, that old man was a complete basket case."

"Nobody who has actually *seen* Bozeman is in condition to talk about him," Frank mused. "Unless—"

He turned to Belknap. "What's the latest word on Commissioner DeCampo and Rod Vernon? Have either of them regained consciousness yet?"

Their questioner didn't mind side conversations that took up more time, but he shook his head. "They're still more dead than alive, and they're still in the intensive care unit. With luck they'll pull through. So Collig won't go up for a murder rap." Belknap smiled nastily. "Just attempted murder."

"Collig isn't the one who tried to kill those guys," Joe burst out. "It's his old police partner, Ray Bozeman. Bozeman took shots at us. He threw a bomb at us on the interstate."

"Hold on, hold on, now. You haven't mentioned anything about a bomb so far." Belknap checked the point on his pencil and prepared to start writing again.

"Do you have guards at the hospital?" Frank interrupted.

"I suppose so. Why?"

"Because those two unconscious men are the only ones who can name Bozeman as the one behind the accusations. He tried to kill us when we started getting close to his secret." Frank turned to Belknap, grim-faced. "What do you think he'd do to people who could *prove* it?"

Joe leaned toward the man. "The last time we saw him, Bozeman was driving a tan station wagon, maybe ten years old. At least tell Lawrence to keep a lookout for it. If he turns up near the hospital, those men are in danger."

"Yeah." Belknap started to rise from his chair. "I'd better tell—"

Then he froze in midmovement. The expression on his face was the kind that usually appeared on practical-joke victims.

"You really had me going there for a second."
The man plopped down in his seat. "Sure. Go
tell Lawrence to put out an all-points bulletin on
a guy who exists only in your imagination. That
would put me in real good with the chief."

"Acting chief," Frank corrected him.

Belknap gave him a dirty look. "He'll be chief
soon enough, after we put Collig away. And then
he'll need a captain to run the I.A. unit."

Before he could say any more, the door to
the interrogation room opened. Con Riley stood
framed in the doorway. "Hey, Belknap, the acting chief needs some backup. He's tracking
down a report that Collig has been seen near
Bayport General, and he wants all his best people patrolling the area. Take Krebs and a squad
car."

"Near the hospital, huh?" Belknap flashed the
boys a triumphant smile. Then he rushed out the
door, hefting the pistol holster under his arm.

Con waited until Belknap was well gone. Then
he suddenly acted as if he'd just noticed the
boys. "Why, Frank and Joe Hardy! What are
you doing here?" It wasn't very good acting,
Frank decided.

"Parker Lawrence is holding us for 'questioning,' " Joe said. "We've been trapped with
that idiot for more than an hour."

"Well, there's no one to question you now,"
Riley said. "I guess you can go."

Frank studied Con intently. "What's going on

here? You weren't around before. How did you know we were here?''

"As one of you suggested a little earlier, the walls here have ears—and eyes.'' Con nodded toward the wall-length mirror. "That thing is two-way. Anybody next door can see and hear everything going on in here.''

He smiled. "And sometimes I do paperwork in that room, away from the hustle and bustle.''

"Thanks, Con.'' Joe rose from his chair. "We're out of here.''

"Now, boys.'' Con waved a finger at them. "I want you to go straight home. No going off with your friends for pizza or stopping by the hospital to see if there's any excitement there.'' He gave them a broad wink.

"You mean that Collig was actually spotted near Bayport General?'' Frank asked.

"Yes, indeed. I wouldn't think of sending crack investigators like Belknap and Krebs on a wild-goose chase. We got a call from the owner of a candy store in that area. Chief Collig had stopped in to buy some Sen-sen. Funny thing about that,'' Con said. "The chief *hates* Sen-sen.''

"You think it's a phony?'' Joe said.

"No, the store owner knows Collig—he's sure he recognized him.'' Riley steered them out of the interrogation room and toward the front entrance. "Maybe the chief thinks like you—and made a brief personal appearance to draw a lot of cops to the streets around Bayport General. Maybe there's a good reason for them to be there."

They were outside now. Riley waved them off.

"Thanks, Con," Frank said. "We owe you."

The boys dashed down the front stairs and out to their van. "Next stop, Bayport General," Frank announced.

"Lawrence took that tip pretty seriously," Joe said, looking out the van window. "Half the force must be cruising these streets."

Joe wasn't looking for police cars, though. He was scanning the streets for a glimpse of a tan station wagon. "I guess there's one good thing about having a bomb thrown at you. You're sure to remember the car it came from."

The streets were crowded with parked cars of every description, but Joe saw no tan station wagons.

"Okay. What do you say we check the hospital parking lot— Frank! There it is!" Joe nearly went out the window, pointing at a car parked under a light in a corner of the lot. These were the least convenient parking spaces—the ones farthest from the hospital entrance. As a result, cars were pretty sparse.

Frank whipped the van into an empty spot on the street. "Anyone in the wagon?" he asked.

Joe peered over at the target vehicle. "Doesn't seem to be."

"I think we'd better get over there and check it out, fast." Frank opened his door and stepped from the van. "Any holes in the fence?"

Joe had always been a shortcut-spotter. In a moment he found where someone had cut a slit in the Cyclone fencing around the lot.

The Hardys slipped through and were halfway to the station wagon when Frank suddenly said, "Funny."

"What's funny?" Joe turned to look where Frank was staring.

"That little fenced-off area in that far corner— they always have a chain and padlock on the gate."

"What for?"

Frank gave his brother a look. "That's where they store the tanks of ether and oxygen. The hospital needs both gases for surgery, but keeps them on the far end of the property because they're too flammable. A spark could set off a terrible fire or explosion."

His eyes suddenly grew wide. "Oh, no."

Joe was already running for the open gate.

Inside the fence a waist-high brick wall surrounded the gas stockpile. The big metal canisters were taller than the boys.

"There's the lock and chain," Joe said. "One link snipped through."

"And here's something that sure doesn't belong." Frank pointed at a reddish brown bundle of waxy sticks, wired up and attached to some kind of mechanism. It was jammed into the middle of the gas tanks.

"That dynamite plus the gas—if it went off, we'd probably need a new hospital." Frank whispered as if he were afraid to wake the bomb up.

"Good thing we found it," Joe said. "Bozeman must have planted it, then headed out of range."

"Almost, kid—except for one thing," a voice said from behind them.

Joe whirled around, then froze under the glare of a tall, pale man. It wasn't the glare that stopped him. It was the big, blue steel .38 revolver in the man's hand.

"I haven't left yet," Ray Bozeman said.

Chapter

14

"HELLO, MR. BOZEMAN." It took every bit of nerve Frank Hardy had to keep his voice steady as he faced Ezra Collig's old partner.

Maybe once, Frank thought, Ray Bozeman had had a handsome face. But age and a hard life had changed it. Bozeman's blond hair had receded and gone a dingy gray. His flesh had shriveled up until his face looked as tight as a fist—all nose and cheekbones. His skin was pasty white, as if he'd been living under a rock—or in prison.

The only thing alive in Bozeman's face were his faded blue eyes. They glittered with a mad intensity.

"Don't try anything stupid," Bozeman snapped as Frank and Joe took a step toward the gate to get out of the enclosure. "I was the best shot on the Millerton force. Did Collig ever tell you that? *I said don't move!*"

Bozeman kicked the gate shut. "Back up till you've got that brick wall behind you. Good. Now sit on the ground. I want your legs straight out and your hands under your butts. *Move!*"

Frank realized they had no choice. The gun was scary enough, but Bozeman's eyes left no doubt of what he'd do if they tried anything.

Frank and Joe took the position that Bozeman ordered them into. They knew that without the use of their legs or hands, there was no way they could move quickly. They were helpless, a hundred feet from the hospital, shut into a little-used corner of the parking lot.

Bozeman allowed himself a brief, wolfish grin. Stained dentures flashed at them—the cheap kind made for prison inmates. "Smart boys," Bozeman said. "I don't know what a bullet in those gas tanks would do, but it's better not to find out, eh?"

Now his eyes glowed with evil triumph. "After all, we've got to save them for the *big* bang. I don't think it will be as powerful as you said, but it should be enough to take out Vernon and DeCampo—and at least half the hospital."

He smiled again, showing his cheap teeth. "It will also blow away Ezra Collig's last hope for clearing himself."

Bozeman flashed the butt of the gun at them

for an instant. There was a big gold stamp on it, with the seal of the Bayport Police. "I stopped off at Collig's house earlier and picked this up. Good and recognizable. It was one of the awards he got as a national top cop. I'll leave it someplace where it can be found after the explosion. Even that empty uniform of an acting chief should be able to handle things from there."

"Do you actually know Parker Lawrence?" Frank said. "We wondered about that."

"I know *about* him, the big jerk." Bozeman gave them another wolfish grin. "But he doesn't know about me. Soon no one will."

"What about Len Potts?" Joe spoke up desperately. "He recognized you in the alley, you know."

"Big deal," Bozeman sneered. "I know what the sound of shots does to him. If they get him back together again—and that's a big if—he may not even remember. By then Collig will already be in the joint. And who's going to listen to some crazy man? No," he finished proudly, "I planned it right. Collig will rot in jail, just like I did."

Bozeman's fish-belly face was the picture of successful revenge. "I had a long time to think while I was in the joint—about mistakes I made, chances I missed, people I blamed. I realized finally there was only one person responsible for all the trouble in my life—that blasted Collig."

His face twitched with hate. "If that stupid

kid had only kept his mouth shut, I woulda made sergeant, back there in Millerton. Sergeant, with a sweet racket—''

Frank blinked. From the tone of Bozeman's voice, it sounded as if he were describing paradise.

"And I didn't have to stop with sergeant, you know. A go-getter could get promoted in those days, even if he didn't have some fancy college-boy degree.''

"Chief Bozeman?" Joe scoffed.

"Nah. But Lieutenant Bozeman, maybe captain. That's all I would have needed. I'd have been running that town." For a second his face softened with thoughts of what might have been.

Then his features tightened up. "But no. A dumb rookie just off the turnip truck had to play saint, open his mouth, and ruin everything.''

"Collig really didn't know about your scam with the Policemen's Fund," Frank said. "He really thought it was a charity.''

Bozeman grinned mockingly. "I needed an honest man to make the collections. When any of my pals took the bag around, they always skimmed off the top." His face went cold. "If I'd thought Collig would rat on me, I'd have shot him like a dog thirty-five years ago.''

"Some cop you were," Joe muttered.

"I was a good cop!" Bozeman snarled. "Smart enough to catch a lot of crooks—and catch myself some extra change. I had a sweet racket set up until Collig finked. Then I couldn't keep jobs long enough. Sooner or later it came out. 'Weren't you the guy in Millerton . . . ?' They watched me like a hawk. Every time I got a little action started, I was out. Then I couldn't even *get* a job. So I started working the other side of the street."

"Until that bank job put you away," Joe said.

Bozeman nodded. "I was coming up for parole when I read this article in a magazine about the national top cop awards. And who do I see but Ezra Collig, Chief of Bayport P.D."

Frank and Joe exchanged glances. It was just as they'd thought. "So then you started checking out your old partner," Frank said.

"I still had time on my hands and the prison library." Bozeman leaned forward. "So I read all about Bayport and Collig—like the big scandal when the town supervisor got killed."

He chuckled. "Old Ezra sure mutted that case, didn't he?" Then his face went cold again. "Now that I think about it, you were in on that, too. Frank and Joe Hardy. I should have known to watch out for you."

"Collig came through that case pretty well," Joe said. "He arrested the bad guys and kept his job."

"Yeah, Honest Ezra, the only one to keep his job from the old administration. But I know politicians, and I figured someone would have the knives out for the chief."

129

"Mark DeCampo," Frank said.

"I could always figure the angles," Bozeman said. "DeCampo was hot to find corruption. He even brought in his own stooge, Lawrence, to probe for it. Then I saw this new guy on the local news—Rod Vernon, a great investigative reporter in his own mind. He got bounced from the network and needed a story to get back."

"So you gave it to him," Joe said.

Bozeman smirked. "I thought Vernon was going to bust a blood vessel when I started leaking stuff to him. He took the ball and ran with it."

"Vernon was a lousy journalist," Frank said flatly. "He never bothered to double-check anything you passed on to him."

"Which made him perfect for my purposes," Bozeman said. "Besides, how could he check my story? It happened so long ago, many of the people involved are dead or have moved away. Collig had this one little chink in the armor of his reputation, and I managed to fill it full of dirt."

Bozeman smiled so widely, Frank almost expected his false teeth to pop out.

"I figured a nice quiet whispering campaign would be enough to ruin Collig, but Vernon wanted to turn it into a circus, and so did DeCampo. He wanted hearings, an investigation, the whole nine yards. They were too clumsy in nailing Collig, so people began feeling

130

sorry for him—the big drip!" He frowned. "I could see the handwriting on the wall when that editorial came out, asking for solid proof."

"DeCampo and Vernon wanted you to step forward." The picture was shaping up just as Frank had suspected. "And you didn't dare do that."

"They expected me on that dock with all sorts of goods on Collig. DeCampo was planning a major news conference to unveil me or something. Vernon, of course, would have a front-row seat. But I had a better idea, one that would really nail old Ezra. I blew up the dock and the two guys howling loudest for his blood."

"You figured that Collig would be the prime suspect," Frank said.

"And that Parker Lawrence would railroad him right to prison," Joe added.

"All it took was a midnight visit to a local construction site for some dynamite. Vernon played into my hands, telling me about that rental car he was going to use." Bozeman tried to act modest. "I always had a way with auto locks."

"But it didn't work as you planned," Joe pointed out. "Vernon and DeCampo didn't die, and Collig didn't let himself get arrested."

"And you two came sticking your noses in." Bozeman gave them a cold glare. "You turned up at the dock—following Vernon, I guess."

Frank and Joe nodded. "Then we found the

chief's car, and we were broadcast saying that we were going to Millerton," Frank said. "You must have heard it on the morning news and followed us."

Their captor looked hard at Frank. "You called me Bozeman, so I guess you found out everything. Right?"

"Enough," Joe said. "The only problem is, we don't have enough proof."

Bozeman gave them a savage grin. "Good. That was the only thing that worried me when I tried to blow you up. But after this blast, my troubles will be over."

Behind them, they heard a rattle from the Cyclone fencing.

"Bozeman!" a voice yelled raggedly.

Frank stared as Chief Collig stalked toward them. He had bags under his eyes, and his clothes were soiled and rumpled.

But the gun in his hand looked all business—and it was pointed at Ray Bozeman.

Chapter

15

THIS IS LIKE the final gunfight scene in an old western flick, Joe thought.

He and Frank were the helpless audience, just like the townspeople in those ancient cowboy movies. The question was, would the guy in the white hat win this time?

The two men squared off, guns in hand. They made a strange contrast after thirty-five years. Back then Collig had been a raw-boned, skinny kid; Bozeman, tough, a leader. Now Collig had grown, and Bozeman had shrunk. His pale, gaunt face was like a skull as he stood glaring at the chief.

"How's it going, Ez?" Bozeman's voice was soft and silky.

Collig's eyes widened at the use of his old nickname.

"You know," Bozeman went on, "I was telling these kids how I was the best shot in the old Millerton days. You were always so bad, Ez. I bet I could still aim, plug you, and blow away the kids before you could shoot me."

He smiled. "That is, if I wanted to play fair."

Bozeman whipped around, his gun aimed straight at Frank's head. "Drop the gun, Collig, or I put a bullet in the smart boy's brain. You know I mean it." The ex-con's voice was flat and deadly. "Even if you shoot me, you lose him."

Silence seemed to stretch for an eternity. Then came a clatter as Collig let his gun fall to the pavement.

Ray Bozeman turned so he could keep one eye on the Hardys, the other on Collig. "Kick the gun over here, Ez."

Collig bristled. "Don't call me Ez. That's what my friends used to call me, and you were never my friend."

Bozeman's face grew even more pinched. "You're in no position to give orders," he said, raising his gun. "I can call you anything I like. If you don't kick that thing over, I'll call you dead."

Face frozen, Collig kicked his revolver over. He tensed as Bozeman stood over it.

His old partner chuckled, a chilling sound.

"Gonna rush me when I bend to pick it up? Dream on, rookie." He gestured with the gun again. "On the ground, belly down, hands behind your head. *Now!*"

It took a moment for Collig to assume that humiliating position. Frank and Joe could only watch, sitting on their hands. Only when the chief was completely helpless did Bozeman stoop for the other gun.

"They can call me Two-Gun Bozeman," he said, slipping Collig's piece into his pocket. He kept the chief's .38 revolver aimed at Collig's head.

Bozeman walked over to the prone police chief. Suddenly he whirled around, his gun covering Joe. "No moving," he said, waggling a finger. "Someone could get hurt." His gun shifted to aim at Collig's head. "Do you want the chief to go before his time?"

Joe sagged back, giving up his attempt to surge to his feet. There was no way to rise quickly from his stupid position.

Keeping his gun behind Collig's ear, Bozeman began to frisk the chief.

"And what do we have here?" he asked, searching a rear pocket. Bozeman began to laugh. "Good old Ez, a cop to the end," he said, drawing out a pair of handcuffs.

"Well, I may just have a use for these." The ex-con snapped one of the bracelets onto Collig's right wrist. "Now up." He stepped back as the chief ponderously struggled to his feet. "Walk over to that gate." Bozeman stayed out of reach, his gun trained on Collig's head.

When Collig reached the gate, Bozeman stopped him at the fence beside it. "Assume the position," he ordered.

The chief leaned his hands against the Cyclone fence, in the traditional position of a captured felon. The empty handcuff bracelet rattled against the metal fence.

"Come on, how long have you been a cop? You know better than that!" Bozeman's foot hooked Collig's shins, forcing his feet back. The crook's free hand shoved into the small of the chief's back. Collig was forced off balance, forced to hold his weight on his hands, helpless again.

Bozeman smiled and clicked the free handcuff bracelet around the gatepost and gate. The entrance to the gas storage area was locked again, trapping the boys inside, with Ezra Collig chained to the fence.

"To show you what a nice guy I am, I'll let your last moments be comfortable. See those bottles of dangerous gas in there, Ez? That's a bomb. It'll blow you, DeCampo, Vernon, and these kids to kingdom come. But till it goes off, I'll let you stand up."

Collig staggered back to his feet. Joe and Frank rose, too, stretching cramped muscles.

Bozeman still played his parody of a concerned host. "Glad to see you could make it, Ez. How'd you get here?" He pointed his gun to make it clear he wanted an answer.

"I hitched on a truck," Collig answered gruffly. "It was easy sneaking back to Bayport. I got out of Millerton before they sealed the place up, and the roadblocks here stopped only cars heading out."

"Well, I can't say how happy I am that you're here." Bozeman's voice suddenly turned cold and ominous. "Because I want to see your face when I talk to you, you miserable—"

Thirty years of hatred poured out in a torrent of abuse. Again the Hardys heard Bozeman's complaint, in fouler words because the supposed cause of Bozeman's misfortune was there to hear it.

"If you're a cop today, it's because I *made* you one!" Bozeman screamed. "You owed me, and how did you pay me back? You ratted on me!"

"You used me!" Collig shouted back. "You were my partner, and partners are supposed to look out for each other. Instead, you turned me into the bagman for your cheap little racket!"

"What? You were annoyed because I didn't tell you what the scam was? I was thinking of letting you in on it—"

"If you had," Collig cut him off, "I'd have turned you in sooner."

Bozeman looked like a complete maniac as he

137

raised his gun. Frank was sure he was going to blow the chief away.

With an effort, though, Bozeman brought his arm down. "No. That was what I wanted at first. I wanted to kill you," he said in a hoarse voice. "Then I thought how much better it would be if I ruined your life first. I wanted to rip away your honor, drag your pride through the mud. Everything you built up, I wanted to dirty. And you see how easy it was?"

Bozeman's laugh didn't sound quite human. It was more the howl of a triumphant beast. "Your reputation? Vernon was happy to smear that with just the barest suggestion of a story. Your career? DeCampo and Lawrence couldn't wait to break that in little pieces. And after tonight—well, see this?"

Out of reach Bozeman showed the chief the butt of the gun he'd stolen from Collig's house. A cruel smile twisted his lips as he watched as Collig recognized it. "I thought it only fitting. You got this as a national award for being a top cop. That's how I found out where you've been all these years. After this bomb goes off, there won't be enough of you around to identify. But if I leave this, it's sure to implicate you in the blast."

He laughed. "After tonight, anytime anyone mentions your name, there'll only be disgusted silence."

Collig hung his head.

Bozeman loved it. "The only thing I regret is that your old lady croaked before I got things rolling. That would have been perfect." He started talking in a high-pitched voice. " 'Oh, Ezra, these awful things can't be true, can they?' " He gave a brutal guffaw. "And if that didn't kill her, I'd have done the job myself—a hit-and-run, maybe."

Frank caught the flash in Collig's eye as he heard that. It wasn't the look of a man in pain. Why is he staring at the ground, then? Frank wondered. What's he thinking of?

He realized then that Collig wasn't gazing at the ground, he was staring fixedly at Frank's feet. Frank glanced down. No, it wasn't his feet. There was a small metal ring on the ground, with a tiny key. The chief had managed to toss the key to his handcuffs next to Frank!

Frank dropped to the ground, doing his best to act as if he'd given up all hope.

"You—up!" Bozeman shouted, whirling on Frank. "Stand up and take it like a man."

While I take it from a maniac, Frank thought as he pushed himself up. While his hand was on the ground, he palmed the key. Then, on his feet, he faced Bozeman while flashing the key behind his back to Joe.

Frank held out the key, the movement hidden by his body. Joe immediately grabbed their ticket to freedom. "On my signal," Frank whispered.

It was probably a hopeless fight, but they had to try. If Joe could unlock the chief's handcuff from the gate, he and the chief might be able to overpower Bozeman. Frank would have to disable the bomb. Bozeman might shoot them all, but they might just save the hospital. Any gunfire would draw the cops prowling the immediate area.

"You won't get away with this, Bozeman," Collig said. "I knew you were behind everything since I headed for Millerton. Finally that stupid picture came back to me—the two of us and the moose head at Minty's. I realized you must have been working with Vernon and DeCampo and that you had to finish them off. They needed protection. I couldn't order it, but I could draw it here."

"How?" Bozeman sneered.

"Easy. I walked into a store where the owner knew me and bought some candy. This area is now crawling with cops."

"Even so, they're looking for you, not me," Bozeman said. "But thanks for the tip, old buddy. I'd better get started. There's a radio detonator in my car. I'll take it a safe distance, hit the button, and watch the fireworks."

He stepped away from the enclosure, then turned back. "I'll be safe, but I'll still be able to see you. Don't try anything, because I can still shoot and hit you. And remember—"

"Yeah, right," Joe said. "You were the best shot on the Millerton force."

Bozeman brought his gun up. "You know, kid, if I had more time, I'd teach you some manners. But it would be a waste, what with your short life expectancy."

He turned and was halfway to his car when Frank whispered, "Now!"

Joe grabbed the handcuff bracelet locking the gate, jammed in the key, and twisted it.

Frank leapt for the bomb amid the gas cylinders. Whatever happened, he had to disarm it!

Ezra Collig tore the handcuff loose and flung open the gate. The moment it was open, Joe charged out. It was probably hopeless, but he was going to try to tackle Bozeman.

The chief's old partner whirled around at the noise. He was aiming the chief's revolver in his left hand before Joe had taken two steps. Joe hurled himself forward anyway.

With his right hand, Bozeman whipped out the gun he'd just taken from Collig.

Collig was moving his right hand, too. It slid to his waistband. As Joe raced past, he saw the little automatic appear in the chief's fingers.

Then, at the same time, the three guns exploded.

Chapter
16

JOE KNEW WHERE one of Bozeman's bullets went. It whistled just past his right ear.

He had no idea where Bozeman's other bullet flew.

But he knew where Ezra Collig's shot went.

Ray Bozeman twisted and fell as if he'd been kicked. The big, blue steel revolver flew from his suddenly nerveless fingers, but the gun in his right hand came up for another try at the chief.

Collig, trained police officer that he was, cried, "Freeze, Bozeman!"

Ray Bozeman just smiled. He didn't have to play by police rules.

Joe kept charging. Bozeman wavered for a second, choosing his target—Collig or Joe. To Joe's eyes, the muzzle of the gun appeared large enough to fire cannonballs.

Okay, he told himself. When in doubt, punt.

Still on the run, he launched a kick at Bozeman's gun hand. His foot caught the gun and tore it from the ex-con's grasp, sending it arcing fifteen feet away.

"Three points for our side!" Joe crowed.

Chief Collig came trotting over, his little automatic at the ready. Shaking his head at Joe, he said, "That was the bravest stunt I ever saw anyone try."

Joe grinned.

"It was also the stupidest. What if he'd shot you?"

"Um," Joe said.

"You've got guts, but it wouldn't hurt to use your brains once in a while." Collig turned to keep Bozeman covered.

Joe stared in fascination at the tiny gun, scarcely larger than the chief's palm. "What *is* that?" he asked.

"A backup pistol," Collig replied. "Also known as a belly gun because it's small enough to fit inside the waist of your pants." He kicked the big blue revolver farther away from Bozeman. His ex-partner glared helplessly up at him.

"You always were lousy at patting people down, Ray," Collig said. "And I've gotten to be a better shot over the years."

Then he turned to Joe. "How's your first aid,

young man? I believe this gent has a bullet in his shoulder."

Frank joined them. "The bomb is dead," he announced. "But not Mr. Bozeman, I'm glad to see."

"No, I think he'll be back among his friends in the state pen pretty soon," Joe said, using Bozeman's shirt to stanch his wound. "After all, we heard him admit that the chief was innocent in that extortion scam."

"Your word against mine," Bozeman gasped.

"And your fingerprints on the bomb," Frank pointed out. "I think that will help make a case."

Bayport P.D. squad cars came screaming from all four directions into the parking lot.

"Somebody should tell Lawrence not to run the sirens by the hospital," Collig said. "This is supposed to be a quiet zone."

The cars pulled into a semicircle, pinning them in a wall of headlights. Doors flew open and officers braced behind them, aiming their guns two-handed. Parker Lawrence's voice came over a bullhorn: "Collig! Put down the gun! We have you surrounded!"

"Okay, Lawrence." Collig tossed the gun to the side and raised his hands. "We've got a wounded man here." He nodded toward the hospital. "Maybe you should get him some medical attention."

As soon as the gun was down, several men

approached the chief. In fact, the area was swarming with police units and officers, all drawn from the surrounding blocks by the sound of shots.

"Another attempted murder charge," Detective Belknap said importantly, reaching out to grab Collig's shoulder. "You have the right to remain silent, Collig."

"It was self-defense," Joe said.

"That's what they all say." Then Belknap recognized him. "What are *you* doing here?"

"Just what I was about to ask." Parker Lawrence advanced on them grimly. He looked very impressive, a police warm-up jacket over his bullet-proof vest—all ready for any camera crews.

"I warned you what would happen if you kept interfering in this case." Lawrence poked a finger into Frank's chest. "You could be considered accessories to this crime. So answer the officer. What where you doing here?"

"Stopping a second murder attempt on DeCampo and Vernon," Frank answered crisply. "This is the man who made both tries." He pointed at Bozeman, who was still groaning. "In there you'll see the bomb he planted." Frank pointed to the gas tank storage enclosure.

"Bomb?" Lawrence repeated.

Frank sighed. "It's been deactivated."

"His name is Ray Bozeman, by the way," Joe added. "He started the smear campaign that

145

DeCampo, Vernon, and—'' He smiled at Lawrence. "Well, I guess you know who else was involved in that."

Parker Lawrence was standing with his mouth open as the news van arrived from WBPT. Obviously, Frank thought, things were moving too fast for him.

Grinning, Chief Collig turned around and put his hands behind him. He jingled the handcuffs that still hung from one wrist. "Well, come on, acting chief. Clap these on and take me to headquarters. You can get the keys from Joe Hardy, there."

He glanced at Lawrence over his shoulder. "And by the way," he added, "I wouldn't get too attached to the job of acting chief, if I were you."

Two days later the boys sat in their living room over a copy of the *Bayport Times*. The banner headline read "Out of the Bag." A big photo showed a grinning Chief Collig holding out his handcuffs—and the key to them.

"So, Bozeman finally cracked," Joe said, reading the article.

"He didn't have much choice," Frank pointed out. "The evidence was piled up against him. It wasn't just his fingerprints on the bomb. The truth about his old extortion scam started to surface."

"How?" Joe started to read faster.

146

"It's on page four. Using the list of phone numbers for Millerton police retirees, the *Times* finally found somebody who knew the inside story about Collig's turning Bozeman in. It was some guy living in Arizona. He was a pal of the police captain there—Frazee—who'd told him the whole thing."

Frank grinned. "Needless to say, the Internal Affairs Unit is very embarrassed."

"Sounds like they may need a new boss," Joe said.

"There is talk of Captain Parker Lawrence going back wherever he came from," Frank agreed. "By the way, did you read the sidebar about Rod Vernon? He's conscious, and he's admitted that Bozeman was his primary source on the corruption story."

"Another straw that broke Bozeman's back," Joe guessed.

"It may also do a job on DeCampo," Frank said. "Vernon had to admit why he was meeting DeCampo on the dock. So the whole story of their secret association is out now. There are a lot of red faces at City Hall. The first thing they did was give Collig his job back."

"Sounds like DeCampo may come out of his coma to find he's in political limbo," Joe said. "Couldn't happen to a nicer guy."

He flopped back on the couch. "Well, thanks, Frank. Guess I won't have to read all this now."

Frank was opening his mouth to reply when the phone rang. Frank picked it up.

"It's Con Riley," he told Joe, putting a hand over the receiver. "So, Con," he said, "what can we poor amateurs do for you?"

Frank's grin suddenly changed. "Really?" he said. "We'd completely forgotten about that. Just found them on the desk, huh?"

He listened a bit more. "We can? Great! No, we're leaving right away!"

Frank hung up and turned to Joe. "Come on. We have unfinished business at police headquarters."

"Unfinished?" Joe repeated.

"Dad's papers finally turned up from wherever Parker Lawrence had hidden them. You do want Dad to keep his P.I. license, don't you?"

The atmosphere at police headquarters was very different from that of their last visit. The only nervous officers were the ones from the Internal Affairs Unit. Frank watched their interrogator, Belknap, scurrying around in the background. Instead of wearing a suit, he was back in uniform and carrying a big stack of files.

Con Riley gave the Hardys a cheerful greeting from the booking desk. "Go right in, gentlemen. Straight down the hall—I think you know the way."

The pebbled glass door with the word *Chief*

in gold letters was half open. "Come in," Chief Collig invited.

He was seated behind the same old wooden desk with new piles of paper. Parker Lawrence's TV and VCR were gone, but Frank noticed that the computer remained.

"I'm going to take a stab at learning to use that thing," Collig said, following Frank's eyes. "Have to keep up with the times, you know."

A good night's sleep had erased the dark rings from under his eyes. In fact, Joe couldn't remember seeing the chief look better. It was as if ten years had rolled off him.

Chief Collig held up a familiar-looking manila envelope. "Here are your father's papers, signed and sealed," he said. "I've already spoken with the people in the licensing authority to explain why they'll be late."

"Thanks, Chief," Frank and Joe said.

"It was the least I could do to thank you two." Collig put his palms on the desk and stared up at the boys. "And I do want to thank you. Without your help, I'd probably still be hiding under a bush somewhere."

"I'm sure things would have worked out," Frank said.

"At some point," Collig said. "But thanks to you, the nightmare is over *now*. I really appreciate how you stood by me in spite of any past differences we might have had." The chief grinned. "And in spite of some rough moments along the way."

He stood up. "This was an odd case, taking me back to when I was young. It sort of reminded me of what it was like to be your age."

"It was pretty weird for us, too," Joe admitted.

"Yes, like a trip back in time, seeing what policing was like years back," Frank said. "I don't think I'll ever dismiss the old days as being simpler, though."

He met Collig's eyes. "It must have taken a whole lot of courage to break through the blue wall of silence."

The chief lowered his eyes for a second, saying nothing. Then he handed over Fenton Hardy's papers.

"Thanks again, men," he said, shaking hands with Frank and Joe. "I guess, in a way, we know one another a little better now."

"I guess so," Joe said.

Collig sat down again.

"Well, goodbye, Chief." Envelope tucked under his arm, Frank headed for the door.

"Hey, Hardys," Collig called after them as they stepped into the hallway. "Just remember. This won't cut any ice if you come horning in on one of my cases tomorrow."

Frank and Joe laughed.

"Okay," Joe said. "It'll be enemies as usual—the next time."

SPIKED!

Chapter

1

"GAME, LENZ AND OSTEEN." The voice over the loudspeakers drowned out the sound of crashing breakers at the beach volleyball court on southern California's Laguna Beach. "Match score: one, Lenz and Osteen; zero, Conlin and Donahue."

The crowd of approximately a thousand, which filled the bleachers on both sides of the court, erupted in raucous cheers. Joe Hardy, sitting in the center of the third row next to his brother, Frank, absently wiped the sweat trickling from his blond hair.

"What is it, a hundred and ten degrees out here?" he demanded.

"I told you to change clothes before we came to the games," Frank reminded him, sipping a jumbo-size Hi-Kick soda. Frank, who at eighteen was a year older than his brother, looked cool in colorful surfer's shorts, tank top, and sunglasses, with a bicycle cap covering his dark hair. He glanced at Joe, who was so pink he looked like uncooked steak in a polo shirt and long khaki pants.

"We were late," Joe protested. "It took me half an hour to sweet-talk two press passes from the hotel desk clerk. By the time she gave in, the tournament had already started. No way was I going to miss more of it to unpack!"

He grabbed Frank's soda and took a long sip. "Ugh," he said. "Too sweet."

"It's all they're selling at the refreshment stand," Frank said wryly. "Could that be because the tournament's sponsored by the Frosty Company, manufacturers of Hi-Kick soda?"

"They'll never make money with a taste like this." Joe handed the cup back.

The brothers turned back to await the start of the second game of the tournament's first set. Ever since the previous summer, when Joe had been introduced to the sport in Florida, he'd become a fanatic about beach volleyball. The regular game of six to a side he could take or leave, but beach volleyball with two to a side was fast and exciting—everything that appealed to him. When Frank and Joe had arrived at the South Coast Surf Club that morning, Joe had immediately spotted the poster announcing the First Annual Hi-Kick Beach Volleyball Tournament.

"Now I can show you how the game's really

played!'' he'd said enthusiastically as he read off the list of players from a bulletin board in the hotel lobby. "Wow, I've heard of these guys! Scooter Lenz and Peter Osteen from La Jolla. They're one of the top teams. Look, they're playing the U.S. champions this morning—Brad Conlin and Mark Donahue.'' Still reading, Joe had whistled softly. "Frosty's put a hundred thousand dollars in prize money into this competition. Fifty thousand each to the winning men's and women's teams!''

"Very interesting,'' Frank had said with a yawn as he picked up his suitcase to go to their room. The brothers' parents had sprung this summer getaway on them as a surprise just a couple of days before, and Frank hadn't had a good night's sleep the past two nights because of packing for the trip and the overnight flight to California. "I'm going upstairs to take a shower. Then I'm going to hit the beach.''

Well, they *were* on the beach, Frank reminded himself—bunched in with 998 other fans to watch four guys punch a volleyball back and forth over a net. The sun was so blindingly bright that Frank could hardly see the game even with sunglasses on. But in the distance, beyond the court, he could make out surfers gliding atop the Pacific breakers and closer in beautiful girls and body-builder guys sauntering along the crescent-shaped southern California beach. He was really tempted to make a break for it and join them. The Hardys hadn't been to California

3

in a while, and Frank wanted to enjoy the beaches.

The sound of the referee's whistle interrupted Frank's thoughts as game two of the match began. While the referee climbed a ladder at one side of center court, Frank watched Mark Donahue cradle the ball in his right hand. Joe had told him that at six feet two inches Donahue was the shortest male player in the entire competition. The muscles that bulged on his arms and legs as he took a step away from the back line made it obvious why he was among the top beach volleyball contenders in the world.

His partner, Brad Conlin, had the leaner build and long blond hair of a surfer. His muscles were tensed like those of a weight lifter as Mark prepared to serve.

As Frank watched, Donahue charged forward, threw the ball high, then leapt about three feet off the sand to slam the ball with an overhead smash.

As the ball hummed over the net faster than a cruise missile, Frank decided there was no way for Lenz or Osteen to return the serve. Even as he was telling himself this, Frank saw Peter Osteen fling himself toward the ball to land full length on the sand. He got one hand under the ball and bumped it up to his partner. As Scooter Lenz tapped the ball straight up, Osteen sprang to his feet and slammed the ball down into the sand halfway between the opposing team.

4

"That was incredible!" Frank leapt to his feet as the crowd went wild. "Did you see the way he smashed that ball?"

"What'd I tell you?" Joe said over the noise of the loudspeakers. "These guys are amazing athletes! It takes muscle to make those moves on loose sand, and skill to maneuver with only one guy to back you up."

"Like a combination of pro tennis and regular volleyball," Frank agreed, impressed in spite of himself.

Frank watched Lenz and Osteen giving each other a high five. Osteen, with his curly red hair and six-foot-six, heavily muscled build, looked like a Viking in surfing baggies, blue tank top, and white Hi-Kick cap with the bill folded up. Lenz was much darker but just as large, with black curls escaping from under his Hi-Kick cap and a determined set to his strong jaw. Frank could see from the way they treated each other that the partners were good friends as well as teammates.

"These are permanent teams, right?" he asked his brother as the audience settled down and the next play began.

"Sure," Joe answered. "Men and women, both. There're major bucks in this sport, Frank. I read that Conlin and Donahue made about seventy-five thousand dollars each last year, *plus* endorsements and stuff."

Frank nodded. "The Frosty Company's sure getting its advertising value out of sponsoring

5

this contest." His eyes took in one of the six-foot-tall inflated mock-ups of Hi-Kick soft drink bottles that adorned each corner of the court and the table near the court covered with coolers and paper cups filled with Hi-Kick. Even the teenage ball-catchers who hovered behind each team wore Hi-Kick caps and T-shirts. There was no way the crews of TV news teams could avoid filming the Hi-Kick logo.

"Yeah, they'd better," replied Joe, fanning himself with a brochure, "if they expect to cut into SuperJuice's business. SuperJuice has always been number one in the sports drink market."

"Hey, wait," Frank said, interrupting as he peered at the huge scoreboard, also decorated with the blue-and-gold Hi-Kick logo. "The scoreboard says this game's tied at zero. I thought Osteen won the point."

"You have to be serving to get a point," Joe corrected. "Otherwise, it's just a 'side out.' The next serve switches to your side."

Frank nodded and turned back to watch Scooter Lenz serve. He stood just behind the back line and hit the ball underhand so that it soared over thirty feet in the air before coming down in the other court.

"All right, Scooter!" a fan yelled right in Frank's ear. "Dynamite high-ball!"

Trying to ignore the ringing in his ear, Frank watched as Conlin positioned himself under the serve and popped the ball to his partner, moving close to the net to await the setup. As Donahue hit it up in perfect position for a spike like the one Osteen had just made, Conlin jumped high. Across the net, Osteen leapt up, too, expecting the spike. But at the last second, Conlin only tapped the ball, causing it to arc over Osteen's outstretched arms and drop dead in the sand. Side out, Frank told himself, letting his breath out.

"Way to go, Marco! Fantastic dink!" called out a fan, making Frank's other ear buzz.

"Still zero–zero," Frank commented. "It could be a long time between points at this rate. A game's what, fifteen?"

"Fifteen points," Joe agreed. "And you have to win by at least two points."

"They're going to be totally wiped out," Frank said. "In this heat, playing that hard—"

"Whoever wants it most will win," Joe finished for him, wiping sweat from his face as he followed the action.

"Well, you were right about one thing. They earn their money."

As the match continued, Frank found himself captivated by the impressive jump serves, towering high-ball serves, perfectly timed blocks, and soft dink shots hit just out of reach. Because there were so many more side outs than points, the sun had climbed to the top of the sky and started to descend before the score evened up at two games to two.

"Next team to win a game wins the match." Joe sat up taller in his seat as the exhausted players took a break in the shade of a Hi-Kick awning. "Osteen looks bad."

Frank peered at Osteen, who was resting on one knee under the awning and breathing heavily. His face was flushed and sweaty, and when he stood up, his legs looked a little shaky. Scooter Lenz, his teammate, muttered something to him. Osteen shook his head, then walked back out to start the next game.

"You're right," Frank said. "Looks like he has sunstroke or something."

He wondered privately whether the game would be called, but the referee didn't seem to notice Osteen's condition. He climbed the ladder to the top of the net and blew his whistle so play could begin.

"Way to go, Osteen!" Joe yelled. At least the rest of the crowd had quieted down somewhat, Frank thought thankfully. The heat seemed to have affected them as well.

"Set point!" announced the loudspeakers nearly an hour later. Frank snapped out of his heat-induced doldrums to see a score of 14–15, Conlin-Donahue, on the board. He looked at the court. All four players appeared ragged and were dripping with sweat, but Osteen was by far the worst off. Swaying a little on his feet, he signaled a pause and then trudged through the sand to the Hi-Kick table. As he grabbed a blue paper cup and gulped down the soda, the crowd supporting the current champions rumbled impatiently.

"Play ball," the referee called finally, and Osteen, looking a little revived, trudged back to the court.

When play resumed, Brad Conlin was serving. Osteen hit the serve first and passed the ball to Scooter Lenz in the middle of the court. Lenz bent at the knees, clasped his hands low, and tapped the ball straight up in a perfect set. Osteen leapt to spike the ball down at an angle that couldn't be returned.

His jump wasn't high enough, though. Frank yelled as Conlin, who was ready and waiting, smashed Osteen's shot back over the net.

Lenz saw the ball coming and made a desperate lunge to retrieve it. It landed inches from him, just inside the boundary of the court.

"Match to Conlin and Donahue!" Joe cried as the crowd cheered and rose in a standing ovation for all four players.

Frank watched the exhausted players—two triumphant and two destroyed—move toward the net to shake hands with their opponents. Scooter Lenz's head was hanging low on his chest. He was the perfect picture of defeat, Frank thought.

"Boy, what a game!" Joe said, forgetting all about the heat in his enthusiasm. "Did you see how Conlin—"

"Joe, look!" Frank interrupted, standing up and pointing at the court. As Joe followed his gaze, the older Hardy stared at Peter Osteen.

9

The redheaded player had crumpled to the sand and was lying there, his body twitching and his legs thrashing uncontrollably. His fellow players had turned toward him in shock.

"Osteen's down!" a fan screamed and suddenly there was a rush of spectators from the bleachers.

"Come on!" Frank shouted, moving down to the front of the bleachers. He pushed toward the edge of the court, where a group of players, coaches, and Hi-Kick officials huddled over the downed player. Several television crews had crowded around, too, their camera lenses aimed at Osteen. They backed off only after one of the officials agreed to give them an interview.

"Give him air!" A pair of medics with Hi-Kick patches on their white jackets ran toward Osteen. The fans moved closer, anyway, their curiosity overpowering their caution.

Frank and Joe broke through to the front ranks of the crowd. From where he was standing Frank could see that Osteen's face had turned a dangerous shade of green. As the medics bent over him, the spasms in the player's limbs were growing weaker. Staring at the stricken teen, Frank only heard Joe's voice.

"Frank," Joe was whispering, staring at the player in shock. "It looks like he's stopped breathing!"

Chapter

2

"COME ON, OSTEEN. Breathe!" Joe clenched his fists, frustrated at not being able to help. Both Frank and Joe were experts at CPR, but Joe knew the tournament officials would never let a couple of teenagers near a player in trouble.

"The ambulance," someone in the crowd announced as the noise of a siren approached. The hundreds of fans who'd surrounded the court turned to watch as a team of paramedics leapt out of their ambulance and raced with a stretcher to the scene.

"Ladies and gentlemen," announced a voice on the loudspeakers, "we have a medical emergency. Repeat, a medical emergency. The remainder of today's tournament will be delayed until further notice. Those who desire ticket refunds should go to the tournament office at the Surf Club. Please avoid the court area as you leave."

11

"Okay, move back," Joe ordered the crowd, turning to push the fans gently backward. "Give the medics room to move."

Frank came to his aid. Several fans grumbled angrily, but gradually they either wandered away or returned to their seats to await word on Osteen's condition.

Then Joe heard more sirens and peered down the road. "Police," he said to Frank.

Joe stepped back as one of the tournament officials, a short, middle-aged man in white pants and a blue knit shirt with the Hi-Kick logo made his way to the stretcher. He seemed very tense and kept wiping his forehead with a soggy handkerchief. As soon as he heard the wailing of the sirens, the man froze midstep and frowned. "Who called the cops?" he demanded.

"Uh, I did, sir." It was Osteen's partner, Scooter Lenz. Joe had noticed him following anxiously beside the official and had felt sorry for him. "We need the cops, right?"

"What for?" the little man shouted hoarsely, applying his handkerchief to his face again. "Because Peter keeled over from too much sun? That's illegal now?"

"Sir?" Joe Hardy stepped forward hesitantly, glancing down at Peter Osteen's inert body as the paramedics carried it past him. What he saw made his heart skip a beat. Peter's mouth hung open, his eyes were closed, and his body lay still. "Uh, is Peter still alive?"

"Alive? Alive!" The question seemed to send

the official into a fit of rage. "Of course he's alive. Dead people don't play beach volleyball tournaments, young man."

"I was just wondering. Because if he had died, the police would have to ask questions and decide on the cause of death."

"Questions?" The nervous man glanced toward the ambulance, where the paramedics were just slamming the back doors shut.

"It's standard procedure," said Frank, backing up his brother. "Besides, you'll need help handling this crowd."

"Who *are* you guys?" the official demanded as the ambulance pulled away and two police cruisers pulled into its place. "You act like cops."

"Our dad was a cop," Joe explained quickly. "And we've done a lot of detective work ourselves. You might have read about us in the papers a while back when we solved a case for a movie studio in L.A. I'm Joe Hardy, and this is my brother, Frank."

The man's eyes bugged out, and his handkerchief hung forgotten from his fist. *"You're* the Hardy brothers?" Then slowly his eyes lit up. He looked like a condemned prisoner who'd just figured out how to escape, Joe thought.

"This could be a stroke of luck," the man said, lowering his voice. "I'm Richard Prindle, head of promotion for the Frosty Company. This tournament was my idea, and I have to make

13

sure it generates great publicity for Hi-Kick or I'm in big trouble. Maybe we could—''

The sirens cut off abruptly. Three men in uniform and two in civilian clothes were climbing out of the cars. "Just what I need," Prindle moaned. "A sick volleyball champ *and* a scandal for the newspapers. Excuse me, boys. Might as well get this over with.''

Prindle marched over to meet the officers. The other officials and players watched him go. Everyone was very upset, and one of the female players had begun crying.

"It wasn't the sun that did it," a voice said in Joe's ear.

Startled, Joe turned to find Scooter Lenz standing next to him. "It wasn't?" he said, taken off guard at having one of his favorite athletes speak to him. "What did do it, then?''

"Too much sugar." Scooter's eyes flicked from Joe to Frank. "Or too little. Osteen was a diabetic. Prindle didn't tell you 'cause he thinks any weakness in the players weakens the show.''

"You're saying he had a diabetic reaction?'' Frank said, taking a step closer. "Did you tell the paramedics? If they know, they may be able to save him.''

"Sure I told them," Scooter said, offended. "What do you think, I'd let him die to keep Prindle happy?''

"Sorry," Frank said, embarrassed. "It's just— well, we flew in from the East Coast this morning and I guess we're pretty beat.''

14

"Yeah, but you're detectives, right? I heard you talking to Prindle. Are you going to hang around for a while?"

"Yeah," said Joe. "We're staying at the Surf Club. Why?"

"Well," he said, kicking at the sand with one huge foot, "I'm sure what my partner had was one of those seizures, all right, but what I wonder is, how come? I mean, a diabetic's blood sugar level has to get either real high or real low to set off a reaction like that, and Osteen double-checks his blood sugar so many times during a tourney, it couldn't possibly have gotten out of hand."

"Then what do you think caused the attack?"

Scooter shrugged. "I don't know enough about it, I guess. But I do have a funny feeling about this, and I figure it can't hurt to know how to reach you guys."

While Frank gave Scooter their room number at the Surf Club, Joe noticed one of the plainclothes detectives, a burly redhead, approaching them across the sand.

"Scooter Lenz?" the man asked. He flashed a leather case with a gold badge inside. "Detective Sergeant Dan O'Boyle, Laguna Beach P.D. Could I have a word with you, please?"

"Sure," the volleyball champion said uneasily. "Uh, how is he?"

The detective closed his eyes and sucked in a lungful of hot air. "He died on the way to the hospital, I'm afraid. He went into a brief coma,

15

then slipped away. I'm sorry." He hesitated, then said more gently, "Mr. Prindle tells me you were the last person to see him alone."

At the news that his partner was dead, Scooter had become deathly pale. Now he stammered as he tried to answer the detective without crying.

Joe felt as though he'd been hit with a sledgehammer. He'd been following Peter Osteen's career for months. He couldn't believe that the nineteen-year-old champ could actually die moments after playing so well.

"Excuse us," Frank said to the detective and Scooter, pulling Joe away. "I think Mr. Prindle wants to talk to us."

"I can't get over it," Joe kept saying as his older brother steered him over the firm, hard sand. "He looked great out there one instant. Then the next—"

"Here's what we're going to do," Frank said in a low breath, tightening his grip on his brother's arm. "We're going to find Prindle and offer to look into the situation for him. We'll convince Prindle that finding out what really happened to Osteen is better for the Frosty Company than everybody thinking it was careless about a player's health."

"What do you mean, 'what really happened to Osteen'?" Joe asked. "You think Scooter's right about something being fishy?"

"I think more than that," Frank said grimly. "Remember that volunteer stint I did at Bayport Hospital? We had diabetics come into the emergency room. People with hyperglycemic reactions don't usually jerk and twitch like Osteen did. They just slow down, like they're falling asleep, and quietly slip into a coma. People who twitch around a lot, *then* fall unconscious, are more likely to have been poisoned."

Joe stared at him. "How sure are you about this?" he demanded.

"It's only a hunch," Frank admitted, "but I definitely smell a rat. Besides," he added dryly, "we're here for two weeks, right? Two whole weeks with nothing to do."

"Yeah," Joe said as they continued their search for Prindle. "Nothing but surfing, swimming, lying around on the beach, talking to pretty girls—"

The loudspeakers announced just then that the tournament would close for the day—without mentioning Peter's death. Hundreds of grumbling fans began moving toward the parking lot as Joe and Frank found Prindle standing near the cruisers. They presented him with their offer. Prindle, looking haggard, merely nodded his head meekly.

"Meet me at the Surf Club in twenty minutes," he finally said. "Our tournament offices are in two large Winnebago trailers in the parking lot. The one closer to the clubhouse is mine."

"We'll be there," Frank agreed.

As Prindle hurried away, Joe asked his brother, "What now?"

"Let's find the other team—Brad Conlin and

17

Mark Donahue," Frank said, leading the way back toward the court. "If we're looking for suspects, those two would have had a lot to lose, right?"

"Yeah, but they're all volleyball players, Frank," Joe protested. "You don't think—" He paused midsentence, noticing that Detective O'Boyle was now interviewing the Hi-Kick film crew. He wanted to listen in on their conversation and said so to Frank. Joe filled his brother in when he returned. "He asked them if they'd noticed anything suspicious this morning. But the guy who spoke for them said no. He said something about just minding their business and getting the job done."

"Great," Frank said. "With friends like that, Osteen didn't need enemies. Look, there are Conlin and Donahue."

Joe followed Frank toward the two players, who were talking at the far end of the net with their backs to the Hardys.

Motioning to Joe to be quiet, Frank moved closer toward the two. But even Joe could hear Donahue when he erupted loudly, "A lot of nerve, asking those questions! Like we're criminals! I should have—"

"Take it easy," Joe heard Conlin answer. "Just keep cool, and don't blow it. You don't want to—"

Joe wasn't able to hear any more. Afraid the players would notice them, Frank had backed off and signaled to Joe to move off with him.

"Those two aren't in the mood for questions," Frank muttered to Joe. "It's time to go see Prindle anyway."

They walked the short distance down the beach to the Surf Club complex. Joe took in the beautiful curved beach with sunbathers settled in on blankets and a group of hotel guests tucked under identical yellow beach umbrellas. A boy and a girl were flying a kite while a German shepherd that had escaped from somewhere frolicked illegally in the waves. It looked exactly the way Joe had pictured it when his father had first told them about their trip. Now that they were here, though, all Joe could think about was a volleyball player's death and how he and Frank might have to solve another mystery. Joe sighed. He guessed the detecting urge was in the Hardy blood.

"Wow. Air conditioning!" Joe said as he and Frank entered Mr. Prindle's comfortable trailer office. "Does that feel good."

"Sit down, sit down." Prindle, still obviously distraught, was gesturing to two chairs facing his desk. "Make yourselves at home. Can I get you something to drink?"

Joe sat in the chair nearer the desk, noting the piles of manila folders, glossy photographs, and printed literature that cluttered every inch of available space. "Thanks," he said to Prindle. "What do you have?"

Prindle opened the door of a small refrigerator beside his desk and peered inside. "Frosty Cola,

Frosty Orange, Frosty Lemon—and plenty of Hi-Kick."

Joe exchanged a glance with his brother. "Two orange sodas would be fine," he said.

As Prindle pulled out two cans, popped the tops, and handed them to the brothers, Joe noticed that the executive's hands were shaking.

"I'm very worried," Prindle blurted out abruptly as he sat back down at his desk. "There's been some funny business going on around here. Now that Peter is dead—" He hesitated, then said, "Sorry, I can't really believe it. But if you two think there might be something—irregular—about his death, the rest of what's happened might turn out to be more important than I'd thought. Or maybe there's no connection, after all. I hope not, but—"

Frank raised a hand in the air to stop Prindle's nervous chatter. "Just start from the top, sir."

"Sorry." Prindle cleared his throat. "First of all, this Hi-Kick assignment is my big break at the Frosty Company. We're trying to carve out a place for ourselves in the sports drink market, and using pro beach volleyball was my idea. This is a sport with a future. It gets lots of TV time already, and the players are becoming known. But they are still a lot cheaper to sign for endorsements than pro football players. So you get value for your money."

Joe sipped his soda and nodded. Prindle was talking very fast. Either he was in shock, Joe

20

decided, or he was trying to hide something. Or maybe both.

"It's been a lot of work so far," the promotion man continued. "Arranging to get the top players in the game and hiring a good filmmaker. A lot of work. But finally everything was coming together," Prindle went on. "And then we started getting letters."

"What letters?" asked Frank.

Prindle unlocked the middle drawer of his desk and pulled out a manila folder. "Someone's been trying to scare us out of holding the tournament," he explained. "We started getting threatening notes at our office headquarters." He opened the folder to let the brothers see. "Then a couple of players received anonymous phone calls telling them to drop out of the competition."

"Which players?" Joe asked, watching Frank page through the notes. The messages were made up of individual letters in all sizes and styles cut from magazines.

"Conlin and Donahue for certain. Maybe others who haven't told me. And now a player is dead. I knew Peter had diabetes, but I never knew a guy so careful about his physical health."

Joe read the letter Frank was looking at out loud. " 'The Frosty Company sells junk to its customers! The time has come to pay for your crimes! Stop the Hi-Kick tournament or else!' Sounds like a pretty extreme reaction to a soft drink," he joked to Prindle.

Prindle wasn't laughing. He had become silent and his gaze was fixed. "What's that?" he finally asked out loud, continuing to stare at the same spot.

The boys turned and saw a sheet of paper lying on the floor near the door. Joe stood up and moved over to pick up the paper. He wasn't surprised to see another message written from letters cut out of magazines.

Joe laid it on Prindle's desk.

Prindle read the short note silently, and a moan escaped his throat. "This one's really insane," he said, handing it to Frank.

" 'Frosty can be dangerous to people's health!' " Frank read out loud. " 'Stop the games, or you'll regret it!' "

Chapter

3

SO THERE REALLY IS something going on here!
Frank thought grimly.

Prindle rested his forearms on his desk and
leaned over them. "Listen," he said, quietly taking in both boys. "The tournament is scheduled
to end here in four days, even with today's post-
ponement. After that, we take the winners on a
tour along the East and West coasts. I need to
know that no more disasters are going to happen. If someone is after my players, I want that
person stopped. Can I count on you to find out
whatever's going on here?"

Before Frank or Joe could answer, the door
swung open and a short, skinny man with
slicked-back dark hair popped his head inside.
"Great match, Prindle!" he said as Frank and
Joe turned to gaze at him. He wore a flower-

23

print shirt and bright red pants. "Shame about your player, Osteen, though. If there's anything I can do—"

"I don't need any help, Auerbach," Prindle growled. "And right now I'm busy."

"Don't let me interrupt," said the newcomer. "See you around."

"He sure seemed happy," Frank remarked after the man left. "Kind of inappropriate after the death of a player. Who *was* he?"

"Todd Auerbach," said Prindle angrily. "He's the public relations man for our biggest competitor, SuperJuice. They're based in Santa Ana, near here. He's been nosing around, offering endorsement contracts to some of the players. I saw him at the games this morning, so I'm not surprised that he stopped by to gloat. So—will you take this case?"

"You bet," said Joe. "We've already taken it, actually."

"Great." Prindle appeared to relax a little. "What can I do to help you?"

"You could use us as tournament workers," suggested Frank. "You know—say we're big volleyball fans and we've volunteered to help out. That way, maybe we can pick up information on the inside."

"No problem," said Prindle. "You can start tomorrow, first thing in the—"

Just then, the office door swung in again and an agitated-looking man strode in. Frank recognized the tall, thin man with the blond mustache

24

as one of the Hi-Kick filmmakers who'd been talking to Detective O'Boyle earlier. He still wore his Hi-Kick T-shirt, but he'd switched his Hi-Kick cap for a regular baseball cap.

"Those cops confiscated every foot of film I shot today!" the man roared at Prindle before the executive could greet him. "They said it was *evidence!* I *need* that footage! I mean, I'm sorry Peter's dead, but it's not like they're going to find somebody taking a shot at him on my film."

"Hey, Ken, lighten up," said Prindle, smiling nervously. "I'm sure you'll get the film back and in good condition. We have to cooperate with the law, right?"

The blond man hesitated, then calmed down a little. "I guess so," he admitted. "But if they ruin one frame of that film—"

"Ken Chaplin, I want to you meet Frank and Joe Hardy," Prindle interrupted. "They love beach volleyball and have volunteered to work at the tournament. Can you use some help?"

Frank smiled to look friendly as Ken sized them up, his gripe already forgotten.

"Actually, I could use a couple of guys tomorrow. We're scheduled to shoot Chris Welles demonstrating the jump serve."

"Just tell us where to go, and we'll be there," said Joe.

"All right," said Chaplin with a nod. "Tomorrow morning, nine o'clock. Just ask for Chris Welles, and someone will show you where to go. See you then."

He started out the door, saying to Prindle, "Just do me a favor, okay? Could you push the cops to give back my film right away?"

That evening, after an early seafood dinner at the huge outdoor dining area on the beach, Frank and Joe relaxed on the terrace of their second-story hotel room. Right then, the boys were enjoying a perfect sunset while their feet were propped up on the railing.

But their minds weren't on the scenery.

"Maybe someone's trying to get some money out of the company," Joe suggested, shifting in his plastic chair. "Someone figures Frosty is a big, rich conglomerate with a reputation to protect. It might pay plenty to avoid trouble."

"But the notes haven't mentioned money. Not yet, anyway." Frank frowned, gazing out into the distance. "We'll have to find out if Osteen had any enemies. It's possible the letters and his death aren't even connected."

"I don't know, Frank. I have a feeling they are. And if they are, we're dealing with some rough customers."

Frank nodded. He thought about all the people he'd met who were connected with the Frosty Company. He recalled Conlin telling Donahue to "Keep cool, and don't blow it," and wondered what that meant. He thought about that weird-looking Todd Auerbach and wondered if he was capable of murder. And why, he asked himself, was Richard Prindle so nervous all the time? Was he hiding something—something that the Hardys needed to know?

"I wish Dad were here," he said to Joe. "I'd like to know his thoughts on this."

"I'll tell you his thoughts," Joe said with a short laugh. "Summed up in two words: Be careful."

The next morning the Hardys had breakfast in their room so they could join the tournament workers early. From the lobby, they followed a winding corridor to the opposite end of the rambling hotel complex, where an entire wing that housed a gym, locker rooms, saunas, and spa had been rented for the volleyball players' use.

"Let's check this out," Frank said at the entrance to the men's locker room. He and Joe entered the low-ceilinged room to find a small group of players huddled together near the showers. They were talking in low tones and ignored Frank and Joe. They all had downcast expressions, Frank noticed and wondered if they were discussing Osteen.

"Frank. Over here." Joe was motioning to him from a row of lockers partway across the room. Frank joined him, reading the players' names on strips of masking tape stuck to each locker. Joe stood beside a locker with a tape that read 'Osteen.'

"It's unlocked," Joe whispered excitedly. He swung the door open and instantly saw that the locker had been cleared out.

27

"That must be his stuff." Frank nodded toward a stool near the locker. A pile of items was stacked on top of it. "They must be getting ready to ship it back to his family."

"How do you know it's Osteen's?"

"Look what's on top." Frank picked up a small black box with an LCD display window at the top and the word *Glucograph* in white block letters across the bottom. He turned it over to inspect the buttons and slot at one end and the hinged door in the bottom where batteries went. "I saw one of these once at the hospital. It's for monitoring blood sugar—"

"Can I help you guys?"

Frank stopped midsentence to stare up at the tallest volleyball player he'd seen so far. His incredible muscle tone was obvious even under his shirt, and the frown on his face was very threatening.

"Yes, you can," Joe said easily. "I'm Joe Hardy. This is my brother, Frank. We've just been hired on as general assistants for the tournament, and we're supposed to find Chris Welles. Do you know where he is?"

A flicker of amusement appeared on the player's face. "I'm not sure." He gazed over Joe's shoulder and called out, "Hey, George! This guy wants to know where Chris is."

Two powerful hands clamped down on Joe's shoulders and spun him around. Joe found himself staring up at a handsome, scowling face framed by curly, blond hair.

28

Frank figured the stranger was at least five inches taller than Joe, and even more muscular than the first guy.

"What do you want with Chris Welles?" the blond giant demanded.

The big hands remained clenched on Joe's shoulders. Frank stepped forward protectively. "Take it easy," he said to the athlete, and Joe pulled back a step to get loose.

The volleyball player named George didn't want to take it easy, though. He stepped forward, grabbed a handful of Frank's shirt, and pushed him back. Frank didn't have a chance to brace himself and was propelled straight through a swinging door that led to an outdoor lounge area. Before Joe could react, the giant had grabbed his shirt, too, and Joe was sailing through the swinging door after his brother.

As Frank and Joe struggled to regain their balance, the blond athlete strode out after them. Shaking a fist under Joe's nose, he growled, "Mess around with Chris and I'll bust your face for you! Understand?"

Chapter

4

JOE *DIDN'T* UNDERSTAND, and it was clear from Frank's expression that he didn't either. Who *was* this guy, and why was he pulling this caveman routine? Joe swatted the hand away from his face and glared at his attacker.

"What's your problem?" he protested. "I was just—"

George bored in, sticking an index finger in Joe's chest. "I don't have a problem. *You* have a problem."

Joe felt the anger building inside. A voice in the back of his mind told him to be cool, but this dude was primed to fight, and Joe wasn't going to be pushed around any more.

"Listen, whoever you are, get out of my face! I won't tell you again!"

The stranger's scowl gave way to an ugly grin. "Okay. That's it. You asked for it."

As Joe braced himself for the guy's first move, a girl's voice shouted behind them. *"George!"* she cried, sounding very angry.

The volleyball player flinched, then backed away in confusion and embarrassment.

"What do you think you're doing?" demanded the voice.

Over the athlete's shoulder, Joe spotted a beautiful, blond girl. When she approached him, Joe saw that she was as tall as he was. He looked directly into her deep blue eyes. She glanced at Joe long enough to make him realize his mouth was hanging open. Then she turned to glare at George again. "Uh, h-hi," George stammered, staring down at his feet. "I was just—I mean—this guy here—" He stopped, not knowing what to say.

The girl's eyes shifted impatiently to Joe. "Are you okay?" she asked matter-of-factly. "I'm Chris Welles, this lunk's unofficial nursemaid."

Joe returned the smile. Then he realized what she'd said.

"Chris. You're Chris? Oh! Uh, I'm—Joe. Joe Hardy. This is my brother, Frank. We were supposed to find you this morning—that is, until this guy tried to stop us. We're assisting with the film shoot."

"Ah. My chance at the big screen," Chris joked, reaching out to shake Joe's hand. She smiled brightly at him, ignoring George's low growl. Joe glanced nervously at George, noting that his face had turned a bright, angry red.

31

"Don't worry, George, I'll introduce you," Chris said, and laughed. She released Joe's hand, saying, "The big clown with no manners is George Ritt. Go on, George, say hello, and try to smile."

George obviously didn't feel like smiling, but he forced his face into an almost pleasant expression and muttered something Joe couldn't decipher. Then he turned abruptly and reentered the men's locker room.

"Sorry about that," Chris said to Joe and Frank after he'd gone. "He has it in his head that I'm his property. I wish I knew where he got that idea. He has a habit of attacking any male who even mentions my name."

"Sounds like a nice guy," Frank said.

"You meet all types in this sport." Chris's expression suddenly brightened. "This film is going to be great. Wait till you see Tammy's serve. She's my partner. Let's go find her. The crew's probably setting up."

As the brothers followed her away from the clubhouse, Joe felt someone watching him. He glanced back to see that George had reappeared in the outdoor lounge area and was following their departure with a nasty expression on his face. Joe had the feeling there was going to be more trouble with the massive player sometime when Chris wasn't around.

Turning forward again, Joe saw that several volleyball courts had been set up on the beach behind the clubhouse. Ken Chaplin's helper was clearing the area of sunbathers and onlookers as Ken set up the equipment. Joe gave a low whistle, impressed with the quality of the cameras, lights, reflectors, and insulated film cases that lay in a pile on a plastic sheet.

A little to one side of the film crew, Joe saw a girl sitting on a beach chair, catching some sun. She spotted Chris and the Hardys coming and waved, smiling. As they walked across the court, she stood up—revealing that she was a couple of inches taller than Chris.

"This is my partner, Tammy Strauss," Chris said. "Tammy, meet Frank and Joe Hardy."

As Joe shook hands with Tammy, he marveled that two such good-looking and tall women could be partners. Tammy's light brown hair, cut very short, and her high cheekbones and friendly brown eyes, made her almost as attractive as Chris. He could tell from Frank's expression that he was thinking the same thing. Because of Frank's attachment to his girl, Callie Shaw, he barely noticed most other girls. These two were stunning, though. The fact that he had to look *up* to Tammy might have something to do with it, too, Joe thought slyly.

"Frank? Joe?" Chaplin, who was dressed in a Hi-Kick T-shirt and baseball cap as he had been the day before, motioned to them to join him. His helper—a muscular, older guy with wiry black hair going gray at the temples— looked up as the Hardys approached.

"I want to introduce you to my assistant

33

before we start," Chaplin said. "Vern Elliott's my right-hand man—assistant director, cameraman, lighting expert, editor—you name it. There's nothing in the film business he hasn't done. Vern, Frank and Joe Hardy. They'll be our gofers for today's shoot."

Vern winked, then went back to work. Joe thought he had seen a coldness in the older man's eyes, but it had all happened too quick to tell for sure. He did notice the tattoos on both of Vern's arms as he reached for a reflector, though. One depicted a dragon devouring a snake. The other one looked like a wild dog with a knife held between its teeth.

Ken continued briskly, "We'll be using two cameras. Vern will be stationary here, using the tripod. I'll use a hand-held camera, to get shots from different angles. I need you guys to retrieve the balls as the girls serve them."

He pointed to a huge bag next to the net that bulged with volleyballs. "Chris and Tammy will alternate, serving from opposite ends of the court, and you'll grab the balls and stuff them into these empty bags here, so we can keep filming without long breaks. We're on a tight schedule; they have a match this afternoon, and I promised their coach they wouldn't be out here too long. So stay on your toes. Understood?"

"No problem," Joe said, watching Chris warm up with a couple of stretching exercises.

"Isn't this net too low?" Frank asked Tammy.

"It's lower for women," she explained with a smile. "Seven and a half feet for us, eight and a half for men."

She was about to say more when Chaplin called, "Ready, girls? Crew? Frank, slate the cameras!"

Luckily, Frank had worked on small films before. He knew to pick up a set of clappers that was lying on the plastic sheet, hold it in front of Vern's camera and say, "*A* camera, mark!" Then he stuck the clappers in front of Chaplin's hand-held camera. "*B* camera, mark!" Then he ran back to his place opposite Tammy, ready to retrieve the balls.

"Okay, Chris," Chaplin shouted as he knelt and steadied the camera on his shoulder. "Let's see a monster serve, now."

Chris set herself five yards behind the end line and ran forward. Joe admired her coordination as she tossed the ball high and leapt up after it. Her body arched as her arm swung back, so that when the arm came forward all her strength was behind it.

Slamming the ball with an open palm, Chris sent it whizzing over the net, straight at Joe. Before he could bring up his hands to catch it, it caught *him*—hard, in the stomach.

"Are you all right?" called Chris. Joe looked up in time to catch a combination of concern and amusement on her face.

"Sure, fine," he insisted, refusing to rub his sore belly. "It surprised me, that's all." He stuffed the ball into the empty bag and decided to stand clear and just chase the balls wherever they rolled from then on. He wasn't crazy about being laughed at by beautiful girls.

Tammy's serve, Joe thought resentfully, wasn't quite so fast as Chris's, but since Tammy was so tall she was able to smash the ball at a steep angle. Joe watched as Frank ran helplessly after it and felt better.

The women alternated serves and Chaplin moved around them, sometimes kneeling, sometimes standing, and even lying on his back with the camera pointed straight up at the server.

When one of Tammy's serves bounced off the sand so hard that it rolled over to Joe's end of the court, Joe retrieved it for his brother.

Joe grabbed the runaway ball and trotted back with it, watching as Chris launched herself, preparing to strike the ball.

It was such a beautiful preparation that Joe felt like applauding. But before he could, Chris's hand struck the ball. To Joe's horror, instead of the expected *thwack* of hand against leather there was a sudden, blinding flash and a deafening explosion!

Chapter

5

"CHRIS!"

Joe dropped the volleyball and raced toward the player. Tammy made it to Chris just as Joe had snatched Chris's hand to see if it was okay. By the time Vern and Chaplin had joined them, it was obvious that no major harm had been done.

"I'm okay," Chris said shakily, staring at her hand as if it didn't belong to her. It had several minor burn marks on it, but they were already fading. "I can't believe it didn't hurt more than it did. It was so loud." She smiled sheepishly at the small crowd of onlookers that had gathered. "What happened? Did the ball just—explode?"

Frank had been picking up the shreds of exploded volleyball that lay on the court. Now he joined Joe, holding the rubber bits in his hand.

"The shreds are scorched," he said. "Maybe nitrous oxide."

The athletes and the film crew stared at him. "You mean it was a—a bomb?" Tammy demanded.

Joe picked out one piece of rubber, turned it over to inspect the back, and nodded. "A *kind* of bomb—the kind that's meant to scare and not hurt."

"What do you mean?" asked Chaplin.

"Someone planted a booby-trapped ball in the bag," Joe explained. "All they had to do was inflate a volleyball with an explosive gas like nitrous oxide. Then they'd paint the outside of the ball with an ammonium tri-iodide solution or something like it. That would act like a trigger, and the first time something smacked against it, it would set off an explosion. Unfortunately, that something was Chris's hand."

"The explosion is really pretty minor," Frank added. "So there was no real danger of anyone getting hurt."

"You and your brother certainly know an awful lot about bombs," Chaplin said, eyeing Frank suspiciously.

Frank shrugged modestly. "We've read detective novels since we were little kids. You learn a lot that way."

"But who would do something like this?" Chris asked.

Tammy frowned. "Maybe it has something to do with that phone call."

"What call?" Joe glanced at Frank.

"We thought it was just a dumb joke," said Chris. "Tammy has a house here, and I'm staying with her during the tournament. A few nights ago some weirdo called and started saying we'd better quit the tournament or we'd be sorry."

"Was it a man or a woman?" Frank asked.

"I couldn't be sure," replied Tammy. "The voice was obviously disguised."

"Great," said Chaplin, disgusted. "So now the maniac's trying to sabotage us."

Joe eyed him curiously. "What do you mean?"

"You haven't heard?" Chaplin answered. "A bunch of players have gotten phone calls like Tammy's. Some of my equipment was damaged—one of my telephoto lenses was scratched up, and I had to send my best tape deck to the shop."

"Where did all this happen?" Frank asked.

"In our trailer, next to Prindle's. Someone picked the lock a couple of nights back. I've put in a security system since then, because people keep—"

He was interrupted by a gasp from Chris.

"Could Peter Osteen's death have any connection with this?"

"Whoa." Joe put a hand on Chris's shoulder. "As far as we know now, Osteen probably died of hypoglycemic shock. And as for this stuff, who can tell? It could be just coincidence. A practical joker who happens to like beach volleyball."

Chaplin smiled thinly. "Fat chance that they're

39

not connected. Believe me, brother, if I didn't need the money, I wouldn't stick around.''

Chris turned away abruptly.

"Are you okay?" Joe asked, moving over to her.

She nodded, swallowing hard. "Sorry. I was thinking about Peter Osteen. We dated last year." She smiled furtively. "He sent Nadia into incredible fits."

"Nadia?" echoed Joe.

"Nadia Galinova, our coach. She believes that mixing dating and sports is lethal. She told Peter to stay away from me, and he told her to mind her own business. She said he didn't care about my career, which was silly. But they got at each other so much that I finally stopped seeing Peter."

"You play a lot." Frank tactfully changed the subject.

"Three months is all this year," she answered, forcing a smile. "I start college this fall, so I won't play professionally again until next summer. This is the big event of the year for us. Unless they cancel it because of what's been happening." Chris was obviously unhappy at the thought.

"I doubt that they will," said Tammy. "They've put an awful lot of money into this event. I can't imagine the Frosty Company throwing away all of that unless we get some really ghastly publicity or some solid proof that something's wrong."

"Speaking of publicity," said Chaplin, "it's almost eleven o'clock, and we have all the shots we need. Besides, I don't want to risk another exploding volleyball. Let's pack up."

The small crowd of onlookers faded away as Frank joined in taking down the equipment, and Tammy collapsed onto a beach chair. Joe steered Chris to a spot a short distance from the others. "Uh, I was wondering," he said self-consciously, "do *you* think sports and dating mix?"

Chris laughed. "You bet. I don't go out that much, but not because I'm against it. Professional athletes don't usually have time for a great social life. There's the traveling and the training—"

As she was talking, two of the men's teams arrived to work out on one of the neighboring courts. Joe realized that one of them was George Ritt's team and that he was directing a very angry scowl their way. Chris saw him, too, and her words to Joe faded to a defeated sigh.

"I don't know what to do about Junior," she admitted.

"Junior?"

"His full name is George Ritt, Jr. Most of us call him Junior—behind his back. He has no reason to act like I'm his personal property. We've never even gone out. He gets on my nerves, but I can't help feeling sorry for him sometimes."

Joe stared in disbelief. *"Sorry? Why?"*

Chris grinned. "Wait till you meet George

41

senior. You will, if you stick around long enough.''

Joe started to ask Chris what she meant, but their conversation was interrupted by a new voice. "Chris! Tammy!" A gray-haired woman strode across the sand toward them. She wore a gray sweatsuit, and a whistle hung from her neck. As she drew closer, Joe saw that the expression on her square face was very stern. He was glad when Frank walked over to join them.

"It's time for training now," the woman announced in a thick Eastern European accent. A volleyball from the men's court landed at her feet. She picked it up and expertly served it back to the players.

"Nadia," Chris said, a little flustered, "meet Joe Hardy and his brother, Frank. Guys, this is our trainer, Nadia Galinova."

Nadia nodded to each brother. Then she addressed the girls.

"Come. Now."

"But I want to take a swim."

Nadia fixed Tammy with a commanding stare. "There will be no swimming. You will be competing soon. Now come." Then she turned and rapidly strode back toward the clubhouse, paying no more attention to the group on the court. The girls reluctantly trailed along behind her. After a few steps Chris turned and waved mischievously to Joe.

"Tough lady," Frank commented, watching them go.

"You wouldn't believe *how* tough," agreed Chaplin as Joe and Frank helped him with his gear. "She was a top coach in regular volleyball in Czechoslovakia before she came here. Over there, her word was law, and it still is as far as she's concerned. You don't want to get on her bad side."

Joe stared after the three women. "What's so bad about mixing dating with sports?"

Chaplin smirked at Joe. "Interested in Chris, huh? Can't blame you. But watch out for Nadia. And Junior, too, while you're at it. He can be vicious, and his father is worse."

"Great," Joe remarked. "Nice bunch you have around here."

Frank straightened up from loading the larger camera into its hard case and wiped the sweat from his face with a towel. "Hey, Joe," he called, maintaining a casual expression. "Didn't Prindle tell us to check in for a new assignment after this?"

"Oh, right," Joe said, catching on immediately. "Okay if we go now, Ken?"

Ken gave his permission, and Joe followed Frank toward the far end of the surf club building. "What was that about?" he asked his brother as soon as they were out of earshot of the crew.

"We need to tell Prindle about the explosion," Frank explained. He took the incriminating pieces of rubber from his pocket. "It might give him some new ideas about who's doing this."

But when the boys found Prindle in his trailer and showed him the pieces of the exploded volleyball, the executive only turned a shade paler. "No one was hurt?" he repeated. "That's a break, anyway."

He then showed them a collection of fresh newspaper clippings piled on his desk. One of the headlines read, "Hi-Kick Contender Dies of Diabetic Attack."

"Whoever's doing this to the team must be planning to demand money before they'll stop— unless they're just plain crazy. I'm sure the company will pay—if it means no more trouble for the tour."

"But you can't pay someone when you don't know who or where they are," Frank pointed out. "Maybe there's a motive we don't know about yet."

"Yeah," said Joe. "And by the way, I was wondering if you could give us some background on Nadia Galinova. We ran into her today."

"She came here from Czechoslovakia twenty years ago," Prindle said, seemingly surprised at the switch in the conversation. "She used to coach regular volleyball, but when the beach version started getting popular, she was one of the first coaches to take it up. She coaches nearly all the top women players. Chris and Tammy, for instance—"

The phone on Prindle's desk rang, interrupting him.

"Prindle," he said into the receiver. Then his expression sharpened. "Yeah. Uh-huh. Oh, I see."

Frank and Joe watched as Prindle sat up straighter, his expression puzzled and upset. "B-but—" he stammered. Then his expression flattened, and he sagged back in his chair. "Okay. Thanks. Right."

He hung up the phone and took a deep breath.

"What was that about?" Joe asked. "More trouble?"

"That was the police," Prindle said resignedly. They want me to know that they've almost concluded that the cause of Osteen's death was hypoglycemic shock. Tests showed that his blood sugar took a nose dive just half an hour before he died."

"Then it wasn't murder," Frank said, surprised and oddly uneasy. "That's good news, right?"

"Not really." Prindle stared at the papers on his desk. Then he looked up at the boys. "The doctors said his blood sugar dropped. A diabetic's blood sugar drops only when he doesn't get enough sugar. But Peter had about half a gallon of Hi-Kick soda several hours before his death. And that was all he had."

Joe stared at him. "So?"

45

"So," Prindle said with a sigh, "Hi-Kick is loaded with sugar. Low blood sugar couldn't have killed him.

"The police told me their forensic department will be doing a complete tox screen on Osteen— a detailed analysis of his blood—just as a formality.

"And?" Joe demanded.

"And," said Frank, leaning toward Prindle, "you think it will prove Osteen was poisoned!"

Chapter

6

"YOU MEAN YOU can prove Osteen was poisoned?" Joe glanced at Frank for an explanation.

"Of course not!" Prindle ran a finger around the inside of his collar. "But I do know that Hi-Kick didn't kill him! Unfortunately, when this story comes out, everyone's going to *believe* our soda somehow killed him. It's a catastrophe!"

"What *did* kill him, then?" Frank asked. "Did someone put something in the drink? The police didn't find anything, though."

Prindle shook his head. "All they said was that the results of the tox screen would be ready tomorrow or the next day. Anyway, it doesn't matter. Even if the poor kid drank pure poison, people would still connect what happened with Hi-Kick. Believe me, I know. I've been in the promotion business over fifteen years."

"Maybe there's hope, though," Frank said, frowning. "After all, if Osteen *was* murdered, we need to know who did it and why. When the public finds out who did it and why, the bad press for Hi-Kick soda will have to die down."

Prindle appeared unconvinced. The three thought in silence for a moment until the office door opened and a burly man charged in. The reddish blond hair was receding on his head, but it grew thick on his powerful arms. His two small eyes were set close together, and his face was flushed with anger.

"Prindle, I want to talk to you!" he bellowed. Then he noticed Frank and Joe.

"Is one of you two named Hardy?" he demanded.

"Both of us are," Joe replied.

"Mr. Ritt," said Prindle, getting to his feet, "won't you come in?"

"Don't get smart with me," snarled the red-faced man. "These two young punks here—get rid of them, you hear me? Throw them out!"

"May I introduce George Ritt, Sr.," Prindle said to the Hardys. "George, Frank and Joe Hardy. Mr. Ritt's son is a player in the tournament, and George here takes a strong interest in his son's career."

"We met George junior this morning," said Frank.

"That's right, wise guy. He told me all about it." Mr. Ritt turned to Richard Prindle. "They were rifling through Peter Osteen's things, and

48

when my son called them on it, they started getting fresh with one of the girls. George took them to task for it—and I want them out of here."

"Wait a second," said Joe, getting out of his chair. "That's not the way it was."

"Relax, Joe," said Prindle, also getting up and stepping between Joe and George senior. "I'm not getting rid of anyone. George, your son has had problems with a lot of people around here, and it never seems to be his fault."

Mr. Ritt's face turned red. "Are you calling me a liar?"

"No," Prindle shouted in disgust. "But I don't take orders from you, and Frank and Joe are my employees. If any female player has a complaint, she can come to me herself."

"But—"

"George, I'd like to get back to work." Prindle walked to his office door and gestured for Ritt to leave. The older man glared at the Hardys for a long moment before starting out.

"And, George?" added Prindle. Ritt stopped on the trailer steps.

"Knock next time, will you?"

Ritt slammed the door hard enough to shake the trailer.

Prindle took a deep breath and returned to his desk. "Ritt inherited a lot of money when he was young and used it to make a fortune in real estate. Now he's retired and devotes his entire life to nothing but making his son the number-

49

one player in the country. Believe me, you get to know some pushy parents in this business, but Ritt beats them all.''

"*Is* Junior number one?" asked Frank.

Prindle smiled wanly. "He's young, and he has talent. But volleyball is a team game. The best teams stay together, learn from each other. Junior can't keep a partner. He's had some good ones, but sooner or later his dad drives them away.''

"Who's he with now?" Frank prodded.

"Buzz Maestren," Prindle replied. "He's young, too, and wants to get onto the pro circuit. But I'll bet anything George'll drive him out.''

He shook his head. "Osteen and Lenz were the surest bets to take the trophy from Conlin and Donahue—if anyone could.''

Joe's ears perked up at this. "So Osteen was standing between Junior and the championship, in a way?" he asked.

Prindle blinked. "Hard to say. The tournament has just started. George junior hasn't even played yet.''

"What's happening to Scooter?" Frank wanted to know.

"He's still in the competition," Prindle said. "He's hoping to line up another partner and come back later in the tournament.''

"So," mused Frank, "we have a bunch of people who could benefit from Osteen's death. The Ritts, who want Junior to win the tournament,

Conlin and Donahue, who want to keep their place at the top—"

"And Nadia Galinova," Joe said, interrupting. "Chris said Nadia thought Osteen was a threat to Chris's career. Maybe Nadia would try to eliminate a threat like that."

"Now hold on a second," Prindle protested. "I never meant to imply for one second that Brad Conlin or Mark Donahue would—"

Joe held up a hand. "We're just going over people who might have motives. Besides, you'd be amazed how many murderers are 'wonderful people.'"

They heard a knock at the door just then and a voice calling, "Richard? Mark Donahue."

"Speak of the devil," Prindle murmured. Then he called, "Come in, Mark."

Mark and Brad Conlin walked in, saw the Hardys, and paused uncertainly. "Sorry," Mark said. "I didn't know you had company."

"That's okay, we're nearly finished here." Prindle motioned to Brad to close the door. At the appearance of the athletes, Prindle had become almost joyful. He seemed delighted to see the players and eager to know what was on their minds. Joe watched, amused. He knew that the promotion director's main job was to keep the competitors happy.

"Mark and Brad, meet Frank and Joe Hardy," Prindle said. They're volunteer workers. Now, what can I do for you guys?"

The players stared at Frank and Joe with more

51

interest. "Didn't one of you have a run-in with Junior this morning?" Brad Conlin asked.

"That was me," Joe admitted sheepishly. "I was looking for Chris Welles," he explained, "and the guy just attacked me."

Mark Donahue grimaced. "You're not the first one he's done that to. The guy's a stick of dynamite with a very short fuse. You never know what's going to set him off."

"He's like that with you guys, too?" Joe asked innocently.

Conlin laughed. "He doesn't try much. A lot of us are stronger than him. He did lay into Peter Osteen once, though, right in the locker room after he'd lost a match."

"Oh, yeah, I remember that," Donahue said. "Santa Barbara, right? Junior said Peter had palmed the ball—carried it instead of hitting it," he explained to the Hardys. "Junior protested to the ref, but the ref allowed the play. So poor Junior lost the match. It was beautiful."

"You sound like you don't like Junior much," Frank remarked.

Both players hesitated. "Well," Conlin said carefully, "he's not that bad. He just has a tendency to spout off when he ought to keep quiet. That time, he and Osteen got in a fight. The tournament officials had to come in and break it up themselves. I can still remember it. They kept on yelling at each other even when they were in separate rooms. Junior swore he'd get even."

"Right," Donahue said. "He was yelling stuff like, 'Nobody messes with George Ritt! I'll get you for this, Osteen!' "

Voicing both brothers' thoughts, Joe said in a low voice, "Sounds like a maniac."

Chapter

7

PRINDLE GLARED at the brothers. "Oh, come on," he said.

Ignoring him, Joe asked the athletes, "What happened then? Did Ritt and Osteen have any more problems?"

"Not that I know of," said Donahue. "Junior was put on probation for six months, but his dad got him out of it almost right away. After that, he and Osteen stayed away from each other." A funny expression fell over Donahue's face. "Why are we talking about this?" he asked. "Brad and I just came in to find out when we're doing the shoot for the Hi-Kick commercials."

"Yeah," said Conlin, only half-joking. "If Junior gets wind of what we've been saying, his dad'll have our necks."

"Don't worry." Joe made sure his laugh sounded casual. "I won't tell. I'm a fan."

Donahue grinned at Joe, then turned to Prindle. "So? When's the shoot?"

"Why don't you have a seat while I iron out a few details?" Prindle suggested. "We can go over the revised schedules, too. Oh, by the way, boys, take the rest of the day off. You deserve it."

Frank and Joe vacated their chairs. "Good luck in the games."

"Thanks," Donahue said. "The way this tournament's going, we can use all the luck we can get."

"Where to now?" Joe asked his brother as they stepped out of the trailer into the blinding sun.

"Our hotel room." Frank strode ahead across the parking lot. "I need to call Dad to ask him to check out George Ritt, Sr. I want to know if he has a record, or if anyone's ever sued him—that kind of thing."

"Good idea." Joe jogged to keep up with his brother. "Ask him to check out Nadia Galinova, too. She gives me the creeps."

Frank glanced at Joe. "That has nothing to do with Chris Welles, of course."

"I just want to cover all bases."

"Right." Frank couldn't resist teasing. "While I'm at it, maybe I should ask Dad to check whether Chris is married?"

Fifteen minutes after speaking to their dad, Frank and Joe left the hotel by the beach

55

entrance to head for the surf's edge. In trunks and sandals, they'd walked about twenty yards when Joe held out an arm to stop his brother.

"Isn't that Mark Donahue out there?" Joe pointed toward the volleyball courts some distance to their right, where a tallish guy stood listening as a short, dark-haired man talked effusively with both hands and his mouth.

"Yeah. I recognize the other guy, too. He works for Frosty's competitors—uh, SuperJuice." Frank snapped his fingers. "Auerbach!"

"Right." Joe nodded. "Todd Auerbach."

As Joe spoke, Frank saw Auerbach glance in their direction, do a double take, and then abruptly shake Donahue's hand and walk off in the opposite direction toward the hotel parking lot.

"That was weird," said Joe. "Do you think he was trying to lure Donahue away from Frosty? So SuperJuice can sponsor Donahue instead?"

"It looks like it, doesn't it?" Frank agreed. "Maybe we should put Auerbach on our list of suspects."

"He stands to gain as much as the others if this tournament gets derailed," Joe agreed. He glanced over at the smooth, rolling waves. A blond male surfer was riding in on one of the crests, his legs bent perfectly and his board hardly moving. "But enough already," Joe added. "It's time to catch some rays."

As the brothers trudged past the gym area at the far end of the hotel, Joe glanced hopefully in the direction of the outdoor lounge. Chris Welles appeared just as he went by. She waved cheerfully at him.

"I thought you were warming up for your game," Joe called.

"We did." She strode across the sand toward him. "We just finished. Our match is at two o'clock this afternoon. Nadia wants us to jog on the beach, then go inside for a nap. Are you coming to the game?"

"You bet." Glancing over Chris's shoulder, Joe spotted Nadia Galinova watching them. He lowered his voice. "Maybe after the match I can take you for a victory dinner."

"What if we lose?" Chris asked, smiling.

"No problem," Frank chimed in. "Then he'll take you to a consolation dinner."

"Not that that's going to happen, of course," Joe assured her.

Chris laughed. "Sounds good," she said. "But it'll have to be early. I have a strict curfew."

"Great!" Joe's face brightened. "Are you going to run now? I'll walk you down the beach."

"You guys go ahead," Frank said. "I just remembered something I need to do at the hotel. Joe, I'll catch you later, either on the beach or at the hotel."

Joe barely glanced at his brother. "Ready, Chris?"

Chris winked mischievously at Frank, then set off with Joe. Frank could hear her chatting animatedly as the two of them crossed the sand to the water's edge. Smiling to himself, Frank heard a harsh voice just behind him.

"You. Tell your brother to mind his own business. Otherwise, there could be trouble."

Frank turned, already knowing he would see Nadia Galinova standing behind him. "What kind of trouble?" he demanded.

The coach didn't answer. She folded her arms across her chest, and her face grew even more stony and forbidding.

"Stay away from Chris and Tammy or you will be very, very sorry," she said forcefully. Then she turned back toward the gym.

Frank understood what Joe meant when he'd said that Galinova gave him the creeps.

Frank called his father again and added Todd Auerbach's name to the list of those he wanted investigated. Then he called Richard Prindle to describe the scene he and Joe had witnessed between Mark Donahue and Todd Auerbach.

"He's been sniffing around since we got set up here," Prindle said, annoyed. "He'd love to cause trouble."

"But you already have all the players under contract, right?" said Frank.

"Yes, but if the tournament is scrapped, the

contracts are worthless, and Auerbach could sign up anyone he wants for endorsements. He's probably making sure they keep him in mind— just in case."

Prindle paused, then blurted out, "I sure hope you boys get this whole business straightened out soon. I'm getting worn out."

"Don't worry," Frank assured him. "We're looking forward to winding it up so we can start our vacation, too."

Meanwhile, Joe Hardy had finally found the perfect spot to lay out his towel—just above the high-water mark. He stripped off his T-shirt and walked the few feet to the water. The surf was low, and the water not very cold. Some small children were splashing and laughing in the shallower waves.

Joe had left Chris and Tammy to their jogging, but all he could think about was dinner with Chris as he waded out into the ocean. He was only waist-deep even after he'd walked more than fifty yards. The wet sand was firm under his feet, and the chill of the water contrasted perfectly with the heat from the sun.

Joe dived forward and began swimming farther out. Soon he could barely hear the laughter of the children playing. He rolled onto his back and closed his eyes against the sun. His mind wandered to the Osteen case and what they'd learned about Peter's death so far.

Plenty of people, it seemed, had a reason to

wish Peter Osteen out of the picture. But were any of them capable of killing a person? Joe let the images of Nadia, George Ritt and his son, and Auerbach run through his mind. He really couldn't imagine any of them brutally ending a young man's life. Besides, whoever was causing the trouble seemed interested in more than Osteen. After all, the threatening phone calls had been made to plenty of people, and Chaplin's equipment had been vandalized.

It felt as if he'd been drifting a lifetime when Joe suddenly heard someone splash up beside him. It took Frank long enough to get here, he thought idly, not bothering to open his eyes.

An angry voice jarred him out of his pleasant mood.

"I warned you to stay away from Chris, and you came down to the beach with her. I guess I'm going to have to teach you a lesson."

It was Junior.

Instinctively, Joe swung around in the water to face his enemy. Glancing over Junior's shoulder, he realized Frank was nowhere in sight. But standing on the shore George senior was watching them.

"Okay, just a second—" Joe said, stalling.

Junior didn't feel like waiting. He looped one strong arm around Joe's throat and yanked hard.

Joe was being pulled under!

Chapter

8

DON'T PANIC, Joe told himself as Junior forced his head under. He thrashed helplessly, trying to pry Junior's hands loose from his throat. But he couldn't do it. Junior was too strong for him. Joe needed air—right then!

Think of something! he thought wildly as the pressure on his lungs grew more painful. But the athlete's grip remained tight on his throat. Joe started feeling dizzy, and his legs stopped kicking. Junior was going to kill him, he realized dimly. Gradually, unable to resist, Joe started to relax.

As his body began to go limp, Joe sensed that Junior was relaxing, too. He willed himself to stay awake and wait for an opening. Just when Junior seemed about to let go, Joe gathered his strength and exploded. Jabbing his elbow in

Junior's stomach just below his rib cage, Joe pushed him down and away as hard as he could.

Abruptly, the powerful arm loosened its grip, and Joe bobbed free to the surface to inhale a lungful of air. He was still gasping when Junior broke the surface nearby.

"You don't own her, Junior," Joe said hotly, treading water and glaring at his attacker.

The volleyball player's eyes popped wide open. "Don't call me that!" He took a slow-motion punch through the water at Joe's head. Joe easily avoided it.

"Watch out, George. You're out of your depth. I don't have my back turned now."

"I'll show you—" Junior plunged toward Joe, but Joe was more maneuverable in the water and had no trouble staying out of reach. As Joe turned to swim back toward the beach, Junior grabbed hold of Joe's left ankle and twisted it. Joe went with the motion, and rolled over on his back. Kicking out with his free leg, he caught the athlete in the jaw with his heel. Junior fell back, stunned.

I should leave him here, Joe thought angrily. Even though he was sure Junior wouldn't do the same for him, Joe knew he'd have to save him from drowning. Joe threw an arm around Junior's chest and slowly pulled him toward shore. He let him go when he could stand, and the athlete staggered in behind him on his own rubbery legs.

It didn't surprise Joe to see George Ritt, Sr., storming toward him.

"You could have drowned my boy out there!" the older man was shouting. "I'll have you arrested for assault!"

Still trying to catch his breath, Joe glanced at Ritt and shook his head. "Your son started this," he said, checking for witnesses. A girl and two boys were watching them with expressions of alarm.

He turned back to Mr. Ritt. "I was just defending myself."

"Oh, yeah?" growled the elder Ritt. "We'll see what the police have to say about that. In any case, you'll be getting the bill for his hospital costs. And if he loses his match tomorrow, we'll sue!"

"What's going on here?" To Joe's great relief, Frank was approaching. He took in Junior, who was still gasping as he made his way to the shore.

"Don't tell me *Junior's* been acting up again," Frank said loudly. To Joe's satisfaction, Junior's jaw muscles tightened, and he glowered at Frank.

"Now you've done it," Joe commented. "If he tries to drown someone who only speaks to Chris Welles, who knows what he'd do to someone who calls him Junior."

"I wasn't trying to drown you," Junior growled. "Just knock some respect into you, that's all. I'm not a murderer, no matter what—"

"Shut your mouth!" Mr. Ritt's voice lashed

out like a whip, and his son stopped in midsentence. "Come on, George. Time to go." But before they left, he gave Joe a long, cold stare.

"Don't think you've seen the last of us," he said. "Nobody messes with the Ritts."

Joe was looking from son to father, wondering what George had started to say before his father interrupted him. "Did Peter Osteen mess with the Ritts?" he asked abruptly. "Is that why he's dead now?"

Neither man answered. The older Ritt stared stonily at the Hardys, but Joe thought he noted a slight change in his expression.

Before anyone said anything more, Joe heard a dune buggy approaching. The group turned to see Vern Elliott, the assistant film director, and his boss, Ken Chaplin, approaching in a red buggy with a blue-and-gold Hi-Kick logo painted on the hood. Chaplin held a large camera on his lap, while Vern drove. Joe wondered if the dune buggy was a prop for a promotional film.

"What's going on, guys?" Chaplin shouted over the noise of the engine. "Is Ritt giving you a hard time?"

"Mind your own business, Chaplin," Ritt growled. "You want to keep your job, right? I know you need the money."

Vern cut the engine, and Chaplin deliberately set his camera on the floor of the vehicle and slowly climbed out onto the sand. "Are you threatening me, Ritt?" he asked, standing up to the retired magnate. "It's none of your business whether I need the money or how much I need. Richard Prindle pays my salary, not you. Or maybe you're trying to do to me what you did to Chuck Herrick last year."

George Ritt's face turned reddish purple. "That's slander, Chaplin!" he roared. "No one ever proved we did anything to Herrick. I'd take you to court for that, if you weren't such a loser that it wouldn't be worth it. How much do you owe for your gambling debts, anyway? I hear it's so much you'll be doing hack work for the rest of your life."

Chaplin's jaw was clenched, but he remained in tight control as Ritt collected his son and left without another word.

"You were sure right to warn me about Junior," Joe told Chaplin when the Ritts were out of earshot. "He attacked me out in the water because he saw me walking on the beach with Chris."

Chaplin nodded, acting very tired all of a sudden. "Yeah. Steer clear of the Ritts. That's still my advice."

"What happened between you two in the past?" Frank asked.

Chaplin shrugged ruefully. "I was hired to shoot a documentary last year for the Beach Volleyball Federation, to publicize the sport. Old man Ritt instantly started giving me grief over it. He accused me of not devoting enough film

65

time to his son. He said that since Junior was going to be the game's top player, I owed him more exposure than the other players. It started to irritate me, so I finally told him that if he pestered me any more I'd cut his son out of the film altogether.''

Joe gave a low whistle. "I bet that went over big," he said.

"Right." Chaplin backed up onto the sand as a wave lapped at his canvas shoe. "Next thing I knew, the federation called me on the carpet and told me I was through. They said they couldn't have people offending their major backers.''

"What about this Chuck Herrick you mentioned?" Frank asked.

Chaplin seemed taken aback. "I'm not supposed to talk about this stuff. Anyway, we've got to get ready to shoot the women's match soon. Are you guys assigned to me again today?''

Ignoring the question, Frank assessed Chaplin's reaction. "You're still scared of Ritt, aren't you?''

Anger flickered across the filmmaker's face. "Sure I'm scared," he said. "The man has a very long, strong arm. Listen, some of us have work to do. See you two later at the court.''

He climbed back in the buggy and was driven off. "Well, I don't know who's more suspicious of us now," Joe said, picking up his towel and briskly drying himself off. "Ritt senior or

Chaplin. We haven't been acting much like lowly assistants lately.''

"Maybe not," replied Frank. "But at least we're getting some information. I want to find out more about this Chuck Herrick. I wonder what Ritt did to him that was never proved.''

"Maybe Chris knows about it," Joe suggested. "I could ask her at dinner.''

Frank grinned. "Sure you don't want to be off duty tonight? She might not like being pumped for information. And you might make her suspicious.''

"I don't like not being able to tell her who I really am. You think there's any chance of wrapping up this case before the tournament's over?''

"Only if we quit lazing around on the beach and get back to work.'' Frank grinned at his brother. "In fact, I'm going to skip my swim and go ask Prindle a few questions. Like what kind of gambling problems Chaplin has. And what he knows about Ritt getting Chaplin fired. Then we need to be at the court for Chris and Tammy's match.''

As they talked, Frank and Joe started toward the hotel parking lot. "You think Chaplin was telling the truth about Ritt firing him?'' Joe asked.

"Who knows? He hates Ritt enough to stretch the truth, that's obvious. By the way, I called Dad from the hotel and asked him to run a check on Todd Auerbach. And—oh, yes—I had a wonderful chat with Nadia Galinova."

"I'll bet that was fun," said Joe with a laugh. "Did she say she'd put a contract out on me if I didn't leave Chris alone?"

"Not in so many words," said Frank. "But I bet you're right—she is hiding something."

"Do you think she could have had something to do with Osteen's death?" Joe asked in surprise.

"The motive is really weak—you don't kill somebody just to keep your athletes from getting distracted."

"Not if you're sane. But judging from what Chaplin and Prindle have said about her, Galinova seems a little out of touch with reality. Like she's still in the old country, where she can crack the whip."

Frank nodded. "Let's see what Prindle can tell us," he said. "Then we'll have just enough time to grab some lunch before Chris and Tammy's match. Who are they playing, anyway?"

Joe shrugged. "It doesn't matter. Chris and Tammy will roll right over them. Like a machine."

Frank grinned at his brother. "Just don't go shouting advice to them from behind the court. That's all they need—some would-be boyfriend getting them disqualified."

"Don't worry." Joe's smile gleamed against his new layer of tan. "The last thing Chris needs is my advice."

Spiked!

When the brothers reached Prindle's trailer at the edge of the parking lot, Joe pushed the door open, forgetting to knock, and the two brothers stepped inside.

Prindle wasn't there. Someone else was sitting at his desk, leafing through stacks of papers. Todd Auerbach!

Chapter

9

"WHAT ARE YOU doing here?" Frank asked, astounded.

"What do you mean?" Auerbach seemed to be puzzled. Then his face brightened. "Oh! You mean going through Richard's things! Don't worry, boys, he knows all about it. Can I help you with something? You need a work schedule or what?"

"Wait a minute," said Joe, stepping closer. "You work for SuperJuice, right? I don't think Mr. Prindle would want you poking around his desk. You'd better stop. Right now."

Auerbach glared disdainfully at Joe. "Why don't you take a hike?" he said smoothly. "Let the grown-ups do their jobs."

"Fine." Joe's voice shook with anger. "I'll take a hike. Straight to the police."

Auerbach's grin faded. "Look, boys," he said icily. "I don't like being threatened."

"Then why don't you leave?" said Frank, standing beside his brother and presenting an obvious threat to Auerbach.

Auerbach blinked several times. Then he stood up, backed around the desk chair, and edged toward the door. "Fine," he said. "No need to flex your muscles. But believe me—your boss will hear about the way you treat guests in his office!"

"You bet he'll hear about it," Joe called after Auerbach as he hustled out the door. "The minute we find him."

The door slammed, and the brothers glanced at each other, perplexed. "What was he looking for?"

"Beats me," Joe answered. "He's got a lot of nerve, though, just walking in when no one's around."

"There's a list of players' phone numbers and addresses here on top," Frank said, picking up a piece of paper. "And some contracts. Maybe he was looking for loopholes to get the athletes out of their agreements with Frosty. I bet SuperJuice wants to get into the beach volleyball business, too."

"He'll probably contact the players at home, in private," Joe agreed. "I wish we'd asked him a few questions while we had him here."

Frank shook his head. "A guy like that would have a reasonable answer for whatever we asked him. Anyway, he'd start wondering pretty quick why a couple of gofers wanted to know so much. He looks smart, even if he is slime."

"If he's so smart, why doesn't he come up with his own promotion idea? Why steal Frosty's?" Joe asked.

"Good question. Another thing I wonder, is he the kind of person who'd murder to get what he wanted?"

"While we're here, why don't you call Dad to see if he has the info on our suspects yet," Joe said.

It took only five minutes for Frank to listen to all the information his father had called up on his computer regarding the murder suspects.

"First of all, he says George Ritt did really well with his real estate business," Frank began telling Joe. "He's a major big shot in southern California. No arrest record, but he's been sued a few times for shoddy business practices. He has a reputation for being a very tough businessman."

"Big surprise," Joe commented dryly. "What about Auerbach?"

"Nothing on him yet. No federal record or anything. Nadia Galinova's a different story, though. Dad says she's still a registered alien after almost twenty years in this country. She's never applied for American citizenship, which is a little unusual but not unheard of. No criminal record for her, either."

"Great. That gives us just about nothing new to work on." Joe sighed, then said, "I'm starved. Let's go eat. We can tell Prindle what happened when we see him at the tournament.''

As the brothers left the office, they saw Vern hastily unlocking a padlock on the film trailer door. "Hi, Vern," Frank said in a friendly voice. "How's the setup going?"

"We're running late," the middle-aged man said gruffly. "And now, after opening this lock, I have to fiddle with this dumb security system."

"What's wrong with it?" Frank approached the film office, watching intently as Vern punched in a code on an expensive-looking switch box next to the door.

"Nothing's wrong with it," Vern grumbled absentmindedly. "I just have to remember the code every time I need a lousy roll of film. Chaplin tried to make the code something I'd always remember," he said. "But I still have to think before I punch it in."

Vern entered the office, and Frank noted that the security system Chaplin had bragged about consisted only of an alarm system and a single padlock.

"See you at the court this afternoon." Frank called up to Vern from the bottom of the steps. "I was hoping I could get a look at all your equipment. I'm kind of interested in film myself."

"You'll have to ask Chaplin." Vern's voice floated out of the trailer's dim interior. "Can't be too security minded around here."

* * *

73

"Vern acted like he didn't quite trust us," Joe observed as he and Frank finished their sandwiches.

The restaurant was nearly empty. Frank figured nearly everyone had gone to watch the women's match. They'd have to hurry if they were going to get to work on time.

"They *did* have some equipment ruined. How can they be sure we didn't do it?"

As they left the snack bar and headed for the tournament down the beach, Frank glanced wistfully at the rolling waves. Two full days there and he hadn't been in the ocean once. It was getting ridiculous. He felt like jumping in and swimming out far enough to escape his frustrations.

"We're just in time," Joe said as they approached the near end of the court. Frank nodded. The bleachers were overflowing with people, and tense-looking tournament officials were rushing everywhere. The bad publicity of the day before hadn't hurt attendance any.

"There you are!" Frank heard Prindle call. "Just in time. Frank, you'll be retrieving balls on the far side, over there. Joe, I want you right here. You'll both have a perfect view of everything that goes on, and you can keep your cover intact, too."

"Thanks, Mr. Prindle," Joe said. "Listen, we have something we need to tell you about—"

"Sorry, boys. Can't talk now. Tell me after the match."

Prindle hurried off. Joe shrugged at his

brother. Then he beamed at someone over Frank's shoulder.

Frank turned and saw Chris peeling off her warm-ups and smiling back at Joe. Nadia Galinova was standing at one side of center court, glaring at the boys. Frank felt a chill run down his spine at the look on the coach's face. He wondered what had happened in her past to make her so hateful.

"I see you've been spotted," Frank said ironically to Joe as he started toward the far end of the court. "Good luck catching balls."

"Right." Joe ran a hand through his hair to get it out of his eyes. A strong breeze had started blowing in off the ocean. He wondered how much the wind would affect the competition.

With mock salutes, the two Hardys took up their positions, facing each other across the court. Frank watched as Chris and Tammy jogged in place to warm up. Then he looked over at the other team—a redhead nearly as tall as Tammy, and a slightly shorter, stockier brunette with a very determined expression.

The loudspeakers announced the players, the audience burst out in loud applause, and the match began. It started out so exciting that Frank forgot everything but the game.

Chris and Tammy were ahead one game to none when Frank noticed a high, whining noise from somewhere nearby. He glanced around, trying to locate the source of the sound.

It must be the wind blowing past those guy wires, he decided, eyeing the huge Hi-Kick bottles at the corners of the court that were held in place by heavy metal cable. The cables were held down by anchors that looked like giant hooks screwed partway into the sand. The hooks looked as secure as granite.

But Frank was wrong. As Tammy prepared to serve and Chris stood poised near the net, Frank heard a loud metallic twang at his left. Out of the corner of his eye he saw one of the giant Hi-Kick models flap free. He spun to his left just in time to see one cable anchor tear itself free from the ground and fly into the air, straight at Chris!

Chapter

10

JOE ALSO SAW the heavy anchor flying through the air. "Chris! Duck!" he yelled, charging forward. Chris whirled around in confusion as Joe ran across the court to smash into Chris with his best running buck tackle. He was just in time to knock her flat as the anchor flew over her and fell back to the sand.

As everyone screamed, Joe stayed where he was and tried to calm Chris. He could feel her trembling.

"What happened?" she whispered to Joe as all the officials descended on them.

"The cable and anchor," Joe said falteringly. "They pulled loose. Someone must have—"

"Oh, no!" Chris covered her face with her hands. "Not again."

"Are you all right, Chris?" It was Richard

77

Prindle, with Nadia Galinova, Tammy, and Frank right behind him.

"Yes. I think so," she said shakily. "I just don't understand—"

"It was an accident with those stupid bottles," Nadia interrupted furiously. "I told you they weren't safe, Mr. Prindle. But you had to advertise, you said. Well, you might have just lost another valuable athlete because of your greed—"

"Please, Nadia," Chris interrupted. "I don't think there was anything wrong with the anchors. I think this was deliberate."

Prindle stared at her, slightly green. The television news crews began crowding in, and Prindle leapt to his feet to order them off the court.

"Come, Chris," Nadia ordered, helping her up. "We'll take you to the hospital."

"No," Chris said as she got to her feet and brushed herself off. "I want to finish the game, Nadia." Her eyes went to Tammy, who hung back, waiting to talk to her friend. "That is, if it's okay with my partner."

Tammy nodded mutely. As the teammates walked over to the television cameras to announce their decision, they were trailed by a fuming coach.

Frank and Joe made their way to where the anchor had pulled out of the sand.

"It doesn't make sense," Joe said over the noise of the crowd's cheers as they learned that the match would go on. "This kind of cable and

78

its anchor are made to last for years. All of a sudden they can't hold an inflated model up for two or three days?"

"Someone sabotaged the cable, no doubt about it," Frank agreed, straightening up. "The question is, did they do it just to disrupt the tourney?"

"I can't wait till we catch this guy. I have a long list of questions I want to throw at him," Joe said.

The brothers were unable to investigate further because the match was about to start again. Prindle was motioning wildly for them to take their places at either end of the court.

The crowd belonged completely to Chris for the remainder of the match, and Joe proudly witnessed her team win. After she and Tammy had shaken hands with the competition, Joe jogged over to ask her when she'd be ready to go out and celebrate.

"Pick me up at Tammy's in two hours," she said. She gave him the address and directions.

"Thanks." Joe backed away to let other well-wishers approach her.

Joe saw Junior beaming at Chris from the edge of the crowd. He was so tall, he didn't need to move closer to be able to see her. "How about celebrating with me tonight?" he yelled to Chris.

"Sorry, George. I have other plans," Chris called back.

As Joe passed Junior he gave him a slap on

the back. "That's the way it goes, George," he said.

Junior was ready to fight right then, but for some reason he wheeled around and walked away instead, brushing past people without noticing them.

"Hey, Chris and Tammy, way to go!" Joe saw Brad Conlin, Mark Donahue, and Scooter Lenz approaching from the direction of the bleachers. He guessed most of the players had watched this match. Frank brought up the rear, holding the winning volleyball.

"Thanks, guys. Hi, Scooter," Chris said, her smile faltering for an instant. "Thanks for coming. I'll show up at all your games, too."

The male players laughed. Tammy asked, "Scooter, have you found a new partner yet?"

The others went silent as Lenz stared down at the sand. "Haven't come up with anyone yet," he admitted. "It's kind of hard to replace Osteen, you know? He had guts."

Joe moved closer to Scooter, and Frank joined the two of them as they were shunted aside by eager officials, Chaplin's film crew, and the television news crews.

"Scooter, you said you wanted us to help out about Peter," Joe said, keeping his voice low.

Scooter nodded.

"Well, we're still working on it," Frank said gently. "But we have a couple of questions. We saw the machine Peter used to monitor his blood sugar. He did that regularly, right?"

"Before every match and workout," Lenz replied. "He'd had diabetes since he was a kid so he knew the ropes. Doing the kind of exercise he did, the amount of sugar in his blood could go way up or down in a short period of time. If it ever went too far in either direction, he'd—well, he'd die. So he kept fresh fruit by his locker to keep his sugar level high enough. He also carried a kit with insulin and hypodermic needles."

"The insulin would lower his blood sugar level, right?" asked Frank.

"Right," Scooter replied. "Just before yesterday's match, he took out one of those syringes and gave himself a shot. 'This is to make up for all that sweet Hi-Kick soda we're going to have to drown ourselves in on the court,' he said to me. He stayed away from the fruit that day for the same reason." Scooter's voice faltered.

"Thanks, man," Joe said, patting him on the shoulder. To make Scooter feel better, he added, "I guess he hadn't counted on such a long, hard match in such hot weather." But he knew Frank was thinking the same thing he was. It was more likely that someone had been out to get Osteen, and that was why he had died.

Two hours later Joe arrived in slacks, jacket, and tie at the front door of Tammy's cottage. "You sure look handsome," Chris teased, answering the door in a pretty silk blouse and

81

skirt. "Are you selling something door to door?"

"Just giving stuff away." Joe brought a bouquet of flowers out from behind his back. Pleased, Chris gave him a kiss on the cheek.

"I know a perfect seafood place on the beach," she said. "And since you're new here, you have to go where I say."

"Sounds perfect," he said.

The road to the restaurant wound among spectacular cliffs and canyons, past towering palm trees, and lush tropical flowers. They caught an occasional glimpse of the Pacific Ocean between the trees. "Sometimes I wonder why my parents ever decided to live in Bayport," Joe admitted, admiring the view, "when they could have picked a place as great as this."

"But then you'd have grown up as just another California surfer boy," Chris teased, "and I would never have noticed you."

Joe liked the seafood restaurant right away because Chris was known there, and they were led to the very best, most private table on the open-air terrace.

Joe dug into his order of shrimp and steak and enjoyed the sight of Chris eating hungrily.

"This food is great!" she said.

"Hey, that's my line," he joked. "I think you're the only girl I've ever met who can out-eat me."

"Yeah, and that worries me," she admitted cheerfully. "I mean, I'm not going to play beach volleyball all my life. What'll happen to me if I stop playing but my appetite stays?''

"You can always become a food writer," he suggested. "Then when you get fat everyone will think you're just doing your job."

Chris laughed. Then she stopped abruptly.

"What's wrong?" asked Joe.

Chris didn't answer for a moment. She finally relaxed again and smiled shakily at Joe. "Nothing. I saw Junior's dad over there, and I was afraid Junior was with him. But it looks like he's alone."

Joe glanced through a large window into the interior of the restaurant. He spotted Ritt in a booth, talking to someone who looked familiar. Joe realized with a jolt that it was Todd Auerbach.

"What's he doing with Auerbach?" he muttered.

"Oh, Auerbach's been trying to get us to break our Frosty contracts and sign endorsement deals with SuperJuice," Chris said calmly. "George senior is Junior's manager, so Auerbach is probably giving him a big sell."

Joe nodded, but noted that Ritt was doing the talking. "By the way, I wanted to ask you—do you know Chuck Herrick?"

Chris was obviously surprised. "Sure. But where did you hear about him? He hasn't played for a year now."

"Ken Chaplin said something nasty about the

Ritts and Chuck Herrick. It got Ritt all huffed up. What's that about, anyway?''

Chris got serious. "I don't know if I should talk about it because nobody knows anything for sure." Then she smiled. "Well, I owe you one after you saved my life today. This is strictly rumor, understand?''

"Understood," Joe replied.

"Chuck was a good player, but last year, just before a match with Junior and his partner, he suddenly got real sick. He had to go to the hospital. Of course, he had to forfeit the match and Junior won. People thought 'someone' might have put something into his pregame food, but nothing could be proved.

"Then, right after the tournament," Chris continued, "Junior's partner had a big argument with Junior and walked out on him. No one knows what it was about. He just cleared out and left the circuit. He won't even talk to his old volleyball buddies on the phone. It was all kind of suspicious, but no one's ever been accused or anything."

Chris checked her watch and smiled at Joe. "Nine o'clock. I'd better be getting home," she said, "or Nadia will ground me for the rest of the year."

Joe asked for the check, paid it, and the two of them left the terrace for the inside of the restaurant.

"I don't think they've seen us," Chris whispered, referring to Auerbach and George Ritt.

"Let's try to sneak out without their noticing us. I'm really not in the mood for small talk."

"Fine with me," Joe said, and led her the long way around the booths.

As they passed the rest rooms on the way out, Chris said, "I'll meet you outside, okay? My hair could use a touch-up after all it's been through today."

Joe wandered out to the parking lot to wait for Chris as she'd asked. Outside, his eyes fell on a luxury convertible parked near the building. A gold monogram on the driver's door read "G.R."

This must be Ritt senior's, Joe thought derisively. He ran a hand along the smooth paint, admiring the car in spite of himself. The top was down, and he could see the all-leather interior, the CD player, the cruise control.

It occurred to Joe that this might be the perfect opportunity to do a little sleuthing. He made sure no one was watching. The car appeared to be empty, but Joe wondered if something incriminating might be hidden in the glove compartment or in the trunk.

He tried the glove compartment. It wasn't locked. Popping the door open, Joe found a sheaf of receipts and papers. He rifled through them.

The receipts were all made out to George Ritt. Most of them were restaurant, gas, and garage receipts, but one bill stood out. It was for a small-size container of something called Biodane, bought at the Meadowlark Garden Center somewhere around Laguna Beach. Joe tried to imagine George Ritt gardening, but that seemed impossible. Joe stuffed the receipt in his pocket and returned the rest of the papers to the glove compartment. He turned away just as Chris appeared at the entrance to the restaurant. She walked out to join him and tucked her arm through his.

"Like the car?" she asked.

"Not my style."

"Mine, neither." She sighed. "I hate to say this, but I'd better get back pronto."

"I know," Joe said. "Maybe we can do this again sometime. When you have no curfew."

Chris smiled and squeezed Joe's arm. "I'd like that."

They began the drive back up the beautiful Coast Highway in silence, lost in their own thoughts. "I wish Frank could see this," Joe said after a while. "He was looking forward to rediscovering California, and he's hardly left the hotel. Tonight he's having an early dinner and watching a movie on TV."

"Poor guy. We'll invite both of you over to Tammy's sometime," Chris said with a smile. "That way he can experience how the natives live."

Joe turned off the Coast Highway and onto the narrow road where Tammy lived. Tammy's cottage was in a quiet neighborhood with no streetlights along the winding canyon road.

Spiked!

"I had a great time," Joe said after he'd walked Chris to the front door.

"Me, too," Chris replied. "Let's—"

A loud *thump* sounded from inside the house and stopped Chris's next comment. It was quickly followed by a muffled cry.

Then Tammy's voice rang out in the evening air.

"No!"

Joe and Chris stared at each other.

Tammy was in trouble!

Chapter

11

"WAIT HERE," Joe snapped. He found the door
unlocked and charged in. Tammy was kneeling
on the living room floor, struggling with a man
standing above her in a baggy gray sweatsuit and
a rubber mask that covered his whole head. The
man had Tammy in a choke hold with her right
arm bent up sharply behind her back. Another
man in a similar getup stood nearby doubled
over and gasping.

Joe lowered his shoulder and drove it into
Tammy's attacker at waist level. The impact
made the man let Tammy go, and she flew forward onto the floor. Her attacker was thrown
off balance long enough for Joe to throw a short
but potent uppercut punch to his jaw. The man
stumbled back, dazed.

Joe turned toward the second man, who had

just managed to stand upright. Backing away from Joe, he croaked, "Let's split!" and turned for the door.

Joe started after him, but just as he reached out to grab him, a tremendous blow fell on the back of his head. The room exploded with stars as Joe pitched forward, crashing into a low table that collapsed under his weight. Through a haze of pain, he saw something bright and hard fall on the floor beside him and heard the assailants race out the door.

A car engine roared to life outside as Chris raced in.

"Tammy!" she gasped, ignoring the squeal of tires as the attackers made their getaway. "Joe! What—how—"

"Don't worry about me," Tammy said, her voice hoarse from the stranglehold she'd just been subjected to. "See about Joe."

"I'm okay." Joe carefully disentangled himself from the splintered table. He stared down, still feeling a little dizzy, and saw that the hard, shiny object was a volleyball trophy. The intruder must have hit him over the head with it.

"Good thing that trophy was kind of tinny," he said, "or I'd be in a lot worse shape."

Chris led Joe to the kitchen table and sat him down on one of the wooden chairs, then began carefully examining the back of his head. Tammy joined them.

"No blood," Chris announced to Joe. "But you'll have a nasty bump there for a few days."

"I've had worse. Sorry about the table," Joe added. "Tammy, what happened?"

Tammy's eyes widened as she started to talk. "I was sitting here, listening to music," she said, "when the door burst open and those two goons stormed in and grabbed me. I think they were trying to kidnap me. I kicked one in the stomach, but the other one got a choke hold on me. And that was when you showed up."

"Do you have any idea who they were?"

"None." Tammy shook her head firmly. "I was too busy fighting them to worry about who they were."

Joe sighed. "Where's the phone?" he asked.

"Right there," Tammy asked, indicating the kitchen counter. "Why?"

"I'm calling the police."

Tammy groaned. "Prindle will murder us!"

"Tammy, you were assaulted," Joe said sharply. "This isn't the kind of thing to cover up."

"But, Joe," Chris said tentatively, "there's a clause in our endorsement contracts that says if we defame the company in any way—you know, by causing a scandal or attracting any kind of negative attention—the Frosty Company doesn't have to pay us anymore. Tammy would be in big trouble, income-wise, if her contract was broken."

"Yeah," said Tammy, lifting her chin. "Besides, Nadia would have my head if she knew I hadn't locked my door.''

Joe frowned. He didn't like the idea of not reporting the incident. What if the men came back, or something similar happened again? He knew he'd blame himself.

''All right,'' he said at last. ''How about this? We'll call them and give them just the plain facts without the lurid details. They can draw their own conclusions. And I think I can get them not to leak any of it to the papers.''

At last Tammy agreed and Joe made the call. Ten minutes later two squad cars pulled up in front of the cottage. Two detectives and two uniformed officers knocked at the front door and entered. One of the men was Detective Dan O'Boyle. He introduced his partner as Detective Ericsson, and they joined the group at the kitchen table while the uniformed officers searched for clues.

After Tammy had given her brief account of what happened, Detective O'Boyle asked Joe, ''Did you notice their car when you drove up?''

''I'm afraid not. I must have seen it, but it didn't register. There aren't any streetlights, so I couldn't see much of anything.''

Detective Ericsson asked Joe a few more questions about the attackers' height and weight, and then the two detectives stood up. ''We don't have much, do we?'' said O'Boyle. ''No good descriptions, no prints, no license number, nothing. But I have the feeling that someone around here doesn't like volleyball players very much.''

"It could be, I guess,'' Joe said uncomfortably.

"Anyone want to add anything?'' O'Boyle looked at Tammy, Chris, and Joe in turn. None of them spoke. O'Boyle coughed. "You, young ladies, lock your doors from now on. Good night.''

After the police had left, Joe said to Chris, "I'd better go, too. Will you be all right?''

Chris nodded, and Tammy bragged, "They don't scare me. If there had been just one of them, I could have taken him, easy.''

"I bet.'' Joe saluted her with a smile. "Call if there's a problem, okay?''

"We will.'' Chris got up from the table and walked him to the front door. "Thanks, Joe,'' she said as he walked outside. "For everything.''

Joe hurried to his car, a goofy grin plastered across his face.

It was nearly eleven o'clock when Frank was startled awake by the sound of angry voices shouting. Still confused by sleep, he thought at first that the sounds were coming from the television set in his room.

Finally he realized that the voices were coming from somewhere outside, drifting through his open door that led to the terrace. He strained his ears to try to identify the voices. One of them sounded like Nadia Galinova's!

After getting off the bed, Frank moved silently

toward the open door, listening to Nadia's angry voice shouting at some unknown victim. Now a low voice rumbled an answer. Frank realized that that voice belonged to George Ritt, Sr.

No matter how hard he tried, Frank couldn't decipher what the older man was saying. But Nadia's voice came loud and clear in reply: *"No! I cannot!"*

Another man's voice joined in, speaking more softly, apparently urging Nadia to be quieter. The voices started to move away, growing softer. Frustrated, Frank leaned over the rail.

He spotted three people walking close along the wall of the hotel, their backs to Frank. Ritt and Nadia were recognizable to him—the other man was not.

He leaned farther out to get a better look. As he did, the trio reached the corner of the building and turned. Curious about the identity of the second man, Frank slipped over the second-story railing and dropped to the sand below. Moving swiftly but silently, he raced after the little group, keeping close to the wall.

The other man wasn't Junior because he was much too short.

At the corner of the building, Frank pressed against the wall and cautiously peered around it. The trio was on the way to one of the parking lots that served the beach crowds—now deserted in the night. Frank saw that Ritt had a grip on Galinova's arm just above the elbow. The woman was dragging her feet, appearing to be

93

afraid as she tried to pull away from his powerful grasp.

Then Frank heard the second man speak. "Take it easy, George."

The voice was familiar, but Frank couldn't place it. Just then the three of them moved into the bright circle of light from a street lamp. Frank stared. The other man was Todd Auerbach!

Ritt and Auerbach—what was the connection, Frank wondered. And what did they want with Galinova?

Not wanting to be discovered, Frank turned and started noiselessly back. He was so involved in his own thoughts that he failed to hear someone moving up behind him until the last second.

By then it was too late. Frank started to turn just as something heavy and solid crashed into his skull. He dropped to the ground, unconscious.

Chapter

12

FRANK AWOKE to the sound of surf filtered through a splitting headache. He rolled over and struggled to his feet. He was on the beach—the lights of the Surf Club about fifty yards away. In the dim moonlight, Frank could make out a blurred trail in the sand leading from the edge of the parking lot where he had been slugged. He had evidently been dragged here, where there would be no casual passersby to spot him.

I feel dizzy, he thought as he trudged back toward the hotel. Who did this to me? He remembered watching Ritt, Auerbach, and Nadia Galinova and wondered whether one of them had attacked him. He checked his watch. It was eleven-thirty.

He entered the Surf Club from the beach entrance in the back and slipped up the back stairs without anyone noticing his sandy, disheveled appearance. He walked down the corridor to his second-floor room, only to remember that he didn't have a key. He knocked on the door. A moment later it opened and Joe was there, staring at him.

"Where've *you* been?" Joe demanded.

"Out on the beach. How was dinner?" Frank stepped inside and sat down on the edge of his bed.

"Great. Chris is fantastic. Just one problem. When we—" Joe stopped when he saw Frank reach for the back of his head and wince.

"Okay, let's have it," he demanded. "What happened, and let's look at that head."

As Joe probed Frank's scalp, Frank gave him a rundown on how he had tried to find out what Auerbach and Ritt had been doing with Galinova.

"The only thing I was able to work out— *ouch!*—watch it back there!—was that Nadia seems really scared of Ritt," he concluded.

"Ritt and Auerbach are up to something, all right," Joe said excitedly. "I saw them together earlier, at the restaurant where I ate with Chris." He filled Frank in on the events of his own evening, including the attempted abduction of Tammy and the receipt for Biodane he had found in Ritt's car.

"Ritt and Auerbach must have driven straight over here after dinner," Joe surmised. "I bet we

can crack this case by tomorrow, now that we
know about Chuck Herrick—"

"Herrick? What about him?"

"Oh! I forgot to tell you." As he cleaned
Frank's wound, Joe told his brother about Herrick. "That kind of makes the Ritts front-runners
in Peter Osteen's death," Joe concluded.

Frank frowned. 'Yeah, but they wouldn't be
crazy enough to try the same stunt more than
once. Especially when people are already suspicious about the last time."

Joe tossed the towel over a chair. "Ritt might
figure he can always pull the right strings to
make a police problem go away."

Frank stood up and began pacing back and
forth. "If Ritt *knows* that this tour is not going
to come off, that the whole Hi-Kick promotional
scheme will fail, then he'll want to get Junior in
with SuperJuice."

Joe considered this. "So he sets up a meeting
with Auerbach to make a pitch for Junior. Chris
thought it was the other way around. But what
do they want with Galinova?"

Frank stopped pacing. "Galinova has a lot of
influence on Chris and Tammy. So Ritt tells
Auerbach to lean on her to persuade the girls to
commit to SuperJuice. One question—"

"What can Ritt use to pressure Nadia?" Joe
finished.

They thought about that one for a while, but
came up with nothing. "It's late," Frank admitted with a yawn. "Tomorrow we'll tackle the

97

Nadia question—and we'll visit that gardening store where Ritt bought the Biodane.''

"You think there's any chance of looking at the film of Chaplin's that the police impounded?" Joe wondered, unbuttoning his shirt.

Frank yawned again, and headed for the shower. "We could try, I guess. That is, if we can drag ourselves out of bed tomorrow. Some vacation," he remarked.

The next morning Frank went right to Prindle's office. Prindle greeted them eagerly and asked to hear any news.

The Hardys ran through the events of the previous day, and Prindle groaned when Joe mentioned calling the police the night before.

"I know you had to do it, but if any more of this stuff gets leaked to the press, I'm done for," he said gloomily.

"Any new clippings today?"

"Just a few small pieces on the cable accident yesterday. But that's been played down as an accident because of my own efforts." He made a wry face. "There is a feature on Peter's death coming out in one of the major tabloids next week, though."

Suddenly Joe's eyes widened. "Oh, wow!" he said. "Frank, we forgot to tell him about Auerbach!"

"Auerbach? Something else about Auerbach?" Prindle asked, getting nervous all over again.

Frank turned to Prindle. "We tried to tell you

at the tournament yesterday, but you didn't have time. We found Auerbach in your office yesterday, going through the papers on your desk."

Prindle's eyes got large and round. "He *what? My desk?*"

Frank nodded. "We think he was copying down the addresses and phone numbers of some of your players. We told him to hit the road."

Prindle slammed a hand on his desk. "The nerve of that guy! I oughta—if you find him in here again, call the cops! That's exactly the kind of stuff he used to do when he worked for us—"

"He worked for you?" Joe interrupted, shocked.

"Didn't I tell you that? He was with us for three years. He moved over to SuperJuice eighteen months ago, when I got this job instead of him. Officially, he left on good terms, but I know he's been sulking ever since. He'd give anything to see me fail on this project."

"The thing is," Frank said, "he's hanging around with Ritt, and Ritt's starting to look really suspicious. Ken Chaplin told us Ritt may have doctored a player's food last year. Do you think there's anything to that?"

Prindle blinked. "Could be. I wouldn't put a lot past that guy. On the other hand, I don't trust Ken Chaplin either."

"Why not?" Joe asked, even more astonished. "I thought you hired him."

"I did because he was cheap. Chaplin's a good filmmaker, but he has a gambling habit that keeps him in debt. He does a good job, but personally, he's not a guy I'd trust.''

"Does anyone else on the tourney know about our being detectives?'' Frank asked Prindle suddenly.

Prindle pursed his lips. "Nadia Galinova seems to."

"Nadia?'' Frank frowned. "How?''

"I don't know.'' Prindle seemed perplexed. "She marched in here yesterday evening and chewed my ear off for about half an hour about how we shouldn't let people pry into her private life. I asked her who she meant, and she named you two. She said she had half a mind to resign, but she cares too much about Chris and Tammy. I figured Joe must have told Chris who you guys really are, and Chris told Nadia."

"No way," said Joe, glancing at his brother. "I wanted to tell her, but I figured it would just put her in more danger. So who told Nadia?'' he asked, but got no reply.

The Hardys got up to leave, more confused than when they'd arrived. "If I can help any more, let me know,'' said Prindle, walking them to the door.

"With help like that, we may still be working on this case in ten years,'' Joe muttered to Frank as the office door closed behind them.

"Let's drive out to that garden store you told me about. I want to get something solid on Ritt if we can,'' Frank said.

"Great idea." Joe led the way to their rented car. "That's one guy I wouldn't mind nailing."

It didn't take long to find the Meadowlark Garden Center address. It was located on a major road leading from Laguna Beach to Anaheim. Joe figured the drive would take half an hour, tops.

"After this case is over, we ought to explore the area around here," Frank said as he maneuvered the car out of the lot and onto the highway.

"But then again we might not get a chance to do that," Frank said, when he looked up at the rearview mirror.

"Someone is following us. And after what Prindle told us, I figure these guys play for keeps!"

Chapter

13

THE NAVY BLUE four-by-four truck that had been a few car lengths back was now so close it was practically kissing the rental car's back bumper.

"I guess they want us to know they're following us," Frank said to Joe. "Maybe they're hoping to scare us off. I can't see their faces. Can you?"

Joe turned to peer back, not caring whether the pursuers saw him. "No," he said. "The truck's too high and the windshield's too dark. But if they want to make a statement, maybe we should go ahead and answer them."

Frank glanced over at his brother, a grin flickering across his face. "Are you thinking what I'm thinking?"

Joe nodded solemnly. "My seat belt's fastened. Let 'er fly."

Frank smashed his foot down as hard as he could on the accelerator. The effect was as dramatic as the Hardys intended it to be. The small rental car screamed as it kicked into high gear and peeled out ahead of the lumbering four-wheel-drive truck.

"Did they take the bait?" Frank asked, steering the car onto the Santa Ana Freeway and passing several cars as he moved into the fast lane.

"Yep," Joe said after a moment. "They're coming up fast. That baby definitely is not stock. Someone has done a job on the engine. This rental is no match for it." He laughed. "Looks like you're going to have to do all the work."

"Dad always said that brains can beat muscle any day." Frank gave his brother a quick grin.

As the boys talked, the truck was catching up to them in a series of bull-like rushes, cutting off one driver after another as it changed lanes. Frank, on the other hand, drove smooth and straight.

"You know, if we were on a dirt road, this guy would catch us in a minute," Frank said.

"Then it's a good thing we're on the freeway," Joe said.

"He's still going to catch up to us in a minute if we don't think of something fast," Frank said in reply. Just then a gray-haired man in a glistening black luxury car pulled in front of them, cutting them off. The man was talking on his car phone and clearly hadn't noticed their car.

"Joe, I've got it!" Frank exclaimed as he

slowed to avoid hitting the preoccupied phoner. "And all you have to do is act like your usual crazy self."

The truck was right behind them, one lane to the right to block the Hardys from pulling off quickly at an exit. Frank punched the accelerator after the black luxury car pulled away from them.

As they moved along, the brothers watched not only the pursuing truck, but other cars they were passing. When they overtook a bright yellow van two lanes over, Frank deliberately cut it off, veering into its lane and hitting the brakes. The driver of the van had to hit his brakes, too, to keep from hitting the boys' car. Meanwhile, the Hardys' pursuers shot by them like a rocket.

Just as quickly as he had slowed down, Frank again put the gas to the floor.

Within less than a mile, the boys passed the truck crawling along on their right in the slowest lane. As they went by, the truck accelerated once again.

Very soon the Hardys saw and heard two California Highway Patrol officers on motorcycles enter the highway behind them with lights flashing and sirens screaming. So did the driver of the truck, Joe noted with satisfaction as it finally used all its power to pull away. Within seconds, the police were alongside the brothers' car, waving them off to the shoulder.

When the officer walked up beside Frank's

window, he found, to his surprise, two grinning faces staring up at him.

"Officer, you're never going to believe how glad I am to see you," said Frank.

All Joe could do was laugh.

Frank led Joe into the Meadowlark Garden Center's large greenhouse, where he'd spotted the shop's manager squatting and snipping leaves from some potted plants.

"These grow like weeds in this climate," said the manager, a cheerful older man with a fringe of white hair around a bald, shiny scalp. "May I help you gentlemen?"

"We'd appreciate a little information," Frank replied. "Do you carry something called Biodane?"

"Biodane?" echoed the manager, getting to his feet. "You fellas want to be real careful with Biodane. It's nasty stuff."

"We aren't planning to use it," Joe assured him. "We just want to know what it is."

"It's a heavy-duty pesticide. And I mean *heavy-duty*. Active ingredient is nicotine, and in concentrated form it'd kill off a herd of buffalo. Most folks wouldn't want it around the house, and I think they're perfectly right."

"We were wondering if you had a customer buy some a few days back," Joe said. "Do you remember?"

"Well, yes, as a matter of fact," the manager

said without hesitating. "An impatient fella, I recall."

"What did he look like?" Frank asked, trying to stifle his own impatience.

The manager reflected. "He was kind of husky, middle-aged, with curly reddish blond hair. I warned him how strong it was, and he got kind of angry. Said he just wanted Biodane, not advice." The manager shook his head. "Nasty fella."

Frank and Joe exchanged a quick look. The man had given them a fine thumbnail description of George Ritt, Sr.

"Nicotine," Frank said as the brothers got back in their car. "Colorless and tasteless. And about as toxic as poison gets."

"Okay. Ritt had the means to kill Osteen," Joe said. "And he had motivation—maybe. But what about opportunity? And, anyway, you don't think Ritt put Biodane in the Hi-Kick, do you? All the players drank it, and the other three didn't get sick."

"Right," answered Frank. "But I don't think Ritt bought it for his rose garden, either."

The brothers rode in silence for a while, pondering all the pieces of the puzzle. "Well, we always suspected George Ritt," Joe said finally. "Now we have one more reason to suspect him. But what about Auerbach? And Galinova? What does she know about us, and how did she find out?"

"Maybe she doesn't really know anything. She might just have wanted us fired. She sure doesn't like the idea of you distracting Chris from volleyball."

"Yeah, but she talked about our snooping," Joe reminded him. "She could have just told Prindle we were bothering Chris and Tammy."

"But then Prindle might not have backed her up," Frank suggested. "This story is just her word against ours. And she knows she carries a lot of weight within the sport."

"The weird thing about this—if you take the different elements—" Joe said, "the anonymous letters, the phone calls, the attempted kidnapping, the exploding volleyball, the poison, and that truck that tried to run us down, they all seem as if they must have been done by different people. It's hard to put all those things on any one suspect. On the other hand, it's even harder to imagine a lot of people working together to destroy Hi-Kick's investment."

"Yeah, I know what you mean," Frank said. "But if, for instance, Galinova is in on this, she's not alone. She'd have to be working with someone else. Maybe Ritt, maybe Auerbach."

"So now what?" Joe asked with a sigh.

"Now we drop in on Detective O'Boyle and see if the tox screen turned up anything interesting. And maybe we can ask to see Ken Chaplin's confiscated film."

"Sounds good," Joe said. "Then we can get

lunch and maybe watch a little volleyball. What time—"

Whap!

A sharp explosive sound cut Joe off in midsentence, and acrid smoke drifted into the car.

"What was that?" demanded Joe.

"I don't know," replied Frank.

"Great. What'd our horoscope say today? 'Avoid all transportation, especially rental cars'?" He waited. "Well, what's up?"

They were riding at just under the forty-five-mile-per-hour speed limit, but a yellow sign up ahead warned of unusually sharp curves. Frank turned the steering wheel.

The car failed to respond.

"That 'bang' left us without any steering!" Frank shouted.

He hit the brake pedal. The car started to slow, but then, to Frank's horror, the pedal suddenly gave way and sank to the floor.

"Uh-oh," said Joe. "I don't think I want to know any more."

"You have to!" Frank shouted. "It took the brakes, too! Brace yourself!"

The road curved to the left. Straight ahead, a clump of tall palms loomed.

"We're going to hit them!" Frank yelled. "Hold on, Joe!"

Chapter

14

"CAN WE JUMP?" yelled Joe.

"Nope. Too fast!" Frank shouted, downshifting before he yanked the handle of the emergency brake. The forward motion still sent the car lurching off the road, the right front bumper slamming into the trunk of a palm. Sliding sideways and raising a huge cloud of dust, the rear swung around and smashed into another palm. The car was wedged in solidly.

Frank felt as though his seat belt had nearly cut him in half. He looked across at Joe. His brother's eyes were shut.

"Joe? Can you hear me? Are you hurt? *Joe!*"

Joe grunted, his eyes still closed. "My shoulder feels like someone hit it with a sledgehammer," he mumbled finally. "Otherwise, I feel great."

Frank opened his door, and they struggled out on his side, since Joe's door was jammed. "Not that it makes much difference at this point, but let's find out what caused this," Frank said, checking to make sure none of his bones was broken before moving to the front of the car.

"Score two for seat belts," Joe muttered as he joined his brother.

Frank managed to pop the hood of the wrecked car, and he and Joe peered into the battered interior. "Just what I thought," Frank said, noting the grease splattered all over the left side of the engine and scratches on the inside of the fender from flying bits of metal. "Someone put a small explosive on the steering box. The brake lines must have been cut by one of the exploding pieces of metal." He slammed the hood down in disgust.

"Who?" Joe asked, voicing what was in both their minds. "The guy who chased us in the truck?"

Frank shrugged. "All I know is, I'm checking out every vehicle belonging to everyone connected with the tournament. Anyone who turns up with a customized truck had better watch out for me."

"Yeah," agreed Joe. "And while we're at it, we might as well look around for any explosives experts, too."

Just then a battered, dusty station wagon pulled up by the side of the road, and two long-haired, shirtless surfers, their boards on a rack on top of the car, stared at the scene.

"You dudes all right?" called the driver.

"We're fine," called Joe. "But the car—"

"The car is a total wipeout," said the driver's friend. "Strictly scrap metal."

"We need to get to Laguna Beach," Frank said.

"No sweat," replied the driver. "Hop in back. You sure you're all in one piece?"

"Almost," Joe replied, sliding into the wagon and flexing his arm.

Half an hour later Frank and Joe were in Laguna Beach police headquarters, sitting in Dan O'Boyle's cramped cubicle of an office. O'Boyle had arranged for a tow truck to pick up the rental car, and now he was studying the brothers.

"This isn't a big city," O'Boyle said philosophically, "and I'm an easygoing kind of guy. Some people might even think of me as a dumb hick cop. You don't, though, do you?"

"No, sir," Frank said dully.

"Good. Because since I first saw you two at that tournament on the beach, we've had an unexpected death, an attempted abduction, and now a mysterious and very nasty road accident. These are the things I *know* about you." He paused. "I think it's time for some straight talk."

"Actually," said Joe, "believe it or not, we

111

were on our way here when our car got wrecked. To have that straight talk."

O'Boyle pulled out a pad of lined, yellow paper and a pen. "Let's hear it," he said briefly.

"Our father is Fenton Hardy," said Frank, "a private investigator back East. We work on cases, too, sometimes. We happened to be around when weird stuff started happening at the tournament, and Mr. Prindle asked us to investigate."

"Investigate what?" asked the detective.

Frank and Joe quickly described the anonymous letters, the phone calls, the exploding volleyball, and the truck that had chased them that morning. The detective already knew about the other incidents.

When the Hardys had finished, O'Boyle said nothing—he only stared. Finally he spoke up, "Aren't you boys a little young for this kind of thing? Meaning no offense, of course."

"We can handle it," Joe said tersely. "If you want confirmation, you can call our dad."

O'Boyle stood up. "I think I have to do just that," he said. "In some other office, where I can have a little privacy. You boys wait here."

When O'Boyle returned ten minutes later, his pained expression had been replaced with an amused grin. "Well, now," he boomed as he sat down at his desk. "I thought I'd heard the name Fenton Hardy before, and it turns out we have some common friends in the law enforcement business. So you were coming in to see me, anyway, were you? What was it you wanted to ask?"

"We were wondering about the tox screen you're doing on Peter Osteen," Frank said. "Are the results in yet?"

"We expect them in this afternoon," the detective replied. "What else?"

"Have you looked at the film you confiscated from Ken Chaplin yet?" Joe spoke up. "Did anything in it seem out of line?"

"We've run that film half a dozen times," O'Boyle said with a sigh. "It's got pretty shots of the beach, a bunch of volleyball action sequences, and some folks drinking that Hi-Kick gunk and smacking their lips. Not a thing you could use, though. You're welcome to look yourselves."

"That would be great," said Frank.

"I'll have it set up for you." O'Boyle reached for his phone. "One thing, though," he said before he dialed. "No more hush-hush stuff, okay? We share what we know from now on."

"Yes, sir," Joe replied.

O'Boyle led them to a room with a projector and screen, then left the Hardys alone to watch the film.

Joe sat back and watched the series of shots, all of them exactly as O'Boyle had described. Halfway through, the film switched to shots of the tournament's first match—mostly of players drinking cups of Hi-Kick between plays.

As Joe watched a shot of Peter Osteen, he

113

wondered again if the poison had been in that cup. But if so, how did it get there without hurting the others? Joe peered intently at the screen as the scene changed to one of the cheering crowd. There had to be something there they could use.

Suddenly Frank reached over and pressed the Pause button. "Wait a minute," he said. "Look at that."

Joe studied the still shot of the front row of the bleachers, where the Ritts were sitting, deep in conversation. Frank ran the film in slow motion, and Joe watched as Junior spoke to his father. Junior seemed nervous and was pointing at the court. In response the older Ritt swung his head around and said something short and angry. Junior shut his mouth and looked even more unhappy.

"Junior's worried," said Frank.

"Yeah, and his dad told him to keep his mouth shut," Joe agreed.

A shot of the players between serves showed all four of them breathing hard and sweating.

The final sequence showed Peter Osteen pitching forward onto the sand.

"No shot of Ritt pouring Biodane into the cooler," Joe said. "Too bad."

Frank stood up. "Let's see about getting another car. We need to talk to Prindle."

It was midafternoon when the Hardys reached the Surf Club's parking lot and knocked on Prindle's door. There was no answer, but as they turned to leave they saw Ken Chaplin drive up and head for the film crew trailer.

"Mr. Chaplin!" called Frank.

"Can't talk now, Frank," called Chaplin. "Got to hurry back. We're between matches."

After he punched in the security code on the alarm system, unlocked the front door, and opened it, Frank and Joe peered inside. It looked as though every inch of the limited space was filled with equipment, plastic containers of chemicals, and boxes.

"Have you seen Mr. Prindle?" Joe called into the trailer.

"If he's not in the men's locker room," Chaplin answered, "he's at the court."

The Hardys found Prindle in the locker room, where most of the players had gathered until it was time to take their places on the court or in the bleachers for the next match.

"What's up?" Prindle asked as he joined the Hardys in the empty gym for a little privacy.

"Plenty." Joe filled Prindle in on all that had happened so far that day.

"Listen," he said when Joe had finished, "You sure you guys are all right? I don't want to be responsible for your getting hurt or anything—"

"Too late now," Frank quipped. "Actually, what we need from you is information. Do you know anyone connected with the tournament who owns a truck like the one that chased us?''

"No," Prindle replied. "And it sounds like a truck I'd remember. Of course, I don't notice what everyone who works here drives." He paused. "Anything else?"

"Yeah," said Joe. "I was wondering, the day Peter died, did the players seem more burned out than usual? It was hard for us to tell, but you've seen a lot of these games up close."

"Maybe." Prindle looked perplexed. Then he checked his watch. "Listen, the match is going to start soon. I've got to get back to work. Why don't you talk to the players about how they felt?"

"Good idea," said Frank as Prindle hurried off. "Why don't you do that, Joe? I'm going back to the room."

"How come?"

"I want to call O'Boyle to find out if those test results came in. I'll meet you in the room in, say, half an hour."

Joe returned to the locker room, and was relieved to see that Junior had wandered off. The other players were laughing and joking in small groups. Brad Conlin was stretched out on a bench, talking with Mark Donahue. They looked up when Joe entered and waved him over.

"Aren't you working today?" Brad asked. "Just twenty minutes till match time."

"Uh, right." Joe was taken off guard. He'd been so involved in the case that he'd almost forgotten he was supposed to be a working volunteer. "Prindle gave us the day off," he improvised. "I guess he figured some other guys ought to get a chance to field volleyballs on national TV."

The players laughed, and Joe sat down on the bench next to Conlin. "I'll be in the bleachers, though," Joe added. "It's Junior and Buzz Maestren against Scooter Lenz and his new partner, right?"

The players nodded. Pretending to make small talk, Joe then asked, "How are you two feeling, anyway?"

"How are we feeling," Donahue echoed, mystified. "Fine. Why?"

"No reason," Joe hedged. "You looked so beat after that match the other day. But I guess that's normal after something like that, huh?"

"I wouldn't say normal, exactly," Donahue replied. "I mean, I felt bad all that day. So did you, right, Conlin? A bug must have been going around. That's why we didn't react right away when Peter started slowing down."

"Yeah," Conlin remembered. "At first he looked like the rest of us felt."

Just then one of the other players checked his watch and called out, "It's time!" There was a general hubbub in the locker room as the players got ready to hit the bleachers.

"Coming, Joe?" Donahue asked as he and Conlin headed for the door.

"Go ahead." Joe waved them on. "I'm supposed to meet Frank at our room. We'll see you at the match."

By the time Joe was finishing his conversation with Conlin and Donahue, Frank had arrived at their room.

As he punched in the first few digits of O'Boyle's phone number, Frank had the feeling that something had moved across the room. Instantly alert, he spun around—and saw that the closet door was open.

Out of the closet sprang Nadia Galinova, eyes fixed and staring. In her upraised hand was a long, gleaming knife!

Chapter

15

FRANK HIT THE FLOOR as Galinova's razor-sharp blade buried itself in the bedding where he'd been sitting a moment before. Instantly he scrambled to his feet and backed away from the knife, which she had retrieved.

Nadia slowly advanced toward him, holding the weapon waist high. The limited space gave Frank little room to maneuver.

"Nadia, you're making a big mistake. I don't mean you any harm."

Nadia paid no attention and continued to advance. Frank took one more step back—and found himself up against a wall. Realizing he was trapped, he searched for a weapon—any kind of weapon. Just then Galinova made her move and threw herself at him with the knife in her out-stretched hand.

"No, you don't!" Frank pivoted and grabbed her knife hand. Pulling her off balance, he chopped down on her wrist with the edge of his hand. Nadia's weapon fell to the floor. Frank stooped quickly to retrieve it as Nadia crumpled to the floor in a heap.

"Nadia?" called Frank.

She made no response.

"Nadia?" Frank knelt down on the floor beside her just as the room door opened and Joe rushed in.

"Frank, Conlin and Donahue said—"

He stopped as he rounded the corner of the bed.

"What happened here?"

Frank explained. Astounded, Joe stared at the hunched figure. "Nadia?" he said softly. "Tell us why."

"You can talk to us or to the police," Frank pointed out. "It's your choice."

She raised her head and, with Frank's help, got up and sat on the edge of the bed. Her face was pale.

"I didn't want to hurt you," she said to Frank, her eyes lowered. "I meant to scare you, that's all. Not that it makes a difference now." Her voice sounded thick and mechanical.

"But why scare him?" Joe demanded.

"Because you were about to ruin my life!" she cried, and then forced herself to settle down again.

Joe sighed and sat down on the other bed,

facing her. "Nadia," he said, trying to be patient, "I think you'd better tell us the whole story."

Slowly and with difficulty, Nadia began to talk. She began by telling the Hardys how she had defected to America eighteen years earlier, leaving her family behind. Her defection caused her family to be badly treated by the government.

Five years ago, Galinova explained, she had learned that her younger sister, Hana, was seriously ill. There was then no treatment available for her in Eastern Europe. If Hana remained there, she would die. Only with medical help in the West might she survive.

But there was no way to bring Hana to this country. Nevertheless, Nadia had gone to powerful people and told them her problem. Hana had been smuggled out of the country, and she illegally entered the United States, where her life had been saved.

"So what's the problem?" Joe asked, perplexed.

Galinova eyed him coolly.

Somehow, she told the brothers, George Ritt had discovered Hana's illegal status. He had threatened Nadia with having Hana arrested and either put in jail or deported unless Nadia did as Ritt demanded.

"Which was?" prompted Frank.

"He and a man who works for another drink company—"

"Auerbach," said Joe.

"Yes. They want me to get Chris and Tammy to sign a contract with this SuperJuice. Then Mr. Ritt's son will also sign a contract, and the others will follow. I tried to do this, but Chris and Tammy said they would not."

"But what does that have to do with us?" Frank asked. "Why'd you go after me?"

"Because Ritt told me who you are," she said. "Detectives for the INS—the Immigration and Naturalization Service. He told me you want to find Hana and take her away." She was fighting tears now. "This I cannot allow."

Frank and Joe stared at her, astonished. "And you believed him?" Frank asked.

"Of course I did," she said with a small shrug. "This is not something to joke about."

"Nadia," Joe said urgently, "listen to me. Ritt lied to you. We're not from the INS. We have no interest in your sister. Ritt and Auerbach have treated you very badly. But if you'll trust us, we'll see that they pay for what they've done."

Galinova seemed almost hopeful now. "How?"

"We can't say right now," Frank answered. "But no harm will come to Hana—or to you. For the time being, don't let them know that we've had this talk. Pretend things are just as they were between you."

Then they persuaded Galinova to leave without telling her any more. After she had gone, Frank turned to Joe. He was steaming.

122

"Let's make sure Ritt and Auerbach get what they deserve. They've fooled around with too many people's lives."

"The best way to get Ritt is to nail him for murder," Joe pointed out. "Did you get the results from the tox screen yet?"

"No, I was interrupted," Frank said wryly, picking up the receiver that he'd dropped by the bed. "I'll do it now."

"Not a trace of nicotine in Osteen's body," he told Joe after he'd hung up.

"Then Ritt didn't poison him." Joe sounded almost disappointed.

"Not with Biodane." He thought for a moment. Then he said, "Time for the tournament. Let's go root against Junior."

The match between the Ritt-Maestren team and that of Lenz and his new partner, Whitey Mullins of Redondo Beach, was tied at two-two when Joe and Frank squeezed into the front-row section.

Richard Prindle paced nervously along the side of the court directly in front of the boys. When he noticed Frank and Joe, he went up to them.

"How's the match going?" Frank asked.

"Junior's off his game, and he's losing his cool. He keeps trying jump serves, and they keep hitting the net or landing way out of bounds."

Frank glanced over Prindle's shoulder in time

123

to watch Buzz Maestren serve to Whitey Mullins, who bumped the ball to Scooter Lenz. Junior came forward, assuming Lenz would set for Mullins to spike. Instead, Scooter leapt up and slammed the ball down just behind Junior. "Side out," Frank murmured along with the announcer. He watched as Junior whirled around to face his partner.

"Where were you?" Junior screamed. "I can't play this game by myself."

His display of temper drew scattered catcalls. Frank noticed that several tournament players were delighting in booing Junior. Mark Donahue leaned toward Frank and muttered, "Want to bet Junior is going to need a new partner next week?"

Joe overheard him and laughed. Frank faced front again and noticed for the first time that George Ritt, Sr., was seated in the third row of the bleachers directly across the court. He was watching his son with a stern, rigid expression. Beside him sat Todd Auerbach, whose expression was equally grim.

The audience roared as a perfect jump serve by Scooter Lenz gave his team the lead. No question who most of this crowd was rooting for, Frank noted.

The ball was back in play. Junior jumped to spike the ball. Whitey Mullins leapt with his hands high to block it. The ball hung frozen between their hands, then dropped to the sand on Junior's side of the net.

"Ten–eight," the loudspeakers echoed. Frank watched as Junior kicked the ball savagely. The audience responded with louder boos. The referee leaned toward the surly player, apparently giving him a warning. Frank glanced across the court to see that George senior had risen to his feet. Auerbach was trying to pull him back down.

Junior had lost his poise, and five minutes later his team had lost the match, the score three games to two. Head down, he stomped off the court, not stopping to shake hands with the winners.

Buzz Maestren gave George senior an icy look. "Find another sucker!" the Hardys heard him shout. "I've had it!"

"Look, there are Chris and Tammy," Joe said to Frank, pointing at them in the crowd filing out across the court. "Be right back." He sprinted across to the girls, dodging through the milling fans like a broken-field runner.

Frank remained in his seat, watching Ken Chaplin and his crew set up for an interview with the winning team.

He watched Vern's expert maneuverings with the camera while Ken did the interviewing. It must take years to become a really good technician, he reflected.

Then he got an idea. He blinked, concentrating hard.

A moment later Joe was back in his seat, reporting breathlessly to Frank, "Chris and

Tammy want to make dinner for us at their place tonight. I told them we'd be there at seven o'clock.''

"Fine," Frank said absently, still watching the interview. "Listen, did you talk to the players about being tired the other day?"

"Oh, yeah," Joe said. "I forgot to tell you. They said they felt out of it all through the match. That's why they didn't react to Osteen's staggering around right away. They all felt pretty much that way." He glanced at his brother. "What do you think it means?"

"Tell you later. Right now, how do you like the idea of confronting the Ritts?"

Joe's eyes lit up, and his fists involuntarily clenched. "I *like* it. When?"

"First, I want to have a look around Chaplin's trailer. I've got an idea about that, too, and it looks like the crew's going to be tied up here for a while. Then we go after George junior and senior."

Frank spotted Prindle and called his name. When Prindle came over, Frank asked him for the Ritts' address. Prindle wasn't eager to give it to him, but he finally did relent. As soon as Frank had pocketed the slip of paper with the address, he took off.

"What's the hurry?" Joe asked.

"I want to be out of Chaplin's trailer before Chaplin shows up."

Joe slowed down a little. "I see your point."

126

It was a simple matter to get past the trailer's newly installed security system, since Frank had made a note of the letters Vern had punched to silence the alarm. "Real hard to remember," he commented as he punched in the code. " 'Vern.' Nobody'd think of trying that."

Joe was the expert at lock-picking, and Frank stood back as he worked the padlock.

Five minutes later the boys were inside. Joe closed the door, and Frank switched on the light. He looked around at the piles of technical gear and shelves lined with huge plastic bottles labeled "Toner," "Acetone," and "Distilled Water."

Quickly and efficiently, he began his search. It didn't take long. Fifteen minutes later he straightened up and said, "Okay. Let's go."

"Great." Joe headed for the door. "But are you going to tell me what you were looking for?"

"Sure, but not now. First I want to talk to the Ritts."

"Wonderful," Joe said as they left the trailer, being careful to lock it and reset the alarm. "My own brother's playing guessing games with me."

The address Prindle had given the Hardys was that of a house George Ritt owned in Laguna Hills. Despite their mission, Frank found himself distracted again by the spectacular views as their new rented car wound up among the rocky heights.

Frank drove on past the large, two-story, white-columned house and down the road about twenty yards farther. He parked on the shoulder, and got out.

"Why'd you park here?" Joe asked, walking back toward the house beside his brother.

Frank smiled enigmatically. "I want to take them by surprise."

As they approached the massive front doors of the impressive mansion, Frank and Joe could hear the muffled sounds of angry voices inside.

"Doesn't sound like a happy family," Joe remarked as the brothers mounted the front steps.

"Surprise, surprise," said Frank. He started to ring the doorbell.

At the sound of the chimes, the yelling stopped abruptly. The door swung open and Junior stood there, red-faced and scowling.

"What do *you* want?"

"We need to talk," said Frank.

"We've got nothing to say to you."

"Okay, then, just listen."

Junior muttered something and stepped back to let the brothers in.

He led them to a large living room where Ritt, Sr., was sitting. He jumped up, startled and annoyed.

"You've got some nerve, waltzing in here. Beat it, or I'll call the cops!" he said.

"Go ahead." Frank gestured to a phone on a

nearby table. "Then we can have a nice conversation about gardening supplies."

Junior's eyes widened. "Dad—" he said in a surprisingly small voice.

"Shut your mouth!" growled his father. He turned to Frank. "I don't know what you mean."

"We mean Biodane," said Frank. "A toxic pesticide, which we can prove you bought recently. To kill bugs in the roses, was it? Or moles in the potato patch?"

Ritt flashed him a cruel, hard grin.

"You wise guys have been snooping around, haven't you. Not smart. You picked the wrong man to mess with."

He strolled over to a fancy cabinet and opened a drawer. He pulled out a large, blue-steel automatic pistol, which he pointed straight at Joe. To both Hardys, the barrel looked as big as the mouth of a tunnel.

"See? Biodane isn't the only way to get rid of annoying pests," said Ritt.

He cocked the automatic with a loud, metallic click.

Chapter

16

"DAD!" JUNIOR SQUAWKED. "What are you—"

"Keep quiet, boy!" Ritt kept his eyes and the gun fixed on the Hardys. "These squirts can put us both in prison, don't you see that? No one is going to do that to George Ritt—or his son."

"There's something you should understand," said Frank. "About Peter Osteen—"

"We didn't want him to die!" Junior cried out.

"I told you to shut up!" his father snarled. "Don't turn gutless on me, son."

"It wasn't Biodane that killed Osteen," Joe said. "If that's what you're scared about, you can relax." He couldn't take his eyes off the gun muzzle that was now aimed at his stomach.

"What do you mean?" asked Junior. "Dad, did you hear what he said?"

"It's a trick, son, that's all. They'll say anything to save their necks. But it's too late."

Frank said, "We just learned the results of a tox screen the police ordered. There was no nicotine in Osteen's body. That means no Biodane. Scooter Lenz says Peter didn't eat any fruit before the match. That's how you tried to get him, right? You made a weak solution of Biodane that you figured would make him sick. Then you injected it into the fruit. When he died, you thought you'd miscalculated."

"What we're going to do," said Ritt, ignoring him completely, "is take a little drive to a nice, out-of-the-way canyon I know of, where your bodies won't be found for days, maybe weeks—"

"*Dad!* He says we didn't kill Peter!"

"If he murders us," Joe said to Junior, "you're an accessory. Is that what you want?"

Junior, stupefied, opened his mouth, then closed it again. Then he shook his head.

"Shut up, you," Ritt, Sr., roared at Joe, "or I'll finish you right here and now. Son, do what I say. Don't I always do what's best for you?"

"What's *best* for me?" said Junior, astounded. "Sure, right, what's *best* for me! Like wasting my life trying to make me into a champion athlete, when I don't *want* to be one! Now you want to make me a murderer, too. Well, sorry, Dad. I *won't* be!"

Junior lunged forward and grabbed his father's gun arm. Before Frank or Joe could go for the weapon, it went off with an earsplitting report that echoed through the room.

In the shocked silence that followed, Joe was able to snatch the gun out of the older man's hand. He held it on both the Ritts while Frank moved to the telephone and called the police.

"What's *best* for me," Frank heard Junior mutter to his father as he hung up the phone. Frank looked again at the two of them, and was surprised at the extreme hate in the son's eyes and the uncertainty and fear in the father's.

"One thing I want to know before the police arrive," Frank said crisply. "Why did you try to force Nadia to go after us?"

"Auerbach told me you were professional snoops," the elder Ritt snarled. "He wanted you gone."

"How'd *he* know who we were?" Joe asked.

Ritt shrugged. "He didn't say."

Sirens sounded in the distance. Detective O'Boyle and his partner, Ericsson, entered the mansion. O'Boyle took in the situation quickly and turned to the Hardys.

"All right. Let's have it."

Frank told him everything that had happened—except for Auerbach's part and the attack by Galinova. Nadia would be terrified if she thought the police knew about her.

"Why didn't you call me before you came up here?" O'Boyle demanded sternly.

Frank shook his head. "Maybe we were wrong. I didn't expect Ritt to go for a gun."

"It was *his* idea," said Junior, his face red with fear and anger. "All his doing."

"Son!" exclaimed Ritt, obviously hurt.

"That Biodane stuff—the rest of it is hidden in the basement."

"You're willing to testify against your father?" asked Ericsson.

"Yes, sir." Junior met Ericsson's gaze. "I'm no murderer. He belongs in jail."

As Ericsson handcuffed the two Ritts and herded them out to the police car, O'Boyle paused to say goodbye to the Hardys. "Call me if you find anything. And watch out for yourselves. If you got killed around here it would be a definite black mark on my record."

The brothers smiled wanly, and O'Boyle followed the others out.

As Frank and Joe returned to their car, Joe said, "That felt good, but why do I get the feeling we were only dealing with small fry here?"

Frank nodded. "The way I see it, George Ritt thought he was masterminding a plot to eliminate the competition for his son. But what was really happening was that Auerbach was manipulating him to help destroy Frosty's reputation."

"Right." Joe climbed into the passenger seat. "Auerbach wanted revenge for getting passed over at Frosty."

"And to make his reputation at SuperJuice by stealing the world's best players," Frank added.

"Yeah. Ritt was his most powerful tool for doing that. But he probably had others."

"Bingo." Frank started the car's engine. "See if you can guess who."

It took about two seconds for Joe to come up with the name. "Ken Chaplin, isn't it?" he demanded.

Frank nodded. "And I think his assistant, Vern, must be in on it, too."

"Shouldn't we tell the police?" Joe wanted to know.

"We don't have any proof, but later I think we might be able to come up with it."

"So what do you figure? Junior chased us down the highway in the four-by-four? With his money he'd have access to any truck he wanted," Joe said.

"The anonymous notes and phone calls we can chalk up to Auerbach's warming up while he figured out how to wreck the tournament. But then there were all those complicated bits of action."

"Right," said Joe. "Like the exploding volleyball."

"And the bomb in our car. And the wire cable pulling the anchor loose at just the right time. I was watching Chaplin and Vern film an interview when it hit me—all those pranks were like movie special effects. And when we searched their trailer, I found everything they'd need to coat exploding volleyballs and install timed explosives."

"I guess they complained about their own equipment being vandalized to throw people off the track."

"And to give them an excuse to add a security system to their trailer. It was really installed to keep people from finding their bomb-making equipment."

"Do you think they attacked Tammy?" Joe asked him.

Frank looked grim. "I don't know yet. But if they did, not only are they more dangerous than I thought, but you and I owe them one."

"I still think we should just turn them all over to the cops," Joe said when he and Frank were dressing to go to dinner at Tammy's house. "Why let them run loose?"

"I don't want them spilling the beans about Nadia's situation with her sister, just yet," Frank reminded him. "It'd be the first thing Auerbach would do, just to make them suffer, too."

"Frank, Nadia tried to stab you, remember?"

Frank bent to tie his shoes. "She was lied to and put under a lot of pressure," he insisted. "She'll have to confess the whole story about her sister eventually. But maybe they'll go easier on her if she helps bring in Auerbach."

"So that's your plan. But what if Ritt tells about Auerbach?"

"I think Mr. George Ritt, Sr., is afraid of Auerbach, and Junior may not know," Frank answered.

"So let me get this straight—you're going to talk Nadia into reporting Auerbach personally?"

"Why not? Then she can testify against him and Ritt. She didn't do anything really wrong concerning her sister, anyway. They'll probably give her a break."

"You think she'll trust us enough to contact the police if we tell her to?"

Frank shrugged. "It's worth a try. I'll call her tonight, after we get back from dinner and before we go back to the film trailer for our proof. That way," he added with a mischievous gleam in his eye, "I'll be able to tell her the girls are safe and at home, too."

Frank started to steer the car out of the hotel parking lot when he glanced in his rearview mirror. What he saw made his hands turn to ice on the steering wheel.

"Uh-oh," Frank said in a low voice.

"What?" Joe said. "Did you forget your—"

Joe's words froze in his throat. As he'd turned toward Frank, a movement in the backseat had caught his eye. He turned to see two figures kneeling on the floor behind them. One had a sawed-off shotgun pressed into the nape of Frank's neck.

"Look straight ahead and keep quiet," said the man holding the gun.

Joe felt something cold and metallic against his own neck.

"Remember, we can kill you both in an instant, so behave."

It was the voice of Ken Chaplin.

Chapter

17

"WELL, WELL," said Frank, eyeing the two men in the mirror. "You *are* in this, too, Vern. I wasn't sure."

"Zip your lip and drive," ordered Chaplin. "Turn left here."

"I guess they *did* try to kidnap Tammy," Joe said to his brother, facing front. "We were wondering about that," he added to their captors.

"We just wanted to scare her." Vern was being drawn into the conversation, as the Hardys had intended. "She wouldn't cooperate, though. That was a problem. That girl has a mean kick."

"Shut up, Vern." Chaplin nudged the shotgun a little deeper into Frank's neck. But Chaplin couldn't seem to resist taunting the Hardys himself.

"We've been onto you for a while now," he bragged. "Ever since you seemed so interested in that volleyball we rigged for Chris. I don't know what kind of snoops you are, but you sure aren't professionals. We saw you coming out of our trailer this afternoon from fifty yards away."

"It was unbelievable," Vern crowed. "There we were, lugging all our equipment back when we looked up and saw you guys locking our door."

They were driving north, with the sun low over the horizon on their left. Traffic was light, and Joe had little hope that the occupants of other cars would see the guns and notify the police.

"Why did you do it?" he heard Frank ask. "Just for money?"

Chaplin laughed derisively. " 'Just for money?' " he mimicked. "You make it sound like nothing. Try living without it for years. You'll come to realize it's the only thing that's important. Vern here has always known that, but I had to learn."

"Yep." Vern cackled, making the cold barrel of his gun tickle the back of Joe's neck. "We may not like that George Ritt much, but he pays well. And Auerbach—he's got brains."

"Slow down," Chaplin said abruptly. "You'll see a driveway on the left. Turn into it, and drive toward the water."

The driveway led past a series of old parking lots occasionally used by beach visitors during the day. The pavement was cracked and full of potholes. Grass and weeds sprung up out of the asphalt of the parking lots.

In the lot nearest the beach, a single car was waiting. Joe eyed it apprehensively. It was a red sports car—like the one he'd seen Auerbach drive. Joe could see someone in the driver's seat as Chaplin ordered Frank to pull up next to the car.

"Turn off the engine," Chaplin ordered next. "Leave the key in the ignition."

Frank did as he was told. Joe peered toward the ocean, squinting into the sun, which hung just at the horizon. He made out a small building at the edge of the water. It was faded and weather-beaten—clearly long unused. Behind the building a run-down pier jutted into the Pacific. Some of its pilings tilted at odd angles, and much of the planking was broken.

Vern got out and covered Frank and Joe with his sawed-off shotgun.

"Out," he said. "Take it real easy."

As the Hardys got out of their car, Todd Auerbach got out of the other one with a canvas athletic bag.

Joe stared at the man who had masterminded so much trouble. Auerbach was calm and looked as if he were going for a swim instead of planning to murder two teenagers. He greeted the Hardys. "Let's walk."

The beach was deserted as they walked toward the old pier. Auerbach led the way. Chaplin and Vern, guns in hand, brought up the rear.

"So is SuperJuice worth it?" Joe couldn't resist asking as they crossed the sand.

Auerbach gave a sharp bark of laughter. "SuperJuice is worth nothing," he replied. "I, on the other hand, am worth more every day because of my brilliant coup over Hi-Kick soda."

"You won't get away with it," Frank informed him. "You know Ritt's already under arrest. He'll eventually tell the police about you if it will lighten his sentence."

"He'll have to," Joe added. "They're going to charge him with murder."

"He'll get off," Auerbach said smoothly.

"How do you figure that?" Frank asked.

"Because he didn't commit murder," Auerbach replied, amused. "If anyone did, it was me."

Joe took a quick step toward Auerbach before Vern's shotgun was jammed against his lower back, reminding him to stay back. "What do you mean?" he said then in a low, carefully controlled voice.

"Simple." Auerbach seemed to be enjoying himself. "I was snooping around in the locker room before the match, checking to make sure Ritt hadn't bungled things again and forgotten to put the Biodane in the fruit, and I saw that

Osteen hadn't eaten any of it. I put two and two together and figured he was holding back because of Hi-Kick's high sugar content."

"So?" Joe prodded.

"So I switched the contents of the cooler," Auerbach bragged. "I convinced a ballboy that a cooler full of SuperJuice, which contains no sugar, would be much better for the athletes than that gooey stuff Prindle makes them drink."

Joe's step faltered as Auerbach stepped out onto the pier and he and Frank were herded after him. Osteen really had died of hypoglycemic shock! But it was deliberately induced—not an accident!

"Fortunately, I'll never be caught for that one," Auerbach continued. "I've given Ken and Vern here very large bankrolls and two one-way tickets to faraway places. You boys will soon be out of the way. Ritt has no idea how Osteen really died. And I'll eventually take over SuperJuice myself, just for the fun of running Frosty out of business."

"Vern, Ken," Joe heard Frank say sharply. "You haven't done anything too serious yet. If you kill us, it's Murder One. Nowhere you can go is far enough to hide from a charge like that."

Vern handed his shotgun to Auerbach, went to Frank, and threw a roundhouse right to his jaw. Frank dropped to his knees. Joe moved toward his brother but stopped as two guns

141

swung toward his head. Frank struggled to his feet.

"I've been wanting to do that," growled Vern, taking the shotgun back from Auerbach. "Keep mouthing off and I'll do it again."

Auerbach unzipped his canvas bag and took out two coiled lengths of rope. He gave them to Vern.

"You have to get wet," he said to the boys. "But it *is* summer."

Chaplin and Elliott forced the brothers at gunpoint into the water, next to the pilings of the old pier.

"This is far enough, I think," Chaplin said.

The water was two feet deep. Vern walked to a piling and gestured to Joe with his gun barrel. "Get over here," he ordered.

When Joe did so, Vern said, "Sit."

Joe hesitated, but Vern cocked the hammer on his gun, and Joe sat, feeling the water soak him up to his chest. While Vern held his gun on them, Chaplin tied Joe's outstretched hands to the piling in front of him.

"Your turn," Vern said to Frank.

As Chaplin tied Frank in the same way to the next piling, he said, "You'd better figure out how to hold your breath for six hours or so, because the tide is coming in and you'll be under water soon. We'll be back to pick up your bodies in the morning. And don't worry—we'll tell your parents you had a great time swimming before you drowned."

"Let's go." Auerbach walked away, followed by the other two. None of them looked back.

Already Joe felt the level of the water begin to climb higher. The bigger waves washed over his shoulders. Joe looked at his brother, wondering how long it would be before he could no longer see Frank's head.

Chapter

18

JOE TWISTED HIS HEAD around and saw the cars drive away. He tried moving his arms, but the rope was strong, and the knots were solid. He flexed his hands to keep the circulation going.

"Frank? How are you doing?"

"Okay," he answered over the sound of the waves. "Think there's any chance we can get to our feet?"

"No way," Joe said. "The rope is too tight. It won't slide up the piling."

Joe had a sudden flash of panic as the water crept higher. There must be a way out of this, he told himself. There's got to be.

He tried to rotate his body, hoping the friction of the rope against the rough piling might weaken it. Suddenly a stabbing pain shot through his forearm. He gasped.

"What's the matter?" called Frank.

"I just got jabbed by something—like a splinter. Wait a second."

Joe twisted until his forearm came in contact with the sharp point again.

"I think it's some kind of staple, with one end sticking out of the piling. I'm going to try to get the sharp end into the knot and loosen it."

"I'm with you," called Frank.

Working carefully so as not to snap off the point, Joe struggled to move his arms until the knot was positioned over the piece of jagged metal. It was slow, frustrating work, and the water was continuing to rise.

"Frank! I think I've started it—"

"All right!" Frank exclaimed. A high wave broke over him and drenched his head.

The water had reached Joe's chin when he felt the knot loosen enough for him to work his hands free.

"I've got it!" he yelled. "One more minute—"

"A minute is all we've got," Frank sputtered, spitting out a mouthful of the Pacific.

Thirty seconds later Joe ripped himself free of the binding rope. "We're safe!" he whooped, leaping through the water to untie Frank. He got the rope undone just as Frank's mouth was completely submerged. With Joe's help Frank stood, gasping and choking.

"Let's get out of here," Frank croaked, stumbling toward shore. "Somehow I'm not in the mood for a swim."

Soaked, the Hardys staggered up the beach

145

toward the road. There they tried to flag down a passing car. The first few whizzed by. Then an old station wagon slowed and pulled over. Frank laughed as he recognized the surfers with their boards on the roof rack.

"You dudes again!" said the guy in the passenger's seat, hanging out the window. "What is it this time, you've been taking an evening dip?"

"It'd take too long to explain," Joe said through chattering teeth. "Can you drive us south a few miles?"

"Absolutely," the driver replied. "There are towels in the back."

Frank told the driver they were headed for the South Coast Surf Club, and he offered to drop them off right in front. As they neared the club, Frank leaned forward and said, "You can let us off just past the parking lot."

As they passed the lot, Joe and Frank peered out the window at the early evening.

"There's Auerbach's car and ours, over by Chaplin's trailer," Joe said.

The driver pulled off the road and the Hardys climbed out. "Take it easy, now," the driver's friend said. "And, hey, get out of those wet clothes."

"If you'd like to help a little more—"

"Let's have it, man," said the driver. "Our schedule is totally clear."

"Go to the nearest phone and call the Laguna Beach police. Tell Detective O'Boyle to meet

Frank and Joe at the Surf Club right away. And to bring friends. Got it?"

"Got it," said the driver. "Take it easy."

The old wagon took off.

"Let's go," Joe said to his brother.

The Hardys ran to the edge of the parking lot, and then jogged quietly toward Chaplin's trailer in the early gloom. As they neared it, they heard muffled voices—and Vern's sharp laugh.

Frank and Joe darted close to the trailer's metal wall, out of the occupants' line of sight if any of them looked out the window.

"Okay," Frank whispered. "Now we just hold on until—"

The trailer door opened. Vern Elliott came out, casually holding his shotgun with the barrel down. Frank, who was closer to the front steps, sprang up as Vern sensed a presence and spun around. Vern's eyes widened in shock.

"Hey! It's *them!*" he screamed. He tried to bring up the shotgun.

Frank leapt forward and hit Vern knee-high with his shoulder. The shotgun went off with a deafening roar as Frank's momentum carried him and Vern off the steps and onto the pavement. The gun hit the ground and Vern took a swing at Frank's head, which missed. He locked his legs around Frank's waist and began to squeeze.

Meanwhile, Joe had moved forward next to the door. When Ken Chaplin, pistol in hand, came into the doorway, Joe leapt up and hooked

147

a hand into the filmmaker's belt. He yanked him forward and out of the trailer, sending him sprawling to the ground.

Chaplin got to his knees and lunged for his dropped gun, but Joe was on him and hauled him upright. A short left hook connected with Chaplin's stomach, and he gasped and crumpled to the ground. Joe scooped up the weapon.

"Aaaaugh!" Frank shouted as Vern tried to squeeze his hands around his throat. Frank brought his own hands up hard and broke the hold. He landed a hard left jab to Vern's nose, followed by a looping right that caught him on the point of the chin. Vern collapsed into a limp heap.

As Joe was finishing Chaplin off, he saw Auerbach take off and jump into his car. The car fishtailed with a squeal of tires as it headed for the parking lot entrance.

But before it got there, three police cruisers blocked the path, sirens wailing and lights flashing. O'Boyle and Ericsson leapt out of one of the cars as Auerbach screeched to a halt in front of them.

As Frank and Joe walked toward them, Auerbach got out of his car with a smile on his face.

"Officers!" said Auerbach. "I can explain everything. These two criminals, Chaplin and his henchman, have tried to incriminate me in their plot, and I want to file a complaint—"

"He lies," said Nadia Galinova, getting out of a police car and causing Auerbach to stop in midsentence with his mouth open. "He tells nothing but lies. It is *he* who is the worst criminal. He made others do his evil work, but now I will tell everything, and he will go to jail."

Auerbach spread his hands wide and tried to smile, but the smile was shaky.

"Hey, now, come on! Who are you going to believe, here? She's not even an American—"

"I will become one," Nadia countered regally. "Frank has convinced me. It's time to stop hiding and living in the past."

Frank answered her grateful smile with a very astonished one of his own as he realized she had gathered the courage to approach the police on her own. "That's great!" he blurted out, turning to see if Joe realized what had happened.

But now that he knew Auerbach had been captured, Joe had other things on his mind.

"Quick," he muttered to Frank. "Is there a working phone in Chaplin's trailer?"

"Yeah," Frank answered. "Why?"

"I've got to call Chris and tell her to heat up dinner."

Two hours later Auerbach, Chaplin, and Elliott had been carted off to jail, and the Hardys had told O'Boyle the whole story. "Two dozen times," Joe told Chris over a delicious, if slightly lukewarm, dinner at Tammy's house.

"But what about Nadia?" Chris asked urgently. "Are they going to arrest her?"

"No way," said Frank, swallowing a mouthful

149

of steak. "O'Boyle said he'd help her through the process of getting her sister naturalized if she cooperates in the Auerbach case."

"I still can't believe you guys are detectives!" Tammy said, leaning back in her chair and grinning at them. "You look so—well, kind of *goofy* to solve mysteries for a living."

"Gee, thanks, Tammy," Frank said. "If it makes you feel better, we don't do it for a living yet. We're still in school, remember."

"Chris doesn't think I'm goofy looking, do you, Chris?" Joe demanded, grinning goofily at Tammy's partner.

Chris smiled at him across the table. Frank could see that Joe was going to have a hard time saying goodbye to Chris.

"No, Joe, I don't think you're goofy," she said solemnly. "Look—you've saved the volleyball tournament and helped Tammy fight off a couple of kidnappers and taken me out for a great date. There's just one thing not so great about you, in fact—"

Everyone at the table waited tensely for Chris's final judgment.

"Well?" Joe demanded. "What is it?"

"You still can't catch a volleyball to save your life."

As Joe tossed a blizzard of crumpled paper napkins at Chris, the table erupted in laughter.

OPEN SEASON

Chapter

1

"IF THIS IS A TRAIL," Joe Hardy said, stopping next to his brother, "I'm a grizzly bear. I can't see anything but snow."

Frank Hardy slipped his sunglasses up on top of his head. "It would be kind of hard to get around on cross-country skis *without* snow." He cast a glance at his brother. "And I don't think a bear would be caught dead in that electric blue body suit."

Joe looked at his tight-fitting, one-piece, insulated ski suit. "Hey, this is the cutting edge of ski technology and fashion. It's lightweight, gives me room to move—and it matches my baby blues."

Frank chuckled. "Right. And the neon yellow ski cap matches your hair. But I know what you mean about wanting everything to be as light as

1

possible," he said, shifting his shoulders. "These backpacks are heavy."

Frank's outfit consisted of a dark gray wool sweater and hat and loose-fitting, insulated black nylon ski pants. Underneath it all, he wore synthetic thermal underwear from neck to ankle. The dark colors would absorb the sun's heat better than light ones, but Joe's flashy suit would protect him from the cold just as well. Their choice of clothes simply reflected the difference in their personalities.

With his sunglasses pulled down, Joe scanned the mountain peaks in the distance, ready to kick off again. "We sure have come a long way from Bayport," he said. "It's hard to believe we were on the East Coast yesterday, and now we're in the middle of nowhere."

"I don't think the good citizens of Colorado consider the Rocky Mountains nowhere," Frank replied.

"What citizens?" Joe asked. "We're about eight miles from the nearest town and three miles from the trailhead where we left our rented car. We won't see another human being for the next three days."

"That's the whole point of this trip," Frank said. "No crowds, no noise, nothing between us and nature."

"Nothing except several layers of clothes," Joe pointed out.

"Sorry you came?" Frank asked.

Joe planted his pole behind him and turned to study the terrain. They were halfway down a gentle slope into a valley dotted with pine trees. The sky was the deepest blue Joe had ever seen. The clear air made all colors seem richer and purer, even the blanket of white snow. Every breath he took of the crisp mountain air made him feel more alive.

"Not a bit," he finally said.

Frank smiled, sensing what his brother was feeling.

Joe pushed off with his poles and got back into the kick-and-glide rhythm of cross-country skiing. "Come on!" he shouted with his typical impatient enthusiasm. "Let's see how many miles we can cover today!"

Frank aimed his skis into the twin grooves carved by his brother in front of him. Even though Frank, at eighteen, was a year older, it was usually easier to let Joe lead. In back-country skiing, a broad outline of a trail was mapped out, but each person was left to pick out a specific path over the steep, rolling terrain. This demanded a lot more from a skier than cruising along on well-worn, packed, and groomed paths. So Frank was content to let Joe do the hard work for a while.

Joe wasn't a machine, though, and Frank had no intention of letting him push himself until he collapsed from exhaustion. "Ease up a bit," he called out. "We're not in a hurry to get anywhere, and we're not used to this altitude. The air's a lot thinner here than back home. Just relax and enjoy the scenery. We've got a whole week of vacation left.''

"Yeah," Joe called back. "And that means Christmas break is half over. Eight short days from now we'll be cooped up in a classroom at Bayport High again. I want to see everything there is to see in this national forest before then."

Frank laughed. "In that case, we're doing it the wrong way. If you want to cover the entire Gunnison National Forest, you should have rented a plane."

They were soon on the other side of the small valley, and the trail sloped upward again, slowing Joe down a little. "These new waxless skis Dad gave us for Christmas are great," he said. "Plenty of grip when you need it going uphill, and they don't seem to cut down on the glide. I could keep up this pace all day."

"That's what *you* think," Frank said as they reached the top of the ridge. "Let's stop here for a short rest, anyway. We need to put some fuel into our systems."

"If you mean it's time to eat," Joe replied, "you could easily talk me into that." He didn't like to admit that he was a little tired but could easily confess to being hungry. Just about everything Joe did made him hungry. It wasn't a problem, though, because everything he ate seemed to turn to muscle. At just about six feet, Joe had

4

the body of a serious athlete. But the only thing Joe was ever really serious about for longer than a few days was detective work.

Their passion for solving crimes was one of the few traits the brothers shared and something they inherited from their father. Fenton Hardy was a former New York City detective and was now a successful, internationally known private investigator. Even though Frank and Joe were still in high school, they had cracked plenty of cases already.

Joe slipped out of his skis and jammed the tails into the deep snow so they stood upright. He joined his brother on a rock outcropping at the very crest of the ridge and dug a granola bar out of his backpack. As he munched, he studied the view. It surprised him. It had been a short, easy climb up from the valley, but on the other side, the ground dropped away sharply into a deep gorge.

"We *might* be able to ski down," Joe remarked with some doubt. "It'll be a little rough getting up the other side."

Frank's pack was leaning against a tree. He reached over, unzipped a side pocket, and took out a map of the national forest. "We don't have to worry about it," he said. "The trail follows the top of this ridge for a way."

Joe leaned over and peeked at the map. "Can you tell how high up we are from this thing?" he asked.

"Not exactly," Frank answered. "It's not a detailed terrain map. Some elevations are marked, so maybe I could make a fairly good guess."

"Never mind the guesswork," Joe said. "Where's that gizmo that tells you everything— except how to meet girls? The monocle or moniker—whatever you call it?"

"The monocular," Frank said, pulling a palm-size object out of his pack. It was a compact, lightweight telescope. It was also a lot more: a rangefinder, compass, clock, and altimeter. Frank held it up to his eye and pressed a button on the top. A digital display winked on at the bottom of the circular view of the magnified countryside. "If this thing is accurate, we're at about eighty-one hundred feet."

Joe let out a long, low whistle. "That's over a mile and a half straight up!"

"Well, yes and no," Frank said. "The altimeter measures elevation from sea level, but we didn't start out at the sea."

"Sure we did," Joe countered. "Bayport's at sea level."

Frank shot a look at his brother. "I mean *today,* from the trailhead where we left the car. We were at about seven thousand, seven hundred feet. So even though we've gone about three miles, we've covered only three hundred vertical feet."

"Let me take a look," Joe said.

"Don't believe me?" Frank asked.

6

"Sure I do," Joe replied. "Three hundred feet uphill in the snow on skis is pretty good, if you ask me. I just want to check out the view."

Frank handed the gadget to his brother, and Joe peered down into the gorge. He followed the winding path of what was probably a frozen stream.

"What are you looking for?" Frank asked after a few minutes.

"I don't know," Joe said, sounding slightly disappointed. "An elk or a deer or something. What's the point of being out in the wild if you don't see any wildlife?" Just then he caught a glimpse of movement in the distance.

"Hang on, there's something down there." He spotted it again. This time there was more than one "something" moving.

Joe handed the monocular back to Frank and pointed. "Remember what I said about not seeing another human being for the next three days? I was wrong."

Frank studied the scene through the telescopic lens. At first he didn't see anything but trees, snow, and rocks. Then he saw it: a bright orange shape moving slowly across an open patch of snow. Three more brightly colored shapes came into view moving up the gorge, and the glint of metal flashed in the midday sun. At least two of the figures were carrying rifles.

"Hunters," he concluded. "They're probably after bighorn sheep."

"Let's hope they don't mistake us for a couple of rams," Joe said.

Frank took another look at his brother's bright blue ski suit. "I don't think you have much to worry about."

Joe jumped to his feet. "Right, but let's put some distance between us and them, anyway." He eyed the subdued earth tones of his brother's outfit. "Maybe you should wear this," he added, holding out his neon yellow ski cap.

"Good idea," Frank said, trading hats with his brother. "This is almost as good as one of those orange safety vests."

The Hardys didn't see the hunters again and quickly forgot about them. It was a beautiful day, and they were surrounded by spectacular scenery. A few hours after they left the ridge, the trail led them into a narrow canyon. Frank was leading the way, for a change, when he stopped suddenly. Joe almost crashed into him.

"Time for another snack break?" Joe asked hopefully.

"Maybe," Frank replied slowly. "I guess it depends on who's doing the snacking."

Then Joe noticed what had stopped his brother cold. "Wow. Are those what I think they are?"

Frank nodded. "Mountain lion tracks. Judging from the size of the prints, it's a pretty big cat." He stooped down to take a closer look. "The edges are a bit blurred. They don't look too fresh. They might be from yesterday or even the day before. This canyon is pretty well sheltered from the wind."

"It's probably long gone," Joe said, scanning the immediate area. A mound of snow by the canyon wall caught his eye. "It looks like he left his calling card, though."

Frank followed to where his brother was pointing to something sticking out of the snow. It appeared to be a frozen animal hoof. "Well, there's that elk you wanted to see," he said grimly. "But I don't think there'll be much to look at now."

"Let's check it out, anyway," Joe said, already gliding toward the half-buried carcass. He wasn't really interested in a dead elk but was very curious about the habits of one of the last big predators still roaming free in North America.

"I don't think that's a good idea," Frank started to say.

Too late, Joe realized that his brother was right. A hissing growl made him freeze in his tracks. He lifted his head slowly and stared up into the snarling fangs of a cougar perched on the ledge above him. Its tan fur blended in perfectly with the surrounding rocks. The mountain lion was crouched low on the rock, every muscle taut, ready to spring.

Joe could see his own pale image in the cat's cold, yellow eyes. There was no compassion in those eyes—only the hunger of a deadly hunter.

Chapter

2

JOE KNEW IT WAS useless to try to make a run for it—the big cat could bring him down and tear him to pieces in seconds.

The cougar bared its fangs and snarled again. Joe slowly lowered one ski pole to the ground and clutched the other with both hands. The fiberglass shaft with the steel tip was his only weapon. Joe Hardy wouldn't go down without a fight.

Suddenly a sharp crack rang out. The cat shrieked and leapt high in the air. Joe ducked, thrusting the ski pole up and out in front of him. He braced for the impact of several hundred pounds of fur and teeth and claws.

It never came. The cougar didn't touch him. After it jumped straight up, it thumped right back down on the ledge, whirling around and swatting at its flank as if it had been stung by a bee.

Joe saw doubt and confusion in the big cat's eyes now. The cougar paced nervously across the ledge. Then, all of a sudden, its back legs buckled. It snapped its head around, surprised that half its body had decided to take a nap. Its front legs gave way next, and the cat slumped down on the rock. It gave one last, halfhearted hiss. Its eyes closed slowly, and the mighty predator forgot about having Joe for lunch.

Joe stood up warily, not sure what had happened. A camouflage-clad figure, gripping a high-powered rifle, dropped out of a nearby pine. "Nobody move!" a commanding voice ordered through a dark ski mask. The stranger who had just saved Joe's life stomped toward him, thrust the rifle at him, and gruffly said, "Here, hold this."

The ski mask came off—and the hunter shook out her long brown hair. "I've been sitting in that tree for eight hours, waiting for that cat to come back. Then you two come along and almost blow it."

Joe was too stunned to say anything. First, he was almost cougar chow. Now he was being scolded by an angry female hunter.

The woman gave him a sharp look. "What are you doing with that rifle? Don't point it at the ground. Keep it trained on the cat. If he starts to move, put another round into his flank." She

11

turned and started to trudge back toward her pine tree.

"Hey, wait a minute," Joe called. "I'm not going to kill that mountain lion for you!"

"You'd better not!" she shouted back. "I've spent the last decade trying to keep him alive!"

Frank wandered over for a closer look and nudged his brother. "Notice anything strange about that cougar?"

That was when Joe spotted the dart sticking in the cat's side and the thick black collar around its neck.

"She hit him with a tranquilizer dart," Frank said. "He's out cold, but when the drug wears off, he'll be fine."

Joe pointed at a short metal strand poking out of a boxy bulge in the cat's collar. "That looks like some kind of antenna."

"Very good," the woman remarked. "For a couple of smart guys, you sure do some dumb things."

Frank hadn't even heard her come up behind them. His attention had been focused on the mountain lion. "I'll admit that my brother doesn't always use the best judgment," he said evenly. "But why did you let him walk right into this situation? You could have warned us."

"The cat had just come back," she answered. "I didn't want to scare him off. I was hoping you'd ski right on by. I guess my judgment's not all that great sometimes, either. Sorry you got caught in the middle of my research." She stuck out her hand. "I'm K. D. Becker."

Frank and Joe both shook hands with her, Frank supplying the introductions.

Becker set down the red backpack that was slung over her shoulder. Frank noticed a two-foot-long, arrow-shaped antenna and a blue metal box lashed to the back of the pack. There was a signal meter set into the top of the box. A socket in the side held an electric cable that led to the antenna.

"I'll bet you knew that cat was coming long before he climbed down the canyon wall," Frank said, nodding toward the blue box. "There's a radio in the cougar's collar, right? You were tracking him with electronic equipment."

"I knew he was heading this way," Becker admitted, "but I didn't know how close he was. It's not a very sophisticated setup."

Joe stooped down to examine the radio telemetry gear. "How does it work?"

"It's a directional antenna," she explained. "You aim it around until you get a signal. Then you head off in that direction and hope you find something."

Frank nodded. "The higher the meter needle jumps, the closer you are."

Becker stared at Frank curiously. "You seem to know a lot about my business."

"Not really," Frank replied. "I don't even

know what your business is. I know something about electronics, that's all."

Frank studied the woman for a moment. She had a long, lean face that suggested a slim body under the bulky clothes. There were a few lines on her face, mostly around her alert green eyes, which told Frank more about her outdoor life than about her age. If he had to guess, he'd say she was in her early thirties, even though she looked younger.

"What did you mean when you said you spent the last decade trying to keep that mountain lion alive?"

"Not just that one," Becker said. "All the cougars in these mountains. The world's closing in on them. We keep carving up the wilderness for towns and resorts. Whatever's left we turn into cattle ranches and mines. A single mountain lion needs thirty or forty square miles for a hunting range. We're running out of space, and the big cats are going to be the losers."

Joe glanced over at the dead elk. "I don't think the other animals would share your concern."

"Mountain lions keep herds healthy," Becker replied. "They hunt the old and the sick, like this one. The cat made the kill about two days ago. He ate all he could and then covered up the rest for later. I knew he'd be back, so I just sat in the tree and waited."

Joe raised his head to eye the slumbering pred-

14

ator. "Now that you've got him, what are you going to do with him?"

"Give him a quick checkup and change the battery in his collar."

"How long do the batteries last?" Frank asked.

"They're *supposed* to be good for at least a year," Becker answered. "Lately some of them have fizzled out after a few months. I've lost track of three cats in the last six weeks. I must have gotten a defective batch of batteries, so I'm trying to replace them all.

"I should be in Washington right now," she continued, "pestering senators and convincing the Fish and Wildlife Service to extend my research grant, but I decided that this is more important."

She walked over to the canyon wall. "It's also fairly important to do it *before* he wakes up." She glanced back at the Hardys. "Could you help me get him down? It'll be a lot easier for me to do my work on the ground."

"No problem," Joe volunteered.

The lip of the ledge was just out of reach. Frank gave Joe a boost, and Joe scrambled up to the cat. Following Becker's instructions, they managed to grapple the cougar down. It was a lot harder than Joe had expected.

"This overgrown kitten must weigh close to two hundred pounds," he groaned as they carefully set the big cat on the ground.

"He tipped the scale at one hundred seventy-nine back in September," Becker said. "He's the biggest cat I've collared." She crouched down, pushed up the cougar's lip, and looked at its teeth.

"How many cats are you tracking?" Frank asked.

"Listen," she replied as she pulled a stethoscope out of her pack, "I love to talk about my work, *except* when I'm working. I also don't want to have to worry about you when my furry friend wakes up. That'll be in about thirty minutes."

She paused. "I'm grateful for your help, but I'd feel a lot better if you were away from here when he wakes up."

"Sounds good to me," Joe said. He wasn't eager for a rematch with the cat. "Will you be okay?"

Becker chuckled. "I've had a lot of practice. I can manage."

With some reluctance, Frank and Joe left K. D. Becker in the canyon with the mountain lion. They skied for an hour and a half more, until dark storm clouds started to push toward them over the mountain peaks in the north. Frank picked out a campsite halfway up a gently sloping hill, where they would be sheltered from the rising wind. They pitched their lightweight dome tent, made a simple dinner on a tiny butane

stove, and jumped into their sleeping bags soon
after the sun set.

After all the fresh air and exercise, they were
soon asleep. Joe was startled awake several
times during the night by howling winds buf-
feting the thin tent walls. At least, he *hoped* it
was the wind.

By dawn the tent was half-buried in new snow.
It wasn't a problem—in fact, it helped insulate the
tent, making it warmer inside. The Hardys ate a
breakfast of high-protein granola bars while they
waited out the storm. The snow let up once for
about fifteen minutes at 9:05, but the sun didn't
really come out until a little before ten.

"So where does the trail go from here?" Joe
asked as they rolled up the tent.

Frank checked out the trees, their branches
sagging under the weight of the new snow. "I
think it's time to head back."

Joe stared at him. "What do you mean? We've
got enough food and supplies for five days."

"This is avalanche country," Frank explained.
"There has been a lot of snow recently, and that
big storm last night didn't help the situation. If
we keep going, we might get in over our heads—
literally."

Joe shrugged his shoulders. "It's your call.
This whole trip was your idea, anyway. If we
hurry, maybe we can catch a movie tonight. If
they have a movie theater in that one-horse

town." He paused for a second. "What was it called? Elk Grove?"

"Elk Springs," Frank said.

Joe smiled. "Yeah, that's it. Let's find out if there's anything to do up here that doesn't involve fur and big teeth."

It was late morning when they found themselves back in the canyon where they had met K. D. Becker and the hungry mountain lion.

"Looks like she spent the night here," Frank observed, nodding toward a small mound of white. Peeking out from under the half-inch accumulation was K.D.'s red backpack, propped up against a pine tree.

Joe's ski scraped against something buried in the snow. He glanced down and caught a glimpse of bare metal. Curious, he stopped and prodded it. Brushing away the snow, he uncovered a six-inch-long cylinder with a tiny antenna attached. Joe was surprised by how heavy it was.

"Maybe she was looking for this," he said.

"I don't think she's looking for anything anymore," Frank said grimly. His eyes were fixed on something beyond the red backpack, on the far side of the pine tree. It was another splash of red, but this one was darker and round. Under the blood-soaked patch of snow, deathly still, lay K. D. Becker.

Chapter

3

FRANK AND JOE rushed over to the motionless body. K.D. was flat on her back, her face to the side. A blanket of white covered her except for her chest, which was blood red.

Frank took off his skis and knelt down beside the woman. He put two fingers against the side of her neck and felt a weak pulse. "She's still alive," he told Joe. "If we can get her to a hospital, she may have a chance."

"We should never have left her alone with that cat," Joe said bitterly.

Frank probed the woman's chest gently, feeling for the wound. What he found stunned him. "No mountain lion did this, unless they've got secrets even Becker doesn't know about."

"What do you mean?" Joe asked.

Frank raised his eyes to his brother's. "She's been shot."

"Shot?" Joe echoed. "Why would anyone shoot her?"

"We'll worry about that later," Frank said. "Right now we've got to rig something to carry her on."

"Do you think it's a good idea to move her?" Joe asked, remembering his first-aid training.

"We don't have a choice," Frank replied.

"I could stay with her while you go for help," Joe suggested.

Frank shook his head. "That's three trips instead of one. I'd have to go all the way to Elk Springs to get a doctor or a paramedic, bring the person back here, and then we'd still have to get Becker to a hospital. I don't think she'd last that long, even if the return trips were by chopper.

"But we are in luck," Frank continued. "She got here the same way we did—on cross-country skis."

Joe gave him a blank look. "So what? I don't think she can ski her way out of this."

"Maybe she can," Frank responded while bandaging her wound. "With a little help from us. We can improvise a rescue toboggan from her skis and poles. We'll lash tree branches to the skis across the tips, tails, and bindings to keep the skis about two feet apart. Then we'll lash her poles diagonally to make the whole frame rigid and stronger. To protect her we'll pad the sled with pine boughs and wrap her in her sleeping bag and tent.''

"There's just one problem—we have only one rope," Joe said.

"We'll tie it to the skis through the little holes in the tips and drag the sled behind us. For the lashings we'll use any drawstrings in our clothes or packs.''

"All right. Let's do it," Joe quickly agreed. He peeled off his ski gloves and stuffed them in his pockets. His hand touched cold metal and came out holding the small cylinder he had found in the snow. "I think this is one of her transmitters," he said, showing the object to his brother.

"Stick it in her pack," Frank said, breaking branches off pines.

Working furiously, they rigged up a pretty stable ski-stretcher. Heading out of the canyon, dragging K.D. behind them, Frank and Joe were soon in a sweat from the long and frustrating haul.

It was afternoon when they finally reached the small, nearly deserted parking lot at the trailhead. They laid Becker in the backseat of their rented sedan, and Frank held her secure while Joe cajoled the car through the fresh layer of snow.

The five-mile trip to Elk Springs took almost an hour on the slippery mountain road. Joe managed to find a way around the worst of the snow-drifts, narrowly avoiding spinning out of control on an icy curve, and breathed a heavy sigh of relief when he saw a blue sign with a large white *H* on it.

"We're in luck," he said. "There's a hospital in this town."

Frank felt Becker's pulse—it was barely more than a flutter now. "We need a little more luck. We're not there yet."

Joe followed the blue signs to a county hospital that was newer and larger than he would have expected. The emergency room doctor took one look at Becker's chest wound and whisked her off to surgery.

The Hardys then had to tackle the questions posed by a stern admitting nurse. Who were they? When was Becker shot? How did it happen? Frank and Joe ran out of useful answers after the first one.

They spent the next hour in the waiting room until the surgeon came out and gave them the news. Becker was alive, but only barely. She was in a coma, and the doctor couldn't say when, or if, she'd come out of it.

"We've got to find the police station and report this," Frank said after the doctor had left.

"You don't have to," a burly man with a droopy mustache drawled. He had been sitting with them in the waiting room, but the Hardys hadn't paid much attention to him. There were streaks of gray in his mustache and hair, at least in the hair that wasn't covered by his Stetson. He was dressed like a rancher—bulky down vest, checked shirt, faded jeans, and work boots.

"Who are you?" Frank asked.

The man tipped back his hat and stood up casually. "I'm Bruce Stevens," he replied in a measured, friendly voice. He opened the vest, reached into his shirt pocket, and took out a thin leather case. He flipped it open with practiced ease. A gold badge glinted in the harsh, fluorescent light. "I'm the town sheriff. I was visiting a friend here when you boys came in with K.D."

"I guess you heard us say that somebody shot her," Frank said. "And I guess you've been sitting there, sizing us up before you identified yourself."

The sheriff offered a lazy smile. "After twenty years on the job, you learn a few tricks that cut through the preliminaries." There was a sparkle in the man's deep-set eyes that told Frank he was still sizing them up.

"I'm Frank Hardy, and this is my brother, Joe," said Frank. "We're here on vacation."

"So you boys found K.D., is that right?" Stevens continued after a brief pause.

"That's right," Joe answered. "You talk like you know her."

The sheriff chuckled softly. "Everybody around

here knows K.D. Her father was one of the biggest ranchers in the state.

"And now that I've answered your question, mind if I ask a few?"

"Fire away," Joe replied.

"What were you doing out in the mountains?"

"Skiing," Frank said simply.

"Where exactly?" the sheriff asked.

Frank got out his map and showed the sheriff where they had found K.D. and where they had been skiing.

The sheriff studied the two brothers silently for a minute. "You weren't doing a little hunting, maybe? You didn't maybe accidentally shoot her?"

Frank wasn't really surprised by the question. He knew that a good detective always looks for the simplest explanation first, and he suspected that Stevens was a fairly effective investigator, in his own way.

"No," he responded calmly. "We're not hunters. You can check our gear if you want. You won't find anything remotely connected to hunting."

Stevens shrugged. "I don't think that'll be necessary. You don't act like a couple of boys staring up out of a deep hole, trying to figure a way to squirm out." He stroked his mustache thoughtfully. "What time did you find her?"

"Assuming my watch is accurate," Frank said, "it was eleven-seventeen."

Joe was surprised. There was so much going on when they found Becker, it would never have occurred to him to check the time. Then he reminded himself that checking the time was the kind of thing that Frank would automatically do, even in a nuclear attack.

"That means you got there about a half hour after the shooting," the sheriff said.

Frank looked at him. "We figured she was shot this morning because she wasn't buried deep in snow, but how did you know the exact time?"

"She was wearing a watch," Stevens explained. "It stopped at ten forty-six. The face was smashed, so I figure it broke when she fell."

This information startled Frank. He had missed the watch completely. He called up a mental image of the crime scene. Becker had been wearing gloves, so the watch would have been covered, and he wouldn't have seen it. Still, something didn't quite fit.

Frank's thoughts were cut off when a tall man wearing a ski jacket burst into the waiting room. He stared briefly at the Hardys and then turned to the sheriff. "I came to find out about K.D.," he said. "How is she?"

Frank studied the newcomer. He had ice blue eyes and short, light brown hair. He had the wiry build of a marathon runner, and his deeply tanned face spoke of long hours in the winter sun and wind.

25

"She's not in very good shape," the sheriff said candidly. "At least she's alive, thanks to these boys here. Dick Oberman, say hello to Frank and Joe Hardy. Why don't you all get acquainted while I go check on a few details." He paused in the doorway and glanced back over his shoulder. "I'm sure you boys will still be here when I get back, right?" He left without waiting for a response.

Oberman gave the Hardys a puzzled look. "I don't understand. Were you working with K.D.?"

"We just happened to be in the neighborhood at the right time," Joe answered. "Are you her husband?"

That brought a slight smile to the man's strained features. "No. She's married to those mountain lions. But we've been friends a long time. I even spent a few summers helping her with her research."

"Can you think of anyone who might want to hurt her for any reason?" Frank asked.

Oberman's eyes widened. "You think somebody shot her deliberately?"

"I wouldn't rule it out," Frank replied. "What do you think?"

Oberman moved over to the window and gazed out at the mountains. "I guess it's possible," he said in a hesitant tone. "This is mostly a cattle town, and to a rancher a cougar is just a large pest that preys on his livestock. K.D. is trying to protect the cougars. Hunting them is already restricted to one cat per hunter during a limited winter season, but K.D. thinks that's too much. She's been working with an animal rights group in Washington to set up a protected reserve in the national forest. This has some of the local cattle barons pretty hot."

"Anybody in particular?" Frank asked.

"Well," Oberman said slowly, "the biggest rancher in the area is Walt Crawford, and he's had more than one run-in with K.D. She even tried to get him arrested once because she claimed his men were poaching cats out of season. She couldn't prove it, and nobody was ever arrested."

"Anybody else?" Frank pressed.

"Yes," Oberman answered after a slight pause. "There's Ted Gentry, a Native American who's trying to reclaim a big chunk of the national forest for the Ute tribe, including the area that K.D. and her group are fighting for."

Joe frowned. "Gentry doesn't sound like an Indian name."

"It's not," Oberman replied. "His mother was a full-blooded Ute, but his father was white, from one of the old cattle families."

"I should have guessed," Joe muttered. "Is there anybody around here who isn't connected with cows?"

Oberman smiled. "They're cattle—not cows.

But I'm not connected with them in any way. I run a camping supply store here in town.''

"We could use some new gear,'' Frank said. "Maybe we'll come by your store, if we have time before we go home.''

"Oh, I don't think you'll be going home just yet,'' Sheriff Stevens commented from the doorway. The Hardys had no idea how long he had been standing there listening to their conversation.

"We've got some unfinished business,'' he added with a frown. There was certainly nothing friendly about the two stone-faced deputies standing behind him. Stevens nodded to Frank and Joe. "You boys had better come along with us.''

Chapter

4

"IF YOU'RE GOING to arrest us," Frank said in a steady voice, looking straight into the sheriff's eyes, "you'd better have some good evidence."

"Arrest you?" the sheriff responded, raising his bushy eyebrows. "Why would I do that? I just wanted you to know that I booked a room for you at the Tri-Star Motel, compliments of the city." He jerked his thumb over his shoulder at the two deputies. "Harlan here will drive you there, and Gary will bring your car over directly."

Frank knew that "directly" meant after a complete search. He also knew that Stevens would probably back off if the Hardys refused to play along, but he kept his mouth shut and indicated to Joe that he was to do the same. For the time being, it was best to stay on the sheriff's good side. It also wouldn't hurt to let Stevens think he had outwitted the teenage "boys."

Harlan, the taciturn deputy in the creaky leather jacket with a fleece lining, knocked on the Hardys' room door at exactly seven the next morning.

"Some vacation this turned out to be," Joe grumbled as the deputy drove them to an undisclosed destination.

It turned out to be a helipad, located just behind the hospital. There was a helicopter waiting, the rotor already slicing through the crisp morning air. Frank noted that the chopper didn't have any identifying markings. Inside were the pilot and Sheriff Stevens.

The Hardys wedged into the cramped backseat and covered their ears with headsets just like the ones the sheriff and pilot were wearing. The large, cupped headphones and the microphones made it possible to carry on a conversation over the thundering clatter of the whirling rotor blades.

"For a small town, you sure have a fancy hospital," Frank commented.

"The hospital serves the whole county," Stevens explained. "The landing pad is for ambulance choppers. This bird is just a loaner, compliments of a friend."

"So where are we going?" Joe asked.

"Do you really need to ask?" The sheriff's voice sounded loud in his ears.

Joe shrugged to himself. The sheriff was right. He did know the itinerary for this trip.

The route that had taken the Hardys hours took only a few minutes by helicopter. Stevens motioned the pilot to land a healthy distance from the site of the shooting. They walked up to the site, following the ruts carved by the Hardys' skis the previous day.

The sheriff made a quick tour of the area, stooping down every now and then to take closer looks. When he got to the bloodstained spot near the pine tree, he stopped and did a slow, complete turn, scanning the canyon from all sides. "This is where you found her, right?"

"That's right," Joe said.

The sheriff tipped back his hat and scratched his head. "Well, I think we can safely say that nobody strolled up and shot her at point-blank range."

"What makes you so sure of that?" Joe asked.

"Because there are only two sets of tracks," Frank answered. "The ones you and I made yesterday."

"It was probably a stray bullet from some hunter who didn't know he'd hit anything," Stevens said.

"I don't think so," Frank responded.

The sheriff raised his eyebrows. "Why not?"

"You already know why," Frank said bluntly. "Since there aren't any tracks down here, the shooter must have been somewhere up along the canyon wall. He would have had a clear view of the area after the snowstorm." There was something about what he'd just said that didn't ring true to Frank, but he couldn't bring it to the front of his mind.

"It was an accident," Stevens said. "Because right now I don't have a better explanation." He looked at the Hardys. "You boys are free to leave town whenever you want."

"We'll think about it," Joe said.

They spent a few more minutes going over the site. Frank could tell that the sheriff wasn't putting a lot of effort into the search. His mind was already made up.

The morning was still young when the Hardys found themselves back at their motel. Frank had a theory about why the sheriff was reluctant to give the case a lot of attention. "The rancher that Dick Oberman told us about—Walt Crawford—probably has a lot of influence around here," he ventured.

"So even if Stevens did suspect him," Joe said, picking up his brother's idea, "he just might not investigate fully."

"Something like that," Frank agreed. "But I do think he'd go after Crawford with everything he's got if he thought he could make the case stick.''

A wide grin spread across Joe's face. "Looks like it's time to trade in our skis for spurs and go round up some 'cows' for questioning.''

Crawford's ranch wasn't hard to find. In fact, it probably would have been difficult to find anybody in Elk Springs who *didn't* know how to get to the two-thousand-acre spread called the Lazy W.

It wasn't an exact duplicate of the Old West ranch that Joe had conjured up in his head. The sprawling log house, barn, and bunkhouse inside the main gate fit the image perfectly, but the snowmobiles and all-terrain vehicles brought the picture squarely into the late twentieth century.

The guard at the gate looked like a cowboy with his Stetson and blue jeans. The only difference was that the belt strapped around his waist held a walkie-talkie instead of a six-shooter. Frank drove past the gate without stopping.

"Correct me if I'm wrong," Joe said, "but didn't we just pass the place we're looking for?''

"I'm always happy to correct you when you're wrong," Frank replied amiably. "Sometimes it's a full-time job." He steered the rented sedan around a few turns and glanced in the rearview mirror before pulling over to the side of the road in a wooded area. "Did you think we'd

33

just drive up to the front door and then be invited in?"

Joe zipped up his parka, yanked his ski cap down over his ears, and stuffed his hands in his thick gloves. "I thought it was worth a shot," he grumbled as he opened the door to an icy blast of wind.

They hopped over a low barbed-wire fence, which was built to keep cows in and not people out, and then trudged through the woods toward the house. Joe could feel the cold seeping in through his several layers of clothes as they stalked up to the bunkhouse at the edge of the clearing.

"What are we looking for?" he asked, stomping his feet while Frank carefully studied the layout of the small complex of buildings.

"I don't know," Frank admitted with a casual shrug. "I thought we should take a look around. If we don't find anything, we'll go see Mr. Crawford and just ask him if he's shot any wildlife researchers lately."

"Okay," Joe muttered, watching the plumes of his breath crystallize into tiny weather systems. "I get the point."

Two ranch hands came out of the bunkhouse and walked over to one of the snowmobiles parked nearby. They were both carrying rifles. Frank and Joe quickly ducked behind a thick tree trunk in the shade of the forest.

"I hope we get lucky today," one of the men said. "I sure could use the extra cash."

"I know what you mean," the other one said as he fitted his rifle into a leather case strapped to the vehicle. He swung a leg over the side, settled into the seat, and slid the key into the ignition in a single, easy motion. "If Mr. Crawford paid the bounty by the pound instead of by the head," he shouted as he revved the engine, "the tracks I spotted this morning could lead us to a small fortune. Those paw prints were made by one big old cougar."

Frank and Joe were both remembering what Dick Oberman had told them about the strict controls on hunting mountain lions.

"If Crawford is paying his men a bounty to kill cougars . . ." Frank began.

"And if K. D. Becker caught them in the act—" Joe continued.

The end of the sentence was abruptly cut off by a high-pitched drone from the woods behind them. Frank and Joe spun around as the steady noise grew louder. They had no place to hide.

They didn't even see the snowmobile until it was almost on top of them. "Whoa!" the driver cried out, skidding to a halt as the Hardys dove off to the side. "I almost turned you boys into a hood orna—"

He cut himself off, whipped off his mirrored sunglasses, and squinted at the Hardys suspiciously. "I don't believe I know you young fellas," he said sternly. "What are you doing around here?"

"We're with the federal safety bureau," Joe said, stomping boldy toward the snowmobile. "Why doesn't this vehicle have a seat belt?"

The man's eyes narrowed. "Hey, boys!" he called out sharply. "Get out here and give me a hand! Looks like we caught us a couple of tres-pass—"

The man interrupted himself by jumping off the snowmobile and lunging for Joe. Meaty hands were around Joe's neck in an instant. Joe reacted instinctively and dropped to his knees. The man loosened his grip and Joe squirmed away.

Frank moved without thinking and jumped on the snowmobile, grabbed the controls, and gunned the throttle. "Come on!" he shouted. "Let's get out of here!"

Joe hopped on behind his brother. The snow-mobile lurched forward as the studded treads churned through the snow and spewed out a coarse spray that showered the stunned ranch hand.

The only thing wrong with the escape, Frank realized as they shot out into the open, was that they were headed the wrong way. He spun the snowmobile around, just as a bunch of men poured out of the bunkhouse to find out what the ruckus was all about.

"What's going on here?" Frank heard someone yell. "Stop those boys!"

"Hang on!" Frank shouted, jerking the handlebars and swerving off across an open field, almost losing his brother in the process.

Joe tightened his grip as the snowmobile flew over a small hillock, airborne for a brief moment before it slammed back to earth with a jarring thud. Under better circumstances, he tried to convince himself, this might actually be fun.

His exercise in positive thinking was cut short when the snowmobile twisted violently and jolted to an abrupt stop. Joe lost his grip and pitched off headfirst into the snow.

Frank leapt off the snowmobile and yanked his brother to his feet. "Are you all right?"

Joe gave a shaky nod. "I think so. What happened?"

Frank pointed straight ahead, the way they had been aimed. "That's what happened."

Joe stared into the empty space. His eyes drifted downward, then bulged out in alarm. A few feet from where they had plowed to a stop, the world dropped away over a steep, bleak cliff.

Behind them they could hear the angry whine of snowmobiles and the coarse rumble of all-terrain vehicles. They were closing in for the kill.

Chapter

5

JOE SMILED WEAKLY at his brother. "I don't suppose you brought a very long rope ladder."

Frank moved forward and stared down into the harsh shadows of the deep canyon. "I don't think they make one long enough," he replied grimly.

Joe joined his brother at the edge and peered over. The constant wind howling down the canyon had blown the snow off the cliffside, exposing jagged, barren rocks. He took a deep breath and started moving forward before his brain had a chance to complain.

"Don't even think about doing it," Frank warned as Joe started to lower himself over the edge. "We have to be at least one hundred feet up."

"We have no choice," Joe said, grinning up at his brother as he slowly worked his way down. "This sort of thing is much easier if you don't think about it."

Frank debated—and quickly rejected—grabbing his brother and hauling him back up. One wrong move could get them both killed. "This is a bad idea," he said firmly.

"Probably," Joe admitted, probing the cracks for his next foothold and hoping he wouldn't find ice instead. "But it was the only one I had."

Roaring engines and harsh shouts signaled that Crawford's men would be arriving soon. Frank glanced over his shoulder and decided not to hang around to find out what they'd do if they caught him.

"Race you to the bottom," Joe called up when he saw his brother start to climb down after him.

"No way!" Frank shouted back. "You'd probably jump just to beat me!"

Nobody else took up the challenge, and soon the cowboys' derisive yells dwindled away, drowned out by the whistling winds. Joe moved slowly, selecting his footholds carefully. Although he was anxious to reach the bottom, he knew that one careless move on a patch of ice could lead to disaster. Halfway down, Joe resolved that he'd never take up rock climbing as a hobby. Near the bottom, he decided it wasn't really all that bad. By the time his feet hit

39

the deep snow on the ground, he had convinced himself that it might even be fun.

Any happy thoughts Frank might have had as he reached the bottom were blotted out by a dark shadow and a loud thrumming noise overhead. He glanced up and discovered what the underside of a helicopter looked like. It hovered for a moment before swinging away and landing on a flat stretch of ground a short distance from them.

Joe sighed. "Oh, well, at least we won't have to worry about how we're going to get out of here." He took a harder look at the unmarked helicopter. "Haven't we seen that bird somewhere before?"

Frank nodded. "That's the chopper we took this morning."

The helicopter just squatted there like some fat, ugly bug, the rotor blades spinning round in a hectic blur, whipping up whirlwinds of snow from the ground. The Hardys watched and waited as the door swung open. They waited some more. After a minute or so, they realized that no one was getting out. They were expected to go to the helicopter.

Frank raised his eyebrows, and Joe responded with a shrug. Side by side, they plodded over to the cold steel bird, heads low against the icy sting of the man-made wind.

Frank poked his head inside the cockpit. The pilot gave him a smug grin. "Can I give you boys a lift?'' he shouted over the clatter of the turbine engine.

"Do we have any choice?'' Frank responded. He was mildly surprised that the pilot was alone in the cockpit.

The pilot's grin widened. "Not really.'' He patted the empty seat next to him. "Come on. Don't be sore losers.''

Frank hadn't paid much attention to the pilot the last time. If he had, he might have noticed the sideways letter *W* that was stitched across the front of his visored cap, confirming what Frank had concluded the moment the chopper swooped down. "So this rig belongs to the Lazy W ranch,'' he said as he climbed in.

The man sitting at the controls nodded. "Yep. She's only a few weeks old. We haven't gotten around to branding her yet.''

Frank crawled into the backseat, and Joe strapped himself in next to the pilot. "Walt Crawford must be a very rich man,'' he said bluntly as the helicopter took off. "A private helicopter and a pilot to go with it can't be cheap.''

"You're right about the bird,'' the pilot answered. "But I don't charge Mr. Crawford a penny to fly it for him.''

Joe gave him a puzzled look. "Why not?''

The pilot responded with a chilly smile. "Because I *am* Walt Crawford.''

That put a lid on the conversation for the rest

of the short flight back to the ranch. Frank used the time to make a careful study of the rancher.

Crawford handled the helicopter with relaxed grace, probably reflecting years of practical experience. Frank guessed the clean-shaven, sharp-jawed pilot was around forty-five or fifty years old. A closer look revealed a hint of slack skin and wrinkles where his neck disappeared under his coat collar. Frank upped his age estimate to a healthy sixty.

They touched down on a patch of ground surrounded by a circular driveway that led to an expansive, two-story log house. A boxy, four-door jeep with fat, oversize tires rolled up the drive as the Hardys hopped out of the helicopter. The pair of blue emergency lights perched on the jeep's roof announced that this was not a casual visitor.

Sheriff Stevens burst out of the jeep, and he did not look like a happy man. "I was hoping you boys would be halfway to Denver by now," he said with a stern scowl.

"We get a special rate if we keep the car for a week," Joe quipped. "Our travel agent told us we'd have to pay a substantial penalty if we changed our airline reservations, so we decided to hang around for the rest of the week."

"You may be here a lot longer than that," the sheriff replied. "I hear you stole a snowmobile. That's grand theft. A conviction would get you an extended vacation at one of the state's finest penal resorts."

"Now, hold on Bruce," the rancher spoke up. "When I called you, I thought my men had cornered a couple of cattle rustlers. I didn't realize they were the same brave boys who saved Ms. Becker. I'm sure there's a reasonable explanation for their actions."

The sheriff glowered at the Hardys. "I'm eager to hear it."

Frank turned his steady gaze on Crawford. "I think it would be more interesting to hear your reasonable explanation for paying your men to hunt down mountain lions. I bet that's a felony, too." He glanced over at the sheriff. "Unless some people are above the law."

"Not in my jurisdiction," the sheriff replied flatly.

"I'm afraid there's been a simple misunderstanding," the rancher said smoothly to Bruce Stevens. "I told you about that old tomcat that's been preying on my herd. He got a heifer the day before yesterday, and just the scent of him makes the cattle skittish. Maybe next time he'll cause a stampede or go after one of the men."

The sheriff cut him off with a disgruntled sigh. "So you offered a bonus to any man who could take care of the problem, and the only way to do that is to kill the cat. We've been through this before, Walt. You know I don't like it."

Joe stared at the sheriff in disbelief. "You don't *like* it? That's *all?*"

"There's not much I can do," the sheriff answered. "There's no crime in shooting a cougar on private property if the cat is a threat to people and livestock."

"My men know," Crawford added, "that they're authorized to shoot only if the cat is on my land. Anyplace else is off limits. Those are my strict orders."

"But you have no way of knowing if they'll obey your orders," Frank countered. "They haul in a dead mountain lion, tell you they bagged it on the ranch, and you just take their word for it and pay them."

The rancher smiled thinly. "I trust my men, and I trust that you won't cause any more unwarranted trouble. I'm going to forget this whole trespassing and theft incident."

"That's fine with me," the sheriff responded. "It's a lot less paperwork if I don't have to arrest these boys. Come on, I'll give you two a lift back to your car," Stevens said.

Frank and Joe said their goodbyes and piled into the sheriff's car.

"Did you believe his story?" Joe demanded.

"More or less," the sheriff replied.

"What does that mean?"

"It means I think Crawford's men probably bend the rules a little sometimes, and he looks the other way."

"And what do you think would happen if somebody like K. D. Becker caught them in the act?" Frank prodded.

"I don't know," Stevens said. "And since she was shot roughly thirty-five miles away from the Lazy W Ranch, I'm not going to give it much thought."

"Maybe Crawford was offering a bonus on more than cougars," Joe suggested.

The sheriff shook his head slowly. "K. D. Becker is a nuisance to Walt Crawford, and that's about all. Her big campaign to save the cougars won't put much of a dent in his cattle ranching business.

"Besides," he continued patiently, "this isn't exactly the criminal underworld we're dealing with here. Walt Crawford is a respected rancher, and his men are basically honest, hardworking cowboys."

Frank wondered whether the sheriff was blind to Crawford, since the two were friends.

"And before you ask," Stevens added, "Walt Crawford was in Montana yesterday at a cattle auction. So unless he's a really good shot, I think we can safely assume that he didn't pull the trigger."

"Speaking of shots," Frank responded, "do you have any idea what kind of gun was used in the shooting?"

The sheriff nodded. "We're not sure of the exact caliber yet. Preliminary ballistics tests on the slug the doctor took out of K.D. indicate a high-power hunting rifle. Since the bullet didn't penetrate very deep—"

"It was probably shot from a long distance," Frank cut in, finishing the sentence. "Any closer, and she wouldn't be alive."

The sheriff stopped the jeep next to the Hardys' car. He turned his head and gave Frank a curious look. "You're just full of surprises, aren't you? Where'd you learn that stuff?"

"He just has a bright, inquisitive mind," Joe said offhandedly.

"I don't doubt it," the sheriff replied, his eyes still on Frank. "And does that bright mind find anything inconsistent with the theory of a simple hunting accident?"

"No," Frank readily admitted. "Are you checking out hunting parties that might have been in the area?"

"That's what they pay me for," the sheriff said with more than a hint of impatience. "I'm also working on some other leads."

"Like what?" Joe asked.

The two-way radio clamped to the dashboard squawked just then. "Ah, come in, Sheriff Stevens—do you copy? This is Alpha Tango One Niner—"

The sheriff grabbed the handset and thumbed the Talk button. "I don't need your license plate number, Harlan. What have you got for me? Did you find anything?"

"Ah, that's a roger," the radio crackled.

"Speak English," the sheriff snapped. "Did you find the rifle or not?"

"Yes, sir," the static-filled voice replied. "It was right where you told me to look."

"Okay," Stevens said. "Take it down to headquarters. I'll be there in a little while." He hung up the handset without waiting for a response.

"What was that all about?" Joe asked.

"Looks like your theory about somebody deliberately trying to kill K.D. may be right," the sheriff answered. "If this lead checks out, I'll have the culprit behind bars within twenty-four hours."

Chapter

6

"HOW DID YOU FIND the weapon?" Frank asked. "Did it just turn itself in?"

"Did you know," the sheriff replied in his relaxed drawl, "that most criminals are caught because someone they know turns them in?"

"So who shot Becker?" Joe responded. "And who turned him in?"

"The *alleged* perpetrator," the sheriff said carefully, "is a Native American activist named Ted Gentry. The name probably doesn't mean anything to you. I doubt if he's made headlines outside our immediate area."

"We know who he is," Frank said. "What makes you think he's your man?"

"I got an anonymous phone tip," Stevens explained. "The caller said he heard a shot and

48

saw Gentry leave the canyon where K.D. was found. Then he said he found a rifle stashed in Gentry's truck. Harlan picked up the rifle and says it was fired recently."

Frank frowned. "That doesn't make a lot of sense. Why would Gentry drive around with the rifle? You'd think he'd hide it."

"Maybe he did, sort of," the sheriff replied. "His cabin is off the beaten path, and no one plows his road, so Gentry stores his truck in a garage in town during the winter and gets around on skis and with help from his friends. He probably thought the rifle would be safe there."

"And maybe somebody set him up," Joe countered. "Doesn't just about everyone have a hunting rifle in Elk Springs? How do you know his is the right rifle? Maybe it's not even his rifle."

The sheriff grunted. "You boys don't give up, do you? What do you want me to do—arrest every single person in Elk Springs?"

"We just want to make sure you get the right man," Frank answered.

"Or woman," Joe added.

"I'll tell you what," the sheriff said coolly. "I'll track down the criminals, and you boys go do whatever it is teenagers do."

"So you haven't arrested Gentry yet?" Frank prodded.

"No," Stevens said. "But I plan to have a talk with him as soon as I ditch the two of you." He nodded out the window. "There's your car.

Get in it and go someplace—anyplace. I don't care where, just as long as you're out of my hair.''

The Hardys took the hint.

"So what do we do now?'' Joe asked as they sat in their car and watched the sheriff's jeep roll off down the road.

Frank started the engine. "We do exactly what the sheriff said.'' There was a glint in his eyes.

Joe smiled. "Right. We stay out of his hair, but we don't let him get out of sight.''

Frank was careful to keep distance between them and the jeep. As there was very little traffic, nothing but empty road separated the two vehicles.

"Boy, he sure wasn't kidding about Gentry living off the beaten path,'' Joe observed as they bumped along a twisting mountain road.

"He's got to know we're following him,'' Frank said pensively. "If he hasn't noticed us by now, his rearview mirror must have fallen off.''

"Do you think he's leading us on a wild-goose chase?'' Joe ventured.

Frank shook his head. "I doubt it. I don't think he'd waste that kind of time.''

The jeep disappeared around a sharp curve, but Frank wasn't worried. It would come back into view when the sedan poked around the bend. At least, that's what he assumed. But on the other side of the curve there was nothing but empty road. The jeep was gone.

Joe, eyes wide, jerked his head from side to side. "What happened? Where'd he go?"

Frank stopped the car, his eyes making a detailed sweep of both sides of the road. He twisted around and stared back toward the curve.

"I should have known," he muttered when he saw the new set of tire tracks in the snow snaking up a steep incline through a long, narrow clearing in the trees. "Sheriff Stevens told us Gentry lived off the beaten path—on an unplowed road."

"No wonder the sheriff wasn't worried about us following him," Joe said. "With four-wheel drive and huge snow tires, Stevens doesn't even need a road, plowed or not. But we wouldn't get ten feet up that path in this thing."

"Then we'll just have to leave the car here," Frank said simply.

Joe gaped at his brother. "You mean we're going to walk? We don't know how far it is to Gentry's cabin."

"We'll know when we get there," Frank replied. He got out of the car and patted the ski rack on the roof. "If you don't like walking, there are other ways to get around in the snow."

Joe wasn't sure which would be worse, slogging through knee-deep snow or sidestepping with long cross-country skis uphill. He took another look at the narrow path and convinced himself that the slope flattened out beyond the first bend. "Oh, well," he said as he helped his brother get out their gear. "We came here to ski, so let's do it."

They didn't get far before the jeep with police lights and big, fat, knobby tires came rumbling back down the trail and stopped a few inches from the tips of Joe's skis. The sheriff stuck his head out the window. His face held a mix of emotions, as if he couldn't decide whether to laugh at the persistent pair or lock them up.

"Beautiful scenery around here," Joe remarked nonchalantly. "Did you come up to see some natural wonder, like we did?"

The sheriff struggled to suppress a grin. "You boys sure have a lot of spunk," he said. "I'll give you that." He took off his cowboy hat and wiped his forehead with the back of his hand. "I hate to tell you that you're wasting your time, though. Mr. Gentry isn't at home today."

Joe pursed his lips in a pout. "Aw, shucks. No one there to buy our Boy Scout cookies?"

"Fun's fun," the sheriff responded, shifting into a serious tone, "but this is police business. Gentry may be armed and dangerous."

"All you have so far is a rifle that *might* belong to Gentry and *might* be the one used in the shooting," Frank pointed out. "That's not exactly what I'd call any kind of case against him."

"I've found it's always safest to assume the worst," the sheriff replied. He paused and scratched his thick mustache. "You'll live longer that way."

"You're probably right," Frank said in a subdued voice. He didn't want to start an argument after they'd managed to get the sheriff in a relatively good mood.

The sheriff eyed him warily. "I should escort you boys off this mountain." He glanced down at his watch. "But I don't have time. So you're on your own. Try to stay out of trouble.

"And stay clear of Gentry's place!" he shouted back out the window as he drove off.

Frank and Joe smiled cheerfully and waved goodbye vigorously. As soon as the jeep was out of sight, they continued up the trail.

As Joe had hoped, the steep grade soon tapered off. It was still mostly uphill, but by cutting diagonally back and forth across the rise, they made pretty good time. "This is like trying to run a marathon on your hands," Joe panted after about a half hour.

"I know," Frank huffed. "There's nothing quite like it to keep the old cardiovascular system in shape."

"Yeah, right," Joe grumbled. "There's nothing like giving yourself a heart attack now to prevent having one later."

THE HARDY BOYS CASEFILES

Frank stopped and turned to smile at Joe. "If you can't handle it, I can go on by myself. Just go back to the car and wait for me. It's all downhill from here."

Joe couldn't ignore the challenge. "I'm fine," he said with a forced grin. "I was just worried about you."

Soon they were both furiously stabbing the snow with their poles and racing straight up the trail in a silent duel. That was how they worked. They pushed each other to stretch their limits and then go a little further. Other people saw only a couple of teenagers. They didn't see the serious, dedicated detective team.

The trail left the woods, and the furrows in the snow meandered across a wide, flat meadow. Frank didn't need a compass to know what direction they were going. They were chasing the late-afternoon sun, already low in the western sky.

Too low, Frank told himself. He stopped and checked his watch. "Time for a break!" he called out as Joe shot ahead.

Joe glided to a halt and looked back over his shoulder. "What's the matter? Can't keep up with me?"

Frank shook his head. "I can't keep up with the sun, and neither can you. We've got to go back."

Joe shielded his eyes with a cupped hand and squinted ahead. "We can't stop now," he protested. "We've got to be close. It didn't take Sheriff Stevens that long to drive there and back. Gentry's cabin is probably right over that next rise."

"It'll still be there tomorrow," Frank replied. "After dark we could freeze to death out here without any protection."

Joe had to admit that his brother was right. Reluctantly, he swung around and followed Frank out of the meadow and back into the trees.

The shaded pine forest was dark compared to the glare off the stark white meadow. Joe shivered with a sudden chill. He tried to shake it off, but the effort made him dizzy. He staggered and groped for a nearby tree trunk. He leaned against it heavily and gulped air.

Frank came over and gently took hold of his arm to steady him. "Relax and take slow, deep breaths. You probably have a mild case of over-exertion. Remember this is thin mountain air. It can sneak up on you sometimes."

Joe nodded slowly. The woozy, spinning feeling gradually faded. He was feeling almost normal when he heard a rustling in the branches above him.

Frank heard it, too. He raised his head and caught a glimpse of movement.

"What is it?" Joe whispered hoarsely.

Frank put a finger to his lips and kept his eyes on the tree limbs overhead.

"I have a bad feeling about this," Joe muttered softly.

Frank stared intently, trying to see through the tangled network of branches and pine boughs. There was another faint rustling—then a branch creaked. Something was definitely moving around up there—something large. Suddenly a dark shape appeared over Frank's head in a blur of motion and hurtled straight down toward him.

Chapter

7

FRANK DOVE out of the path of the plummeting shape. As a muffled thud sounded behind him, Frank unfastened his skis and steeled himself, grimly prepared for the worst.

He wasn't prepared for what did happen next, though.

"Um—hi there," Joe ventured in a tentative voice. "I'm Joe Hardy. That guy sprawled in the snow over there is my brother, Frank."

Frank twisted around and saw the back of a figure clad in winter camouflage towering over his brother. A long, jet black ponytail hung down his back and stood out against the mottled streaks of brown, green, and white. An elaborately curved hunting bow with a steel cable drawstring was slung over one shoulder.

57

A serious face with keen, black eyes turned to scrutinize Frank. "This is private property," the man announced in a deep, resonant voice.

"Sorry," Frank said as he got up. "We didn't see any signs."

"I don't believe in them," the man said. "Barbed wire fences and ugly, hostile signs mar the beauty of the land. People should respect the rights of others without threats.

"No trespassing. Violators will be prosecuted," he intoned derisively. "Where was our fine legal system when the white man was violating Native American land?"

"You must be Ted Gentry," Frank responded, avoiding the question since he didn't have a good answer.

The man nodded. "Now that we've all been properly introduced, perhaps you could tell me what you're doing here."

"Looking for you," Joe replied.

"I seem to be a popular guy today," Gentry remarked. "First Sheriff Stevens, and now you."

"You saw the sheriff?" Joe asked.

Gentry gestured at the tread marks in the snow. "I didn't actually see him, but I do recognize the tracks." His dark eyes flicked between the two brothers. "I don't suppose you'd have any idea why the sheriff drove all the way up here to see me?"

Frank decided to gamble with the truth. "He

58

wanted to question you about the shooting of K. D. Becker."

Gentry focused his full attention on Frank. "I just heard about K.D. today—a friend let me know on the shortwave. But what makes Stevens think I know anything about it?"

"They found a rifle in your truck," Frank explained. "They think it might be the weapon used in the attack."

Gentry let out a short, bitter laugh. "Without my truck I'm restricted to skis, which I'm not great on. How could I have skied out to shoot K.D.—in a snowstorm—and then skied back to town to hide a rifle in my own truck? Why would I hide it there, anyway? Then I supposedly would have to ski all the way back here. You know how far out I live—I'd still be skiing. But who knows, maybe they'll uncover a signed confession before they get around to questioning me.

"By the way, what's your connection to all this?" Gentry asked.

Frank shrugged his shoulders and started to speak.

"Never mind," Gentry said. "I just figured out who you are. You must be the guys who found K.D. and got her to the hospital." Frank and Joe nodded. "Nice work. I hope she pulls through. She's doing such important research, and she's working for a good cause."

"You mean the wildlife refuge?" Frank responded. "We heard you had other plans for the same land."

"Our goals aren't that far apart," Gentry said. "The Utes and other tribes lived in harmony with nature for centuries—and we have a special respect for the cougars. We call them the spirit of the mountains."

"So you don't see her as a threat to your claims that the land should be returned to the Utes?" Frank probed.

Gentry sighed. "Just between you and me and the woodchucks, I stand a better chance of winning the state lottery than convincing the federal government to give back *anything* it stole from my people. And if we can't have our ancestral lands, I wouldn't mind seeing a piece of it saved for those magnificent beasts."

"Okay," Joe said. "So let's say you really didn't have motive or opportunity. What about the rifle in your truck? If ballistics tests indicate it fired the bullet, the sheriff's still going to ask you to do a lot of explaining. He'll figure someone could have driven you around."

Gentry looked at the sky. "It's getting dark," he said. "I'm ready for a warm fire and a hot dinner. You're welcome to join me, unless you have other plans."

"None that we can think of," Joe said with a smile.

* * *

Gentry's home, nestled in a grove of aspen trees, was a simple, one-story log house. Inside there was a single spacious room with a sleeping loft at one end and a massive stone fireplace at the other. Most of the furniture appeared to be hand carved.

Only three things spoiled the image of its being a rustic cabin: a fairly new refrigerator in one corner, a shortwave radio, and a personal computer perched on the end of a long worktable. "I didn't see any power lines," Joe noted. "Where does the electricity come from?"

"There's a generator powered by an ugly tank of liquid propane out back," Gentry explained, grabbing up an armload of logs from a stack outside. "It also supplies most of the heat. This beautiful old fireplace makes a lousy furnace. Most of the heat goes right up the chimney."

He took a match from the scarred oak mantel and lit the kindling in the grate. "Still, there's nothing like a blazing fire to keep you company when winds howl outside."

Joe warmed his hands by the growing flame. "I know what you mean."

Frank wandered over to the worktable. What had looked like a jumble of rocks and pebbles from the far side of the room resolved themselves into an assortment of small clay pottery shards and stone arrowheads. "Looks like somebody's doing some archaeological research."

"You might call it a hobby of mine," Gentry replied casually.

Frank's eyes moved to the computer. "Just a hobby?"

Gentry smiled. "Okay, you caught me. I'm an escaped college professor. The university became a little too stuffy for me, so I took a sabbatical to become politically active for my tribe."

Frank studied the tall man with the long black hair. 'I'd like to hear more about your politics."

Gentry shrugged his wide, muscular shoulders. "There's not much more to hear. I've been working with a group of tribal activists and lawyers for a few years now. We don't really expect to get our land back. We *do* have a real shot at a financial settlement, though. That would mean better schools, better hospitals, and maybe a chance at a better life for a lot of Native Americans."

"So the land is the focal point of your cause," Frank pointed out. "If Becker gets her wildlife refuge, you'd have a harder time getting public support to return the land to your people."

"I told you before that I'm sympathetic to Becker's cause. I'm also peace loving. Do you honestly think I'd attempt to kill one human being to help others?"

"But what about all these weapons?" Joe asked. He pointed out a rack that held three intricate hunting bows, similar to the one Gentry had been carrying when they met him. They were all compound bows—molded, curved fiberglass jobs with steel cable drawstrings looped around a pulley-like cam assembly at each end. Joe knew the design made them more powerful. It also made them much more deadly.

His eyes moved on. One end of the worktable contained an array of hand tools and a variety of half-finished, high-tech arrows. The coat rack on the wall was made of elk antlers. The rug on the floor might have come from the same animal.

"These are the signs of a serious hunter who knows his business," Joe finished.

"What else?" Gentry prodded.

"Isn't that enough?" Joe replied.

"I think it's what we *don't* see," Frank ventured.

Gentry smiled. "Very good."

"I don't get it," Joe said with a frown.

Frank picked up an arrow with a razor-sharp steel head. "You see all the signs of a dedicated bow hunter. There aren't any guns of any kind. Becker was shot with a rifle."

"Exactly," Gentry said. "I'm a sustenance hunter. I don't hunt for sport. I kill what I need to eat, and I do it the way my ancestors did. I don't own any firearms."

"I doubt if your ancestors had bows like these," Joe said. "Just because we don't see any guns here doesn't mean you don't own one."

63

"No, it doesn't," Gentry admitted. "But it gives you something to think about." He walked over to the small kitchen area and opened a cupboard above the stove. "I hope you guys like canned beans. Tonight's menu would have included venison. Unfortunately, the main course got wind of me before I could get off a clean shot."

"Whatever you have is fine," Frank said politely.

Joe stretched his arms and yawned. "I think I'm more tired than hungry, anyway. I could probably fall asleep right here in this chair by the fire."

"That's good," Gentry said. "Because those are the best accommodations I have to offer, and you're sort of stuck here until morning."

Joe didn't reply. He was already asleep.

Shortly after sunrise, Frank woke to a gust of arctic air and the sound of the cabin door closing. A note on the table said Gentry had gone out hunting and wouldn't be back until late in the day. It also said they shouldn't have any trouble finding their way back down the trail. The unspoken message was clear: Don't be here when I get back.

That wasn't a problem. Frank was anxious to get back to town. He wanted to find out if there was any improvement in Becker's condition. But to avoid a continuous series of complaints all the way back to the car, he let Joe sleep a while longer.

He decided to enjoy the early-morning daylight and go outside. He was also making a conscious effort not to snoop around the cabin.

Frank quietly opened the door and stepped out onto the porch. He shivered as the frigid mountain air gusted around him. As he started to pull the door shut behind him, a chunk of the door frame next to his head exploded into splinters. A sharp pain sliced through Frank's skull, and the world went black.

Chapter

8

A PEAL OF THUNDER ripped through Joe's dream of a summer day at the beach, jolting him awake.

Someone yelled, "I got him!"

Another voice shouted, "What in tarnation do you think you're doing?"

Joe's bleary eyes slowly focused on a form lying in the cabin doorway. Any hope of returning to sleep was blasted away when the shape resolved itself into a body.

"Frank!" he cried out, leaping to his feet. He rushed to his brother's side, not even considering what might be on the other side of the door.

Joe knelt down and saw a red welt on the side of Frank's head, just above the temple. He heard talking and spotted three armed men coming out of the woods.

Sheriff Stevens threw his hat at one of his deputies. "Put that thing down, Harlan!" he barked. "It might go off again."

The deputy gave him a wounded look. "You said we should consider him armed and dangerous."

The sheriff picked up his cowboy hat and brushed off the snow. "Does either of those boys look like Gentry? Are they armed—with anything?"

Frank groaned and opened his eyes. "What happened?"

"A piece of door frame hit you on the head," Joe answered.

"Shot out by an overanxious deputy," the sheriff said. He was clearly relieved to hear Frank speak.

With Joe's help, Frank struggled to a sitting position. "Yesterday you just wanted to talk to Gentry. Today you shoot first and ask questions later. What's going on? Did ballistics match the rifle with the bullet?" Frank asked.

"The results were inconclusive," the sheriff answered.

"Did you check to make sure Gentry is the registered owner of the rifle?" Joe asked.

"As far as the state computer files are concerned, Ted Gentry doesn't own a gun," Stevens said. "And since the serial number's been filed off the rifle, we may never find out whose name is on the registration. It's a mighty fine weapon, a brand-new bolt-action Winchester with one of those fancy German scopes.''

"Let me get this straight,'' Joe said. "You don't even know if the rifle you have was used in the shooting, or if it belongs to Gentry. So why the trigger-happy posse?''

"We have a witness,'' the sheriff said.

"Somebody, other than an anonymous caller, who actually saw Gentry shoot Becker?'' Frank asked.

"Not exactly,'' the sheriff replied. "But somebody did see him in the area that morning. A hunting party was camped about three miles north of there. The guide's a local fellow named Mark Pearson. I had paid him a visit to ask if he'd seen anything that might help us out.

"He couldn't recall anything unusual,'' the sheriff continued. "But he did suggest that I ask Gentry, since he had seen him near the canyon.''

"Maybe Pearson is lying because he did the shooting,'' Joe suggested.

"I thought of that,'' Stevens replied. "So I checked his story with the folks in the hunting party. They all said the same thing—nobody left the group that morning, and nobody fired a shot.''

"But there was a storm that morning—how could any of them have seen anyone until it ended at ten?'' Joe asked.

"There was that short period of time when it stopped snowing, around nine,'' Frank reminded him. Frank then turned to the sheriff with a sharp look. "What were they hunting? Can you tell us that, at least?"

Sheriff Stevens cleared his throat and stood up. "Cougars," he said stiffly. He walked brusquely into the cabin and looked around. "What are you doing here, anyway?"

"Just paying a social visit," Joe said lightly.

The sheriff turned and gave him a cold stare. "I could charge you boys as accessories."

Frank got to his feet slowly, rubbing at the dull ache in his temple. "We could probably sue you for wrongful injury."

The sheriff was silent for a moment. Then he pushed up the brim of his hat and turned on the smile again. "What are we arguing about? We're all on the same side, right? And just to show you there's no hard feelings, let me give you a lift back to your car." His tone said it wasn't a request.

After the sheriff dropped them off, the Hardys drove straight to the Elk Springs Hospital to check on Becker. Dick Oberman was just coming out as they were going in.

"How is she?" Frank asked.

"Stable," Oberman answered. "She's still in a coma."

Frank tried to be optimistic. "At least she's not any worse. If she's stable, she still has a good chance."

"I've heard that talking and reading to coma

69

victims sometimes helps them recover faster,'' Joe said. "Maybe we should do that."

Oberman didn't seem very receptive to the idea. "I doubt if they'll even let you see her. An aunt and uncle were here earlier. You're not relatives. You barely even know her. I got in only because I know one of the nurses in the intensive care unit."

"So you can put in a good word for us," Joe said.

Oberman glanced at his watch. "I can't, right now. I've got to get back to the store."

"I almost forgot about that," Frank said. "You have a camping supply store. Is it far from here?"

Oberman laughed. "Nothing's very far from anything else in Elk Springs. It's only a couple blocks away."

"Terrific," Frank said. "I think I could use a new sleeping bag—a much warmer one. Mind if we tag along?"

"Not at all," Oberman replied. "I'll even give you a special discount. I wouldn't want you to leave town without at least one pleasant memory."

"This is my kind of town," Frank remarked as they walked down the street. "Most of these stores look like they've always been here and always will be. There are no instant neon fast-food minimalls. No highrise office complexes."

"No tourist traps hawking genuine Native

70

American artifacts fresh from Taiwan," Joe added.

Oberman stopped at a storefront with a rustic wooden sign above the door. Carved into the wood was the name Adventure Outfitters. "Well, I wouldn't mind if Elk Springs attracted a *few* more tourists," he said, pushing the door open. "Things may change a lot around here if the new state highway project gets approved."

"If it were easier to get here," Joe argued, "this would turn into another resort town like Aspen."

Oberman smiled. "I think I could live with that."

Frank browsed through the aisles of daypacks and duffel bags, canteens and cook stoves. The rain gear and clothes leaned heavily toward camouflage styles. So did the tents and packs. A locked glass case displayed an assortment of colorful shotgun shells, fat deer slugs, and sleek, steel-jacketed, high-caliber rifle ammunition.

"Are a lot of your customers hunters?" he asked.

Oberman nodded. "Most of my business comes from the hunting crowd. I can't say I understand the appeal. I never got into it, myself."

Joe pointed to a row of trophies on a shelf behind the counter. The largest one was topped with the figure of a man on skis, a rifle slung over his shoulder. "If you're not into hunting, what are those for?"

"Biathlon competition," Oberman explained. "It's a combination of cross-country skiing and target shooting. Most hunters would laugh at the kind of rifle I use—a twenty-two. It's great for target accuracy, but it wouldn't stop anything bigger than a squirrel."

"Isn't the biathlon an Olympic event?" Joe asked.

"That's right," Oberman answered. His voice took on a wistful tone. "In fact, I was on the Olympic team. Well, I was an alternate, anyway. Nobody got sick or broke a leg or anything, so I never got my chance to go for the gold."

"Do you know many of the local hunting guides?" Frank asked, steering the conversation back on track.

"Sure," Oberman said, his eyes still on the trophy case.

"What about Mark Pearson?" Frank asked.

That seemed to get Oberman's attention. "Where did you hear that name?"

"The sheriff told us about him," Joe said. "Pearson claims he saw Ted Gentry near the canyon where K.D. was shot."

"Mark Pearson isn't going to win any awards for honesty," Oberman said. "He used to be a state game warden. He got fired for taking payoffs from hunters who wanted their own private, extended hunting season. Now he runs his own 'big game' operation."

"Do you think he might be lying about Gentry?" Joe responded.

Oberman shrugged his shoulders. "I wouldn't put it past him—if he had a reason." His eyes widened. "You don't think Pearson shot her, do you?"

"It wouldn't hurt to ask," Frank said.

Joe glanced at his brother. "It might—but when has that ever stopped us?"

Oberman gave them directions to Pearson's place, a short distance outside town. As the Hardys neared the old farmhouse, a weathered blue pickup truck with a trailer attached drove out of the driveway. There were three men in the cab. The bed of the truck was loaded with crates of some kind, and the trailer carried two black snowmobiles.

Frank slowed and let the truck gain some distance. "Looks like the intrepid guide is on the job," he said. "If we stick with him, maybe we can pick up a few tips on hunting safety."

Joe grinned. "There's no telling what you might learn if you keep your eyes open and pay attention."

Frank matched the truck's speed but hung back, following from a safe distance.

"If you let them get any farther ahead," Joe remarked, "they'll be in a different time zone."

"I don't want them to spot us," Frank replied.

"If we're very careful and a little lucky, they may not notice anything behind them."

The truck slowly weaved along the snowy and icy mountain roads and eventually pulled off to the side on a high ridge. Frank quickly backed his car around a curve and out of sight. He grabbed his pack out of the backseat and fished out the monocular.

Hiding in a jumble of boulders, the two brothers took turns with the palm-size telescope, watching the action around the truck. After unloading the snowmobiles from the trailer, a heavyset man with a rusty red beard jumped into the bed of the truck.

"That must be Pearson," Frank whispered as he peered through the magnifying lens. He took a close look at one of the crates and realized what it was, just as the burly man flung it open and the contents bounded out. "Dog carriers," he murmured, handing the monocular to Joe.

By the time Joe brought the scene into focus, a half dozen brown-and-white-spotted beagles with floppy ears and frantic tails were leaping out of the truck and scampering in the snow. The bearded man jumped down to the ground and walked around to the cab. He took out something that almost made Joe drop the compact telescope.

Joe gave his brother a sharp nudge and thrust the monocular back in his face. "Take a look at this," he whispered.

Frank peered through the lens, but all he could see was the man's back. Then Pearson started to turn slowly, as if he were looking for something small and hard to find. He continued to circle—and eventually Frank could see what had jolted his brother.

In one hand the man gripped a blue metal box with wires attached to it. With the other hand he was aiming something down the sloping ridge. It was a small arrow-shaped antenna—just like the one K. D. Becker used to track her mountain lions.

Chapter

9

FRANK MET his brother's eyes. "Are you think-ing the same thing I'm thinking?"

"He's not using that thing to tune in the Weather Channel," Joe replied. "I also don't think this kind of hunting is much of a sport."

Frank nodded. "Exactly what I was thinking."

He took another look through the monocular. The wide man with the thick red beard barked out a few words, and the hounds took off down the slope. Then he loaded a rifle case and some supplies onto the back of one of the snow-mobiles. The other two men busied themselves by strapping their own gun cases onto the other snowmobile. The three men had a short conver-sation. The bearded man waved the antenna around and stared intently at the blue metal box.

76

He exchanged a few more words with the other men and pointed off in the distance. Then the three of them hopped on and roared away on the two snowmobiles.

Joe jumped up when he heard the engines. "They're getting away!" he shouted.

Frank grabbed his arm and jerked him back down behind the rock. "They'll come back," he said firmly. "If we move fast, we can get the sheriff and bring him back here before they return."

"If we move fast," Joe shot back hotly, "we can stop Pearson before he kills another one of Becker's mountain lions. He might as well shoot animals in the zoo! With their radio collars on, those cats can't hide from him!" He whirled around and stomped off toward the car.

Frank ran after his brother. "What are you going to do?" He had seen that expression on Joe's face before, usually right before Joe did something they were both sorry about later.

"I'm going to do something," Joe growled. He yanked his skis off the rack on top of the car, flung open the trunk, and snatched his ski boots.

"Joe," Frank began, trying to reason with his brother, "they're on snowmobiles, and they have guns—*big* guns with bullets the size of small cruise missiles. We'll never catch them. And if we do, we might end up as tragic victims of a fatal hunting 'accident.' "

Joe ripped off his hiking boots and jammed his feet into his ski boots with fierce, single-minded determination. "I don't care much about hunting one way or the other," he said. The edge in his voice was razor sharp and hard enough to cut glass. "But I like to think that most of the time the animals have a fighting chance."

He stuffed his hands deep into his gloves and curled his fists tightly around his ski poles. "I'm going to do whatever I can to give at least one cougar that fighting chance."

Frank sighed. "Once you get an idea stuck in your head, not even heavy explosives can jar it loose. Hold on while I get my gear. If you're going to get killed, I don't want to be left alive to explain it to Mom and Dad."

They got off to a fast start, going downhill on a steep ridge. They easily followed the snowmobile tracks that snaked along in tandem.

Joe could hear the faint whine of the snowmobiles, the distant sound doubling his determination. "I think we're gaining on them," he said.

Frank didn't answer right away. He didn't want to break his rhythm. He kept his breathing deep and even, planting his poles and moving his skis in a steady flow. "Sound echoes in the hills," he replied, pacing his words between breaths. "They could be miles away."

Joe had already set a fierce pace and was now

78

pushing himself even harder. "And they might be right around the next bend," he insisted.

Frank didn't bother to respond at all—there was no point. Joe would press ahead until he collapsed. So Frank conserved his energy the best he could and blotted out everything but the smooth pumping of his arms, legs, and lungs. Plant, kick, glide, inhale. Plant, kick, glide, exhale. He bent his head and focused on the back of Joe's skis. Plant, kick, glide, inhale. Plant, kick, glide—

The distant buzz dwindled and died. Joe strained to pick up any sound other than the soft scrape of skis across snow and his own labored breathing. He forced himself to go faster.

The long, snaking ravine that they were skiing now spilled out onto a wide, flat plain. The snowmobile tracks cut a pair of ruler-straight furrows across it. The ground was almost *too* flat, Frank thought. They were in a roughly circular clearing, about a half mile wide. Tall fir, pine, and aspen trees crowded the edges of the clearing, but none strayed out into it.

They weren't in a clearing, Frank realized. They were gliding across the frozen surface of a small mountain lake. If the ice could hold the snowmobiles, it wouldn't even notice the weight of two skiers. And the smooth, flat surface was ideal for cross-country skiing. The only thing easier would be going downhill.

What bothered Frank was the fact that the

lake was sitting at the bottom of a deep basin. Beyond the shoreline, the trees marched sharply up steep slopes. The ravine they had just followed was actually a frozen stream that fed the lake. The lake had been carved out because there was no place else for the water to go. This was the end of the line.

The snowmobile tracks pointed to a narrow break in the trees, and Joe kept his eyes focused on that. For now, that was his goal. He couldn't tell where the trail went from there, although he knew that "up" was likely to be the direction.

When they reached the chilly, dark cover of the trees, the trail was still easy to follow. The tracks veered to the right and then zigzagged up a switchback trail cut into the side of the thickly wooded slope. Joe's eyes traced the path to the rim of the basin, at least a hundred vertical feet above. His heart sank. His arms ached, and his legs felt like rubber. He didn't think he could make the climb without a few minutes' rest to get his wind back. Even then it would be slow going. The hunters would get farther away and closer to their prey.

Just then he heard something, though. A faint but frenzied yapping reverberated in the natural amplifier of the lake basin.

Joe saw his brother's eyes light up, too. "The dogs!" he managed to croak out. He put on a burst of speed, tapping an energy reserve he didn't know he had. Pearson's hounds were somewhere just up ahead, barking wildly.

The scramble up the steep slope took about everything Joe and Frank had left. The effort wasn't wasted, though. From the rim, they had a commanding view down into a shallow valley on the other side of the lake basin. Less than a hundred yards away, a thick slab of rock with sheer sides thrust up ten feet out of the ground. The dogs were doing a skittish dance around the base, hopping and yelping and whacking each other with their whipsaw tails. The three hunters were clustered by the snowmobiles, parked a short distance away from them.

A snarling, hissing mountain lion prowled back and forth across the top of the rock slab. Joe could almost feel the cat's anger and fear. The cougar could easily take out one or two of the hounds, but he couldn't take on the whole pack. They were all around him. There was no place to go. He was trapped.

The hunters didn't even notice the Hardys. They were too busy arguing about something. Joe couldn't make any sense of it. He could hear the angry words, but he was just having a hard time accepting the signals his ears were sending to his brain.

"I saw him first!" one of them snapped. "So he's mine!"

"I don't see your name on him!" the other one barked. He was clutching a rifle in one hand.

"I say he belongs to whoever can shoot him first. So get out of my way!"

The two men started to shove each other, and Joe was sure a slugfest was about to break out. But Pearson stepped neatly between them. "Why don't you flip a coin?" he suggested in a polite but forceful voice.

"Because they've already flipped their minds," Joe muttered.

Frank shot a sidelong glance at his brother. After seventeen years of hanging around with him, he could almost read Joe's mind.

Frank's arm shot out a split second too late. Joe was already moving. His skis skimmed across the snow, picking up speed as he slipped down into the valley. He was going to stop the hunters. He didn't know how. He was just going to do it.

The bearded man had whirled around. There was a huge revolver in his hand. From Joe's angle, the thing looked more like a small cannon. Maybe that was because the barrel was pointed right at Joe's head.

Chapter

10

JOE GRITTED HIS TEETH and continued to rocket toward the hunters. He was going too fast to stop now. He crouched low on his skis, trying to make himself a smaller target. It wasn't much, but it was the best he could come up with on short notice.

Behind the gaping barrel of the revolver, a look of surprise and doubt grew in Pearson's eyes. He jerked the gun away at the last second and jumped out of Joe's path, crashing into one of the hunters. Both men tumbled to the ground. The other hunter spun around, still clutching his rifle. Joe slammed into him and knocked the weapon loose. It sailed through the air, flipping end over end, and finally crashed into the side of the rock. The gun went off with a loud boom, something whizzed past Joe's ear, and there was a sharp *spang* behind him of bullet hitting metal.

Joe's momentum pushed him past the hunters. The hounds, already frightened and confused, scattered in all directions as he plowed toward them. The cougar's lips curled back in one last snarl before he leapt into the air and disappeared.

Pearson picked himself up and shoved the revolver into a leather holster. He stormed over to Joe and grabbed him by the collar, lifting him off the ground. "Are you insane, or just brain-dead?" he growled, his face as red as his beard. "You almost got yourself killed."

He dropped Joe roughly and glared at him with raging eyes. "And if I had known you were going to mess up the hunt and be responsible for a hole in my new Sno-Cat, I *would* have pulled the trigger."

Joe peered around the wide man and saw a ragged blotch of bare metal on one of the snow-mobiles, where the black paint had flaked off. "That's not exactly a hole," he observed, trying to sound cool and casual. "It's more like a severe dent."

"That's not the point!" the man roared. He gestured at the two bewildered hunters. "These gentlemen paid good money for a cougar hunt, and you just ruined the whole thing!"

Joe gazed at the man with steady eyes like

cold, blue ice. "What you were doing didn't have much to do with hunting."

"What's that supposed to mean?" the man demanded sharply.

Joe pointed at Frank, who was holding the arrow-shaped antenna over his head. At his feet was a metal box. A pointer on a numbered arc under a clear plastic cover on the top of the box danced as Frank waved the antenna around.

"It means you don't have to be much of a hunter to track mountain lions with this," Frank said. "You just have to be a mediocre meter reader."

"Do you boys have some problem with radio tracking gear?" the man snapped.

"Not when it's used for research," Joe responded. "K. D. Becker didn't put radio collars on those cats to make it easier for you to hunt them down."

The man pointed at the collar on one of the dogs, a thin wisp of wire jutting out from it. "Does that look like a cat to you? I use radio collars on my dogs to keep track of them. Sometimes they get too far ahead. Just about every cougar hunting guide uses them, and it's all perfectly legal.

"And did you actually *see* a collar on that cougar before you blundered in here?" he challenged.

Frank had been too far away, and he knew Joe would have been too busy to notice such details. "If you weren't tracking the cat electronically, how'd you find it so fast? You were out less than an hour."

The man shrugged his wide shoulders. "Just luck, I guess. There's no law against that, either."

Just then something flashed past the men. There was a metallic thunk, and the bearded man jumped backward as if he had been jabbed with an electric cattle prod. He was staring at the ground with a startled look on his face. Joe looked down and saw that the radio signal detector was now neatly skewered by a thin black arrow.

Ted Gentry stepped out from behind a nearby tree. There was already another steel-tipped arrow notched in his bow and pointed at the bearded man. "There may not be a law against luck, Pearson—but there *is* one against hunting on private property without permission.

"Besides, luck had nothing to do with it," he continued. "I heard a few stories about your amazing run of so-called luck and your quick kills. Something about it just didn't sound right." He glanced at Frank. "Nobody would ever accuse Mark Pearson of being a great hunter. So I decided to check it out."

His eyes shifted back to the bearded man. "I've been tailing you for the past three weeks. You took out three hunting parties and bagged three cougars. Two of the hunts lasted less than six hours, and both of those cats were wearing radio collars."

Pearson scowled. "That doesn't prove anything."

"No, it doesn't," Gentry admitted. "You've been pretty careful, and I wasn't sure until today."

"Wait a minute," one of the hunters interrupted. "The dogs never got out of sight, so he didn't even use the radio gear. He just turned it on at the start to make sure it was working."

"That's right," the other one joined in. "And we saw cougar tracks by the road and followed them here."

Gentry laughed. "You saw a few paw prints that didn't go anywhere. Pearson had already located the cat's den, probably sometime yesterday, judging by the snowmobile tracks I followed after I saw him making those fake cat tracks."

He nodded toward a rocky outcropping halfway up the side of the valley. "The cat was living in a small cave up there. All Pearson had to do was turn on the radio once to make sure he was home. And since Pearson was in the lead snowmobile, you never noticed that the only tracks he was following were his own."

Pearson glowered at Gentry. "Everybody knows you're crazy. I don't have to listen to any more of your babbling."

"You're free to leave any time," Gentry said.

"What are we waiting for?" one of the hunters complained. "There's a fresh set of tracks. We can still catch that cougar."

"That's right," Pearson replied, nodding his head firmly. "And that's exactly what we're going to do."

Gentry shook his head slowly. "I don't think so. As I said before, there's a law against hunting on private property without permission."

"That's between me and the owner," Pearson said gruffly. "And you're not the owner."

Gentry smiled. "I think we can safely assume that K. D. Becker didn't give you permission to hunt here, and she *is* the owner."

Pearson's only reply was a silent, stony stare. Finally he spun around and stomped back to his snowmobile, shouted a few terse commands, and the dogs scurried after him as he roared away. Once the two hunters realized what was happening, they hastily jumped on the other snowmobile and took off after him.

"Nice piece of detective work," Joe said as Gentry unnotched the arrow and snapped it back into the row of shafts in the miniquiver attached to the side of the bow. "Pearson must have found out which radio frequency Becker was using and adapted his equipment to tune into it."

"I don't understand people like that," Gentry said. "There's no honor in what he does, no dignity. He'd rather lie and cheat even when it's easier to be honest."

Frank looked at him closely. "He wasn't lying about seeing you that morning near the spot where Becker was shot, was he?"

Gentry didn't respond.

"You were there because you were following Pearson," Frank pressed.

Gentry nodded. "I was there."

"You should come into town with us and explain it to the sheriff," Joe said.

"No," Gentry replied after another pause. "You go back and tell the sheriff. I think I'll stay here in the mountains. This is where I belong."

He didn't say goodbye. He just turned and walked away.

Afternoon had faded to evening by the time Frank and Joe returned to town. Even though they were hungry and tired, they knew they had to see the sheriff before they did anything else. "Downtown" Elk Springs was only a single street lined with small stores and restaurants. At the end of the strip was a single-story brick building with one word on the sign above the door: Police.

The sheriff lumbered out the front door just as Frank and Joe were getting out of their car. "I was just talking about you boys a little while ago," he said in his country drawl.

"Is that good or bad?" Joe responded.

The sheriff chuckled. "Oh, pretty good, I

think. The young lady I was talking to had a fairly high opinion of you.'' He seemed to be enjoying some private joke.

"And who might that be?'' Frank asked. "I don't remember meeting any women in town.''

"You didn't meet her in town,'' the sheriff answered. "But you did run into her at work.''

Comprehension dawned on Joe's face. "You mean Becker's out of the coma? What did she say? Did she see the shooter? Is she all right? Can we see her?'' The words rushed out of his mouth in a rapid stream, the sentences strung together in one long question.

"Whoa,'' the sheriff cut in. "One at a time. Yes, she's out of the coma, and yes, she's talking. Well, it's more like meandering. She's not too coherent yet.''

"What about the shooting?'' Frank prodded. "Does she remember anything?''

"It's hard to say. Her dates are sort of mixed up right now.'' He paused and looked off in a distracted way, as if he were sorting out something in his mind. "Anyway, the doctor thinks she'll make a full recovery. All she needs is rest to give her body time to heal. If you boys are still in town tomorrow, you can visit her. I'm sure she'd like to thank you in person.''

"We'll still be here,'' Frank assured him.

Frank and Joe showed up at the hospital at exactly nine o'clock the next morning. Frank got

90

a bad feeling when he saw the sheriff's jeep parked a few feet from the front entrance in an area clearly marked No Parking. Inside, they found the sheriff having a hushed conversation with a doctor and a nurse in the lobby.

The sheriff spotted the Hardys, said one last thing to the doctor, and strode across the lobby to intercept the two brothers. "I'm afraid K.D.'s had a little setback," he told them.

"What do you mean?" Frank asked. "What happened?"

The sheriff scratched his mustache. "She's been on a respirator ever since they operated on her to remove the bullet. She'd been having a little trouble breathing on her own."

"If she's been on a respirator the whole time," Joe said, "I wouldn't call it a setback."

"I was getting to that part," the sheriff replied. He pushed up the brim of his cowboy hat and stroked his mustache again. "Something went wrong with the respirator during the night. By the time the nurse discovered the problem, K.D. had slipped back into a coma."

Chapter

11

"THE SHERIFF should have put a guard on her room!" Joe muttered as they left the hospital.

"Sheriff Stevens has only two deputies," Frank reminded him. "And we don't know that the respirator problem wasn't an accident of some kind."

Joe stared at his brother. "You don't really believe that, do you?"

Frank hesitated. "Not really. As a general rule, I don't believe in tidy coincidences.'"

"So what do we do about it?"

"For the moment, nothing," Frank said. He turned up his collar against the cold wind as they walked to the car. "The sheriff's a fairly bright guy. I think he can check out this situation without our help."

"While we just sit around our motel and wait?" Joe responded in an abrasive tone. He yanked open the car door and slipped into the driver's seat.

"We could do that," Frank said mildly as he slid into the seat next to Joe. He gazed absently out the window at the clear sky. "I thought it might be a nice day for a drive, though."

Joe jammed the key into the ignition and gave it a sharp twist. The engine complained that it was too cold to start, but it started, anyway. "Any place in particular?" he asked, clutching the steering wheel in a two-fisted choke hold.

Frank shrugged. "We could take in the sights of the bustling metropolis of Elk Springs."

"That should take about five minutes," Joe muttered.

Frank smiled a secret smile. "That sounds about right."

Joe shot a sidelong glance at his brother. "What's going on in that mental computer of yours?"

"Just drive around until you find something that looks like a library," Frank said. "I'll tell you when we get there."

It didn't take long to find the small public library. Inside, a plump, smiling woman stood behind the check-out counter.

"May I help you?" she asked in a bright, cheerful voice.

The place was deserted, and Frank guessed that their visit was a welcome occurrence. That was good. It would make their job easier.

"I sure hope so," he said. He tried to sound both friendly and just a little distraught. "I've been to six libraries in three counties, and this is my last shot."

The woman's smile faltered. "Oh dear. We don't have a very big selection of books. What were you looking for?"

"I'm working on a term paper on historical land-use patterns," Frank explained. He leaned forward and spoke in a hushed tone. "If I don't get a good grade, I'll lose my table tennis scholarship."

The woman made an apologetic face. "I'm afraid all we have is a set of county land maps." She led him over to a table at the back of the room. "They go back about fifty years. They indicate the property owner's name only, not what the land is used for."

Frank tried to look disappointed. "Maybe I can find something out from them," he said somberly.

Actually, he couldn't believe their luck. The huge maps had a wealth of detail: property lines, title owners, locations of houses, even garages and barns.

"What are we looking for?" Joe asked, joining his brother after the woman went back to her desk.

94

"What do Becker and Gentry have in common?"

Joe studied his brother studying the most recent map, which was less than a year old. Then the answer came to him. "They both own land around here."

"Bingo," Frank replied. "And quite a lot of it, if this thing is accurate."

Joe frowned slightly. "What does that have to do with anything?"

"Dick Oberman said a new highway project might bring some new life into town," Frank answered. "If somebody wanted to make a big killing, he could buy real estate cheap now and then sell it for a big profit after the new highway makes the land more attractive to developers." He left the rest unsaid.

Joe filled in the blanks. "Then Becker and Gentry are perfect targets. Neither of them uses the land for ranching, and they both need money for their special causes."

Frank nodded. "What do you think would happen if neither of them wanted to sell?"

Joe smiled grimly. "It would be convenient if one of them killed the other one. With one dead and the other behind bars, somebody could probably buy up their land at bargain prices."

A troubled look passed over his face. "Of course, this is all speculation. With Becker in a coma and Gentry kind of on the run, we can't confirm any of this. We don't know if anybody tried to buy their land—much less who."

"For now, let's just assume that's the way it is," Frank suggested. "Now, who could really benefit from this? Maybe someone who already owns land that abuts theirs. It might make sense to be able to sell a really giant parcel of land—perhaps to a resort developer. Whose land borders on K.D.'s and Ted's?" he asked.

Joe looked down. His brother's finger was running back and forth across the map. He stopped it on the words Lazy W Ranch—Owner: W. Crawford.

"So far, this is all guesswork," Joe pointed out as he steered the car toward the Lazy W.

"That's why we have to check it out on our own and not involve the sheriff yet," Frank replied.

"How are we going to get Crawford to talk to us?" Joe asked as he pulled up next to the main gate of the ranch.

Frank patted a large manila envelope on his lap. It had taken two dollars' worth of quarters and a considerable amount of jockeying with the oversize sheet of paper to make a complete photocopy of the map, but he had succeeded. "Let me handle this," he said. He rolled down his window and beamed at the cowboy sentry. "We have some important papers here for Mr. Crawford," he announced.

The cowboy hunched over and squinted in at

the envelope Frank was waving around. "What kind of papers?"

"How should I know?" Frank responded. "They only pay us to deliver the stuff. All I know is that if the package is marked Urgent, we're supposed to make sure it gets there the same day." He stuck the envelope in the man's face. "See? Right there."

The cowboy pulled back his head and eyed the hand-scrawled red letters. "This doesn't look very official," he remarked doubtfully.

"That's because it's urgent," Frank said. "There wasn't time to make it look pretty."

"All right," the sentry said, reaching out for the envelope. "Give it to me."

Frank held the envelope clutched tight to his chest. "No way. I have to deliver this personally."

"I can't let you in without clearance," the sentry told him.

Frank smiled. "That's okay. We can wait. It's all part of the service. And maybe you'll get some kind of bonus for holding up the delivery of these *urgent* papers."

The man started to scowl, caught himself, and turned it into a resigned shrug. "Aw, what do I care? I signed on to be a cowboy, not a guard dog. I'll just let 'em know you're coming." He trudged over to the small guard house and disappeared inside. A few seconds later the iron gate swung open.

Joe drove up to the big main house and parked. As they walked up the front steps, Walt Crawford came storming out onto the porch. "What's all this about ur—" he started to shout and then cut himself off when he saw the Hardys. "Not you two again. What do you want now?"

"Just a few minutes of your time," Frank said pleasantly. "That's all."

Crawford stood at the top of the steps, staring down at them. "Go ahead, I'm listening."

"Out here?" Joe asked with a shiver, stuffing his hands in his coat pockets.

Crawford nodded. "That's right." Even with no coat, he seemed unaware of the extreme cold.

"I can understand why you might be upset," Frank said. "We thought you should know what we found out."

Crawford arched his eyebrows but didn't say anything.

Frank took a deep breath and plunged in with both feet. "We believe that Ted Gentry is being framed for the shooting of K. D. Becker."

Crawford's hard eyes flicked to the envelope in Frank's hand. "What's in there? Evidence?"

"Evidence that somebody wanted them both out of the way," Frank said evenly.

"I see," Crawford responded in a guarded tone. "And who would want to do that?"

"You know who and why!" Joe blurted out.

98

"With their land combined with what you already own, developers would be throwing money at you once the new highway is finished."

A smug smile spread across Crawford's face. "I have no interest in their property, and I have even less interest in developers. In fact, I've spent a lot of time and money fighting that highway bill."

Joe scowled. "Why?"

"Because I'm in the cattle ranching business," Crawford replied in a calm voice, like a parent patiently lecturing a child. "And it's a good business. If somebody decides to build a resort or hotels next door, my property taxes will skyrocket, and that will eat up most of my profits. That's bad business."

He glanced at an expensive gold watch on his wrist. "Your few minutes are up. Now, get out of here before I have you arrested for trespassing."

"We sure were terrific," Joe grumbled loudly as they drove past the front gate. He gave the steering wheel a hard jerk, and the car swerved out onto the road.

Frank gazed out the window at the cattle and bales of hay that dotted the rolling fields of snow. "The plan was to draw him into a conversation and see if anything slipped out, not hurl accusations in his face."

A sign flashed by outside the window. Frank

kept staring out at the cattle. Something clicked in his head. He sat up stiffly and twisted around. "Stop the car," he said sharply.

Joe glanced over at him. "What?"

"Stop the car and back up," Frank said in a firm, insistent tone.

"Whatever you say," Joe muttered, putting his foot on the brake and shifting into reverse.

When they were past the signpost again, Frank told his brother to stop. He pointed at the sign. "What's wrong with this picture?"

" 'Welcome to Gunnison National Forest,' " Joe said, reading the words out loud. "What's wrong with that?"

Frank jerked his thumb over his shoulder. "Crawford's ranch is there—this is the border between his land and the national forest."

Joe gave him a blank look. "I still don't see what's wrong."

Frank gestured at the cattle on the gentle hills in front of them. "Crawford's cattle are on the wrong side of the sign. They're grazing in the national forest—the same national forest that K. D. Becker wants to turn into a wildlife refuge."

Chapter

12

JOE REACHED OUT and put his hand on his brother's shoulder. "I don't know how to tell you this," he said in a solemn voice, "but cows can't read."

Frank continued to stare straight ahead.

"Don't you think some official person would try to stop them from eating government property?" Joe asked.

Frank was silent for another minute. "Not if there was a lease," he finally said.

"Could you rewind that and play it for me again?" Joe responded in a puzzled voice.

"It's possible to lease parts of national forests," Frank explained. "That's part of what makes them different from national parks. Oil and lumber companies do it all the time."

"And cattle ranchers, too," Joe ventured. "Crawford gets some low-rent grazing land, and the government makes a little money. Everybody comes out ahead."

"Until K. D. Becker comes along with different plans for this part of the national forest," Frank said, filling in the next step.

Joe nodded. "I don't think steers count as wildlife. That means Crawford would have a lot to lose if Becker is successful."

"And if Gentry's people get the land," Frank added, "Crawford still loses. Getting rid of Becker and Gentry might not solve his problems, but it would buy him time."

"Crawford was out of town when Becker was shot," Joe recalled. "But he could have hired somebody to do the job for him. That won't be easy to prove."

Frank drummed his fingers on the dashboard. "We have to link him to the shooter somehow," he said half out loud. "If we had any idea who actually did the shooting, we might be able to put something together. Since we don't, we just have to wait to see if Crawford makes a move. Maybe we rattled him today. If we get lucky and he doesn't just call, he might lead us right to the trigger man."

Joe let out a low groan. "Does that mean what I think it means?"

Frank put on an innocent face. "I don't know. What do you think it means?"

"Stakeout," Joe muttered.

"Bingo," Frank replied with a smile. "There was a little side road about fifty yards from the main gate. We should be able to keep an eye on everything that comes in and out from there."

"Let's go back to town and get something to eat first," Joe suggested hopefully. "By the time we get back, it'll be dark. Nobody will spot us as long as we keep the headlights off."

Frank shook his head. "We can't take the chance. We might miss something important."

Joe sighed. "How long do we hang around and wait?"

Frank shrugged. "If nothing happens by midnight, we'll reconsider our options."

They didn't have to wait that long. The sun had barely slipped behind the jagged mountain peaks, when the gate swung open and a car pulled out. There was still enough light lingering in the sky to give Joe a good look at the driver.

He nudged his brother and switched on the engine. "There goes Crawford. If this trail leads to a restaurant, I'm going to follow him all the way inside, grab a table, and order some dinner. And if he leaves before I'm finished, he's on his own."

"He's going the wrong way for that," Frank said. "Elk Springs is in the opposite direction. The way he's headed, the road climbs into the mountains. That's a good sign."

"Why is it a good sign?" Joe asked, frowning.

"If Crawford is meeting the person he hired to shoot Becker and frame Gentry," Frank began, "he wouldn't want to be seen with the guy in broad daylight, not in town or at the ranch. He'd pick an out-of-the-way meeting. place."

Joe turned on the headlights. "And he'd do it at night, under cover of darkness. Don't forget that part."

Frank smiled. "If I do, I'm sure you'll remind me." He reached over and switched off the headlights. "Just like I'll remind you not to shoot off any flares or fireworks to let Crawford know we're behind him. Keep him on a short leash and let him light the way."

That trick worked fairly well until the road got treacherous, hugging the side of a peak that disappeared into darkness and snaking steadily upward with sharp twists and turns. Joe hoped they wouldn't hit an icy patch and wipe out. Every time the lead car disappeared around a blind curve, the glow from its headlights vanished, too, and Joe had to flick on his own beams to pierce the blackness that swallowed the next treacherous turn. Halfway around the bend, he'd switch them off again. It was all a matter of timing. If he didn't turn them off fast enough, Crawford would spot them. If he didn't turn them *on* fast enough, he might miss the turn.

Frank was studying the road just as intently as his brother. Up ahead, the mountainside jutted outward, and he could clearly see the wide beams of Crawford's headlights moving toward another hairpin turn.

This one was slightly different from the others. It had a wide shoulder and a wooden guard rail. Frank caught a glimpse of what might have been benches facing out over the ledge, and he realized that there was some sort of scenic overlook. That wasn't all he glimpsed.

"Whoa," he said in a low voice, as if somebody might overhear him. "Looks like we just hit the jackpot."

Joe stopped the car and killed the engine. "Either that," he whispered, "or it's another one of those tidy coincidences that you hate so much."

The twin beams of Crawford's headlights lit up the blue metal of a battered pickup truck parked on the shoulder. The car pulled up next to the truck and stopped. Frank got out his monocular and managed to focus it on the scene just as a bulky figure stepped out of the truck. He wasn't surprised to see the red beard of Pearson.

The passenger-side door of Crawford's car swung open. The large, bearded man hesitated for a moment and then got in.

"What's going on?" Joe asked. "What are they doing?"

105

"I can't see inside the car," Frank answered. "It's too dark. It doesn't look like they're going anywhere, so it's a fairly solid bet Crawford and Pearson are having a little chat."

Joe snorted. "I doubt if they're planning a hunting trip, unless they're after more two-legged victims."

"If we don't want to end up on their itiner-ary," Frank said, "we'd better get out of here."

Joe twisted his head around and peered out the rear window. There was no room to turn around, and he couldn't risk turning on the engine. If Crawford or Pearson heard the noise and spotted the car, things might get a little rough.

There was only one way to go. He took a deep breath, released the emergency brake, and let the car roll slowly backward. The cloud cover had lifted and there was just enough light from the moon to outline the first bend behind him. Joe guided the car around it and stopped on the thin shoulder, just out of sight of the overlook.

He turned the key in the ignition and winced as the engine roared in the empty silence. He made a quick, tight U-turn in the narrow space, and headed back down the mountain. Thirty seconds later he managed to hear himself think over the pounding of his heart and remembered to turn on the headlights.

Frank peered out the window. "If you see anything like a side road, take it."

"Coming right up," Joe said. He knew what his brother had in mind. He slowed when he passed a narrow, dark lane. He backed the car into it, drove about twenty feet into the shadows, stopped, and killed the lights.

Then they waited.

Fifteen minutes later, Crawford's car went by. Joe put his foot on the gas pedal and the car rolled forward.

Frank reached out and touched his brother's arm. "Not yet. We got what we wanted from Crawford."

Five more minutes ticked by before the blue pickup truck shot past.

Joe let out a low whistle. "He must be doing at least fifty. That's really pushing it on this road. He must be in a hurry to get someplace."

"Let's find out where and why," Frank said.

"It's about time," Joe replied. He stepped on the gas and took off after the truck.

Joe didn't spend a lot of time worrying about being spotted. It took all his concentration to match the truck's breakneck pace and keep the car on the twisting roadway. A small patch of ice could send them over the edge. "If he's trying to shake us," he observed in a tight voice, "he's doing a good job."

Joe's hands were locked tightly on the steering wheel. His right foot jumped back and forth between the brake and gas pedals as the car screeched around each deadly curve. Joe knew that a thousand feet below, at the bottom of black nothingness, the cold, hard ground waited to embrace them.

Frank kept his eyes on the pickup truck. On the last turn, the outside tires had kicked up snow and gravel from the shoulder. It took the next turn even wider, and the tires kissed the edge of the cliff.

Frank glanced over at the speedometer. The needle was pushing sixty. "He's not trying to shake us," he said with grim certainty. "That truck's out of control—he can't slow it down." Joe gritted his teeth and pressed down on the gas pedal. "Then we'll have to do it for him. I'll get in front of him so he can keep his front bumper against our rear one. Slowly I'll ease off on the gas and apply the brake. That should stop him."

Joe's foot didn't even touch the brake pedal on the next turn. The tires screamed and the back end fishtailed wildly. Joe did manage to keep the car on the pavement. He was even starting to gain on the truck, but not fast enough. He pushed down on the gas pedal again.

The car rocketed down a short straightaway, chewing up the distance. When he was close enough to read Pearson's license plate, he swerved into the outside lane and jammed the gas pedal all the way to the floor.

Even though the speedometer hovered at seventy, the side of the pickup truck seemed to crawl by in slow motion. A yellow warning sign with a curved black arrow symbol flashed past. Frank got a good look at Pearson's frantic, terrified face as the car nosed past the truck. Joe jerked the wheel, cut in front of the truck, and stomped on the brakes. Because of the curve he couldn't afford to ease Pearson's speed down slowly. He had to do it fast.

The tires screeched in protest. The pickup truck slammed into the rear end of the car. Frank's head snapped back as they lurched forward, but his eyes remained locked on what loomed ahead, framed in the harsh glare of the headlights.

The pavement disappeared as the road veered off to the right. The snow on the thin shoulder took on an ugly tinge in the yellow beams. Beyond that, the lights couldn't find anything and just dwindled away.

Frank's fingers sank deep into the armrest on the door as the heavy truck's momentum pushed them closer to the edge. "We're not going to make it!" he yelled. "We're going over!"

Chapter

13

METAL GROANED and rubber smoked as the run-away truck bulldozed the car closer to the edge of the cliff. Joe threw all his strength against the brake pedal, but he couldn't outmuscle the laws of physics. The pickup truck had too much weight and too much momentum. He couldn't stop it from going over the edge. If he didn't do something fast, they'd go down with it.

Joe grappled the steering wheel, cranking it away from the cliff. If he could have pried his hands off the wheel, he might have crossed his fingers. Since he couldn't, he just swallowed hard and did what he had to do.

He yanked his foot off the brake and hit the gas. The car shot forward, away from the over-powering mass of the doomed truck. The back end swung out, and the left rear tire skidded across the snowy shoulder, flirting briefly with the empty darkness beyond. Then the front tires grabbed the snow-covered road and the car swerved around the curve.

Frank looked back and saw the pickup truck desperately trying to follow. It did a half-spin, slid sideways to the edge of the precipice, hung there for a second, and then tumbled into the black void.

Joe braked to a stop, and they both jumped out and ran back up the road to the spot where the truck had gone over. Frank didn't really expect to see much in the deep darkness. So it was quite a jolt when he peered over the edge and saw blazing headlights only about sixty feet below. There was a ledge with two scraggly, twisted pines jutting out of it. The truck was wedged precariously between the trees and the rocky cliff, half off the ledge.

"Hello!" Frank shouted. "Can you hear me down there?"

There was no response and no movement from the truck.

Frank glanced over at his brother. "There's a rope in my pack."

"Not for long," Joe said. He dashed down the road and came back with more than the rope. He brought the car, too.

Joe lashed one end of the rope to the front bumper while Frank looped the other end around his chest. When they were both ready, Joe stood at the edge of the cliff, gripping the rope with both hands. He let out the line a handful at a time so Frank could rappel down the rocky slope.

His feet scrabbled over huge boulders, loose rocks, and pebbles that clattered down into the darkness. Some of them clanked and thunked off the hood and roof of the stranded truck. Frank angled down into the open cargo bed behind the cab. The scrawny trees creaked and swayed. The truck rocked ominously.

He could see Pearson inside the cab, slumped over the steering wheel. Frank hoped he was only unconscious. Using a fist-size rock, he smashed out the glass and then cleared away the jagged shards with his gloved hands.

He leaned into the cab and grabbed Pearson's shoulders. The truck groaned and nosed down sharply. Frank quickly hauled the heavy, limp body out of the cab, and the truck tilted back again.

"Are you all right?" Joe called down.

"Yeah!" Frank shouted up. "For now, anyway. One wrong move, and this truck could go over. You're going to have to pull us up together, and this guy is heavy. He must weigh over two fifty."

"No problem," Joe replied. "I've got a friend here who must weigh a couple *thousand* pounds. Hang on! We'll have you up in a minute."

Joe ran over to the car and took out the floor mats. He lifted up the slack rope, draped the mats over the rough edge of the cliff, and laid the rope back down on top of the layer of protective padding. He knew the mats would keep the rope from fraying. Then he went back to the car, hopped into the driver's seat, started the engine, and backed up slowly.

His head swiveled back and forth between the pavement behind him and the taut rope in front. When he saw Frank's head poke above the cliff, Joe stopped the car, jumped out, and ran over to help his brother wrestle the massive red-bearded man onto the shoulder of the road.

Pearson was still alive. There was an ugly purple lump on his forehead, and he was out cold, but he was still breathing. They loaded him into the backseat and headed down the mountain.

Pearson was still unconscious when a doctor and nurse wheeled him off on a gurney at Elk Springs Hospital. Frank and Joe were about to leave the emergency room, when Sheriff Stevens lumbered in.

"News sure does travel fast in a small town," Joe commented. "We were just about to call you."

"I was already here when I got word you boys had brought in another body," the sheriff said. "As long as you're in town, maybe I should just move my office in here. It would probably save a lot of time and bother."

"Were you here on police business?" Frank asked. "Or was it just a social call?"

113

The sheriff smiled. "A little bit of both. I came over to have a chat with K.D."

"She's awake?" Joe asked eagerly. "Can we see her?"

"I think that can be arranged," the sheriff said, "even though it's after visiting hours. But first, I think you have to fill me in on what hit Mark Pearson and how you fit into it."

The Hardys told him what happened, and the sheriff listened quietly, nodding occasionally. After Joe described how they saved Pearson, Stevens just sat and let the facts sink in.

"I suppose you boys have a theory about all this," he finally said in a relaxed tone.

"What we guess happened is that Crawford hired Pearson to kill Becker. He must have decided that Pearson would go along with it because the wildlife refuge would ruin his hunting business. Then Crawford must have decided to get rid of Pearson."

"And why would he do that—according to your theory, that is?" the sheriff asked softly.

Joe shrugged. "Maybe he got nervous. Maybe Pearson wanted more money, or maybe Crawford just decided he was unreliable. So Crawford asked Pearson to meet him out on a remote mountain road. Then someone, somehow, got under Pearson's truck and cut his brake line."

"Did you hear what Crawford and Pearson talked about?" the sheriff asked.

"No," Joe admitted.

"You think it was one of Crawford's men who tampered with Pearson's brakes?" the sheriff asked.

The boys nodded.

"Did you *see* anyone crawl under Pearson's truck?"

"There was a thick cloud cover," Frank pointed out, "and we weren't watching the whole time, so we didn't see anyone."

"But don't you think Pearson would have seen something? And where did this man come from?" the sheriff questioned, not buying into their theory.

"If Crawford set up the meeting," Frank answered, "he could have sent out a man ahead of time." He paused and ran it over in his mind. "The man could have parked up the road and out of sight, backtracked on foot, and then hid until they arrived."

"If you can pull the truck back onto the road, it should be easy enough to check the brake lines to see if they've been cut," Frank suggested.

Stevens looked at his watch. "It's getting late. If you boys want to have a word with K.D. you'd better do it now," he said, dismissing them and their theory.

A hospital aide directed Frank and Joe to Becker's room. She was propped up in bed, and a nurse was drawing blood from her arm. She was pale but alert and smiled weakly when she saw the Hardys.

"Isn't that just like a hospital?" Joe cracked after the nurse left. "If you're not dead when you get to one, they bleed you to death a teaspoon at a time."

Becker laughed softly. "Are you saying I'd be out of here by now if they didn't keep stealing my blood. Of course, I might have a lot less to steal if you guys hadn't come along when you did. At least, that's what they tell me. I can't remember anything that happened that day."

"You don't remember getting up or having breakfast?" Joe asked.

"Oh, sure, I remember breaking camp and coming back to the canyon. Everything after that is a complete blank, though."

"You came back to the canyon?" Frank responded. "What do you mean? You didn't camp there?"

Becker shook her head. "I camped a few miles farther up in the hills. In the morning, I picked up a new signal on the radio, which led me back to the canyon." She paused, frowning slightly. "According to the meter, the signal source shouldn't have been more than ten feet away, but I didn't see any sign of a cat in the canyon, and the snow had let up right then, so I shouldn't have missed it."

"What time was that?" Frank asked.

"About nine-fifteen," she replied. "I know because I wrote it down in my log book."

"Your watch was broken at ten forty-six," Joe said. "That leaves an hour and a half unaccounted for."

Becker frowned again. "I know. The doctor told me amnesia isn't unusual in severe trauma cases, but it's driving me crazy. I can't figure out what I did there all that time."

"Speaking of time," Frank said, "it's late. We should let you get some rest."

Becker sighed. "I guess so. They tell me that's the only way I'll get out of here." She closed her eyes. "Come back and see me tomorrow."

"It's a date," Frank said over his shoulder as he stepped into the hallway. He was surprised to see Sheriff Stevens leaning against the wall outside the door.

"Do you solve a lot of cases by eavesdropping?" Frank asked coolly.

"A fair number," the sheriff responded. "I had one of my men drive out to take a look at the crash site. He just radioed back to me that that's a dangerous rockslide area. A man could get killed just trying to hook on a tow hitch. I'm not going to order anybody to do it, and I don't think I'm going to find too many volunteers. We have to leave the truck where it is."

* * *

The next morning Frank and Joe were standing on the edge of the road, looking down at the wreck of the pickup truck.

There was a wide ledge about twenty feet below the one the truck had crashed onto. The truck had shifted during the night, and the front end now tilted down at an even sharper angle.

"It could go over any minute," Joe said. "You'll have to put some weight in the back and try to balance the thing while I go under and check the brake line."

"Right idea," Frank replied. "Wrong job assignments. If anybody's going to crawl around under there, it's going to be me." Joe didn't argue.

Tying a rope to their car bumper again, they used it to secure themselves as they worked their way down to the truck. Joe let go of the rope and stepped into the cargo bed. Metal creaked and the truck rocked back a few inches. Frank tried to peer under it.

He was about to tell Joe to shift his weight farther back in the bed, when he felt the side of the cliff tremble and heard a low rumble from above.

Frank raised his head just in time to see an avalanche of rocks and boulders crashing down toward them.

Chapter
14

A GIANT BOULDER cartwheeled down the slope, barely missing the front fender of the pickup. There were more on the way.

Frank jerked open the door of the cab and dove in. He had tossed the rope to Joe who scrambled in behind him. With their extra weight, the truck pitched down at a dizzying angle. Rocks hammered onto the roof with a deafening din. A huge boulder smashed into the cargo bed, and luckily the front end lurched up again.

"What do we do?" Joe cried out, swallowing hard to fight down the sick feeling in his stomach.

Frank snatched up the shoulder harness from behind him and hauled it roughly across his chest. "Buckle up!" he yelled.

"I don't think that's going to help much!" Joe

119

shouted as he slammed the buckle into the slot. Something crashed into the roof, leaving a fist-shaped dent next to his head.

"It couldn't hurt!" Frank screamed over the roaring tide of earth and stone and snow.

A rock shattered the windshield, which was now a maze of tiny cracks. There was a groaning, rending noise. The stunted trees jerked and shuddered as the ledge they had clung to crumbled away. The force of the landslide and the weight of the truck were too much for their root systems. They lost their tenuous grasp, and joined the rocks in their race to the bottom. The truck joined in, too.

Joe felt the world drop out from under him, and his stomach jumped into his throat. Then everything spun around in confusion. He had just enough time to figure out that the truck had flipped over before a searing jolt of pain brought an abrupt halt to all his figuring.

Joe woke up with a sharp ache in his neck and a dull throb across his chest. He coughed and gagged on the thick dust swirling around him. "Well, that's a good sign," he groaned. "I'm still breathing." Peering through the dim haze, he could see that he was still in the truck. Thin shafts of sunlight trickled in through the rocky debris and dirty snow that iced the crumpled cab. Joe was dangling upside down in the shoul-

120

der harness, the straps biting into his skin, his head wedged against the ceiling.

"We're lucky to be alive," Frank said in a hoarse whisper.

Joe tried to laugh. "You call this living?"

Frank thumbed the release button on his shoulder harness and slowly slid down onto the ceiling. He moved his arms and legs carefully, one at a time, then clenched and opened his fists. He swiveled his head from side to side. "Nothing broken. How about you?"

Joe unbuckled himself and joined his brother in the cramped space. "I'm okay, but I don't think anybody will be driving this heap anywhere for quite a while.

"And that brings up an interesting question," he continued. "Why aren't we dead? We should be buried under several thousand tons of rubble at the losing end of a very long drop."

"That's where the luck comes in," Frank explained. "I think the truck plowed into that ledge that was twenty feet below where we were. Something pinned us here while the rockslide rumbled past."

"That's a great theory," Joe replied. "Let's see if we can test it."

He turned himself around in the tight space and faced the door. He tugged on the handle and pushed. Rocks and dirt shifted. More sunlight streamed in. The door opened a crack but wouldn't budge any farther. Joe tried jiggling it back and forth. The rocks moved some more, and a little more light seeped in. The opening was now wide enough for a scrawny, greased cat.

Joe rocked back on his hands and knees, tucked his head down, and slammed his shoulder into the door. Dirt and stones fell away, light flooded in, and the door flew open. Joe toppled forward into clear blue, empty air. He flailed his arms wildly and snagged the door handle with one hand.

He hung there for a few seconds like a human bridge, his toes in the cab, hooked around the rim of the doorway, and one arm stretched across the gulf to the handle of the wide-open door. He stared down in wide-eyed surprise. A bird glided in lazy circles some distance below him. Joe guessed that the distance between him and the bird was about the length of a football field. Another football field below the bird was the base of the cliff.

"Well, your theory passed the first test," Joe remarked after his brother hauled him back inside.

He poked his head out cautiously and looked around. The half-buried truck was less than a foot from the edge of the ledge. He twisted around, grasped the metal running board with both hands, and lifted himself out and onto the bottom of the wreck.

"What about the brakes," Frank asked after Joe helped him out.

Joe gestured at the twisted wreckage. "I don't think they work anymore."

Frank nodded ruefully. "Any signs of tampering were probably destroyed in that landslide."

Joe had brushed away some debris and found the tattered end of their rope. "At least we haven't run out of luck completely."

He tugged on it, and a section of line popped out of the loose layer of dust and small rocks. He gave it another tug and more rope appeared, leading straight up the slope, all the way to the road above. He put all his weight behind one final pull to make sure the line was secure.

He turned to Frank with a wide grin. "Never let anyone accuse the Hardy brothers of buying cheap climbing gear."

The sun was high in the sky when the Hardys drove back into Elk Springs. They wanted to find out about Pearson's condition and have another talk with K. D. Becker, so they made the hospital their first stop.

Frank pushed through the revolving door into the lobby and limped toward the front desk. He winced slightly, trying to ignore a throbbing pain in his left leg.

An orderly rushed over with a wheelchair. "Don't worry," he said in a way that immediately made Frank worry. "We'll get you down to the emergency room, and a doctor will fix you right up." He tried to push Frank into the chair.

Frank waved him off. "There's nothing wrong wi—" He caught a glimpse of his reflection in the spotless, shiny tile floor. He looked down at himself. His pants were ripped in a dozen places. His red down vest had turned dull gray with a thick coat of rock dust. He didn't want to think about the condition of his face and hair. He glanced over at his brother. Joe's thick blond hair was doing an imitation of a dirty brown dust mop. The right sleeve of his coat was torn halfway off at the shoulder.

A grin crossed Joe's grimy face. "You look like you've been playing football in a war zone," he said.

Frank smiled. "So do you." He turned back to the puzzled orderly. "We're okay. Really."

"Yeah," Joe said. "We're just slobs. Is there someplace where we can clean up?"

The orderly gestured vaguely down the hall to a public washroom and wandered off. The Hardys did their best to make themselves presentable. The result weren't pretty, but at least they didn't resemble the living dead anymore.

"We forgot to get visitors' passes," Frank remembered as they walked down the corridor. Doctors and nurses hustled back and forth and bustled in and out of rooms. Nobody stopped the Hardys.

"The halls at Bayport High are more tightly secured than this place," Joe commented.

Frank knocked softly on Becker's door. The door swung open, and he found himself face-to-face with Dick Oberman.

"Oh, hi," Frank said. "I'm sorry. We didn't know you were here."

Oberman motioned them inside. "Come on in. I was just leaving anyway, and K.D. could use the company."

"I sure could," Becker called out from her bed. "This place is boring!"

Oberman glanced at his watch. "Well, I'd better get going. I told my clerk I'd be at the store at ten, and it's almost noon."

"Why didn't you say something earlier?" Becker responded. "You didn't have to sit with me all this time."

He turned and smiled at her. "If you think *this* is boring, you should try retail sales sometime. I'm always finding excuses not to work. In fact, if I hadn't planned on visiting you this morning, I probably would have blown off the whole day and gone skiing instead."

That triggered something in Frank's mind. "What about the day K.D. was shot? Did you go skiing that morning?"

Oberman's cold blue eyes narrowed. "Why do you ask?"

Frank studied him carefully, curious at his reaction. "No special reason. I just thought you

125

might have seen something to help break the case, that's all.''

Oberman relaxed visibly. "Oh, of course. I'm afraid I can't help you out there. I was at the store at eleven sharp that morning. I had to be there to receive a shipment of goods.''

He moved to the door. "I really have to run. I'll try to stop back again tonight, K.D.''

"Not many people have close friends like that," Joe remarked after Oberman left.

Becker gave him a strange look. "What do you mean?''

"Uh, nothing," Joe replied, somewhat flustered. "It's just that it seemed like he spent all his spare time at your bedside while you were in the coma. I guess I just assumed the two of you were pretty tight.''

Becker shook her head slowly. "I've known Dick a long time, but I've hardly seen him the past couple of years. I guess you could say we're still friends, but we were never close.''

Frank's eyes roved around the room. "We brought your gear in with us when we carried you down from the mountain. Do you know what happened to your backpack?''

"Sure," Becker said. "It's in the closet over in the corner. I hope all my equipment is there. I haven't checked." She held up an arm with an IV tube strapped to it. "I've been sort of tied up.''

Frank got out the backpack and quickly found

what he was looking for. He held up the small metal cylinder with the stubby antenna. "We found this near the spot where you were shot and put it in here. Is this one of your radio transmitters?"

Becker studied the object for a moment. "This is similar to the transmitters I used six or seven years ago, but it's not one of mine."

Joe responded with a perplexed frown. "If you didn't lose it, who did?"

Chapter

15

FRANK PULLED a chair over to the bed and sat down heavily. He stared at K. D. Becker for a long moment. The narrow escape from the rockslide that morning really had taken its toll on his body, and the twists and turns in this case were giving his brain the same battered and bruised feeling.

"Oberman mentioned that he used to help you with your research," he finally said. "How much does he know about your radio telemetry equipment?"

"It would be easier to tell you what he *doesn't* know," Becker answered. "Back in the days when Dick was involved, I was making my own transmitter collars. He did a lot of that work. He probably could have been a real electronics whiz if he'd stuck with it. I guess he was more interested in sports."

Frank held up the device. "Do you think he could still build a transmitter?"

Becker shrugged. "Probably. I don't know why he'd want to, though. What would he use it for?"

Frank pushed himself out of the chair. "I'm not sure. Maybe we can find out." He stopped in the doorway and turned around. "I almost forgot. Have you heard anything about Mark Pearson's condition?"

"He had to have some kind of emergency surgery last night," Becker said. "The nurse I asked didn't have too many specifics. He's probably still in recovery."

"I guess that rules out bursting into his room and grilling him relentlessly for hours," Joe remarked.

Frank shot a look at his brother. "You've been reading too many cheap detective novels."

"They don't come much cheaper than us," Joe replied.

A few minutes and a short drive later, the Hardys were back at the Elk Springs Public Library.

"I don't think we're going to find a section on former Olympic hopefuls in here," Joe said as Frank pulled up to the curb and parked.

"What we're looking for isn't in a book," Frank replied.

"Then why are we wasting time at the library?"

Frank turned to his brother and smiled. "Trust me. I have a plan."

Joe rolled his eyes upward and groaned softly. "*Your* plans always get *me* in trouble."

"What kind of trouble can you get into in a library?"

Joe eyed him warily. "I don't know, and I'm not eager to find out."

Frank opened his door and got out of the car. "Have it your way. Stay here while I go inside."

"Really?"

"Really." Frank started to shut the door, paused, and stuck his head back inside. "Just one little thing."

"I knew it," Joe muttered. "What?"

"Wait ten minutes, and then come in and distract the librarian for me."

"Why?"

"Trust me. I have a pl—"

"I know, I know," Joe interrupted. "Take your plan and get going."

Frank walked into the library and found the librarian behind the counter again.

"Did you finish your report?" she asked.

"I'm afraid not," Frank said in a glum tone. "I need to get some more data somewhere. I don't even know where to start. Not that it matters. There's not enough time to go anywhere else."

"Well, if you let me know what you're looking

for, perhaps I could help you somehow," the librarian said.

"Maybe you can," Frank said. "Do you have an interlibrary lending service?"

The librarian's face lit up. "Why, yes, we do. It's a brand-new computerized system, too. I'm still learning how to use it."

Frank smiled. "Maybe *I* can help *you*. Where's the computer?"

She took him to a small office in the back of the library. The personal computer on the desk was a fairly recent model. Frank gave the setup a quick scan before he hit the power switch and sat down at the keyboard.

"Does it have an internal modem?" he asked as the machine started to hum and light flickered on the monitor screen."

"I have no idea," the woman said cheerfully. "They told me it was user-friendly, whatever that means. I don't know anything about how it works."

Frank looked at her with patient eyes. "Is it connected to the phone lines?"

"Oh, yes. Well, it has to be, doesn't it? I mean, how else would it talk to the computers at the other libraries?"

"So you just turn it on, type in some commands, and you're hooked up to the network, right?"

The librarian frowned. "Commands? I just use

131

the mouse gadget to point at what I want on the screen."

Frank looked at the colorful digital version of a desktop glowing on the monitor. It was filled with computerized images of tiny file folders. Inside each folder, Frank knew, there were software programs and data files. He moved the mouse and a pointer on the screen moved the same direction. When the pointer was on a folder marked Telecom, Frank clicked the mouse button.

"Where's the murder mystery section?" a loud voice bellowed from the library. "Doesn't anybody work here?"

The librarian glanced around nervously. "Oh my. I should go see what that man wants."

"Go ahead," Frank said as he studied the contents of the electronic folder. "I'll be fine."

"But I haven't even told you how to—"

"Don't worry," Frank cut in. "I'm sure I can figure it out." In fact, he already had. All he needed now was a little time and a little privacy, and he hoped Joe's little diversion would give him both.

"I can't figure out these numbers at all!" the irate voice complained loudly. "What ever happened to the Dewey decimal system anyway? Why don't they just put the dumb things in alphabetical order?"

The librarian wavered in the doorway. "Are you sure—"

"Yes, yes," Frank assured her. "It sounds like he needs your help more than I do." Frank hoped the librarian didn't recognize Joe. Joe had stayed in the background on their last visit— maybe she wouldn't remember him.

Joe was waiting in the car with a stack of faded, dog-eared whodunits in his lap when Frank came out of the library.

"I now have an Elk Springs Library card that's good for the next three years," Joe said. "What did you get?"

"Nothing that impressive," Frank replied with a grin. "Just the lowdown on the finances of a certain camping supply store owner."

Joe raised his eyebrows. "I didn't know they had a section in the library for that kind of information."

"They don't. I used their computer to link up with our computer at home."

"I didn't know *we* had that kind of information, either," Joe remarked.

"We don't," Frank replied. "But we do have a file on the hard disk memory with telephone numbers and access codes for various electronic bulletin boards, data retrieval systems, and a few credit record services."

"I get it now," Joe said. "You ran a credit check on Dick Oberman." He paused and a puzzled look crossed his face. "What I don't get is why."

"There are many motives for murder," Frank explained. "Money is one of the top ten."

"Is that what you found out from the computer?" Joe asked doubtfully.

"No," Frank said. "I found out that Oberman doesn't have any big debts, not anymore, anyway."

"I'm tired and hungry and my feet hurt," Joe complained. "Could you just hit me with the punchline instead of dangling it over my head?"

"Dick Oberman was in deep debt," Frank revealed. "His combined total credit card debt was over forty thousand dollars. Then, all of a sudden, he has a clean slate—everything paid in full."

Joe held up his hand before Frank could finish. "Don't tell me. Let me guess the rest. The big payoff came—"

"The same day somebody shot K. D. Becker," Frank finished.

"That's more than suspicious coincidence," Joe said. "Do you think forty grand would be enough for him to put a bullet in a friend? Don't forget, he has an alibi."

"We'll work on the alibi later," Frank said. "As for the money, it's not exactly chump change, and it might be only a partial payment, anyway. Whoever hired him might be holding out the rest until Oberman finishes the job."

"I thought you said all his debts were paid off," Joe said.

134

"He probably has other, hidden debts that a routine credit check wouldn't uncover," Frank reasoned. "I didn't have enough time to do a complete rundown."

"Sorry," Joe replied, patting his pile of books. "They didn't have any more detective novels at the library."

"It doesn't matter," Frank told him. "Even the most detailed credit history wouldn't tell us what we really need to know."

Joe looked at his brother. "What's that?"

"Who hired him," Frank said pensively. "Unless Oberman's a professional hit man—which I doubt—whoever hired him would have to be someone who wanted Becker dead and also knew about Oberman's money problems."

"Look on the bright side," Joe responded. "That should narrow down the list of suspects."

Frank gazed out the window. The sun warmed the inside of the car in defiance of the bitter cold on the other side of the thin glass. "I still think Crawford's behind the whole thing."

He twisted the key in the ignition and started the car. "If we don't crack this case in the next twenty-four hours, we never will. We should get home tomorrow night."

"Maybe if we shake things hard enough, the case will break wide open," Joe replied.

Frank nodded. "That's exactly what I was thinking."

"So where do we start?"

"With the sheriff," Frank said as he drove away from the library.

Joe appeared doubtful. "Can we trust him?"

"We have to," Frank answered. "We don't have much choice. Becker's life is still in danger since Oberman has to finish his job. If our theory's right, he'll definitely try again. K.D. needs police protection right now.

"And if I'm wrong about Stevens," he added, "telling him what we've uncovered will definitely shake things up."

Chapter

16

THE HARDYS almost had a head-on collision with the sheriff's jeep when they drove into the small parking lot on the side of the police station. Both cars screeched to a halt, close enough to rub fenders.

The horn on the jeep blared, and the siren whooped. Frank shifted their car into reverse and started to back up.

Joe suddenly shoved his door open, bolted out, and vaulted across the hood. He rushed over to the jeep, jerked open the passenger-side door, and jumped in.

He gave the sheriff a wide, warm smile. "Hi. Where we going?"

The sheriff's face turned an angry red as he glared at Joe. "You've got exactly five seconds to get out of this vehicle," he growled.

"Arrest me if you want," Joe said. "But if you're in a hurry to get someplace, you'll still have to take me with you. Just listen to what I have to say while you're driving, and you can throw me in jail later."

The sheriff scowled out the windshield as Frank pulled his car out of the way. "I suppose the two of you are a package deal."

Joe nodded. "That's right. A matched set. Two for the price of one. What do you say?"

The sheriff's gaze lingered on Joe for a long, silent second. Then he sighed, rolled down his window, and stuck his head out. "Hurry up and get your carcass over here!" he shouted in Frank's direction. "You're holding up police business!"

"So where are we going?" Joe asked again as they blasted down the highway with the siren wailing and the lights flashing.

"There's a state police roadblock up ahead," the sheriff answered. "I had my deputies stake out the garage in town where Gentry stores his truck. I figured he'd need his truck if he wanted to get very far.

"It didn't work out quite the way I planned. Gentry did go for his truck and he also got one of my men.

"The state troopers stopped them at the roadblock," he continued. "What we have now is what you might call a Mexican standoff. Gentry won't let Harlan go, and we can't let Gentry go."

"Gentry's bluffing," Frank said confidently. "He won't hurt your deputy. You know he's not the shooter."

The sheriff snorted. "Still think it's Pearson and Crawford?"

"They're involved," Frank replied. "But I don't think Pearson shot K. D. Becker anymore." He quickly told the sheriff what they'd discovered about Dick Oberman's debts and Walt Crawford's grazing rights. "The only thing missing," he concluded, "is a link between the two."

The sheriff didn't respond right away. Frank couldn't tell if he was lost in thought or just concentrating on the road. When he finally spoke, it was in a heavy voice with a touch of sadness. "I wish I could say there isn't a link. But there is one.

"Walt Crawford owns a lot of buildings in town," he explained. "Oberman's store is in one of them."

"So if Oberman fell behind in his rent," Joe ventured, "Crawford would know he had money trouble."

The sheriff's revelation set off a chain reaction in Frank's head. "I'll bet Crawford also owns the garage where Gentry stores his truck."

"You'd win that bet," the sheriff responded as he hit the brakes and the jeep skidded to a halt at the roadblock.

The state police had Gentry boxed in. Two patrol cars blocked the road ahead, and two more had moved up from behind. Eight uniformed troopers crouched behind the hoods and trunks. Sixteen eyes, three shotguns, and five revolvers were trained on the pickup truck.

"Put those weapons away before somebody gets hurt!" Sheriff Stevens bellowed as he lumbered out of the jeep.

A jittery trooper whirled around, his service revolver gripped tightly in his hand.

The sheriff put his hands on his hips and gazed evenly at the young officer. "Don't point that thing at me, son."

The trooper wavered for a moment and then holstered the gun.

The sheriff smiled softly. "That's more like it. Now let's see if we can undo whatever damage has been done here." He strode past the state police cars and approached the pickup truck. "Gentry!" he called out. "There's a couple of young fellows here who say you've been framed, and they've pretty much convinced me they might be right. If you surrender now, you may end up a free man. That's your best choice. I'd take it if I were you. Otherwise, you'll find yourself on a mighty hard road."

A few hours later Frank and Joe were back at the Elk Springs Police Station, sitting around a table with the cowboy sheriff and the Native American activist.

"You understand we're going to have to hold

you until we get this business cleared up?" the sheriff said.

Gentry nodded. "I only ask to be treated fairly, like anybody else. I trust Frank and Joe. If you're working together, I think I can trust you too."

The sheriff glanced over at Frank. "I can't say I like this idea much. Walt and I go back a long way. I'd rather confront him outright and see what he has to say."

"If you really thought that was a better idea," Frank countered, "you'd be doing it now instead of sitting here with us. You know we don't have any proof that Crawford was involved."

"We don't even have any hard evidence that Oberman pulled the trigger," Joe added. "If we can't shake his alibi, we have to force his hand somehow, get him to incriminate himself."

"And that's what this plan is all about," Frank said.

"I still don't like it," the sheriff muttered through his mustache. "I was hoping I could get some information out of Pearson, but I just wasted an hour at the hospital talking to myself. He's playing deaf, dumb, and blind. He didn't see anything, he didn't hear anything, he's tired and he needs to rest, and he's not going to answer any questions without a lawyer."

"He's either too scared to talk," Joe ventured, "or he's still hoping to use whatever he has to blackmail Crawford."

The sheriff put his hands on the table and pushed himself out of his chair. "All right. Let's do it before I change my mind." He checked his watch. "It's five-thirty now. Oberman's store closes at six."

"Then we'd better get moving," Frank said.

Oberman was alone in the store when the Hardys walked in. He greeted them with a smile. "I was just about to close. I can stay open for a little while if there's something you need, but I want to get over to the hospital to see K.D. before dinner."

"Then you haven't heard the news," Frank said gravely.

Oberman lost his smile. "What news?"

"She seemed just fine," Frank began in a faltering voice. "We were sitting in her room, talking. A nurse came in and gave her some kind of shot. She must have had an allergic reaction."

"What do you mean?" Oberman asked. "What happened? Is she all right?"

"I don't know," Frank said. "She started having trouble breathing. Then all of a sudden she passed out. Joe ran out to get a doctor. An emergency team swarmed into the room. They wouldn't let us stay while they worked on her. When they came out, all they'd say was that she was resting."

"I hope she'll be all right tomorrow morning," Joe said. "She sort of left us on the edge of our seats. She was telling us about what happened the morning she was shot."

Oberman's eyes locked on him. "What did she say?" he snapped. "Did she see anything?"

Joe shrugged his shoulders. "The conversation never got that far."

Frank glanced down at his watch. "We're running late. We were supposed to be at the sheriff's office ten minutes ago."

Oberman's cold blue eyes darted between the two brothers. "Why does the sheriff want to see you?"

"I'm not sure," Frank answered. "Something about what time it was when we found K.D. the morning she was shot."

Joe tugged on his brother's arm. "We really should get going." He gave Oberman a parting smile. "Maybe we'll see you again before we leave town."

The trap was set, and the bait was in place. Now all they could do was wait to see if Oberman would bite.

Peering down at the luminous dial on his watch, Frank realized he must have nodded out for a while. The last time he'd checked, it was a little after midnight. Now it was one-fifteen. He couldn't imagine how he had managed to fall asleep on the cramped, hard floor of the closet, and he hoped it wouldn't happen again. He had to stay awake all night if necessary.

143

The closet door was open just enough for Frank to have a view of the door into the dark room and the lumpy form on Becker's hospital bed. After a few minutes of staring into the gloom, Frank's eyelids started to droop again.

They did pop open, though, when a thin shaft of light leaked in from the hallway. A shadowy figure slipped silently into the room and padded quietly across the floor to hover over the bed for a moment. Then the person picked up a pillow and brought it down over the patient's face, pressing down firmly with both hands.

The patient thrashed around for a few seconds as the intruder pushed down harder. The thrashing grew weaker and weaker and finally died out.

Chapter
17

THE INTRUDER leaned over the still body on the bed. Frank burst out of the closet and lunged at him. Somebody hit the light switch and the room was flooded with harsh, fluorescent light.

Dick Oberman whirled around with the pillow still clutched in his hands. He threw it at Frank and whipped a hunting knife out of his jacket. He slashed wildly, half-blinded by the sudden glare. Frank jumped back, and the ugly, curved blade sliced through the air, inches from his chest. Oberman raised the knife over his head.

The body on the bed lurched up and grabbed the knife-wielding arm. Oberman's face twisted into a contorted grimace. Frank didn't know if it was caused by the shock of the dead coming

145

back to life or the pain of the bone-crushing grip on his wrist.

Oberman howled and the knife clattered to the floor. Joe jumped off the bed, still clutching Oberman's wrist, and twisted the man's arm behind his back.

Frank smiled at his brother. "You've got fast reflexes for a corpse."

Joe grinned back. "Being dead isn't as bad as I thought it would be. In fact, it's a lot like my former life."

Frank looked over at Sheriff Stevens, who was leaning casually against the wall next to the light switch. "Think you can make a case now?" Frank asked.

The sheriff pushed up the brim of his cowboy hat and nodded silently.

"This is all a horrible mistake," Oberman protested.

"That's right," the sheriff drawled. "And you're the one who made it.

"There's only one thing I can't figure," he continued. "I talked to one of the waitresses at the diner across the street from your store. She claims she saw you changing the display in the front window around eleven o'clock on the morning K.D. was shot. But I don't see how that's possible."

"That's because you believed the watch," Frank answered. "Since K.D.'s broken watch said ten forty-six, everybody assumed that was the time of the shooting. But K.D. can't remember doing anything for over an hour and a half before that."

"That doesn't mean anything," Oberman objected. "The doctor said—"

"Why don't you just shut your mouth and listen politely?" the sheriff suggested forcefully. "Even if I can't prove you tried to kill K.D. the first time, I caught you in the act this time." His eyes shifted to Frank. "But I'm still curious."

"It's really pretty simple," Frank said. "He shot her between nine and nine-fifteen. When the snow let up for that short period, he was able to see. He smashed her watch then and moved the hands ahead to ten forty-six. Only a professional skier like Oberman could make it back to town by eleven. None of the rest of us could, but obviously he did. Also, he'd know any shortcuts through the mountains. The storm didn't stop completely until about ten, so the new snow covered his tracks near the crime scene. That's what was bothering me earlier. K.D. had some snow on her, so she couldn't have been shot at ten forty-six. The snow had stopped falling by then."

"Hold on a minute," the sheriff said. "This makes sense so far, but don't you think Oberman would have noticed that Becker was still alive when he came down into the canyon to break the watch?"

147

"Probably," Frank said. "But what could he do about it then? He wanted to make the shooting look like an accident. If he shot her twice, nobody would swallow the accident theory. Framing Gentry with the anonymous phone call and planting the rifle was an afterthought."

"How did you figure out that the watch was smashed deliberately?" Stevens asked.

"Actually," Frank replied, "I'm surprised none of us thought of it before. The watch was under her padded glove, and she fell in a pile of soft, new-fallen snow. Under those conditions, an accidental break would have been a million-to-one shot."

"Well, I've certainly learned a lesson from all this," Joe responded. "From now on, I'm strictly a digital watch man."

The Hardys managed to get a few hours' sleep in what was left of the night after the sheriff hauled Oberman off to jail. Before the long drive back to Denver in the morning, they stopped at the hospital to say goodbye to K.D.

"So you saved my life again," she said. "It's hard to believe that Dick Oberman tried to kill me. I'm kind of confused by it all. Why did you want to know if he could build a radio transmitter? And how was Mark Pearson involved in the whole thing?"

"It's all connected," Frank told her. "Pearson saw two people near the canyon that morn-

ing when he was tracking cougars. He saw Ted
Gentry, and he also saw Dick Oberman. He tried
to blackmail Oberman. Oberman told Crawford,
and Crawford decided to eliminate Pearson."

"So Crawford lured him up to the cliff," Joe
continued, picking up the story. "And while
Crawford distracted Pearson, Oberman cut the
brake lines on Pearson's truck."

Becker still looked confused. "But what does
any of that have to do with my radio telemetry
gear?"

Frank grinned. "That's the best part. Oberman had no way of knowing where you'd be. So
he rigged up a radio transmitter to lure you to
him. He wanted you to think a cat had entered
that area. He probably planned to get rid of the
transmitter after he shot you. Either he couldn't
find it in the snow, or he forgot about it. Discovering you were still alive must have rattled him
badly. Oberman's used to shooting at targets with
a small-caliber weapon, not hitting live victims."

"Right," Joe said. "You're not dead because
Oberman wasn't familiar with hunting rifles. He
didn't consider the stopping power of the gun at
long range. He figured all he had to do was hit
the target."

"It sounds pretty complicated," Becker said.
"How can you prove that Walt Crawford was
behind Oberman?"

Frank chuckled. "We don't have to. Oberman
hasn't stopped talking since he was arrested."

"Looks like your cats will be safe now," a deep voice commented from behind them. Frank turned and saw Ted Gentry standing in the doorway.

Becker smiled. "They're not *my* cats. They don't belong to anybody. They're wild and free. That's the way it's supposed to be."

"It sounds like a good life to me," Gentry replied.

"It sounds like a great first verse for a hit single," Joe ventured. "Let's get a camera and make a music video."

Frank shot a look at his brother. "Let's go home instead. I think you need a rest from your vacation."

THE HARDY BOYS CASEFILES